Ted Lapkin spent the first half of his chil  his Jewish family moved to Israel. He s intelligence officer in the Golani Infan brigade's elite recon company during the l

Graduating summa cum laude from Tel the United States for postgraduate study and began to work in politics as a communications/government-relations strategist. While in Washington D.C., he met an Australian woman whom he later married. Moving to Melbourne, he began a PHD (never finished) and began to write political opinion columns for Australian newspapers. Since then he has written for many publications, including the *Spectator*, *LA Times* and the *Sydney Morning Herald*, as well as speeches for members of the US Congress and Australian Government Cabinet Ministers. He now runs his own consulting firm that advises clients on strategic communications, reputation management and government relations.

Ted lives with his wife Sharon in the Melbourne inner suburb of Fitzroy, described by London's *Daily Telegraph* newspaper as one of "the world's most 'hipster' neighbourhoods." *Righteous Kill* is his first novel.

RIGHTEOUS KILL

Ted Lapkin

SILVERTAIL BOOKS • *London*

First published by Silvertail Books in 2020
www.silvertailbooks.com
Copyright © Ted Lapkin 2020
1
The right of Ted Lapkin to be identified as the author
of this work has been asserted in accordance
with the Copyright, Design and Patents Act 1988
A catalogue record of this book is available from the British Library
978-1-909269-41-5

והתורה אמרה אם בא להרגך השכם להרגו

(תלמוד בבלי — מסכת ברכות, דף נח ע״א)

And the Torah said if someone comes to
kill you arise earlier and kill him first.

(Babylonian Talmud — Brachot 58A)

Primary characters

Israelis

Adivi, Aaron — Emeritus Professor of Physics/Temporal Transport Device Pilot

HarSinai, Michael (radio call sign – 'Mishneh KodKod') — Major, second-in-command (2iC) Agag Force

Klein, Yossi (radio call sign – 'Kodkod') — Major/Lieutenant Colonel, commander Agag Force

Levinson, Baruch — Staff Sergeant, Klein's RTO

Lifshutz, Yochai (radio call sign – 'Toren') — Major, medical officer Agag Force

Meshulam, Erad — Captain, commander Team Three (Blocking West)

Weinstock, Azriel — Captain, commander Team Two (Blocking East)

Germans

Gesche, Bruno — SS Obersturmbannführer, Führerbegleitkommando Commander

Hoffmann, Gerhard — Physicist/ Temporal Transport Device Pilot

Koertig, Peter — Oberleutnant, commander motorcycle platoon Führer-Begleit-Bataillon Schnelle Kompanie

Schultz, Karl-Lothar — Major, commander, III Bataillon, Fallschirmjäger Regiment 1

Warlimont, Walter — Generalmajor, Deputy Chief of the Operations Staff, OKW

Jews

Cohen, Emma — Lawyer, Heidelberg resident

Morency, Danielle — (née Bernheim) Resident of house used as firebase for Team Two

Shipperman, Miriam — Mannheim resident

British

Neville, Ralph — Lieutenant Colonel, British Army Intelligence Officer

Supporting characters

Israelis

Abargil, Roie	Captain, demolitions, officer/deputy operations officer Agag Force
Azoulai, Sagiv	Sergeant, machine gunner Team One
Bar'el, Haim	Major General (ret), Minister of Defense
Ben Gurion, David	Chairman, Jewish Agency Executive Committee and Prime Minister
Beton, Yifach	Mossad Officer, temporal sleeper agent who travels back mid-20th century France under cover name Alexandre Roux
Blumfeld, Shlomo	Sergeant, trooper Team Two
Buzaglo, Uziel	Staff Sergeant, section leader Team Four
Dvir, Tzachi	Chief Inspector, commander Team One (Assault)
Eztioni, Yair	Prime Minister
Farkash, Benjamin	Captain, commander Team Four (Security & UAV Surveillance)
Greenspan, Rotem	Sergeant, machine gunner Team One
Geffen, Hava	Minister for Foreign Affairs
Gluska, Yedidia	Staff Sergeant, medic Team Four
Halevy, Gershon	Staff Sergeant, section leader Team Two
Horman, Gavriel (Gabi)	Staff Sergeant, Klein's driver
Karmi, Ohad	Team Two RTO
Kelman, Abdiel	Sergeant Crye12 shotgun/machine gunner Team One
Kupperberg, Tzvi	Attorney General
Levine, Simcha	Major General, commander, IDF Depth Command
Levinson Maya	Baruch Levinson's sister, PHD student Hebrew University
Levinson Zehava	Baruch Levinson's mother, District Court Judge
Maximoff, Ira	Sergeant, Crye12 shotgun Team One
Mesika	Sergeant, 40 mm grenadier Team One
Mookie	Sergeant, Matador gunner Team One
Moskovitz, Yosef	Staff Sergeant, section leader Team Two
Rivkin, Eldad	Staff Sergeant, section leader/motorcycle scout Team Two
Rosenblum, Gisella	Moshav Secretary, Shavei Tzion
Shaltiel, David	Haganah Intelligence Officer
Sheetrit, Boaz	Staff Sergeant, sniper team leader Team Two
Sneh, Gilad	Major, operations officer Agag Force
Tzipori, Yosef	Staff Sergeant, medic Team One
Yavniel, Amiram	Minister of Finance
Yoram	Sergeant, Matador gunner Team One
Wachtman, Orli	Funeral participant
Zevulun, Haim	Staff Sergeant, section leader Team Two

Germans

Bäker — Stabsfeldwebel, motorcycle platoon Führer-Begleit-Bataillon Schnelle Kompanie

Bormann, Martin — Reichleiter and Chief of the Nazi Party Chancery

Candler — Hauptman, III Bataillon Falshirmjäger Regiment 1

Eisner, Helmut — Richter, Judge of the Landgericht Court

François, Freiherr Bruno von — Rittmeister, commander Führer-Begleit-Bataillon Schnelle Kompanie

Franzman, Siegfried — Oberleutnant, commander 88 mm flakbatterie

Goebbels, Joseph — Reichsministerium für Volksaufklärung und Propaganda, Gauleiter of Berlin

Göering, Hermann — Reichsmarschall des Grossdeutschen Reiches, Luftwaffe Commander

Graber, Richard — Oberleutnant, platoon commander (armoured car), Führer-Begleit-Bataillon Schnelle Kompanie

Himmler, Heinrich — Reichsführer SS

Hitler, Adolf — Reichskanzler des Deutchen Volkes

Huttmacher, Alois — Korvettenkapitän, naval liaison officer, Führerhauptquartiere

Jodl, Alfred — GeneralOberst, Chief of the Operation Staff at OKW

Kahler — Führersonderzug Flak NCO

Keitel, Wilhelm — Generalfeldmarschall, Chief, Oberkommando der Wehrmacht

Knochen, Helmut — SS Obersturmbannführer in command of Sicherheitspolizei/ Sicherheitsdienst des Reichsführers-SS in France

Lannon, Ulbricht — Oberleutnant, III Bataillon Falshirmjäger Regiment 1

Morell, Dr Theodore — Hitler's personal physician widely regarded as a drug-administering quack and known in Nazi circles by the derogatory nickname 'reichsspritzenmeister' (injection master of the Reich'

Ohlendorf, Otto — Law student/SS Officer

Papp, Helmut — Oberstleutnant, commander Nachrichten Bataillon (signals battalion) 247 until relieved of command

Portner — Kriminalrat, Gestapo

Saller — Oberleutnant, operations officer Nachrichten Bataillon (signals battalion) 247

Schädle, Franz — Sturmbannführer, second-in-command (2iC) Führerbegleitkommando

Shriver, Hugo — Luftwaffe Hauptman, flak commander, Châteaudun airbase

Tanzer, Sebastian — Me-109 Pilot

Trost — Major, Kreiskommandant of Vendôme

Warlimont, Walter — Generalmajor, Deputy Chief of the Operations Staff OKW

Weiss — Major, second in command (2iC)/commander Nachrichten Bataillon (signals battalion) 247

Wyzan, Helmut — SS Hauptsturmführer

Jews and Deportees

Cohen, Dvora	Emma's Mother, Heidelberg resident
Cohen, Manfred	Emma's Father, Heidelberg resident
Goldberg, Dr Emanuel	Obstetrician, Heidelberg resident
Lilienthal, Arthur	Businessman, Heidelberg resident
Lilienthal, Sarah & Hanna	Arthur's teenaged twin daughters
Morency, Adele	Danielle's four-year-old daughter
Von Stockhausen, Alois	Former Imperial German Navy officer and navigator of the *Mauritz van Nazzau*

French

Bouvier, Fabienne	Gendarme, Gendarmerie Nationale
Chandlier, René	Adjudant, Gendarmerie Nationale
Gilbert, Maurice	Sous-Lieutenant, Gendarmerie Nationale
Guillaume, Roland	Forester, owner la Hubardière
Jaumont, Jasper	Vendômois Real Estate Agent
Lebrune, Josephine	Lascivious Montoire Innkeeper
Roux, Alexandre	Cover name of temporal sleeper agent Yiftach Beton

British

Cavendish-Bentinck, Sir Victor	Chairman, Joint Intelligence Committee
Churchill, Winston	Prime Minister
Crosswaite	General Davidson's personal assistant
Dill, Sir John	General, Chief of the Imperial General Staff
Davidson, Francis	Major General, Director of Military Intelligence
Portal, Sir Charles	Air Chief Marshall, Chief of the Air Staff
Pound, Sir Dudley	Admiral of the Fleet, First Sea Lord

Italians

Buonarota, Giuseppe	Capitano de Frigata, Regia Marina
Sansonetti, Luigi	Ammiraglo de Squadra, Regia Marina

x

Prologue

Word arrived just as the sun began to peek over the crest of the Anti-Lebanon Mountains, its rays painting the underbellies of scattered cirrus clouds with pastel hues. Ambient light crept across the Beqaa Valley, revealing a checkerboard of cultivated fields beneath the slopes that plummeted 1,200 metres from their alpine perch. A pastoral stillness prevailed, pierced only by the raucous caw of migrating cranes en route to their winter feeding grounds in Africa.

It was this tranquillity that made dawn Yossi Klein's favourite part of the day. But on this particular morning, he was oblivious to the physical beauty of his surroundings. He had other things on his mind.

Today was the raiding party's third day in place, and a clammy coldness leeched from the clay walls of the hide position where Klein and his men lay concealed. Their accommodation was far from luxurious, but the art of being comfortable with being uncomfortable was a skill long since mastered. They were all Matkalistim – soldiers who'd endured the gruelling selection course that was a prerequisite for entry into Sayeret Matkal, Israel's top-tier special operations unit.

Just to qualify for 'gibush', the Hebrew word for selection, recruits had to demonstrate physical and intellectual attributes that were considerably higher than the population average. Yet robust cardiovascular fitness and a 110-plus IQ were not themselves sufficient to make the cut. 'The Unit', as Matkal was colloquially known throughout the IDF, sought a more elusive human quality in its soldiers – unyielding fortitude in the face of stress, fatigue and uncertainty.

Over a seemingly interminable fortnight, gibush candidates were subjected to a brutal and bewildering set of physical and mental challenges, never knowing what was coming next, nor by which standard they were being measured. With their every move monitored by Unit cadre and psychologists, aspirants who flagged or faltered were unceremoniously dismissed from selection. There were no second chances, and attrition

I

rates invariably hovered around the 95 per cent mark. The Matkal philosophy was simple: better to dispense with weakness amidst the coastal sand dunes south of Tel Aviv than have frailty unmasked deep within enemy territory – precisely their current circumstance.

The hide was a four-by-four-metre pit dug into a ledge created fifty years previously as construction crews blasted a roadbed through the Lebanon Mountains. The road below, codenamed 'Route Yakinton', was a narrow ribbon of asphalt that snaked its way eastwards through deep valleys and over steep ridges from the Mediterranean into the Beqaa Valley.

A small sap dug into the hide's rear wall was filled with sealed plastic ziplock bags containing human faeces accumulated over fifty-two hours of their immurement. While every other piece of trash would fastidiously be carried away upon extraction, the excrement would be left in place as a parting gift to the enemy.

"Dried shit tells no tales," as some unnamed Matkal wag put it years ago.

Covering the pit was a frame made of telescoping fibreglass rods and light mesh that had been covered with foliage harvested from adjacent Pistacia and Ceratonia bushes. The end result was an artfully camouflaged position that provided unobstructed observation across an arc of 120 degrees.

"Baz for you," murmured the team RTO, while proffering the Tadiran PRC6020 handset to his commander.

Major Yossi Klein shifted in place, taking care that his lanky frame caused minimum discomfort to the six other troopers crammed into the narrow confines of the hide. He put the HF-band radio handset to his ear and pressed the transmit button. "This is Kodkod," he said sotto voce, identifying himself by the IDF radio call sign for a unit commander. "Go."

"This is Baz," came the soft soprano voice of the UAV mission commander, transmitting from the Israeli Air Force radar station atop Mount Meron in the Galilee, 140 kilometres to their south.

"Target package is on the move eastwards along Route Yakinton in three-vehicle convoy. Lead is a black Toyota Land Cruiser, followed by white Benz S-Class and second black Land Cruiser bringing up the rear. Both Toyotas are carrying the escort, while the package is travelling in the Benz. ETA your position in 20–25, how copy?"

"This is Kodkod Samson, copy three-vehicle convoy approaching along Yakinton with target package in the Benz. ETA circa 20. How many dirties and how are they armed? Over."

"We count thirteen dirties, six in the lead Toyota and five in the follow vehicle. Armed with AKs, plus one RPG and one PKM per vehicle. Two more in the driver and shotgun seats of the Benz with AKs only. Packages are in the rear seat of the Benz; one large and two small. Large package appears unarmed but may be carrying pistol."

"Say again in reference to small packages and verify? Over."

"This is Baz. I verify that the package is travelling with two female children; estimated ages six to ten years."

"Fuck," muttered Klein before once again keying the transmit button. "Get me Kodkod Gladiator."

"Wait."

After a ten-second hiatus, a deep throaty rumble was heard through the handset. "This is Gladiator, go."

"You're aware the package is travelling with children? Over."

"We were surprised as well," confessed Major General Simcha Levine. "We knew the daughters were staying at the house, but no-one expected them to accompany their father to Ba'albek. Especially this early in the morning. According to our freshest info, he's on his way to a confer with some political muckety-mucks from the neighbours to the East. If that intel is accurate, there's no logical reason why the girls should be along on this trip. Could be there are unknowns in play, but that's the situation. That's where we stand."

"What are your orders? Over."

"This is Gladiator. Are you confident can you execute without harming the children?"

"Affirmative. The entire operation revolves around capturing the target package intact. Two small children are well within the mission envelope. How copy?"

"Gladiator, good copy. You have my authorisation to proceed. But you're kodkod in the field and it's your ultimate decision."

Klein pondered for a moment before keying the handset. "We continue as planned."

"This is Gladiator, good copy. Confirming Dardarim" – the IDF radio procedure term for helicopters – "taking off now to the forward loiter point. Returning you to Baz. Good luck. Out."

Another two-second pause. "This is Baz."

Someone of a more traditional mindset might have found incongruity between the dulcet femininity of the UAV commander's voice and the deadly business under discussion. Yet with women integrated into all IDF military occupational specialties, save frontline ground combat roles, the fact that his interlocutor was female would have struck Klein as commonplace had he been inclined to ponder the matter.

"Kodkod Sampson here. I want convoy progress updates every two kilometres and final notice when they're one thousand metres from my position; how copy?"

"This is Baz, good copy. We're shadowing directly above at an altitude of 8,000 AGL."

"Thanks again. Kodkod Sampson out."

Returning the HF PRC6020 handset to his RTO, Klein thumbed the transmit button on his 'Madonna', the IDF nickname for the boom mic of the PRC710 personal tactical radio carried by every trooper in the 28-man ambush team.

"All Sampson stations, this is Kodkod. Sitrep – target convoy is on the move to our position. Three vehicles, two Toyota SUV escorts with the target package in the Benz between them. ETA in 15–20. Count thirteen dirties, six in the lead Toyota, five in the follow and two in the front of the Benz. Armed with AKs and one PKM and one RPG per Toyota. Target package appears unarmed, although may be carrying a pistol. Be aware that two children are travelling with the package in rear of the Benz, so take extra care. Aside from that, we proceed as planned. Team leaders acknowledge status, over."

"This is Two, good to go."

"Three here, ready."

"Four here, ready."

"This is Kodkod. We execute as rehearsed, but be on guard against surprises. Good luck. Out."

Behind him, he heard the soft rustle of equipment being adjusted and weapons being checked. Swivelling his head, he shared a brief smile with the half-dozen young men with whom he had spent the past days living cheek by jowl. Then he focused his gaze through the narrow slit between the hide's parapet and the camouflaged roof towards the straight stretch of Route Yakinton that passed in front of him.

They waited, the silence interrupted only by Klein's murmured acknowledgements as radioed updates arrived every three minutes. Then came the final notification.

"Kodkod Sampson, this is Baz. Convoy is one thousand metres from your position. No change in order of vehicles. ETA ninety seconds to two minutes. Good luck."

"Thank you, Baz. Out," replied Klein, relinquishing the HF handset and thumbing his Madonna's transmit button. "Sampson stations, this is Kodkod. Make ready. Target arriving at our location in less than two."

Just over one hundred seconds later, the lead Toyota Land Cruiser hove into view around a hairpin bend, pausing as the follow-on vehicles negotiated that same sharp turn. Neither driver nor shotgun-seat bodyguard paid any heed to the stone that lay on the interior road shoulder.

In fairness, it appeared to be just one rock amongst many dislodged over the years from the earthen wall created as construction crews hacked their way through this particular stretch of mountain. In reality, it was anything but. The light fibreglass shell, carefully textured and painted to match its surroundings, concealed a five-kilogram shaped charge of TNT. As it detonated, the copper lining that sheathed the dimpled end of the charge generated multiple explosively formed projectiles to produce a giant shotgun effect. Designed to penetrate military light armoured vehicles, the two-dozen marble-sized lumps of molten copper had no difficulty ripping through the frame of the Toyota and the bodies of those seated within it.

The incineration of the lead Land Cruiser served a signal for three ghillie-suited troopers to materialise from the underbrush along the side of the road, each with an RPG18 atop his shoulder. The RPG18 was a Russian knock-off of the American M72 LAW disposable bazooka, and the three rockets dispatched into the follow-on Toyota were the textbook definition of overkill. The fuel tank exploded, sending a gout of flame through the passenger compartment that incinerated the five Hezbollah fighters who were already dead from the blast of the RPG warheads.

Simultaneously, unseen marksmen immobilised the Mercedes-Benz through well-aimed small arms fire that punctured the vehicle's engine casing and shredded its tires.

Klein thumbed his Madonna. "Four this is Kodkod, confirm line-of-sight?"

"This is Four, confirmed," replied the sniper team leader from his overwatch position up the slope. "Vision clear and unobstructed."

"Let's move," announced Klein as he tossed aside the fibreglass camouflage frame. Clambering out of the hide, he glanced right and left to verify that three troopers had assumed their choreographed positions on either flank.

As this was a deniable mission, the Israelis were armed with Russian weaponry – AKM assault rifles, RPD light machine guns, RPG rocket launchers and an SVD Dragunov sniper rifle. The seven Matkal soldiers advanced towards the Mercedes-Benz in line-abreast formation, moving slowly with weapons shouldered and sights centred on the target vehicle.

The forward passenger-side door of the Benz suddenly swung open. But the Hezbollah fighter seated within had only partly emerged from the vehicle when he collapsed in a spray of pink mist generated by the passage of a 7.62 mm Dragunov bullet through his cranium.

As Klein approached the Benz, he saw the driver frozen in place, his hands meekly raised in a gesture of surrender.

"Avshalom and Shimshon, handle him," Klein instructed with a sideways nod of the head.

The two designated troopers peeled off with weapons levelled at the driver's seat, whose occupant apparently decided that the better part of valour was discretion. Within seconds, the chauffeur/bodyguard was unceremoniously deposited face down on the ground with hands plasticuffed behind his back.

Keeping his rifle shouldered with his right hand, Klein yanked open the rear driver's side passenger door. A bearded, bespectacled man of early middle age sat motionless as two hijab-clad little girls clung to him sobbing in terror.

"Achraja meyn sayara," barked Klein, gesturing with his free hand for the passengers to exit the vehicle while keeping his rifle levelled at the father's head.

The bearded man gazed up with quiet contempt. "I speak English."

"I'm well aware," replied Klein in the same language. "In fact, I know a lot about you. Massoud Zeydani, age 41, grand-nephew of Hezbollah Secretary General Nasim Hasbaya. Studied at Oxford. Chairman of the Hezbollah Central Council and rumoured to be your grand-uncle's heir apparent. Now get out of the car."

Massoud calmly kissed each of his daughters on the forehead. Then he clambered out of the rear seat and helped his daughters to follow suit before turning to affix Yossi Klein with a cool, contemptuous gaze.

6

"So this is what the vaunted Israeli army does these days? Make war on children?"

The hot flush of indignation that suffused Klein's cheeks remained invisible beneath the greenish-brown combat cosmetics covering his face. But the Israeli officer's deadpan expression could not hide the sharp-edged irritation in his voice.

"Fine words coming from someone who runs a terrorist militia that places rocket launchers in kindergartens. But I'm not here to argue military ethics. Your children will be fine. Avshalom, search him."

The Israeli rifleman stepped forth and gently detached the two daughters from their father's embrace. A meticulous pat-down of Massoud's body revealed a pistol concealed in the small of his back beneath an impeccably tailored grey suit jacket.

Aharon handed the Walther PPQ to his commander, who examined the weapon with a purse-lipped nod of respect.

"Nice," said Klein. "Glad you had sense enough not to use it."

The elder daughter – all of 11 years old – looked up at Klein with rage-filled eyes. "You are a bad man and I hate you," she spat in a smooth Oxbridge-accent worthy of the BBC.

"You speak English very well," Klein replied as he keyed the Madonna mic of his PRC710 headset and switched to Hebrew.

"Samson stations, this is Kodkod, I confirm packages are secure. Converge on my position in prep for movement to primary LZ. Team leaders conduct headcount and confirm all present."

Beckoning to his RTO, Klein clasped the HF PRC6020 handset to his ear. "Kodkod Gladiator, this is Kodkod Samson, Robespierre. I say again, Robespierre. We have zero casualties and will be moving shortly to the primary LZ. How copy?"

General Levine's deep bass voice came over the HF network in reply. "Gladiator, good copy. And the children?"

"Secured and unharmed along with the package. They'll be coming with us. And one of their security team as well."

"Well done, Samson. There'll be champagne waiting when you get home. The Dardarim are on schedule, but be advised that a civilian truck is travelling in your direction along Route Yakinton west-to-east. ETA your location is five-to-seven minutes. The neighbourhood is waking up. Time to hustle."

7

"Samson, good copy. We'll be on the move in less than two. Out."

With practised efficiency, the Israelis policed the ambush site and shouldered the heavy rucksacks they carried. The only residual testament to their presence were expended RPG-18 tubes and cartridge casings from Russian weapons that were a dime a dozen in Lebanon.

The troopers settled into their appointed places in an infantry formation known in the IDF as 'pi' because of its resemblance to the mathematical symbol. Klein took his place at the head of the π and was flanked by the two RPD gunners, each of whom led staggered parallel columns that constituted the formation's 'legs'. Massoud Zeydani and the Hezbollah security man walked with hands plasticuffed between the two columns along with the two young girls.

As the crow flies, it was only a distance of 1,700 metres from the ambush site to the primary landing zone. But the steep boulder-strewn mountainous terrain made the going extremely tough. The six-year-old began to flag almost immediately and one of the Israeli troopers scooped her up in his arms, depositing the little girl on his shoulders. She giggled in spite of herself, and Klein turned to look at the sound, grinning at the incongruous sight of a laughing hijab-clad girl borne atop a camo face-painted Israeli soldier. But the child's delighted chortles trailed off into a throttled silence under her father's disapproving glare.

Their route took them across the watershed of Lebanon Mountain Range and down to a barren spur that projected westwards from the main north-south ridgeline. The spur afforded a panoramic view of the verdant ridges and valleys that descended from Mount Lebanon to Byblos on the Mediterranean coast. But more importantly, it was the perfect LZ for a helicopter extraction – proximate to the target area, yet beyond line of sight or sound. There were no roads in the immediate vicinity and the flat expanse was large enough to accommodate two UH-60s landing abreast.

The first sign of their approaching deliverance was the distinctive thump of helicopter rotors knifing through the air. The nap-of-the-earth flight profile followed by the incoming choppers meant that they were heard well before they were seen.

Klein beckoned to his RTO for the PRC6020 handset. "Nakar Leader, this is Kodkod Samson. How do you read?"

"Five-by-five," came the voice of the lead helicopter pilot against the backdrop whine of two turbo-shaft engines turning over just two feet above his head. "We'll arrive your position in three. Throw smoke on eye contact."

"This is Kodkod Sampson, copy smoke on eye contact, out." Klein turned to Avi, his RTO. "The purple."

Avi nodded and extracted a violet M18 smoke grenade from his tactical vest.

An Apache Longbow popped into sight out of the valley bordering the spur to the North and settled into a low-altitude hover as Avi threw the smoke grenade off to the southern side of the LZ. After two seconds, it began to hiss and belch clouds of violet-hued smoke.

"I have purple," said the Apache pilot and formation leader while maintaining his hover.

"Affirmative purple," replied Klein.

"This is Nakar Leader. Three and Four are authorised. Five and Six, wait in place while Two takes up overwatch to the South. After the first wave clears the LZ, the second wave – numbers Five and Six – will land and load. Then we all egress in formation per plan. Execute."

A second Apache materialised out of the vale and settled into a hover, its deadly snout pointed westwards to cover their exfiltration route to the Mediterranean. Moments later, a pair of Blackhawks climbed into view and set down in the centre of the spur amidst a massive cloud of brown dust.

With a choreographed efficiency that bespoke intensive rehearsal, every second man of the Israeli force withdrew from the security perimeter and assembled in two kneeling queues opposite the brace of Blackhawks. The commanders of Teams Two and Three, a captain and senior lieutenant, went down the queue, counting off each man with an accompanying smack on the helmet. When finished, both officers turned towards Klein and signified all present with thumbs up gestures. The officers then guided their respective queues of men through the helicopters' side doors, themselves boarding last.

The whirr of the Blackhawks' rotors deepened to a staccato *thwap-thwap* as the feathering angle of the blades shifted to generate lift. The northern chopper took off in another cloud of dust, followed ten seconds later by its twin – and they assumed a hovering position on either side of Apache No. Two.

The second pair of Blackhawks swept into the now vacant LZ and the same procedure was followed – with the remaining Israeli troopers forming into orderly lines opposite each chopper door.

Zeydani and his daughters were loaded into Klein's helicopter while the bound Hezbollah bodyguard was bundled into the sixth chopper. Configured in seatless tactical format, the handcuffed Hezbollah official was placed against the rear bulkhead of the helicopter's cargo compartment with the two girls by his side.

Once the Blackhawk was airborne, Yossi Klein shut his eyes as he felt days of accumulated tension drain away. He could now afford to relax because things were no longer up to him. No more life-and-death tactical decisions; no more ethical dilemmas; no more ever-present anxiety that the wrong move at the wrong time might bring disaster to those for whom he was responsible. Now someone else was in the driver's seat – literally.

It was special operations tactics 101 that a raiding force should never withdraw along the same route previously used to infiltrate enemy territory. And thus, the Israeli helicopter formation skimmed the ridgeline to the North, descending deep into a neighbouring mountain valley that would serve as its path of egress to the Mediterranean. The detour didn't add much to their flight path and the choppers soon debouched from the mountain valley into the heavily populated Lebanese coastal plain. They reached the outskirts of Byblos just as the city was beginning to stir from its nocturnal torpor. A hijab-clad matron hanging laundry on a rooftop clothesline stared open-mouthed at the sight of impudent Zionist infidels skimming past just a few metres above her head.

The helicopters proceeded out to sea for another ten kilometres before turning southwards for home. Beneath the watchful gaze of four F-16Is flying top cover at 30,000 feet, the final leg of exfil was utterly uneventful.

The formation made landfall north of Haifa and set course for Wing 1, the formal military designation of Ramat David airbase located some twenty-five kilometres inland at the edge of the Jezreel Valley. The two Apache Longbows peeled off towards the helicopter refuelling point, while the four Blackhawks flared into landings at the far western end of the base.

As Klein clambered out of the chopper and glanced at the reception party assembled on the tarmac, he wasn't surprised to see a coterie of senior officers waiting amongst the crowd. It was routine for the brass to welcome the safe return of a Matkal detachment from a particularly deep penetration mission into hostile territory.

Major General Simha Levine approached, sporting a broad smile and with hand outstretched. "Well done!" he yelled over the whine of the Blackhawk's engines in his trademark gravelly growl. Levine gestured towards a waiting Scania coach parked at the edge of the landing pad. "Get the boys on the bus. We've laid on a meal at one of the fighter squadron briefing rooms."

Klein glanced back at the choppers as a quartet of men clad in distinctive Shabak bodyguard jackets marched the still-shackled Massoud Zeydani to an unmarked VW Transporter Van. A female captain with a medical corps shoulder tag was ushering the children to a waiting ambulance.

"What will happen with the girls?" Klein enquired.

Levine shrugged. "As we discussed over the net, their presence was a surprise. But the PM has been briefed and tomorrow he'll instruct the Foreign Ministry to contact the International Red Cross. I assume they'll be back home in Beirut within a few days."

Klein nodded. "That's good. The boys will be pleased."

"Speaking of the boys, let's get them fed. You can ride with me."

The two men strode over to the Levine's Range Rover. Klein removed his tactical vest, handing it to the general's driver who deposited it in the SUV's baggage compartment.

"Hope I don't stain the leather," said Klein with a self-deprecating smile as he slid into the rear seat.

"Don't worry about it," said Levine as he passed a packet of baby wipes over his shoulder. Klein spent the short ride across the airfield removing brownish-green camo paint from his face and hands.

The meal that awaited them in the squadron briefing room was sumptuous by Israeli military standards. The normal complement of chairs and desks had been cleared away and replaced by dining tables heaped with platters of chicken schnitzel, accompanied by Israeli salad and bowls of hummus. The promised champagne – five bottles of Yarden Blanc de Blancs 2008 – was apportioned amongst the men. Klein raised his cup of kosher bubbly and commenced the meal with the traditional bor'eay blessing over wine.

The feasting and merriment that followed were brought to an end when Major General Levine clinked his glass with a fork and gestured to the airbase security officer. The air force major took his cue and ushered the mess attendants out of the room while stationing himself outside the now-closed door.

"I'll begin with congratulations on a near flawless mission," said Levine. "Some might say that you performed beyond expectations. But that would be untrue, because the professional excellence you showed at every step of this operation is precisely what we expect of you. So, if there's any champagne left, let's raise another glass and make a lehaim to your accomplishment."

The major general paused until all the other banqueters were on their feet with cups recharged. "Lehaim!"

"Lehaim!" echoed the raiding party members.

"Please be seated," said Levine while remaining upright. He stood silently until the troopers settled in their places and the sound of scraping chair legs subsided.

"While you're obviously aware of what you've done, you've been kept in the dark about why you've done it. Until now. It will be all over the news as of tomorrow morning, but I think you've earned a preview."

Levine motioned to an aide, who quickly opened a tripod easel upon which was placed a 1:100,000 scale map of northern Lebanon. A photograph of Massoud Zeydani was affixed to the northwest corner of the map over the Mediterranean Sea.

"Of course, you all know the identity of our target," said Levine. "Massoud Zeydani, grand-nephew of Hezbollah Secretary General Nasim Hasbaya. Zeydani is also Chairman of the Hezbollah Central Council and rumoured to be his grand-uncle's heir apparent. He has a degree from Oxford and speaks perfect English. He's a favoured guest on CNN and the BBC who has raised jihadi bullshit-peddling into a real art form. He's a real pain in our ass."

Levine paused in his delivery to flash a grin at the assembled troopers, who all faithfully delivered the expected guffawed response. Years of experience as a combat commander had fine-tuned the Israeli general's thespian talent for playing to a military crowd.

"But Zeydani's annoyance factor is not the reason why we snatched him. How many of you know the name Nir Boker?"

A grove of hands shot up.

"You," said Levine, his finger pointing to a trooper seated midway along the table.

"He was a pilot who was shot down over Lebanon," said the fresh-faced trooper.

12

"Nine-and-a-half out of ten," replied Levine. "In fact, he was the navigator of a Phantom fighter that was hit by anti-aircraft fire over Sidon. We managed to rescue the pilot, but Boker was captured by Hezbollah. The object of your operation was to acquire a bargaining chip for negotiating his release. It's about time we bring him home."

Another hand shot up and Levine nodded in acknowledgement of the new questioner.

"Wasn't that tried before?" asked the trooper with the forthright informality that marked the quasi-egalitarian culture of Israel's tier-one special ops unit. Formal military rank did not bestow a monopoly on wisdom in Sayeret Matkal, and the voices of the Unit's most junior soldiers were afforded full hearing alongside those of their officers. "How do we know he's even alive? It's been over thirty years."

"Absolutely correct," conceded Levine. "Back in the 1980s and early 1990s, we snatched two Shia Muslim militia leaders from their homes in southern Lebanon. But neither Abdul Kareem Obeid nor Mustafa Dirani carried enough weight to seal the deal. So, this time we upped the ante. This time we decided to strike a lot closer to home. And by snagging Nasim Hasbaya's much-loved grand-nephew and designated successor, we hope to make an offer the Hezbollah Chairman can't refuse."

"And Boker's status?" persisted the trooper. "How do we know he's still alive?"

"We don't, but at the end of the day it doesn't matter. If he's alive, great. And if he's dead, at least we'll be able to give his remains a proper Jewish burial. The Prime Minister attended the wedding of Boker's daughter last year and promised to do everything possible to bring about her father's return. You are the fulfillment of that promise. That should make you very proud. Further questions?"

None were forthcoming and Levine nodded. "Alright then, let's get you back to Sirkin where you can shower and get some overdue sleep. I'll see you tomorrow evening at 19:00 for a formal after-action debrief. And, once that's complete, you'll be granted a ten-day furlough in recognition of a job well done."

As the happy troopers filed out of the dining room, Levine turned to Yossi Klein and said, "Ride with me. Sirkin is on my way, so I'll drop you at the base. There are a couple of things I want to discuss."

After apprising one of the Matkal team leaders of his alternative travel arrangements, Klein settled into the plush leather of the Land Rover's rear seat and immediately fell asleep.

Awakened by a hand on his shoulder, Klein wiped his eyes and noticed that they were just passing Barkai Junction. Halfway there.

"Sorry, I dozed off."

"Don't worry about it. You've earned a bit of rest, which is precisely the matter I wanted to discuss. What are your plans for the next ten days?"

Klein shrugged. "I haven't given it much thought. There's always work …"

"Cut the crap," interjected General Levine. "Don't forget I've known you since the day you got off the bus as a wet-behind-the-ears recruit. So, listen up; you 'will' put on civvies; you 'will' disappear from the army; and I don't want to hear of you showing your face around base until Sunday next at the earliest. Do I make myself clear?"

"Good copy, over."

Choosing to ignore the undertone of sarcasm in Klein's response, Levine paused before continuing in a tone that radiated paternal concern. "You know, it wouldn't hurt to spend a couple of days around the house. I drove past last week and the grass is getting a little wild."

Klein just shook his head, his eyes gazing through the window at the darkened countryside sporadically illuminated by the headlights of passing cars.

"How about a few days with us, then? Shoshi would love to see you. She's worried about you. We all are."

Klein's mouth curled in a melancholy smile. "Thanks, but I think I'll head to Eilat and do a bit of reef diving."

"Sounds like fun," replied Levine. "Take as much time as you need. Heaven knows you've accrued enough leave."

Klein cast a quizzical look at his superior.

Levine nodded unapologetically. "Yes, I took the liberty of checking your personnel file. But that's beside the point, which is your need for some R&R. So, don't spend all your time communing with the dolphins. Eilat is full of blonde Scandinavians on holiday this time of year and that means lots of fish in that particular sea. It's a target rich environment and you should partake."

Klein's eyes rolled. "Simcha, you've gone from trying to fix me up with every single woman in your extended family to organising a one-night stand with some nameless Danish tourist? Your standards are slipping."

A snort of self-deprecation sounded from the front passenger seat. "It's not good for man to be alone," said Levine, quoting Genesis. "But seriously, your next mission ... and you will choose to accept it ... is to recharge your psychic batteries and get laid in the process. The mission board is empty and there's nothing looming on the horizon."

"Never say never. This is the Middle East after all."

"Acknowledged," replied Levine. "And if something unexpected crops up, we'll have one of the other teams handle it. So don't call us because I certainly won't be calling you."

Events would soon prove him wrong.

MAVO

One

Propelled by force of habit, Gerhard Hoffman's hand swept aside the lapel of his business jacket and made for his left interior pocket. His fingers longingly caressed the rigid outline of the Marlboro packet through the silky softness of the jacket's lining. Hoffman was in dire need of a nicotine hit – but his passion would have to remain unrequited while he graced the grounds of the Charlemagne. Smoking was strictly verboten within the confines of Cologne's swankiest hotel.

Nor was it the only passion he would have to deny himself. He tried not to look as a dolled-to-the-nines platinum blonde swayed by atop a pair of 5-inch Jimmy Choo stiletto heels. With a quiet sigh of regret, he averted his eyes from her come-hither glance. Another place, another time, perhaps. The business that currently engaged him precluded any indulgence in the business of carnal pleasure.

At the core of any valid stereotype resides an indispensable kernel of truth, and the scientists attending the biennial conference of the International Mathematical Physics Society were pretty much what you'd expect. Tortoiseshell spectacles with Coke-bottle lenses, beards of varied lengths and hair notable more for its disarray than any discernible coiffeur. A troop of kangaroos, a pride of lions and a murder of crows. This was a congeries of nerds.

Hoffmann kept a close watch on the crowd flowing into the Charlemagne's lobby from the just-completed session in Conference Room Four. There! A quick glance at the conference program booklet was enough to confirm the identity of his quarry. Hitching the strap of the worn leather messenger bag over his shoulder, he moved to intercept.

"Good afternoon, Professor Adivi," said Hoffmann in German-accented English to a bald, lanky septuagenarian clad in an open-necked shirt and khaki trousers. "My name is Dr Gerhard Hoffmann. I wonder whether I might impose on a few minutes of your time?"

Adivi cast an appraising glance at his interlocutor. "Sorry, but I only have thirty minutes before the next session. Just long enough to grab a bite to eat."

"I fully understand," replied Hoffmann. "And I've taken the liberty of making lunch reservations at the hotel restaurant on the mezzanine floor. I think you'll find the menu infinitely preferable to the assembly line fare offered at these conference events."

Adivi shrugged. "I'm never one to turn down a free meal, so lead the way."

The men ascended to the mezzanine level and made their way towards a sign emblazoned with a hunting horn and the inscription 'Lied von Roland'. They passed beneath it into an establishment where leather furnishings and stained-glass windows reflected a medieval motif.

"Reservierung für Hoffmann, Bitte."

The maître d' cast a barely concealed look of disdain towards the casually clad Adivi before slipping back into his role of gracious host. "Ja, wilkommen Meine Herren. Hier entlang, bitte."

"I hope the food is better than the décor," muttered Adivi with a nod towards the larger-than-life statue of a medieval knight looming over the centre of the main dining area.

Hoffmann laughed. "Yes, they do take the whole Holy Roman Empire thing to an extreme. But you'll find that the spätzle is excellent."

Beckoning for a waitress to follow, the maître d' led Hoffmann and Adivi to a private dining room that hosted two lonely place settings on a table large enough to accommodate ten times that number.

"I was told you don't adhere to Jewish dietary rules," said Hoffmann apologetically. "I hope that's correct."

"Not a problem. But I see you've gone to considerable trouble arranging all this. So perhaps you can get to the point and tell me what I'm doing here?"

Hoffmann opened his messenger bag and extracted a bottle of Bruichladdich Octomore whiskey. "Allow me to begin by offering a token of my respect. This is yours, regardless of whether you accept my proposition."

Adivi examined the amber contents of the bottle for a few moments before looking up to examine his interlocutor with an inquisitive gaze. "Very impressive. You know my favourite brand of scotch whisky and that I don't keep kosher. What else have your enquiries unearthed?"

"Professor Aaron Adivi, Emeritus Professor of Physics at Tel Aviv University. Only child of Holocaust survivors who met after the war in a British detention camp on Cyprus. Graduate of the Israeli army's 'Talpiot' program that recruits the best and brightest into its military R&D program. Earned a doctorate in particle physics at MIT and went on to a tenured faculty position at Tel Aviv University. Awarded visiting teaching and research fellowships at Stanford, Cambridge and the University of Melbourne. Not to mention considerable work at that particular facility in the desert Israelis don't like to mention. Never married and no children. Lover of Verdi opera and the world's most heavily peated brand of scotch whiskey. Need I go on?"

Adivi doffed his head in grudging acknowledgement. "Okay, you've done your homework. Now let's move on to why I'm here. What's this proposition of yours?"

"It's very simple, really. Accompany me to my lab in Göttingen where I'll demonstrate a revolutionary process that will completely upend your understanding of quantum physics."

"So you're a physicist?"

"Of course," replied Hoffmann. "PhD from the Technische Universität München in 1987 and a tenured university position."

Adivi smiled sceptically. "My mother once told me that if something sounds too good to be true, it probably is. Add to that the fact that the world of academic physics is a very small place. I haven't heard about any paradigm-shattering discovery coming out of the Georg-August-Universität Göttingen. So why shouldn't I conclude that you're either delusional or up to no good?"

"I can think of twenty-five thousand reasons," answered Hoffmann. Reaching again into his messenger bag, the German produced a bulky buff A3 envelope that he placed on the table.

Adivi arched his eyebrows, saying nothing.

"Go ahead, open it," invited Hoffmann.

Adivi reached over and picked up the envelope. He opened the flap and peered inside at the neat stacks of crisp, new €100 bills. Looking up from the envelope, he saw Hoffmann grinning with clear enjoyment.

"At the latest rate of exchange, twenty-five thousand euros works out to around one hundred thousand shekels. And they're yours in return for a one-day visit to my lab."

Adivi closed the envelope and pursed his lips sceptically. "How do I know you're not some nutter, or a radical leftist who's made common cause with Hezbollah? How do I know this isn't a kidnap plot that will end with me in some rat-infested Beirut cellar? Or even worse, handed over to the Iranians? Our security officials brief us on such threats, you know."

Hoffmann broke into a low chuckle. "Herr Professor, I can assure you of my pro-Zionist sentiments. The most rudimentary enquiry by your Shin Bet people will be adequate to verify my philosemitic bona fides. But if you're really worried, I'd be quite happy for a security detachment from the Israeli Embassy to tag along. It really doesn't matter because I ultimately hope to be working jointly with your government on this project."

"And what 'project' might that be?"

"Sorry," said Hoffmann with a definitive shake of the head, "but that's something you'll have to see with your own eyes. I'll be happy to provide any explanations you require after witnessing what my project can do. But until then … what do they say, 'a picture's worth a thousand words?'"

"I should be sent to a psychiatrist for even considering this," Adivi said.

"Think about it this way. Göttingen is around three hundred kilometres from Cologne. The way I drive that's about three-hours up the autobahn. With me at the wheel, you could get there and back the same day. Not much effort for 25,000 euros in cash, you must admit."

"Fine," said Adivi. "When?"

"That depends on you. You've given your paper and I didn't see you listed for any other event on the conference program. Do you have any other engagements here in Cologne?"

Adivi shook his head.

"If you're willing to stay overnight, we could leave immediately."

Adivi shook his head. "I'm booked on a 5 pm flight from Frankfurt tomorrow afternoon and that means a change of ticket if I accept your crazy offer."

"What if I take care of the travel logistics and, in the bargain, I cover any added fees or charges? Does that sound fair?"

Adivi shrugged. "I suppose so."

Now that the deal was sealed, Hoffmann's tobacco cravings struck with redoubled force.

"Let's order something to eat, shall we? I recommend the spätzle, which is quite good."

"Yes, so you said."

Hoffmann beckoned the waitress, who loitered discretely outside the door watching for her summons through the porthole-shaped window.

"Eine portion von krautwickle und spätzle für jeden von uns, bitte. Und eine flasche ihres besten rot, ebenso."

"Sehr gut," responded the waitress with a smile, and decamped to convey their meal choice.

"Now, if you'll excuse me, I'll be back in a minute."

Adivi nodded, his attention already transferred to his iPhone.

Hoffmann exited the dining room and made a beeline for the end of the corridor where a door opened onto an open-air courtyard. Nodding in acknowledgement to a fellow smoker puffing away at the far end of the atrium, he lit a Marlboro and sighed as the nicotine hit his system.

But the German physicist's contentment derived not only from the satisfaction of his physical dependence. Seen firsthand, the thing would sell itself. This he had never doubted. And now Adivi had agreed to come, the deal was on the cusp of being sealed.

Stubbing out the end of his cigarette, Hoffmann pushed his way through the hotel side door and retraced the way he had come.

Adivi was examining the wine bottle label as Hoffmann entered the dining room.

"I hope you don't mind that I didn't wait, but this was too good to resist."

Hoffmann took the bottle from the hands of his guest. "2012 Penfolds Cabernet Shiraz. I'm no wine expert, but I did ask for the best red in their cellar. I'm glad you approve."

"I do, indeed. It's delicious."

"I'll order another bottle that we'll take with us tomorrow. Think of it as a fringe benefit."

"My favourite whiskey, my travel expenses, a large payment in cash and now a 100-euro bottle of premium Australian wine. You're beginning to look a bit desperate. How do I know this project of yours is legal?"

"I prefer the word 'eager' rather than 'desperate'," replied Hoffmann with a smile. "And yes, I can assure you everything will be entirely above board from the perspective of the Israeli government."

The door swung open and the waitress entered, arms laden with two platters piled high with stuffed cabbage and pasta.

"Wird es noch etwas anderes geben?" she enquired after distributing food to the two diners.

"Nein danke," replied Hoffmann.

Taking the hint, the waitress withdrew.

"Remind me how to say bon appètit in Hebrew?" asked Hoffmann as he poured himself a glass of wine.

"Beh tayavon."

"Right ... beh tayavon," echoed Hoffmann as he tucked a napkin into his shirt collar.

"Todah Rabbah," replied Adivi.

"That one I remember," said Hoffmann with an impish grin.

And with that the conversation faded, replaced by the tinkling of cutlery on porcelain as both men focused their full attention on the meal in front of them.

Two

NOW

"Good morning Professor," said Hoffmann with a cheery smile as Adivi exited the elevator with a mid-sized suitcase in tow. "Are you checked out?"

"Yes," replied the Israeli. "I'm good to go."

"Well then, come along. We're over on the right."

Hoffmann led the way to an elevator that transported the pair down into the cavernous bowels of a basement garage. Their footfalls echoed off the structure's walls, until the tranquillity of the subterranean parking area was disturbed by the loud chirping of an automobile's keyless entry being activated.

"Ah, there we are," said Hoffmann as he pointed towards flashing lights. The German scientist smiled at the surprised expression on Adivi's face when the Israeli discovered that the vehicle in question was a 2015 Mercedes-Benz SLS AMG Coupé.

"Not exactly what you expected, I take it?" asked Hoffmann with a laugh as he pushed the keyless entry button to swing open the car's distinctive gullwing doors.

"Well, you have to admit it isn't the normal mode of transportation for your average academic," replied Adivi. "I'm more of a Toyota Camry man, myself. There's barely enough room here in the back for my suitcase, and fuel consumption must be nightmarish. But there's no denying it's a beautiful piece of machinery."

"Hope you don't hold it against me," said Hoffmann once they both were seated. "This is the only personal indulgence I've allowed myself from the fruit of my grandfather's ill-gotten gains."

"What was he, a bank robber?"

"I should be so lucky," answered Hoffmann with a rueful smile. "But I said all questions would be answered once you've had an opportunity to inspect the lab. So sit back and enjoy the ride. The scenery is stunning this time of year. The colours are just beginning to show, and the effect can be quite spectacular."

Hoffmann wheeled the Benz smoothly out of the parking garage, maneuvering through the streets of Cologne with a deftness that Adivi found a bit surprising. It took them only fifteen minutes to traverse the city centre and reach the speed-limitless autobahn where the roadster's full potential came into play. Moving at an average speed of 140 kilometres per hour along the A1, they reached the outskirts of Dortmund within 45 minutes. A quick stop for breakfast and they were back on the road, moving quickly through Kassel and northwards up the A7 along the Leine River. Fields of deep brown loam lay naked on either side of the highway, shorn of the summer crop with the harvest now complete. Thickets of oak, maple and elm displayed the first crimson portents of an even more brilliant technicolour autumn to come.

"I'm pretty much a philistine when it comes to aesthetic matters," said Adivi, "but you were right about the scenery. Even I have to admit it's phenomenal."

"A lot like upstate New York," replied Hoffmann.

"Or the Berkshires. I went there one autumn while studying for my PhD."

Hoffmann nodded in silent understanding as a sign announcing their approach to Göttingen loomed in the distance. Hoffmann took the first Göttingen off-ramp, driving across the river and turned south to the Bürgerstrasse, skirting the medieval town centre. As they drove towards the city's periphery, the homes became progressively newer and the lots on which they were built progressively larger.

"Göttingen is primarily a university town, is it not?" enquired Adivi.

"Since 1734," Hoffmann replied.

"What's the population?"

"Just over 100,000 during the academic year, about half of them students. Things are quiet when the students are away during the mid-term holidays, but when the university's in session there are lectures and music recitals. The town has a nice ambience. All in all, it's a pleasant place to live."

The Benz passed through Mittleberg, a neighbourhood nestled in the lee of the hilly Göttinger Wald that overlooked the city from the East. Hoffmann turned on to Vor Dem Walde, the final street of the housing estate before the wooded terrain sloped sharply upward. Roughly halfway down the street, he pulled into the entrance of a driveway blocked by a heavy wrought iron gate set between high ivy-covered brick walls.

Hoffmann pressed the button on a remote control affixed to the sun visor and the gate began to open. Once the way was clear, he nosed the Benz towards a large modern one-storey home standing in the midst of a grassy three-acre lot.

"This is it," he proclaimed as he brought the car to a stop near a path leading to the front door.

Adivi stepped out of the car, stretched and looked around at the wall that encased the entire property in all directions. "You certainly value your privacy."

"With good reason. Please bring your things and we'll go inside."

Adivi removed his suitcase from the trunk and followed Hoffmann through the front door. After a short pit stop, the Israeli physicist was ushered into another room where he stopped to peruse his surroundings.

"Very impressive," observed Adivi. "Is that a Cray?" he asked, with a nod towards the large bank of computers covering almost one entire wall.

"Yeah," responded Hoffmann. "An XC30-AC. The calculations involved in my little enterprise are quite delicate, so I needed something with a little ... computational muscle, shall we say?"

"Muscle indeed," said Adivi. "When you spoke of Göttingen, I assumed you'd be taking me to the departmental physics lab."

"Oh no, I've never had any affiliation with the Georgia Augusta. Frieberg is where I taught. For thirteen years."

"Then why are we here in Göttingen?" asked Adivi. "What's the connection?"

"As I said before, all will become clear."

"There's more and better equipment here in your home than I've seen on many campuses. All purchased with those ill-gotten gains you previously mentioned, I assume?"

"Correct," said Hoffmann. "But we'll talk about that later. Now I want to introduce the pièce de résistance. Through here," he said, as he gestured to an open doorway. Adivi strode through the threshold into a room filled with equipment clearly scientific in function, yet unrecognisable in his experience.

Adivi's attention was immediately drawn to an object that reminded him of a manned space capsule from the 1960s. Even stranger was the fact that this windowless metallic cone was ensconced in a circular aperture inset within the floor. As he approached, he observed that the aperture extended through the entire foundation and the capsule was perched on the bare earth below.

"Where'd you get all this, a NASA yard sale?" asked Adivi, his voice tinged by sarcasm. "Planning a trip to the moon?"

"Not the moon," replied Hoffmann with a cryptic laugh as he walked over to a large wall safe and tapped in a digital combination. The safe swung open and he extracted two thermos-sized metallic cylinders from within. Walking to the capsule, Hoffmann then placed his palm on a slightly recessed rectangle placed at shoulder height. A series of hums and clicks sounded as an electrical lock disengaged and a hatch-like door swung open to reveal two seats positioned Gemini-style, side-by-side within.

"One very important thing. It's vital you stay away from the aperture in the floor," Hoffmann said, as he climbed into the left-hand seat. "Regardless of what happens, of what you see, keep your distance. Are we clear?"

"Clear."

"Then it's show time," proclaimed the German physicist as he pressed a button within the capsule to close the hatch.

Three

Behind his cultivated façade of nonchalance, Adivi grappled with a rising tide of internal suspense as he waited for 'it' to happen. For a few moments, nothing did. Yet, just as his sense of anticipation began to metamorphose into annoyance, the capsule disappeared from view.

For a moment Adivi stood transfixed, his brain at war with his eyes. But then his scientific training kicked in and he began to analyse what he had just witnessed. Some sort of cloaking device, perhaps? He took two steps towards the aperture before remembering Hoffmann's stringent admonition, then looked around and noticed a cheap ballpoint pen on a nearby table. Picking it up, he threw it into the aperture. It bounced once and came to rest on the bare earth.

Before Adivi could speculate further, the capsule suddenly rematerialised in precisely the same location it had previously occupied, crushing the pen into small plastic fragments. With a whirr and click, the hatch opened – and there was Hoffmann, grinning broadly as he unstrapped himself from his seat.

"What the hell was that?" Adivi bellowed, the final vestiges of his affected indifference crumbling beneath waxing excitement.

"My dear Professor, it was a simple demonstration that time travel is not only theoretically feasible, but also practically possible. I went sixty seconds into the future and simply waited until you caught up."

Hoffmann stepped out of the capsule, yawned and stretched rather ostentatiously. "Would you care to join me for an afternoon snack? All this jumping around through time really gives me an appetite."

Hoffmann walked out of the room, leaving the bewildered Adivi to hasten along in his wake like an errant puppy. Crossing through the computer lab, the Hoffmann entered a nicely appointed kitchen with few signs of heavy use. He opened a large stainless-steel refrigerator and peered inside.

"Let me see," he mused, extracting a wooden plate with a large slab of yellow cheese. "We have a very satisfactory Gouda, and is Darjeeling satisfactory?"

"Whatever," replied Adivi with a dismissive wave. "Darjeeling is fine. But I really want to talk about what …"

"Ah, ah, ah," interrupted Hoffmann as he waved his right index finger didactically. "Let's have a nice cup of tea first."

Adivi rolled his eyes in silent frustration, but took a seat as instructed at the large wooden table in the dining alcove. Once Hoffmann had arranged the afternoon repast to his satisfaction, he sat down and poured them both a strong brew of tea.

"What I just saw goes against every principle of physics that has governed my entire professional life!" Adivi erupted, ignoring the steaming hot cup before him. "So please put me out of my suspense. You owe me an explanation."

"Fine, fine," sighed Hoffmann. "It's quite complex, but the fundamentals revolve around helium-2."

"Helium-2? But that's never been isolated."

"Until now," said Hoffmann with a smug smile. "I've been fiddling for a few years now and I've developed a method of extracting two neutrons from helium-4. And, as it turns out, the negative binding energy generated by the Pauli Exclusion Principle opens a portal that allows travel through time. Anyone or anything in physical contact with the helium when this reaction takes place is sucked through the portal."

"So that's why the aperture goes all the way through the floor and the capsule rests on bare ground," said Adivi with a nod of dawning comprehension.

"Quite correct," replied Hoffmann. "If the capsule were touching any part of this house, the entire building would be taken along for the ride. Having a 4,500-square foot home suddenly materialise out of nothing in another era could prove a bit awkward."

"To say the least," observed Adivi. "But we're skimming the surface here. I'm still trying to get my head around this, and more detail would help. What can you tell me about how the helium extraction process works?"

"Sorry," replied Hoffmann with a negative shake of the head. "I'm happy to discuss the other aspects of this proposal, but the mechanics of helium-2 isolation will have to remain off-limits, at least for the time being."

"Then what more is there to say?" said Adivi in a palpable tone of pique. "I think this has been a waste of my time and your money."

30

"Hardly, my dear Professor," replied Hoffmann in a soothing tone. "Surely you have many other questions that I'd be more than pleased to answer."

Adivi pondered for several moments. "Okay, tell me how you're able to calculate the temporal direction of the capsule's travel, and how far forward or backward through time it will go?"

"The temporal direction and length of travel are determined by the quantity of helium-2 unleashed within the machine."

"And you can calculate this?"

Hoffmann nodded. "The computations are quite complex and considerable precision is required to have any confidence in the destination date – hence the Cray. But before we get into the business of crunching numbers, I think it would be useful for you to experience the process yourself. So how about it? Would you care to become the second person ever to travel through time?"

Adivi found himself nodding his head even before he made a conscious decision to vocalise his assent.

"Excellent," said Hoffmann. "Now eat up. Otherwise you'll be ravenous."

Roughly 20 minutes later, Hoffmann pushed his chair away from the table. "I suppose there's no time like the present," he said with a sophomoric grin. Then he sauntered over to a sideboard and picked up a small green backpack. He pointed to a book on the kitchen counter next to the stove. "Could you get that for me?"

Adivi briefly perused the copy of *Believe and Destroy: Intellectuals in the SS War Machine*. "Pretty depressing fare," he observed.

Hoffmann smiled as he placed the book in his backpack. "Didn't Santayana say that those who forget the past are condemned to repeat it?"

Adivi shrugged. "I studied physics, not philosophy."

Hoffmann nodded and conducted Adivi back to the capsule room. In short order, both men were strapped into their respective seats under a closed hatch.

A stainless-steel console with a keypad atop it was situated between the two seats. Hoffmann punched in a code and the top of the console slid aside to reveal a custom-formed space that was a perfect match for the thermos-like cylinders.

"Ready?" he enquired with a smile.

"I suppose so," said Adivi with a nervous gulp.

Hoffmann loaded a cylinder into the console and again punched the keyboard, causing the console's lid to slide shut. Settling himself comfortably in his seat, he glanced over at Adivi. "It takes a while to build up a head of steam, so I'd advise you to relax."

Hoffmann then proceeded to follow his own advice, shutting his eyes in insouciant repose.

Four

The process of time travel itself struck Adivi as quite underwhelming. In fact, it was all rather peaceful, featuring neither the whizzing nor tempestuous buffeting of HG Wells' *Time Machine* or a B-Grade 50s sci-fi flick.

The top of the console suddenly popped open, causing Hoffmann's eyes to do the same.

"That's it," he remarked, hitting another button that opened the hatch to reveal stygian darkness without.

"This isn't your lab," blurted Adivi. "Where are we?"

"Come with me if you want to find out," replied Hoffmann as he clambered out of the capsule. Within moments, he was engulfed by the all-enveloping night.

Adivi hesitated a few moments before following. He smelled the pine needles before his eyes adjusted sufficiently to allow him to discern his surroundings. He was standing in a cedar wood. The floor was crisscrossed by shadows cast by trees in the dim light of a crescent moon.

"Over here," called Hoffmann.

Through the gloom, Adivi was able to make out Hoffmann's silhouette. "This obviously isn't your house. Let me ask again, where are we? Does this mean your device can move spatially as well as temporally?"

"Soon all will become clear," replied Hoffmann as he walked away through the trees.

"Just a minute!" yelled Adivi, but Hoffmann continued on as if oblivious. Rather than be left alone in an unfamiliar place, the Adivi followed suit.

At the edge of the tree line, Hoffmann approached a brace of bicycles chained to a particularly robust cedar. Extracting a key from his pocket, he opened the padlock and released the bicycles, taking one while leaving the other leaning against the tree. Hoffmann gestured towards the bike. "Come along now. We'll have to hurry if we don't want to miss the show."

Hoffmann pushed his bicycle out of the woods into a furrowed field towards a dark ribbon that soon materialised into a dirt road. On reaching this earthen byway, he mounted his bike and began pedalling towards lights that signified human habitation. Adivi followed, careful to avoid the deepest ruts in a rural lane that had clearly seen more use than maintenance.

The air was thick with the sour smell of freshly spread nitrate fertiliser emanating from the fields on either side. A thickly wooded ridge reared up to their left, its stands of cedars extruding from the slope like the bristles of a giant black hedgehog.

After ten minutes of pedalling, Hoffmann and Adivi passed from open farmland into a residential area that featured small homes of wood construction. As they progressed further through suburbia, the quality of the roads and housing improved, with dirt lanes metamorphosing into macadam and the homes becoming larger.

By the time they reached their first fully paved road, the area was illuminated by electrified streetlamps that revealed the street into which they were turning was named Hauptstraße. The poplar trees that lined the road cast crisscrossed shadows that resembled the work of a manic modern artist. Their surroundings were now much more urban, dominated by brick homes and larger public buildings.

As he rode in the wake of his German colleague, Adivi was struck by an ill-defined feeling that there was something odd occurring. He'd noticed that they'd been passing a far greater number of horse-drawn wagons parked along the side of the road than motor vehicles. And now that they were passing through a more urban environment, the cars and trucks looked like exhibits from an automotive museum.

Then it all suddenly clicked. Adivi pedalled furiously, overtaking and forcing Hoffmann to halt. "This is the past, isn't it?" he demanded almost out of breath. "You've taken us back in time!"

Hoffmann frowned in annoyance. "Professor Adivi, what I'm about to demonstrate is the only way to get a complete picture of what this enterprise is all about. But if we dally here that opportunity will be lost, and all will be for naught. Time is of the essence, if you'll excuse the pun. So please, trust me."

Adivi nodded his grudging assent and the two men continued on their way. At a Y-junction, Hoffmann bore left, and Adivi followed into what the signs proclaimed to be Geismar Landstraße. Circumnavigating a small rectangular park, the two pedalled further in what Adivi, orienting himself from Polaris, knew to be a northwards direction. Here they entered a neighbourhood with tiled row houses indicating a more ancient provenance. "Jüdenstraße," proclaimed the white rectangular sign affixed to one of the buildings they passed.

The Street of the Jews curved sharply west and Hoffmann turned at the next intersection into the Weenderstraße. Never one to appreciate being led by the nose, Adivi was once again on the cusp of giving vent to his spleen – but, before he could act, Hoffmann pulled into a plaza that fronted an imposing baroque-style building complete with grand stone steps and massive oak doors.

"We're here," said Hoffmann with a bright smile as he propped his bicycle against a nearby tree.

"Where is 'here' and what are we doing?"

Hoffmann pointed at the baroque building. "That building is known as the 'Alte Auditorium' and it houses the law faculty of the Georg-August-Universität in Göttingen. At least it did in 1929, which is when we are now."

"That's the 'when and the where'," shot back Adivi, "but I'm still waiting to hear the 'what' and the 'why.'"

The evening quiet was suddenly disturbed by the peal of a nearby church bell.

"Good," replied Hoffmann in a tone of voice that conveyed a sense of relief. "We made it just in time."

A few moments later, the Auditorium began to disgorge students by the score. Hoffmann watched carefully as a gaggle of aspiring lawyers made their way down the front steps and into the plaza.

The time travellers were positioned such that anyone leaving through the Auditorium's main entrance would pass directly to their front. And, as a group of twentysomethings came abreast, Hoffmann called out, "Hallo Otto!"

A tall, fair-haired student stopped and turned around with a quizzical expression. "Entschuldigung, aber kenne ich Sie?" the young man enquired politely.

"Nicht wirklich," replied Hoffmann, drawing a pistol from the small of his back and firing four rounds into Otto's chest. The law student collapsed in a welter of blood and the plaza erupted into a scene of panic-stricken flight by screaming students.

Adivi recoiled in horror. "Are you crazy? What in the hell have you done?"

Ignoring the protestations of his Israeli colleague, Hoffmann casually walked over to where Otto lay and knelt, placing his fingers on the young man's neck. After a few moments testing for a carotid pulse, he stood and fired another two bullets into the wounded man's head.

"The police will be here any minute, so it's time to go," said Hoffmann in a preternaturally calm voice. He reached into his pocket and pulled out another pistol that he proffered to Adivi. "Take this, you might need it."

Still fixated by shock, Adivi ignored the offered weapon. But within moments, he was jolted into full situational awareness by an ugly murmur from the gathering crowd. One of the onlookers suddenly pointed at Hoffmann and began yelling, "Da ist er! Es ist der Mörder!"

Hoffmann put a hand on Adivi's shoulder. "We have to move ... now."

Adivi mounted his bicycle and set out in hot pursuit of his partner in temporal crime. He pedalled furiously, as if trying to expunge the bilious taste of panic from his gorge through sheer physical exertion. Looking over his shoulder, he spied the flicker of auto headlights approaching along the road to their rear. A jolt of adrenaline-fuelled fear coursed through his body.

"Hoffmann!" yelled Adivi. "A car!"

Hoffmann skidded his bike to a halt and examined their surroundings. "Into the ditch," he ordered. "If we lie flat they'll never see us."

Hoffmann slid over the roadway's shoulder into the drainage channel pulling his bicycle flat beside him.

Adivi did the same, his fear overcoming his disgust at the malodorous muck that lined the ditch bottom.

"Get your gun ready," ordered Hoffmann as he snicked the safety lever of his pistol to 'fire'.

But Adivi just lay there, half covered by slime, listening anxiously as the growl of a diesel engine waxed, climaxed and waned.

As the sound receded, Hoffmann peered cautiously over the rim of the ditch. "We're clear."

Adivi clambered onto the road and began flinging gobs of gunk from his sleeves and torso.

"Don't worry about that," said Hoffmann. "I'll buy you a new set of clothes once we're home. But now let's move."

The duo retraced the remainder of their route back to the forest with wracked nerves, but no further incident. Casting their bikes aside, they clambered aboard the capsule and Hoffmann repeated the cockpit procedures that previously propelled them through time. And after a hiatus of several uneventful minutes, the centre console slid open to signify their journey's end.

Five

The hatch disengaged and swung aside to reveal that the capsule was once again in Hoffmann's lab, perfectly ensconced within the room's central aperture.

But before Hoffmann could rise from his seat, Adivi placed a restraining hand on his shoulder. "What the fuck was that? You just killed a man in cold blood! Give me one reason why I shouldn't go to the police!"

"I'll give you two," retorted Hoffmann. "First of all, what would you tell them? Some wild story about how I took you for a ride in a time machine back to 1929 in order to commit a murder? In that scenario, the only committing being done would be you to a mental hospital. And the second and more important reason is because the bastard deserved it. Or, to be more precise, he would have deserved it in about twelve years' time."

"What are you talking about? No more 'laters' or enigmatic quasi-explanations!"

Hoffmann flashed a conciliatory smile. "Wouldn't you prefer to wash? That drainage ditch was rather disgusting. I think we both could benefit from a hot shower."

Adivi shook his head. "First we talk. I want to know what's going on. Everything. The full story. No elisions and no evasions. This is your last chance."

Hoffmann raised his palms in a gesture of submission. "Very well, Aaron. I hope you'll allow me to call you by your given name because I'd like very much to work in partnership with you on this project. It will now be my pleasure to provide you with a detailed explanation of what has happened and why. I think the best place to hold such a discussion is in my library. Please follow me."

Hoffmann proceeded to another wing of the house with Adivi in tow, leading the way to a large room with walls lined with bookcases packed primarily with hardcover volumes. Sitting down in a high-backed leather chair behind an oak desk, he motioned Adivi to take a seat.

"You're familiar with the Einsatzgruppe? The SS killing units that operated on the Eastern Front during Operation Barbarossa?"

"Of course. We teach the Shoah in our schools and almost all Israelis have visited Yad Vashem."

"What about Otto Ohlendorf? Ever heard of him?"

Adivi shrugged. "I'm a physicist, not a historian."

"He's the person I shot. But more important is the person he would have become had I not shot him." Hoffmann reached into his backpack and extracted the book he'd placed in it before their trip through time. "Look him up in the index," he invited, pushing the tome across the desk in Adivi's direction.

Adivi spent the next few minutes reading up on Gruppenführer Ohlendorf's bloody record as commander of Einsatzgruppe D. He learned that from June 1941 to July 1942, this particular SS unit executed more than ninety thousand Jews at Babi Yar and other locations throughout Ukraine and Crimea.

Adivi looked up from the book. "Okay, so he was a murdering Nazi bastard in the making, but that still doesn't explain what this is all about."

"No it doesn't," replied Hoffmann. "But the next stage of revelation will come when you bring me the other copy of *Believe and Destroy* that I didn't take along on our jaunt through time. It's over there by the door on the fourth shelf from the top."

His curiosity piqued, Adivi stood up, strode over and pulled the book from the shelf.

"Now look up Otto Ohlendorf in that version," instructed Hoffmann.

Adivi thumbed in vain through the index. "There's no mention of him."

"Because, in the world as it is now, he died in a never-solved homicide while still a law student at university. And if you look up Einsatzgruppe D in the index, you'll see someone else entirely was in command."

Adivi again thumbed through the pages. "Josef Bühler."

"Correct," said Hoffmann. "But had we not intervened in the flow of history, Bühler would have spent the war as a legal officer at SS headquarters in Warsaw. He never would have served a single day in Russia."

"All very interesting, no doubt," grumbled an increasingly annoyed Adivi. "But I'm still waiting for you to get to the point."

"My dear Aaron, the point is very simple. If we have the capacity to change the course of events, why limit ourselves to half measures like eliminating a single SS murderer-to-be? What about a more ambitious agenda? What about something that will save millions of lives, Jewish and non-Jewish alike?"

Adivi sighed. "Don't tell me you're going with this where I think you're going with this."

"Indeed I am," replied Hoffmann, his mouth creasing into a toothy smile. "I believe the relevant military term is 'decapitation'. And what I propose is a raid by Israeli special forces to kill not only Hitler, but Göring, Himmler, Bormann and most of the Wehrmacht High Command."

"But even if such a thing were militarily feasible – and that's a mammoth 'if' – the temporal complications would be incalculable," protested Adivi.

"To the contrary, my friend. They're quite amenable to calculation if you have the correct tools. That Cray you saw isn't there only to compute the amount of helium-2 required for each trip. I've also used it to calculate the downtime impacts that flow from what I propose. And I've been able to find the perfect confluence of opportunity and probability."

"Meaning what, precisely?"

"Meaning a historical event that will see the entire rotten bunch gathered together in one place at one time. And it's not even in Germany, making for a much softer target."

"Professor Hoffmann, I think you're getting way ahead of yourself. I served as a technical officer in a signals intelligence unit, so I make no claim to expertise on military tactics. And, with all due respect, neither should you. Let's leave such matters to the experts – if and when we ever get to that stage. Your present challenge is to convince me that this harebrained scheme has a solid scientific foundation. And on that score, you have your work cut out for you, especially in light of this annoying refusal to discuss the extraction process for helium-2."

"I'm afraid that aspect of the project will have to remain off-limits for the time being," replied Hoffmann, shaking his head. "But I can guarantee all other topics are open to discussion. What else do you wish to know?"

"You spoke about a perfect confluence of opportunity and probability. Probability of what?"

"A very high probability that we can accomplish what I propose while containing temporal disruptions to the world as we know it. Think for a moment about the larger ramifications of what we just did."

"What you just did," corrected Adivi. "I didn't shoot anyone. I was just along for the ride."

"Okay, fine," conceded Hoffmann with a 'whatever' wave of his hands. "What I did – and that was to prove that the Novikov Self-Consistency Principle is invalid."

"But that flies in the face of everything we know about general relativity," demurred Adivi.

"You mean everything we thought we knew," countered Hoffmann. "The Novikov Principle postulates that any attempt to alter the past generates a temporal paradox that nullifies any change, correct?"

Adivi nodded. "Yes, the classic example used in undergraduate physics seminars is someone travelling back through time to kill his grandfather. The gun misfires or some other unforeseen mishap always intervenes to forestall that result."

"Ah," proclaimed Hoffmann. "But we've just demonstrated by means of the late and unlamented Otto Ohlendorf that Novikov is flawed. His pre-emptive death didn't prevent the Einsatzgruppe campaign on the Eastern Front. He was simply replaced by another barbarian. At the very least, this proves that Novikov isn't universal and there's a threshold beneath that changes to the timeline are possible."

"Let's say, for the sake of argument, that Novikov doesn't apply universally, as you say. What's your alternative explanation?"

"As best I understand it, there's a single timeline that can be likened to a stream flowing downhill," replied Hoffmann. "It always seeks the route of least resistance. But what happens in the event of an obstacle? We all know that if you drop a boulder into a stream bed, the water will flow around it seeking the quickest return to that path of least resistance – and that means its original course or the closest possible approximation to it. This is physics at its most elementary."

"And your thesis argues that a similar principle applies to time?"

"Not similar, but functionally identical. I call this the Prime Temporal Imperative. Just as water will deviate from that original course for the bare minimum required, the PTI will force the timeline to do the same. This I've named the principle of Minimal Temporal Disruption – or MTD."

"Does any of this include a capacity for spatial movement from point to point?"

Hoffmann shook his head. "Alas, no such luck. Contrary to the stuff of science fiction, there are no wormholes that combine a capacity for spatial and temporal movement. At least not to my knowledge. The only things altered by my device are the date and the hour. As you personally witnessed, the trip begins and ends in precisely the same geographical location. This is quite unfortunate because it adds danger and difficulty to this project. But we're dealing in reality as opposed to imagination. Besides, I have great confidence in the ability of your Sayeret Matkal to overcome even the most daunting of obstacles."

"Professor Hoffmann, you're once again straying from your area of expertise. Let's stick to the science, and leave the tactical side of things to the military. Looking at this through the prism of temporal physics, I note you're not just talking about killing some dispensable mid-level SS officer. You want to wipe out the entire governing elite of the Third Reich. Even if your MTD theory is correct, the historical consequences of such a significant action would remain colossal. Wouldn't the scope of such an event exceed the threshold of the Novikov Principle and trigger a self-negating temporal paradox?"

"Not necessarily. It all depends on timing. And my data strongly indicates that a decapitation of the Nazi government at an optimal moment in history is not only possible, but highly desirable."

"How so?"

"If Hitler disappears from the equation before June 1941, the power vacuum in Berlin is filled by a junta of German generals who have no ideological impetus to pick a fight with the Soviets," replied Hoffmann. "This means no Operation Barbarossa and no orchestrated Final Solution. A cross-channel invasion of Britain remains well beyond the capabilities of the Wehrmacht, so Germany makes do with consolidating its conquests in France and the Low Countries. When the Japanese attack Hawaii, probably in mid-1942, the Germans stay out of it. For their part, the Americans have no appetite for involvement in Europe and fight a Pacific-only war, which they win by 1947 with a very bloody invasion of the Japanese home islands."

"No American nukes? No Manhattan Program?"

Hoffmann shrugged. "Not during the 1940s or even 1950s. It's quite possible nuclear weapons are developed sometime later, but I didn't do any longer-term calculations on that particular question. The point is that the Wehrmacht generals who are now running Germany have a conservative scepticism about theoretical wonder weapons. They prefer to go with what they know. And, once the Americans figure out that nothing is going on in Germany, they focus their scientific resources on rocketry, jet aircraft and better tanks."

"Then Europe lapses into stalemate?" asked Adivi.

"Quite correct. At a certain point, even Churchill is grudgingly forced to accept the reality of German dominance over the continent. By the mid-1940s, the war peters out into an armed and sullen peace and Labour Prime Minister Clement Attlee signs a formal armistice treaty with Reichskanzler Ludwig Beck in 1946."

"Atlee? What happens to Churchill?"

"Defeated at the ballot box, although in this new world the general election is likely held around March-April 1945, rather than July."

"But wait," Adivi queried, "doesn't that mean our troops would be returning to a now-time France that's occupied by the Germans?"

"Not really," answered Hoffmann. "According to my data, Berlin begins a gradual transition from military dictatorship to democracy by the early-1960s. What ultimately emerges is an EU of sorts, where Germany is the dominant economic power. France, Belgium, the Netherlands, Denmark and Norway gain political autonomy while aligning with Berlin in an economic confederation and defensive military alliance against the Russians."

"Something like NATO, but without the Americans?"

"Precisely."

"What about the UN?"

"Never established," Hoffmann replied. "Roosevelt makes some noise about finding an alternative to the League of Nations, but he dies in 1945 and the idea never develops traction. The League continues to wallow in its impotence and is generally ignored by all and sundry."

"And Russia? How long does Communism endure in this brave new world?"

"It's a scenario that's quite similar to our current reality," explained Hoffmann. "A cold war that sputters along until the economic collapse of the Soviet Union in the early-to-mid 1990s."

"What about the Yishuv? How does the Zionist enterprise fare in all of this?"

"Quite well, in fact," responded a smiling Hoffmann. "The UK still ends up bearing the cost of two world wars within the space of a quarter century. Add to that the burden of maintaining Fortress Britannia in the face of a German-dominated Europe. As a result, the sun begins to set on the British Empire because it's simply too expensive to maintain. My calculations see India gaining independence sometime in the early 1950s. And I found a likelihood of ninety-three to ninety-five per cent that Britain abandons its Palestine mandate by 1951. That means the Zionist project would be slightly delayed, but the newly established State of Israel would boast a much larger Jewish population."

"Just because there's no Shoah doesn't mean those millions of still-living Jews would make Aliya," countered Adivi.

"Ah, but I believe they would in very large numbers," said Hoffmann. "Think of it this way: the social impact from years of Nazi anti-Semitic propaganda doesn't evaporate overnight. A Führer-less German-occupied Europe might not be the scene of orchestrated mass murder, but it still isn't a very happy place to be a Jew. Nor is Russia. Don't forget the Doctors' Plot and murder of the Yiddish poets during the final years of Stalin's rule. American neutrality means US immigration laws remain quite restrictive. My calculations tell me that the combination of all these factors triggers a mass wave of Jewish immigration to the only existing safe haven – the Yishuv. And this movement becomes so large that it simply overwhelms British efforts to stop it. Then there are almost one million Sephardic Jews who are forced to flee their homes throughout the Middle East in the face of epidemic anti-Semitic violence."

"So the Arabs still oppose the creation of a Jewish state by force?" asked Adivi.

"Oh, yes. They go to war just as in the world as we know it. Only, in this version, they lose even more spectacularly."

"Okay, so there may be a certain logic to this on the macro-level, but what about my family? asked Adivi. My parents were both Shoah survivors. If we did this, they'd probably never meet. Wouldn't I be doing away with myself before the fact? Wouldn't I be nipping myself in the bud?"

Hoffmann gave his head a purse-lipped shake. "That's a more difficult proposition to quantify, because the more micro the focus, the less exact the calculations. Yet, I did a little before-and-after digging into Otto Ohlendorf, and it turns out that his would-be wife ended up marrying his younger brother, who would otherwise have remained a bachelor. I see that as a strong indication the law of Minimal Temporal Disruption applies not just to the broad swathes of history, but to individuals as well."

"So by shooting Ohlendorf, we dropped a proverbial rock into the timeline," mused Adivi. "But the rule of Minimal Temporal Disruption caused the woman he would have married to seek out the closest possible facsimile ... his brother."

"Precisely," said Hoffmann.

"You think the forces of temporal physics would conspire to bring my father and mother together, regardless? That they'd find each other and conceive me at precisely the same moment as in our world?"

"That's correct."

"But how can you be sure?" pressed Adivi. "What about all the millions of alternative potential mates who'd still be alive in this world without a Shoah?"

"To be honest, there's no absolute certainty," Hoffmann conceded. "But I believe the case of Ohlendorf's would-have-been wife strongly leads towards that conclusion. Then there's the Novikov Principle. We now know it's not universal. But there still has to be a threshold for temporal intervention that nullifies any self-contradictory paradox. It should still be logically impossible for you, personally, to take retrospective action that would prospectively negate your own later existence. Hence, your direct involvement in the project is, in and of itself, a form of life insurance. Don't take my word for it, though. The Cray is completely at your disposal for all the number crunching you might require."

"Well, I'd certainly need to have a comprehensive look at your calculations before even thinking about signing onto this mad scheme."

"That's all I ask," replied Hoffmann. "You're a world-class physicist. If anyone can poke holes in my thesis, you're the one to do it. If I'm wrong, no harm. But consider the prospect of history's most murderous anti-Semitic bastards being cut down by Jewish soldiers firing Jewish bullets from Jewish rifles. It would be a truly glorious thing to behold."

"All very poetic, no doubt," replied Adivi. "But before anything else, I have to ask you why? This whole operation must have cost you a considerable amount of time, money and effort. Yet you're not even Jewish. You'll have to excuse me if I'm bit curious about your motivation in all this."

Hoffmann grimaced. "Aaron, do you really think Jews are the only people to be repulsed by crimes of the Third Reich?"

Adivi sighed in perfunctory semi-apology.

"As it happens, I do have a personal connection. My grandfather was Obersturmbannführer Wilhelm Hoffmann, deputy chief of Ämter IV in the Reichssicherheitshauptamt, the SS legal office. In other words, dear old grandad was Himmler's lawyer – the guy who dotted all the I's and crossed all the T's to ensure the legality of the Final Solution."

"Your grandfather participated in the Wannsee Conference?"

"Participate in it? Hell, he organised it," spat Hoffmann "But grandpapa wasn't just a legal eagle facilitator of genocide. He was also a thieving bastard who amassed a fortune in looted Jewish valuables. Diamonds, jewellery, rare Bessarabian carpets and even ingots made of melted-down gold teeth; you name it, he stole it. He walked away from the war with millions of dollars stashed in a Swiss bank account."

"Those ill-gotten gains."

Hoffmann nodded. "This project is the perfect way to spend that dirty money. If Wilhelm is spinning in his grave at the idea, it serves him right."

"As much as I hate to say it, I'm impressed," conceded Adivi. "You've put a lot of thought into this. A base of operations in Göttingen – where you neither studied nor taught – for the sole purpose of providing easy access to Otto Ohlendorf as a demonstration project. Then you approach me, knowing that my personal background makes me particularly susceptible to persuasion. I can't fault your logic."

Hoffmann smiled, lifting his palms skyward in a gesture of self-deprecation. "Your personal background and your scientific credentials were essential, of course. So was the fact that you served with Prime Minister Etzioni in the same unit during your army service."

"Wow ... your due diligence is very thorough," said Adivi with a nod of grudging respect.

"Look, Aaron, at the end of the day it's very simple. As a student, I spent several summers as a volunteer on Kibbutz Negba and, in some ways, that was the best time of my life. I fell in love with your country. And I want to set in train a course of events in which Israel at the turn of the 21st century has a Jewish population of twenty million rather than five million. I want Israel and the Jews to thrive. That's my ambition and I'm asking you to join me. I need your help."

Adivi grinned. "Indeed, you do. After all, I'm the one who'd have to sell this crazy concept in Jerusalem if your math turns out to be correct."

Hoffmann hid a cascading sense of inner relief behind a broad smile. "I have full faith in your ability to seal the deal."

Adivi pondered silently for a few moments before nodding his assent. "Now how about that shower?"

Six

The 'Prime Minister's Pit' was a place designed to keep secrets. Built into the rocky Jerusalem hillside at a depth of 120 metres beneath the Ben Gurion Government Office Complex, the facility was impervious to everything short of a direct hit by a hydrogen warhead.

The Government Situation Center, its formal title, was linked to the Foreign Ministry building and the Prime Minister's Office by a series of subterranean corridors, blast doors and elevators. It included sufficient protected space and supplies to accommodate a contingent of one hundred people for up to thirty days.

But the Pit's main feature was a chamber the size of a small auditorium, its walls covered by organic LED screens and a massive digital map scaled to show the Middle East from the Nile to the Euphrates. Thirty computerised workstations, arrayed in tidy rows, consumed most of the chamber's floorspace, all of them dormant except for a skeleton crew tasked with awakening the facility in case of need. An elevated meeting room was built against the rear wall, its soundproof glass wall giving a commanding view of the screens and workstations, much like a VIP box at Mile High Stadium.

That meeting room was occupied by five people of late-middle-age, four males and one female, sitting around a large rectangular oak table. Another woman, much younger, occupied a small desk sited unobtrusively in a corner.

"I hereby convene the Cabinet Committee for National Security Affairs," said the man with a wild shock of grey hair seated at the table's head. "I note the absence of the Minister for Domestic Security who is overseas. This meeting is classified Top Secret, Taboo Most Exclusive and, per protocol, minutes will not be taken. Thank you, Anat."

Prime Minister Yair Etzioni pushed a button on the arm of his executive chair and the vault-type locks on the blast door room disengaged with a hydraulic hum and heavy metallic clank. Once the door was fully open, the attractive young amanuensis gathered up her laptop and departed down the corridor.

"Bring in the Professor, please," Etzioni instructed the officer of his Shabak security detail standing sentry at the open door. The Shabaknik nodded and disappeared, returning several moments later with Adivi in tow.

"Aaron, please take a seat next to me," said Etzioni, with a wave towards the vacant chair on his immediate right.

A loud hum and clank were once again heard as the blast door closed and its locks re-engaged. A light on the wall turned from green to red.

"The matter on our agenda today is quite complex, so I enlisted the assistance of someone who should be able to clarify matters. Allow me to introduce Dr Aaron Adivi, Israel Prize Laureate in Science and Emeritus Professor of Physics at Tel Aviv University. He's also made a tremendous contribution to our work at Dimona, so there's no security clearance issue."

"Welcome Professor," proclaimed Hava Geffen, an elegant woman in her mid-fifties who served as Minister for Foreign Affairs. "I'm certainly no physicist, but your reputation as one of our preeminent scientific minds has preceded you nonetheless."

Adivi smiled by way of polite response.

"And Hava, your reputation for diplomatic savoir-faire is equally well-deserved," said Etzioni. "But let's get down to business. The story you're about to hear may strike you as fanciful or even outlandish. Note, however, that I've known Aaron since we served together in unit Eight Two Hundred. Not only is he one of the smartest people around, he's the most boringly sane person you'll ever meet."

Adivi doffed his head in ironic gratitude as a smattering of polite laughter swept through the room.

"I ask you to keep an open mind while hearing what he has to say," Etzioni continued, turning to his friend. "Aaron, the floor is yours."

"Thank you, Prime Minister," Adivi began. "I'll get straight to the point. Time travel has been the staple of science fiction since HG Wells wrote *The Time Machine* in 1895. It's a concept that has also been the subject of considerable speculation by people in my field of quantum physics. But I'm here to tell you that time travel is not only possible – I've done it myself."

Adivi spent the next twenty minutes detailing his foray through time to an audience whose facial expressions gravitated between doubt and outright disbelief.

Once the presentation had concluded, Prime Minister Etzioni glanced around the room. "I can see you're finding it difficult to get your heads around this news. I don't blame you one bit, as my initial reaction was very much the same. Because Professor Adivi anticipated your understandable scepticism, we took the liberty of making certain evidentiary preparations. A week ago, you each received a sealed, courier-delivered envelope with instructions to bring it unopened to this meeting. Please open your envelope now."

The ministers opened their briefcases, each extracting buff envelopes secured by large plastic seals that they proceeded to tear open.

"As you can see, what you hold in your hands is a copy of today's edition of the *International Herald Tribune*," said Eztioni. He disengaged the door locks and picked up a red phone on the desk in front of him. "You can bring the papers in now, thanks."

The door to the Situation Room swung open and the young stenographer entered bearing a stack of newspapers that she distributed to those seated around the table.

"Thank you again, Anat," said Etzioni with an avuncular nod of dismissal. He waited until the room was sealed once again. "Now, please compare the versions of the *Tribune* freshly delivered from the Government Press Office with those sent to you a week ago. As you can observe, they're perfectly identical."

The assembled ministers spent a few moments studying their newspapers, looking up when Adivi broke the silence.

"They're exactly the same because, a fortnight ago, I travelled forward through time and purchased the newspapers you received by courier. You've all had possession of your copies for a number of days, so any tampering is completely out of the question."

"I apologise for the theatrics," said Etzioni. "I thought it might take more than my endorsement of Professor Adivi's bona fides to convince you this isn't just a wild figment of his imagination. As bizarre as it might sound, I've come to accept this as fact rather science fiction. And I believe it offers the potential to do great things for the Jewish People and the State of Israel."

Etzioni settled back in his chair as the room lapsed into stunned silence.

The assembled ministers exchanged glances around the table until Defense Minister Haim Bar'el finally took the plunge.

"Prime Minister, I'm normally something of a sceptic when it comes to claims of technological panaceas," said the stocky ex-paratroop officer. "But if what Professor Adivi tells us is accurate, this device would create tremendous scope for action by Tzahal. We could reshape the entire Middle East very much to our advantage."

"No doubt, but as Aaron will now explain, our current options are rather narrowly focused," replied Etzioni.

Adivi nodded in agreement. "It's quite simple really. We're all familiar with the phenomenon of younger Germans plagued by a sense of intergenerational guilt for the sins of their ancestors during the Nazi era. In Dr Hoffmann's case, his grandfather was the senior SS legal officer who organised the Wannsee Conference and amassed a fortune in stolen Jewish wealth. As a result, he's quite fixated on forestalling the Shoah."

"The gentleman in question spent two summers as a volunteer on Kibbutz Negba," said Prime Minister Etzioni. "We made some discrete enquiries with his host family and they remember Hoffmann as a very nice young man who was rather passionately pro-Israel. He also spent six years teaching at the University of Wisconsin where he was very active against pro-Palestinian propaganda on campus. We're confident there's no ulterior agenda at work here. We're satisfied his motives are genuine."

"Gerhard Hoffmann describes his personal riches as the fruit of his grandfather's 'ill-gotten gains'," said Adivi. "And he certainly hasn't been shy about spending that money. The private lab he's built to create this technology must have cost at least twenty-five million dollars, if not more. He also told me it was an added bonus that his grandfather might be spinning in the grave at the prospect this stolen fortune would be used to mount an Israeli kill mission against Hitler."

A wave of laughter briefly swept through the room before it was dispelled by a dour interjection from Defense Minister Bar'el. "If he's such a lover of the Jews, he should build his device right here in the Jewish state. We could prevent the Yom Kippur War or eliminate the Mufti before the Arab Revolt of '36. The strategic possibilities would be incredible."

"I broached a very similar suggestion, and in fairness I should report that Dr Hoffmann was open to consideration of other operations on Israel's behalf," Adivi reported. "Only afterwards, though. He's quite insistent

Hitler and his chief lieutenants must be the targets of an initial mission that should be mounted between September 1940 and March 1941."

"What's so special about those dates?" enquired Finance Minister Amiram Yavniel. "If killing Hitler is the objective, why not go back to pre-World War One Vienna when he was a still a nobody?"

"You must always consider Hitler's enormous significance as a historical actor," explained Adivi. "Assassinating him at any time would generate a substantial disruption to the timeline flow."

"Your boulder in the stream metaphor," interjected Yavniel.

"Indeed. The choice of when and how to act must be weighed against the retention of historical continuity. In this case, it would be a balancing act between obviating the Shoah while avoiding changes to the course of events that would render our world unrecognisable. The possible ramifications for the Zionist movement could be particularly profound."

"By killing Hitler too early, would we be setting off changes to the timeline of such scale that they'd jeopardise the establishment of a Jewish state?" asked Geffen.

"It's quite probable," Adivi answered.

"So we have to let things like Kristallnacht just happen, even though we might have the power to stop them?" Foreign Minister Geffen persisted.

"Hava, Jewish history is full of nasty episodes we'd love to prevent," replied Etzioni. "And not just during the 20th century. Who amongst us wouldn't want to go back and put a bullet into Bohdan Khmelnytsky, or protect Jewish communities along the Rhine during the Crusades? We simply can't because the downtime consequences would be far too radical."

"Madam Foreign Minister, I spent the past four months evaluating Dr Hoffmann's data and testing his hypotheses," said Adivi. "I have to say that, with a few minor caveats, he's essentially correct. A successful decapitation of the Nazi government between late-1940 and early-1941 would leave a probability of roughly ninety-five per cent that the State of Israel would be created by 1951 at the very latest, along with a Jewish population quadruple the size."

"You say you've had months to analyse Hoffmann's technology," said Defense Minister Bar'el. "Any chance you've learned enough to recreate his device on your own?"

Adivi smiled. "None at all. I was given free rein to crunch the probability numbers for historical scenarios, but Hoffmann was always very secretive about anything to do with his helium-2 formula. He's no fool."

"Worth a try," Bar'el grunted.

"I have a question about feasibility," said Yavniel. "You tell us this operation must be mounted between autumn 1940 and spring 1941. After the German victory in the West, but before the invasion of Greece and Russia. That means trying to wipe out the governing elite of the Third Reich at the absolute apex of its power. I'm hardly a military expert and will happily defer to the superior experience of the Defense Minister – but perhaps he can explain why this project isn't tantamount to a suicide mission?"

"There's no doubt this would be a complex operation," Bar'el replied. "I remember people saying the same thing before Entebbe. We've identified a possible target date within the relevant six-month period that we think might hold considerable potential for a successful operation. Don't forget that we have some of the finest and most experienced special forces in the world. We all know that, over the years, they've used very unconventional methods to accomplish some astounding things. If anyone would be able to accomplish this task it's our special ops boys. But, you can be certain of this: Tzahal doesn't do suicide missions. I can guarantee that no operation will proceed if it doesn't offer our forces a reasonable chance of survival."

"That's quite reassuring on one level," said Justice Minister General Tzvi Kupperberg, a former academic who'd entered politics after two decades as a professor of international law. "For the moment, I'll leave aside the moral conundrum that arises from killing a man for crimes he has yet to commit, but I'm even more concerned about the personal implications of this project. We're talking here about odds, percentages and theories. In the final equation, this Minimal Temporal Disruption principle is nothing more than a guesstimate."

"I'd respectfully dispute your use of that term," replied Adivi. "I've gone over Hoffmann's calculations several times from top to bottom. I believe they're sound."

"The fact that your dead Nazi's would-have-been wife married his brother can't really be regarded as definitive," Kupperberg retorted.

"It's indicative, not definitive," replied Adivi. "In a strictly technical sense you're quite correct, but does life ever offer us a one hundred per cent guarantee of anything? The next time you get into your car you could wrap yourself around a tree."

"Sorry Professor, but I really don't see that as a valid analogy. There's a vast difference between the consequences of a single auto accident and what you propose," countered Kupperberg. "In one case, a handful of people might die, but in the other, a whole world full of people are never born. You have no way to guarantee that our parents will meet and we'll be conceived at precisely the same moment with precisely the same sperm fertilising precisely the same eggs. By changing the world, we could be snuffing out our own existence."

"I can't deny that possibility," replied Adivi. "But as I previously explained, your involvement in this operation should serve as its own life insurance policy. It should still be impossible for anyone to travel through time to the past and engage in an act that prospectively negates their later existence. The act of approving this mission serves, in essence, as a guarantee for your own survival. I believe the danger you describe is, at most, quite remote. Under four per cent, the statistics tell us."

"Let's not forget the absolute certainties that arise from this situation," chimed in Foreign Minister Geffen. "The most indisputable of those is the fact that six million Jews and millions of others will die if we do nothing. The greatest calamity the world has ever seen will unfold without impediment."

"This is the question that goes to the very essence of who we are as a nation," said Etzioni. "It's axiomatic that each of you is an unabashed Zionist because there's no place in my government for anyone who isn't. The creation of a safe haven for oppressed and persecuted Jews has been the raison d'être of our movement since the days of Herzl. During the 1930s and 40s, it was Aliya Bet. During the 1950s and 60s, we took in almost a million Jewish refugees from the Arab world and Iran. During the 1980s and 90s, it was Russian and Ethiopian Jews, and now it's Jews fleeing rising anti-Semitism in Europe. I can't see how this is any different merely because there's some weird science involved. If we have the opportunity to save myriad Jewish lives, it's morally incumbent on us to act."

"Even if it imperils our families and ourselves?" challenged Kupperberg.

"We're surrounded by millions of hostile neighbours who yearn for our annihilation," answered Geffen. "If absolute safety is what you seek, move to Beverly Hills. As for me, I rather like the idea of an Israel with twenty million Jews by the year 2000. It would alter our entire strategic equation both militarily and economically. And there'd be no question that Israel would trump the Diaspora as the focal point of Jewish civilisation. On the basis of Professor Adivi's data, I think the risk–reward ratio looks pretty good. I'd still support this operation, even if I don't end up as Foreign Minister in the new-and-improved world we would create."

"Thank you, Hava, for those sentiments," said Etzioni. "Are there any additional comments?" The Prime Minister looked around the room, his glance pausing on Kupperberg, who shook his head in the negative. "In that case, we'll now proceed to a vote. Aaron, thank you very much for your attendance today. If you could excuse us and wait upstairs in my anteroom, I'd be grateful."

"Certainly," responded Adivi.

The Prime Minister pushed the button on the arm of his chair and the blast door to the Situation Room whirred open.

"Thank you very much. Good luck to you all," said Adivi to the assembled ministers. Then he turned on his heel and took his leave.

"It's decision time," declared Etzioni once the room had again been sealed. "I move the following: that the Defense Minister be authorised to commence preparations for what we will now refer to as Operation Agag. And I vote yes."

"I'm a yes as well," said Hava Geffen. "Also, I applaud your choice of code name for this mission. Quite appropriate."

Etzioni nodded his thanks and then turned to his Defense Minister.

"I'm on board," declared Haim Bar'el.

Finance Minister Amiram Yavniel spoke up next. "Prime Minister, you used the word 'preparations'. Am I right to presume this means we will have the opportunity to revisit the issue before any operational decisions are made?"

"I can make that commitment," said the Prime Minister.

"In that case, I vote in favour with the proviso that we retain the final word before the mission is launched."

Etzioni turned his attention to his Justice Minister. "That leaves you, Tzvi. I think an enterprise of this magnitude requires unanimous agreement. Where do you stand?"

Kupperberg shook his head decisively. "I'm sorry, Prime Minister. I recognise the moral imperatives here, but the stakes are too high. We'd be risking too much."

"There's another aspect to this business that just occurred to me," interjected Bar'el. "A factor that I think might force our hand. As I said before, the strategic potential of this innovation is immense. Now this particular genie is out of the bottle, so to speak, we can't allow Dr Hoffmann's technology to fall into the hands of anyone else."

"The Defense Minister is quite correct," observed Hava Geffen. "No-one else can be trusted. Not even the Americans."

"But our relationship with Washington is quite good," protested Yavniel.

"That's fine as far as it goes," replied Geffen. "But even the most ardently pro-Israel president wouldn't hesitate to exploit time travel for their country's national interest. I wouldn't expect anything less from the Yanks, or anyone else for that matter."

"Hava's analysis is spot on," confirmed Bar'el. "When push comes to shove, we can't know how much weight Washington would give to the prospect their temporal tinkering might inflict collateral damage on others – including us. Even worse, I couldn't rule out the possibility that the Americans might even target us directly if they think it's strategically warranted. I could easily envisage them going after Dimona."

"I agree with both the Foreign and Defense ministers," said Prime Minister Etzioni in an emphatic tone. "We're fortunate to be offered exclusive access to this technology. Allowing it to come under any sort foreign control, even of the Americans, is completely out of the question. The risks are simply too great. We're left with two options: assume ownership over Hoffmann's technology, or eliminate any possible opportunity it might fall into other hands. This generates a question for you, Tzvi. In light of the moral misgivings you expressed a few moments ago about prospective executions, what do you have to say about this little conundrum?"

"I certainly can't support your second option," mused Kupperberg. "The premeditated killing of this man would be an abomination. He's not our enemy and it would be murder in the worst sense of the term."

"So you're changing your vote?" asked Etzioni.

"I'd like to mull it over for a while," Kupperberg replied.

"Sorry," said the Prime Minister, "but for reasons just discussed, this is a matter that brooks no delay. We must dispatch a Shabak contingent to secure Dr Hoffmann and his lab, or we must choose the other option. In either case, we have to act immediately. It's an exigent issue of national security."

The Justice Minister was silent for a few moments. "All right, I agree, but subject to the conditions you just laid out to Amiram."

Etzioni nodded. "Very well. Now, if there's no other business, I declare this meeting adjourned. I appreciate your attendance and know I can rely on your absolute discretion."

As the assembly prepared to leave, Etzioni looked at one minister in particular. "Haim, if you could stay behind, we have other matters to discuss."

The other ministers remained seated until the blast door opened, whereupon they rose to their feet and filed out. Etzioni waited for the room to clear and reseal before addressing Bar'el with a wan smile. "Thanks for that last-minute intervention. I didn't anticipate Tzvi would be such a hardhead."

"Well he's always been a Yekke Potz," growled Bar'el. "I guess you can take the man out of the Ivory Tower, but you can't take the Ivory Tower out of the man. But we won in the end."

"With more than a little help from you," said Etzioni. "Now it's time for next steps. How do you propose we proceed?"

"I think we set up shop at Sirkin. The Unit is well accustomed to conducting top secret operations. We can cordon off a corner of the base and work in a securely siloed environment. Sirkin is just twenty minutes in distance from the Mitkan Adam base. Close enough to use its facilities for live fire training," said Bar'el. "I already have someone in mind for mission command. Do you know the name Yossi Klein?"

"Should I?"

"He's a former Matkal deputy commander."

The Prime Minister shrugged.

"He's a top-notch special operator who's been posted to a staff job at the Ops Branch of the General Staff," continued the Defense Minister. "Klein has just the sort of talent for unconventional thinking we'll need for this enterprise."

"Yes, I think I remember now," nodded Etzioni. "Didn't he suffer some sort of family tragedy a few years ago?"

"Yes ... a terrible story. Truly heartbreaking."

"How has he coped?"

"That's the remarkable thing," replied Defense Minister Bar'el. "Most people would be shattered by that sort of misfortune. But Klein's military performance has remained exceptional. If anything, he's even more dedicated to the army than before."

"I'm no psychologist, but that sounds a lot like sublimation. Are you sure he's right for this mission?"

"One hundred per cent," answered Bar'el. "Not only is Yossi Klein the best man for the job, I think the challenge of such a uniquely complex operation might even be ... therapeutic."

"His personal situation does simplify matters in the event things don't proceed as planned," Etzioni said.

"There is that," conceded Bar'el, "although I don't like to think along those lines."

"Okay, we're in provisional agreement; but how are you going to handle the Ramatkal? Surely, we have to tell him something?"

"As little as possible, I should think, and that also goes for Rosh Aman and OC Depth Command," replied Bar'el. "We'll say just enough to keep them from sniffing around."

"You can handle the brass, but I'd like to have a talk with Klein before we make a final decision, said Etzioni. "Get some dates from my diary secretary on your way out. We'll bring him down here into the Pit where I can sound him out, and I'll want you in attendance as well."

"Then I should get moving," said Bar'el. "I'll contact Klein first thing."

Seven

With its outmoded mustard-brown decor, the most charitable adjective that could be applied to the provincial hotel was 'quaint'. An attractive thirtysomething woman at the front desk looked at Yossi Klein with a coquettish smile that hinted at more than simple commercial congeniality.

"Bonjour, Monsieur Bradley."

"And Bonjour to you, Madame Lebrune," Klein replied, his mouth frozen in a hesitant half-smile as he hastened through the lobby.

Michael HarSinai cast a cynical smirk at his commander as the civvies-clad Israeli trio entered the elevator hallway. "You know she wants you. We're likely to see hurricane force winds at the rate her eyelashes are fluttering."

"What would you know about it, yeshiva-boy?" replied Klein. "You kippa-wearers are obsessive about modesty before marriage. I don't see a ring on your finger, do I?"

"I'll have you know I have a girlfriend," protested HarSinai.

"Yeah I know," replied Klein. "Shoshana ... nice girl. Have you progressed beyond the hand-holding stage yet?"

Lieutenant Erad Meshulam, a lanky naval commando of Yemenite Jewish extraction, glanced at his companions with an expression of confused concern.

"Don't worry," said a grinning HarSinai. "It's all in good fun. Yossi was my team commander during maslul. He scoffs at me for being a Sabbath-observant West Bank settler fanatic, and I call him a calamari-eating, Hellenising secular Jew – in name only. But we love each other like brothers."

"I've always thought you Matkal types are a bit too inbred for comfort," quipped Meshulam.

"That's funny, coming from a frogman," fired back Klein.

"Ribbet, ribbet," croaked HarSinai.

Klein was pleased to see Meshulam sporting a good-natured grin. Such jibes were an expression of the friendly, but fierce, rivalry that marked relations among the IDF's top-tier special ops units. This biting banter was an indication that the naval commando from Shayetet 13 was integrating well into the Matkal-heavy planning cell assembled for Operation Agag.

Klein cast a dubious look at the antiquated cage elevator that looked like a relic from a 1920s Agatha Christie murder mystery. "Let's do the stairs."

The three Israeli special warfare officers bounded up the stairs to the second floor. Reaching the end of the corridor, HarSinai opened the door with an ancient lever-lock key to reveal three men sitting around a table piled high with aerial photographs, maps, files and two laptop computers.

"Good to see you haven't been slacking off in my absence," said Klein. "I talked to Tel Aviv on the secure line from the Paris Embassy and everything's on track. Now bring me up to speed as to how the ops plan is developing. Roie, you're up."

"We recommend that the Montoire railway station should be considered a definite no-go," answered Captain Roie Abargil of the Combat Engineering Corps' Ya'alom special demolitions unit. "It's not so much the topography or the building's physical layout, but that the Germans will be putting a massive security cordon in place while the summit meetings are ongoing. At least four hundred men in close proximity to the station, with another few hundred within five minutes by foot. All of which makes perfect sense because a stationary train full of high-value individuals is an obvious target for attack."

"And the obvious is something we never like to do," said Klein with a confident smile. "Too bad – it would have been nice to bag Pétain and Laval as well, but if it won't work, it won't work. No point beating our heads against a brick wall. What are our other options?"

"I think the Saint-Rimay rail tunnel shows promise," replied Roie. "The history books say Montoire-sur-le-Loir was chosen as a meeting location because the tunnel was close enough to provide cover for Hitler's train in the event of an RAF air attack."

"How close?" Klein enquired.

Abargil applied a military UTM protractor to a 1:25,000 scale topographical map. "Just over three thousand metres from the town centre."

Klein studied the map for a few moments before looking up. "Not optimal, but it'll do."

"If we could hit the train inside the tunnel, we'd have an almost perfect kill zone," observed HarSinai. "There are two possible targeting options. 'Amerika', the code name for Hitler's special train, passes through southbound at 18:30 hours on 22nd October, and then northbound at around 06:00 on the 25th."

"Erad, you're the mission's intel officer. What can you tell us about 'Amerika'?"

The 25-year-old naval commando officer consulted his notes. "It had ... "

"You mean 'has'," interjected Klein. "I want all references to the enemy expressed in the present tense. Despite the unique nature of this mission, I want everyone to get in the habit of saying 'they are', not 'they were'. And they 'have' not they 'had'. This is a matter of mental discipline, clear?"

Meshulam nodded and began again. "Amerika has sixteen cars with a combined length of just under five hundred metres. It's propelled from the front by two steam locomotives, each with its own attached coal tender. They're followed by an anti-aircraft railcar with a four-barrelled 20 mm auto-cannon mounted at each end. After that comes a luggage car and an auxiliary power car. Next in line is our primary target, Hitler's personal sleeper railcar. Right after that comes the Begleitkommandowagen, where his sixteen-man bodyguard force sleeps. They'll be armed with pistols, stick grenades and MP38 submachine guns. Then we have a conference railcar, a communications car, a dining car and two sleeping cars for staff. A bath car, two VIP guest cars and another anti-aircraft car bring up the rear. Altogether, that's sixteen cars totalling 478.6 metres in length."

"And what's the length of the tunnel?" enquired Klein.

Abargil grabbed a thick binder, thumbing through its contents. "Five hundred and eight metres."

"That means, if we hit the lead locomotives just as they nose out of the tunnel, the train will stop with both anti-aircraft cars still inside. This is absolutely essential because, otherwise, those 20 mm cannon will tear us to pieces."

"We can take out the AA cars from both tunnel entrances by Matador or grenades," Meshulam suggested.

Klein nodded in agreement. "Because the whole thing's underground it'll be a radio dead zone. There'll be no calls for help from that communications car. This is sounding better by the minute. But what about security? Surely Hitler's special train has more than just an eight-man bodyguard team?"

"There are those anti-aircraft railcars," said Meshulam, as he consulted the contents of another binder. "Each has around two dozen gun crewmen. Beyond that, the history books tell us that Amerika travels in a convoy, sandwiched between two escort trains. The lead car of each escort train is armoured and features a Panzer III turret with a 37 mm short-barrelled cannon. Each also carries an infantry company from Hitler's escort battalion, the Führer-Begleit-Bataillon, or FBB. They're equipped with MG34 machine guns, MP38s and Kar98K bolt-action rifles. A weapons company composed of an additional infantry platoon, an 80 mm mortar platoon and a combat engineer platoon is split between the two escort trains. We estimate around one hundred and fifty men in each."

"Let's make sure they never have an opportunity to deploy those mortars," Klein instructed. He gestured for Meshulam to continue.

"The FBB also has a motorised company of armoured cars equipped with 20 mm auto-cannon and motorcycle-sidecar combos mounted with MG34s. Their job is to sweep ahead of the train convoy for ambushes and other threats."

"So presumably it's this FBB that provides the close security cordon around the station during the summit meetings?" asked Klein.

"Yes," Meshulam replied, "although anecdotal evidence from the memoirs of local residents indicates that an SS honor guard is posted on the railway platform. They'll be no more than a platoon in size and armed with Kar98s as well."

"Anybody who bags one of those black-suited bastards gets bonus points in my book," said HarSinai, eliciting grins from those around the table.

Meshulam continued his exposition. "Those same memoirs also talk about German sentries deployed at twenty-metre intervals along the railroad track from Montoire to the western end of the tunnel. The railroad signalman's house, also at the western end of the tunnel, is requisitioned and used as a communications centre. I think we can expect around twenty German signallers armed with Kar98s and pistols. Finally, there's an anecdotal reference to AA batteries deployed around the town, although we have no idea where."

"Do we at least know what type?" asked Klein.

"We have no definitive information," replied Meshulam. "But I think it's most likely they'd be the quad-20 mm guns, the same as on Hitler's train.

The other possibilities would be 37 mm auto-cannon and, of course, the famous 88."

"If they have 88s anywhere in the Montoire area, we could be in serious trouble," said Klein. "What about non-eyeball enemy?"

"There are roughly two hundred soldiers who arrive in Montoire a few days before the 22nd. But they're signals and logistics types, not combat troops. Aside from them, the closest force would be at the Châteaudun airfield about fifty-five kilometres northeast. We estimate it can generate a company-sized reaction force of truck-borne Luftwaffe AA and airbase security troops armed as light infantry. That means nothing heavier than the MG34. The earliest they could be expected is around two hours after the alarm is given. That's if they're very efficient."

"Okay, I'm sold on the tunnel," said Klein. "But we'll operate on the assumption an enemy reaction force of two companies will arrive on scene within ninety minutes. Do we know what kind of aircraft are based at Châteaudun?"

Meshulam turned the pages of his binder. "Around thirty Ju-88 two-engine bombers and a squadron of twelve ME-109Es on temporary deployment to provide fighter cover during the two summit meetings."

"That means we'll also need to bring Stingers along," said Klein. "The fundamental question, though, is whether we hit them coming or going. On October 22nd or 25th?"

"I think the 22nd is problematic," responded Major Gilad Sneh, the 29-year-old Sayeret Matkal squadron leader who'd been appointed the mission's operations officer. "Amerika only reaches the tunnel that evening, which means we'll have to lie up for the entire day. This greatly increases the possibility that a 'Lamed Hay'-style incident would abort the entire mission."

"I agree," said HarSinai. "Assuming we stage from somewhere in the vicinity, we should reach the ambush area in the early morning of the 22nd. Say 03:00 hours local for the sake of argument. BMNT on that date will be 07:11 hours."

"07:11?" asked Klein. "Are you certain? That seems very late for morning nautical twilight in the final week of October."

"Quite correct," replied HarSinai. "Objectively, it should be an hour earlier —except that, after whipping the French in June 1940, the Germans applied summertime to the occupied zone. Instead of making it seasonal, they imposed it over the entire year. So BMNT kicks in at 07:11 hours local instead of 06:11."

"What about evening twilight?"

HarSinai perused his notebook. "EENT comes at 19:54 local summertime."

"That means over twelve hours of daylight before Hitler's southbound arrival on the evening of the 22nd," observed Klein.

"Yes," said Sneh, "and this is prime agricultural country, so the area will be full of farmers working their fields. Even with the best camouflage, it's far too risky."

"Well, you're the kibbutznick, so you would know," said Klein nodding in agreement. "I agree, it would be extremely dumb. Erad, when did you say Amerika would be passing through the tunnel on the 25th?"

"Around 06:00 local," replied Meshulam.

"We'd be mounting the assault while it's still dark, and that would work very much to our advantage. Okay, the 25th it is. What about a staging point? Any ideas?"

"We really haven't had much of a look yet," said HarSinai. "Up to this point, we've been focusing on the target area."

"I don't want any talk about a target area, per se," Klein instructed. "The tunnel is nothing more than the location we've provisionally chosen for the attack. What we're after is a moving object – the train and, more specifically, those travelling in it. Keep this clear in your minds at all times while we're planning this operation."

"Understood," HarSinai replied.

"In reference to our choice of staging point, I should lay out a few preconditions that will save us all time and effort," Klein continued. "One – the temporal transit and staging points have to be one and the same location. We won't be coming through time at one place and then staging for the attack at another. Two – this dual-purpose location must be no more than ten kilometres from the tunnel. And three – it has to be an enclosed warehouse-type building, at least four hundred square metres in size, that's completely secluded from public view both in our time and theirs. That means nothing within line of sight of a major road or even a single isolated farmhouse. Once you come up with a list of candidate sites, we'll have to access local building records to find out if they'll work in terms of what was there in 1940. I'll get Paris Mossad station to take care of that. They won't have to know why."

The four officers scribbled furiously on notepads as Klein spoke. "In the meantime, let's have a look at the map and those aerial photos."

The room fell silent as Klein studied the topographical chart.

"First we'll deploy a security element to defend the staging point and protect our passage home. Beyond that, we'll post blocking forces at both ends of the tunnel to take care of any leakers from within and deal with the escort trains. They'll both require a robust AT capability and machine guns – let's say a Gil and a pair of Negev 7s. A sniper team each wouldn't go amiss either. And they'll need silenced pistols to take down any sentries."

"And mortars?" enquired HarSinai.

"Don't think so," replied Klein. "I'm inclined to go with the MK47 – one per team. The boys will be able to schlep more 40 mm ammunition than mortar rounds and it has both airburst and armor-piercing capability."

"What if they have 88s?" asked Sneh.

"The ATGMs should be enough – although blocking team south should take Gomeds instead of Gills. Those extra fifteen hundred metres of range will give them coverage beyond Montoire. My command group will be positioned on the ridge directly above the tunnel. I'll have the Stingers to provide AA coverage and the medical team with me in the event we take casualties. Finally, there's the main show: the assault team that takes down the train itself. Any thoughts about the most effective tactic for that?"

"We were hoping to avoid clearing the train car by car," replied HarSinai. "But the tunnel's barely wide enough to accommodate the railcars with only a few centimetres of clearance on either side. That means the only option is moving through the train itself."

"That could be messy," said Klein. "Every carriage doorway forms a natural bottleneck. We'll need to move quickly while laying down overwhelming suppressive fire. The number one man should be a Negevist and his number two a GL40 grenadier. What about shotguns?"

"At least four," replied HarSinai. "We know Hitler's car has closed compartments and that means doors with hinges. So I think assaulters with Crye Six12s attached to their X95s will do the job."

"Make it six," responded Klein. "And we should definitely include some Yamamnikim on this operation. They've trained for a railway hostage scenario and they'll be able to advise on the most effective takedown tactics."

"There's a related issue I think we also need to discuss," said Sneh.

"Go," replied Klein.

"The records indicate that there'll be a contingent of female secretaries on the train. Young women in their twenties who'll be killed along with everyone else if we proceed in this manner."

HarSinai snorted sarcastically "What do you want to do? Go from carriage to carriage like a knight-errant seeking damsels in distress?"

"That's enough," said Klein. "Gilad is raising a perfectly legitimate point that's entirely consistent with the Code of Ethics." He turned back to Sneh. "Continue."

"Well, it's just that they're clearly non-combatants and I was hoping there might be some way to spare them."

"What do the rest of you think?" asked Klein.

"Now, go, and you shall smite Amalek, and you shall utterly destroy all that is his, and you shall not have pity on him," replied HarSinai. "Samuel Alef 15:3"

"Typical Gush Emunim," said Sneh dismissively. "I wonder what your Rosh Yeshiva would say about this indifference to the shedding of innocent blood."

"Better Gush Emunim than a kibbutz movement that's bankrupt both literally and spiritually," fired back HarSinai. "The point is, I don't consider anyone on that train innocent, and I'm sure Rabbi Melamed would agree."

"Settle down, people," said Klein. "Remember who we are and what we're doing."

"I think we have to keep an eye on the broader context," observed Erad Meshulam. "This is an operation that will save millions of lives, Jewish and non-Jewish alike. So, with all due respect, Gilad, a handful of women who chose to work as Hitler's secretaries don't really count for that much in the big picture."

"How about you, Roie?"

The combat engineer officer shrugged. "There are also the tactical circumstances of the mission to consider. We're a small force going very deep into enemy territory. Even with our superior technology, we'll be vulnerable to counterattack. We'll have to move very quickly and decisively. There'll be no time to search the train and move these women to safety."

"You're both correct," said Klein. "It just so happens that I studied the law of armed conflict with one of the world's preeminent authorities on the topic, Michael Walzer. You'll probably recall some of this from Bahad Echad, but it's important to understand so I'll refresh your memories anyway. The law of war was codified in The Hague and Geneva Conventions. They stipulate that two conditions must be satisfied for an attack to be lawful. One – it must be targeted against legitimate military objectives with a good faith effort made to avoid, or at least minimise, civilian casualties. This is called the principle of distinction." Klein turned to Sneh. "Gilad, would you agree that Amerika constitutes a military target?"

"Yes, of course."

"And, while we're not deliberately targeting these women, do you believe I'd try to spare their lives if it were tactically feasible?"

Sneh nodded.

"Then we've satisfied the principle of distinction," declared Klein.

"And the second rule?" asked Abargil.

"Proportionality. It states that, although civilian deaths are unintentional, they mustn't be excessive in relation to the direct military advantage gained by the operation. In other words, you can't carpet-bomb an entire city and kill thousands of women and children just to achieve a minor tactical victory."

"But killing those same women and children would be legal if the stakes were high enough," Abargil weighed in. "Like the atom bombing of Hiroshima and Nagasaki."

"Precisely," Klein replied. "The use of nuclear weapons in 1945 forced the Japanese to surrender before the Americans invaded. Historians estimate that President Truman's decision saved over a million lives on both sides. So Gilad, I come back to you. The lives of a dozen young women weighed against cutting a world war short and preventing the Shoah from ever happening. Justified, or unjustified?"

Gilad Sneh shrugged. "Justified, I suppose, but I still don't like it."

"I'm pleased that you don't," said Klein while glancing at HarSinai. "But our distaste for this facet of the mission doesn't make it any less necessary, or any less legal. Now, if there are no more ethics questions, let's return to the matter at hand. We have a very rough outline of an operational concept that will require considerable refinement. I want to start that process right now with another walk-through of the terrain while we still have daylight. Maps and aerial photos only tell you so much. There's nothing that beats the Mark I human eyeball. We have four hours until dark, so let's move."

The five Israelis left the room, trooping quietly along the hall and down the stairs.

"Comment ça va, Monsieur Bradley?" the desk clerk enquired sweetly as the men emerged into the lobby. Switching to heavily accented Franglish, she enquired, "How goes... ah... la recherche for your film?"

"Very well, thank you Madame Lebreune," Klein responded with a brilliant smile. "I'm sorry, but we're already running late for some locations we have to scout. I'll hope to see you this evening. À bientôt."

"I hope so too," replied Juliette Lebreune, her eyes and the curvature of her lips broadcasting an unequivocal message. "Ciao!"

"Not a word," muttered Klein as the Israelis passed through the hotel front door into the circular driveway outside.

HarSinai responded with a theatrical 'who me?' gesture.

The quintet piled into the Peugeot 5008 amidst a gale of locker-room laughter that only faded as the SUV made its way down the driveway to the main road.

Eight

Emma Cohen seethed as she watched her parents wilt at the sudden pounding on their front door. Her mother lapsed into silent tears while her father's dignified demeanour was betrayed by a tremor in his left arm. It was almost Pavlovian, she fumed, how a few years of brutish thuggery could degrade such dignified people to a quivering mess.

Behind her brave face, Emma also struggled to contain a paralysing sense of trepidation as the heavy knocking echoed through the house. It was a grand old 18th-century manse, built on one of the most picturesque cobblestone streets of old town Heidelberg. Yet the interior décor of the Cohen home was strangely inconsonant with its exterior splendour. The unadorned state of its walls combined with a sparsity of fixtures and furniture to generate an ambience of almost spartan austerity.

Swallowing nervously, Emma walked to a nearby mirror and paused to ensure her raven hair and clothing were flawless. The face she saw staring back was that of a slender, green-eyed 28-year-old, who was generally deemed quite stunning, despite her slightly beaked nose. Affecting an air of faux serenity, she successfully concealed the sense of dread that was wrapped like a vice around her stomach. Whatever might be lurking behind that door, Emma Cohen would be damned if she wasn't going to greet it with poise and self-possession.

The appearance of unexpected visitors at the home of a German Jewish family during the autumn of 1940 was rarely a harbinger of glad tidings. At 10 o'clock in the evening, an unforeseen knock was more likely to portend the worst.

Walking into the entry hall, Emma took a deep breath and swung open the door. Rather than a Gestapo flying squad standing there, manacles in hand, she saw an inoffensive middle-aged man glancing furtively over his shoulder.

"Please let me in, Emma. It would be very awkward if anyone were to recognise me."

"Well, we wouldn't want that," replied Emma in a sarcasm-laden voice as her sense of relief gave way to resentment. She savoured his discomfort for a few delicious moments before opening the door and stepping aside.

"You're not being quite fair," complained Helmut Eisner as he passed over the threshold of the Cohen family home. "I've tried to help over the past few years. I worked hard to get the best possible price for those items you wanted to sell."

"Wanted to sell?" replied Emma, her voice rising an octave in outrage. She glanced at the barren walls, angrily noting for the hundredth time the rectangles set apart from their surroundings by their slightly darker shade of yellow. "You think my father would have parted with his Cézanne and those Renoirs if we weren't about to lose the roof over our heads?"

"Is everything alright, Liebling?" came the warbling voice of Emma's mother from the salon.

"Fine, Mutti. I'm just having a quick chat with someone."

"I think I've done the best I can under the circumstances," Eisner replied huffily. "I even managed to get you an exit visa. At no small risk to myself, I might add."

Emma snorted derisively. "As if I'd leave my parents to the mercy of the psychopaths running Germany today." She flashed a caustic smile, pointing to the enamelled swastika badge that adorned Hoff's lapel. "But I see you've done very well out of the system. A judge on the Landgerichte. That's a big step up from being a junior professor of law with a penchant for sleeping with his students."

Eisner blushed. "I cared for you very much, Emma, and I made sure you were able to complete your doctorate, even after things became ... difficult."

Emma sneered. "You mean after all other Jewish students were expelled."

The Potemkin village of Eisner's arrogance collapsed and he lifted his palms skyward in supplication. "You have every right to despise me. A better man would have spoken out, even if it guaranteed him a one-way ticket to Dachau. But I just don't have it in me to make that kind of self-sacrificial gesture. At the end of the day, I'm no Niemöller, just a coward."

"You'll get no argument from me," Emma retorted with barbed contempt. "But that doesn't explain why you're here. Is it to seek redemption? If so, you're too late. Yom Kippur was last Saturday."

"No Emma," said Eisner in a sombre tone. "I came to warn you. I came to tell you that, however bad it's been up to now, it's going to get worse ... and soon."

"What do you mean worse? How could it get any worse?"

"Late this afternoon we were briefed about a plan to expel the entire Jewish population of Baden and the Saar-Palatinate."

"Expel us?" echoed Emma, her voice rising in to an indignant pitch. "When?"

"Soon. No precise date was mentioned, but I got the strong impression they intend to carry out this 'aktion', as they call it, within the next two weeks. For sure it'll happen before the end of the month. They'll have teams of Orpos and Gestapo delivering expulsion notices to every Jewish household in the city. You'll be required to vacate your home within thirty minutes and will only be allowed to bring those possessions you can carry. All luggage will be searched for hidden valuables and you'll be marched under armed guard to the railroad station and placed on trains for removal from Germany."

"Where are we to be taken?"

"I ... I have no clue about that either," said Eisner. "This Eichmann fellow, he's an SS sturmbannführer, was very closed-mouthed about your final destination."

"And you're certain this includes us here in Heidelberg?"

"I'm afraid so," Eisner replied, frowning with dismay. "Wagner wants to be the first Gauleiter to proclaim his region 'judenfrei'. The object of the exercise is to curry favour with Hitler. It's a giant arse-licking competition at your expense."

"Everything's at our expense these days," said Emma, her white-hot rage congealing into a cold, grey sadness.

Eisner opened his briefcase and extracted a leather bag that resembled a large medieval purse. "I may be a craven man, but I'm not a poor one. Over the years, I've put a bit aside for the event of a proverbial rainy day."

Eisner proffered the purse to Emma, who was surprised by its heft. She upended it over the entry hall console table, staring in mute surprise as a cascade of gold coins spilled onto the lacquered wood.

"That's one thousand, seven hundred and forty marks in 20-Mark Kaiserreich gold pieces," said Eisner. "More than a labourer's annual salary. I thought you would need it."

"You know these are completely illegal," said Emma with a bemused smile. "Hitler outlawed the private ownership of gold in '35. I never figured you, of all people, as a black-marketeer."

Eisner flashed a grin. "I guess there's a whole other side to me you don't know."

"I stand corrected," said Emma, her face softening in magnanimity. "What you're doing isn't the act of a coward, it's the act of a brave and kind man. A smart one as well."

"I don't understand."

"Helmut, the fact is you were right. I was being unfair. A public protest would have been a stupid exercise in futility. It would have accomplished nothing of any value. What you're doing now is both meaningful and moral. I apologise for my previous ingratitude and gratefully accept your proposal with the proviso it's to be considered a loan. When all this madness is over, I'll make sure you're repaid to the last pfennig."

Helmut shook his head. "That's not necessary."

"No Helmut, but it is. That's my pre-condition. A loan."

Eisner sighed in grudging capitulation. "Alright, if you insist. But you have to let me know if there's anything else I can do. I dithered out of fear for far too long. There must be something."

"Helmut, this is more than anyone has done. More than any of papa's business partners. They just took advantage of the new laws to force him out of the very company he built from nothing. You've just done us an extraordinary act of kindness and I'll always be thankful."

"I only hope you can use this money to get away."

Emma shook her head. "I can't see where we could go. The whole of the West is now occupied by Germany. Switzerland has shut its doors to the Jews. The only real options would be England. Or perhaps Sweden. But how would we get there?"

Eisner shrugged helplessly. "I have no idea."

"We don't even have any forged papers. Besides, my parents are in no condition to go on the run. The events of these past years have had a terrible impact on their health. We'll just have to take our chances. I'm sure it won't be so bad."

"Let's hope not."

Emma stood on her toes to place a chaste kiss on Eisner's cheek. "This is probably the last time we'll see each other for a while."

"Yes, for a while," he replied gruffly, in a vain attempt to camouflage the tears welling in his eyes. "Make sure you hide the coins. Sew them into your coat or something."

"I will, Helmut. Thank you again."

There was nothing left to say. Emma opened the door, and with a gloomy nod of farewell he left. She returned to the salon, careful to sport a chipper smile.

"What was that all about, Liebling?" asked Dvorah Cohen running her hand over the pin in her silver hair. "You were talking for a very long time."

"Nothing important, Mutti. Just a bit of gossip with an old friend from university. But now I'm feeling a bit tired and think I'll go up to bed."

Emma dispensed goodnight kisses on the foreheads of her mother and father and climbed the stairs to her bedroom. Extracting her sewing kit from her dresser, she opened her closet and took her thickest overcoat off its hanger. Then she set to work.

Nine

Klein drove the rented Benz through the gate of Hoffmann's home, exchanging brief pleasantries with the four Shabak operatives on perimeter duty. The heavy duffel coats worn by the Israelis hadn't been acquired solely for the purpose of warding off the growing cold of a European late autumn. It just so happened that this particular item of clothing also provided perfect concealment for their UziPro 9 mm submachineguns.

Over the two summers he spent as a volunteer on Kibbutz Negba, Hoffmann had developed something of a fascination with the Israeli military. He was absolutely chuffed to have a twenty-man contingent of Shabak security men take up residence in his home.

For their part, the Israelis took great care to remain discreet, keeping a lower-than-low profile within the neighbourhood. They also managed to keep Hoffmann ignorant of the fact they had rigged his entire home for demolition.

Klein pulled up to the front door and entered, nodding again to the on-duty Shabakniks posted within. "What's new, Ilan?" he enquired of the team commander.

"All quiet on the Western Front."

"Where are they?"

"The usual," replied the Shabak commander, his head canting towards the home's interior.

Klein nodded and made his way to the lab, where Hoffmann and Adivi were busily working at their respective computer terminals.

"Ah, Colonel," said Hoffmann, walking over to Klein with an outstretched hand. "It's good to see you again."

"Nice to see you as well," Klein replied, giving Hoffmann's hand a quick shake. "We've been able to hammer out a rough operational concept and I wanted to run it past you."

"Aaron, don't be anti-social," Hoffmann called out. "Come and say hello to Colonel Klein."

Adivi remained glued to his computer screen, waving his hand in perfunctory greeting. "You two go ahead. I'll be with you in a minute. I just need to complete this set of calculations."

Hoffmann pushed his glasses further up the bridge of his nose in mild exasperation and motioned Klein to take a seat at a desk piled high with ring binders and loose sheaves of paper. "So what kind of progress are we making on our little enterprise?"

"We've come up with an operations plan that looks quite promising," Klein replied. "The boys are still refining it, but I wanted to run the fundamentals past you to make sure we're all on the same page."

"Go ahead."

"Okay," said Klein. "We'll need to transport a force of around ninety men and thirteen vehicles. Think of them as Jeeps-on-steroids. They'll each measure roughly six metres in length and three in width, when you factor in all the equipment and ammo they'll be carrying."

"And height?"

"Excuse me?"

"The height of your oversized Jeeps?"

"Let's say two and a half metres when you include weapon mounts."

"I see," said Hoffmann. He reached for a thick ring binder, leafing through its contents and tracing his finger along a spreadsheet foldout. "That will mean transport in several increments. Four, I should think."

"That many waves could create a tactical problem," Klein reflected. "Can't you produce sufficient amounts of this helium-2 stuff to power a vehicle that can take us all through at once? Or in two waves at most?"

"Ah, but as Hamlet said, 'there's the rub'," Hoffmann explained. "Producing helium-2 isn't the problem; that's just a matter of time, if you'll excuse the pun. But the larger the transporter, the larger the amount of helium-2 required to generate the time travel effect. And the larger the amount of helium-2, the greater the distortion in the timeline. That distortion, or warping if you will, degrades the accuracy of our calculations. It's not so important when on the outward leg, because a few seconds here or there won't make a difference. But coming home is a different story."

"Presumably because of that Novikov thing," prompted Klein.

"Quite correct, Colonel. Calculations for the return leg must be ultra-precise to avoid the temporal paradox of having two of you in exactly the same space at exactly the same moment. If the numbers are off, even by a millisecond, you'll be stuck in the past with no possibility of return to your temporal point of departure. The Novikov Self-Consistency Principle will simply prevent the transporter from making the time jump. At any rate, that's my hypothesis. I haven't personally put it to the test for obvious reasons. But there's nothing theoretical about the link between the amount of helium-2 and scope of the timeline distortion. That part is observable fact."

"What's the largest time transporter that would give us reasonable confidence we could get home without incident?"

"It would have enough capacity to take three of your vehicles at once. Let's say internal dimensions of twenty metres by four metres and three metres in height. About the size of an extra-large shipping container."

"I don't like this one bit," frowned Klein.

"It's not as bad as it sounds," explained Hoffmann. "How long do you think it would take your troops to disembark from the transporter at the destination end?"

Klein shrugged. "Three minutes. Maybe two-and-a-half with practice."

"So, from the standpoint of those in 1940, each successive wave would only be delayed by that three-minute unloading time. Plus, perhaps, a sixty-second safety margin."

"And you'd calculate the transporter's arrival time in the past with the shortest possible interval between trips."

"Correct," Hoffmann replied. "And with four waves at four-minute intervals, you'd have the entire force in place within about sixteen minutes LPT, or local past time."

"Still far from optimal," groused Klein. "But you're right, not as bad as I feared. We'll just have to adapt and overcome."

"I have every confidence in the men who pulled off that wonderful Entebbe rescue."

"That was way back in '76," replied Klein with a self-deprecating wave of his hand. "Long before my time, but I appreciate the sentiment."

"My pleasure. But there are a couple of other issues I wanted to discuss."

"Go ahead," replied Klein.

Hoffmann turned towards Adivi, who was still immersed in the figures flowing across his computer screen. "Aaron, I think you'll want to weigh in on this one."

Adivi stood and walked over to join the conclave.

"I think Aaron needs to join us," proposed Hoffmann.

"On the mission?" asked Klein in semi-disbelief. "You don't mean on the mission?"

"That's precisely what he means," replied Adivi.

"Absolutely not!" barked Klein with a shake of the head for emphasis. "It's out of the question."

"And why is that?" enquired Adivi with his eyebrows arched.

"Look, I admire you both tremendously. We wouldn't be here if it weren't for you. But you have to understand that having non-combatants under foot on the battlefield is a serious problem. I realise Professor Hoffmann will be with us to operate the time transport vehicle, but one civilian is more than enough."

"What if something happens to Gerhard?" asked Adivi. "The most routine civilian passenger flight always has a copilot on board. Do you really want to go on such an extraordinary journey with only one person who knows how to operate the device?"

"We wouldn't be a bother," reassured Hoffmann. "We wouldn't stray from base camp and we'd stay out of everyone's way. Besides, I have to insist."

"Insist?" echoed Klein in an incredulous tone. "This is a military operation. You're in no position to insist on anything."

"I beg to differ. As you just pointed out, we're not soldiers and not bound by military discipline. That puts me the perfect position to insist because you need me and I need Aaron."

"Are you really prepared to scuttle this entire operation?"

Hoffmann's mouth curled upwards in a confident grin. "Ah Colonel, I don't think it will come to that. After all, I don't believe your government would appreciate any decision to cancel this mission over such a minor matter."

Momentarily speechless at this open display of effrontery, Klein was pragmatic enough to cut his losses. "Fine," he conceded with a smile of grudging respect, "you've called my bluff – but there's something I'll require in return. You'll both undergo a course of weapons training before we depart. If things go bad, I don't want to see you curled up in a foetal position like whimpering children. I'll expect to see you on the firing line. Agreed?"

"Sounds like fun," said Hoffmann, his grin now impish.

"Also, you'll be under the strict orders of the security team commander during the entire duration of this mission. What he says goes. Acceptable?"

"Yes," chorused Hoffmann and Adivi.

"Alright then," said Klein as he leaned back in his chair. "If there isn't anything else, I should think about heading back to the boys."

"As a matter of fact, I do have a few questions," said Hoffmann. "I'm wondering about the physical location of our temporal transit point. Acknowledging my complete lack of military expertise, am I correct to assume you'll be looking in the vicinity of Montoire?"

Klein nodded in affirmation.

"You're aware it will have to be some sort of structure that is there both in October 1940 and at the present time?"

"Yes indeed," answered Klein, "and somewhere sufficiently off the beaten track that it won't attract undue attention. Our people are currently looking through the title deed history of a few places that might be appropriate."

"What about the issue of property acquisition at both ends of the timeline?" Hoffmann persisted. "Any thoughts as to how that will be handled?"

Klein nodded. "Two properties will be required. The first will serve as the point of transport for someone I'll call our purchasing agent. We're looking for an undeveloped piece of land that's secluded both in past and present. Somewhere we can operate without scrutiny in both time periods. We'll move your Apollo capsule to that location and from there you'll drop him off with sufficient funds to acquire the main transport site near Montoire."

"Did you have any particular date in mind for the 'then' of which you speak?" enquired Adivi.

"We're thinking around mid-1938 should work. Well enough before the war to avoid excessive paranoia about strangers snooping around in search of real estate to buy."

"And how would we know the length of time to allow before pickup for the trip home?"

"There are a couple of options," explained Klein. "One would be to consult property records in our current time. Once they showed the precise date of purchase by our man, we'd travel back at a predetermined time for pickup. Say the stroke of midnight three days later. But I'm inclined towards a more ambitious course of action. I'd like to leave our agent in place until our arrival. The in-depth knowledge of the area he'd be able to accumulate over those two years would be priceless."

"Not an easy thing to ask," mused Hoffmann.

"No, but there's precedent," Klein replied. "Have you ever heard the name Eli Cohen?"

"Of course," interjected Adivi, "the Mossad's man in Syria before the Six Day War."

"Exactly. He lived undercover in Damascus for almost four years."

"Yes, I remember the story, now. Wasn't he ultimately caught and hanged?" asked Hoffmann.

Klein nodded. "That's true. Syrian intelligence homed in on his radio transmissions, but our man won't be doing anything so risky. He'll just be living quietly, seeing what there is to see until the time comes to meet us and greet us."

"All the same, not something I'd want to do," said Hoffmann with a shake of the head.

Klein laughed. "I don't think you're quite suited for that particular job."

Hoffmann flashed a sardonic grin. "Are you implying my schoolboy French and German-accented English might make it difficult to blend into the Loire countryside?"

"The term 'sticking out like a sore thumb' did cross my mind," rejoined Klein with a matching smile of his own. "Besides, even though Professor Adivi is coming along, I'll still need you in the driver's seat for this mission. It just wouldn't do to have you stuck back in the 1930s."

"Fair enough," Hoffmann conceded. "Do you have anyone in mind for this sleeper agent role?"

"Haven't gotten that far," replied Klein, "not that I'd be able to say anything specific for reasons of operational security. But I can tell you this: economic stagnation and rampant anti-Semitism in France have combined to induce the emigration of around 90,000 Jews over the past fifteen years. Most of them ended up in Israel, which means we have a sizeable talent pool from which to choose. It shouldn't be a problem to find someone with the appropriate skills and disposition."

Hoffmann's pushed his glasses back pensively. "Well, whomever he is, I think that Kipling quote from *Gunga Din* is in order: he's certainly a better man than I."

Ten

Jasper Jaumont grimaced as the tyres of his Renault Primaquatre crackled after turning from the bitumen of Chemin Communale 8 onto the gravel lane. "The automobile is brand new," he said with an apologetic smile directed towards the passenger sitting beside him. "You see, in the property business, first impressions are most important."

Alexander Roux nodded in perfunctory acknowledgement, his eyes fixed on the looming hardwood forest that appeared to swallow the gravel lane whole. Roux had far more serious matters on his mind than the pretentious nattering of an oleaginous real estate agent.

The Renault continued its slow progress, passing from sunlit fields into the maw of the hardwood forest, the swaying branches casting a kaleidoscope of shadows across the narrow lane. After several hundred metres, the lane debouched into a forest clearing that was dominated by a large shed and three smaller outbuildings.

From the faded woollen beret on his head to the grey serge overalls he wore, the man who emerged from the nearest outbuilding looked like a middle-aged French labourer from central casting. He pulled a half-smoked Galoises from his lips and cast the butt to the ground, crushing the cigarette beneath the heel of his boot while watching the approaching car with a face that radiated cynicism and mistrust.

"He's not the most congenial type," said Jaumont. "It would be best if you let me do the talking." With that, the realtor hastened to exit the Renault as if his commission were contingent upon him uttering the first words of the coming conversation.

Jaumont strode up with an outstretched hand and an unctuous smile. "Monsieur Guillaume, how are you this wonderful summer's day?"

Guillaume grunted, shaking the realtor's hand with a palpable dearth of enthusiasm. "I know you. You're that shyster from Vendôme who's built a small fortune out of shoddy deals with suckers. Whatever you're selling, I'm not interested."

"That would be buying, not selling," Roux announced as he stepped out of the Renault.

Guillaume's shoulders heaved in a shrug of disinterest. "The answer's still the same. Not interested."

The labourer's snub did nothing to dim Jaumont's million-watt grin as he gestured towards his passenger. "Allow me to introduce Monsieur Roux from Paris. We are here to convey his interest in acquiring la Hubardière."

"And you'll be dealing with me," Roux declared.

Guilliame's mouth curled in a disdainful smirk. "I don't know you and don't care to know you. Besides, with those hands, you wouldn't last a week as a forester."

"Who I am and what I intend to do with this property is no business of yours," snapped Roux, oblivious to the peevish annoyance etched across the face of the sidelined Jaumont. "The only things that should interest you are the one-hundred-and-forty thousand francs I'm prepared to pay for the packing shed, the three outbuildings and the full thirty hectares of forest. You may keep your tractors and other machinery."

"Monsieur Roux, perhaps you should allow me ..." interjected Jaumont in a transparent effort to inveigle himself back into the bargaining process.

"Please be quiet, Monsieur Jaumont. You'll be paid regardless," interrupted Roux as he strode past the estate agent to address Guillaume directly. "Now Monsieur, you heard my offer. What do you say?"

"I say you don't sound like a Parisian. You speak with a Midi accent – as though you're from Provence or Languedoc."

"As it happens, Monsieur," said Roux, "I originate from Marseilles and have lived in Paris these past seven years. But my family history is irrelevant. I'm here to discuss a business transaction. So, I say again, you've heard my proposal. What's your response?"

"It's really quite a generous offer," added Jaumont in his best salesman-like tone. "You should seriously consider it."

"I'll take one hundred and seventy and not a centime less," declared Guillaume.

"One forty-five," replied Roux.

Guillaume shoulders heaved in a dismissive shrug.

Roux nodded. "Thank you for your time." He wheeled around and strode towards the car. Pausing at the passenger door, he called over his shoulder.

"Come, Monsieur Jaumont. There's nothing to be done here. Our search continues."

Jaumont scuttled along in Roux's wake, mumbling semi-audible apologies about Guillaume's peasant obduracy.

Roux had one leg inside the Renault when he heard a yell behind him.

"One hundred and sixty-five."

Roux shook his head and took his seat, with Jaumont following suit on the driver's side.

Guillaume rushed to the now-closed passenger door and rapped his knuckles on the window. "One hundred and sixty."

Roux slowly rolled down his window and examined his interlocutor in silence.

Guillaume shuffled from one foot to the other. "One fifty-five?" he said plaintively.

"One fifty and we have a deal," replied Roux. "I'll have the money transferred to your account the day after the contract is signed."

Guillaume nodded and extended his hand through the window. As they shook, Jaumont got out of the driver's seat and hastened around the car to the passenger side. He placed his expensive leather briefcase on the hood. Extracting a sheaf of official-looking forms, Jaumont scribbled hurriedly with a fountain pen. "Voila, Monsieur Guillaume. Here is the mémorandum 'd'entante for your signature." He proffered the documents and pen with a theatrical flourish and formal bow.

Guillaume examined the forms carefully, nodding his head at the prescribed sum of one hundred and fifty thousand francs. He took the offered pen and signed.

"Thank you, Monsieur," said a beaming Jaumont. "I'll have the formal contract ready for your signature tomorrow at my office. When should I expect you?"

"Three o'clock in the afternoon," Guillaume replied.

"Three it is. À bientôt, Monsieur."

Guillaume responded with a surly nod and strode back towards the outbuilding.

As he maneuvered the Renault down the gravel road, Jaumont glanced at the laconic client seated beside him. "Congratulations, Monsieur Roux. Tomorrow you will become the owner of a healthy slice of the Forêt de Prunay. Might I ask, what do you intend to do with your new property?"

"You indeed may ask," replied Roux laconically, his eyes fixed through the passenger window on the passing countryside.

As it became even more obvious that no further answer would be forthcoming, Jaumont moved to break the awkward silence with a meretricious laugh. "I see you are a man of few words, Monsieur. I can respect that. After all, discretion is an essential element of success in business, hein?"

"I suppose," replied Roux in a cryptic tone clearly meant to discourage further small talk. The petty sensibilities of a small-town estate agent were of no concern to Alexandre Roux – who, in another place at another time, went by the name Yiftach Beton.

This time, the deal had been quick and easy, Beton mused as the Renault turned north on to the Tours-Vendôme highway. Far less haggling than during the negotiations previously conducted over the same piece of real estate in another time.

Beton smiled as he recognised the implicit paradox in his thoughts. *It's absolutely bizarre that I can use the adverb 'previously' to modify something I've already done 80 years in the future. Yet that's just a minor reflection of this operation's essential and unavoidable weirdness. At the end of the day, ruminations on the meaning of life in the twilight zone should be the least of my worries. I have practical matters to consider.*

Over the past two months, Beton had been living in the 14th arrondissemont of Paris near the Gare Montparnasse. It was a working-class neighbourhood, teeming with foreign-born residents whose dubious immigration status left them quite averse to any interaction with French authorities. Within this melting-pot of the illicit and the déclassé – amidst White Russian expatriates, German refugees from Hitler and Spanish Republicans fleeing Franco – Beton's cheap walk-up apartment was the perfect place to keep a low profile.

But now the time had arrived to come out from the shadows. Money wasn't going to be an issue. He had sufficient British Royal sovereigns and US double eagles stashed in a Credit Lyonnaise safe deposit box to support him for the next decade or more. Now he was on the cusp of establishing himself as a legitimate country landowner, slumming was thankfully no longer required.

The next two-and-a-half years were going to be difficult enough without the self-infliction of unnecessary privation. Not ascetically inclined by nature, Beton was determined to soften his temporal exile with as many material comforts the technology of the day, and his cover story, would accommodate. He'd be seeking out a house that combined discreet affluence with proximity to la Hubardière and the Forêt de Prunay. It would be somewhere close enough to allow easy access when the appointed hour finally arrived.

That time would be long in coming, he pondered. Perhaps he'd finally be able to catch up on his reading, and a mistress might help to make things more bearable. The auburn-haired waitress at the hotel restaurant in Vendôme seemed to hold out some promise.

At the end of the day, or 796 days to be precise, there would be no getting around the fact that this journey through yesteryear was going to be a long, hard slog. When all this is over, he thought, the powers in Jerusalem are going to owe him in a major way. Assuming, of course, they even know what he did and when he did it in this brave new world they were in the process of creating.

Eleven

It's a veritable who's who of Tzahal's elite, mused Staff Sergeant Baruch Levinson as he glanced around at the two hundred and fifty olive and tan-uniformed men who filled the auditorium at Bacha 30 in Palmachim. Everybody who's anybody within the special forces community must be here.

The troopers sat together in clusters that reflected their units of origin. Forty-odd operators from Sayeret Matkal occupied the rear two rows, while a similar number from the Shayetet's Raiding Squadron took up seats in the middle. Levinson and his thirty-five mates from Shaldag were down towards the front, alongside about twenty men from the Yahalom special demolitions unit, distinctive in the grey berets of the Combat Engineer Corps.

Scattered throughout were troopers from Maglan and the Palsarim of the Golani, Givati and Parachute Brigades. Completing the picture were around twenty Unit 669 Air Force pararescuemen, and three-dozen operators from the Border Police Yamam counter terror unit.

Most of Levinson's childhood acquaintances and teachers would have been surprised to find him counted amidst such august military company. He was an 'oops baby' who arrived five years after the youngest of his two older sisters. He spent his early childhood in the family quarters at the Ramon Airbase in the Negev desert. But at age five, his fighter pilot father was killed when the F-16 he was flying suffered catastrophic engine failure on a low-altitude training mission. Zehava Levinson never remarried and instead moved to Jerusalem, where she studied law and ultimately became a District Court judge.

As the baby boy in a family otherwise entirely composed of females, Levinson was somewhat cosseted while growing up. By high school, he'd developed into a bookish kid who was more at home in the computer lab than the football pitch or dance floor. He also turned out to be something of a mathematical prodigy who, by special arrangement, was allowed to do university-level coursework while still in Grade 10.

Beyond his academic pursuits, Levinson's teenage years were not particularly happy ones. While he had a small coterie of friends who shared a similar cerebral bent, most of his peers were intimidated by his intellect. Levinson also didn't do his social standing any favours by displaying a seemingly effortless ability to solve problems that defied the more pedestrian efforts of his classmates.

It wasn't so much that Levinson was bullied. He was simply ignored. Rarely invited to social functions, on those few occasions when he worked up the courage to approach a girl, his overtures were invariably rebuffed. After several episodes of humiliation, he took the hint and sought solace in bibliophilic solitude. Thus, Levinson was quite happy when graduation day finally arrived at Jerusalem's University High School.

Like most 17-year-old Israeli Jewish males, the next chapter of Levinson's life revolved around his military service obligation. In light of his exceptional talent for mathematics, it was widely expected that he would wind up in one the IDF's super-secret signals intelligence or cyber-warfare branches.

Levinson had other ideas. He would seize upon the army as a vehicle to forge a whole new social identity. To his family's surprise, he applied for a place in Shaldag – the Air Force commando unit that held pride of place within the top-tier of Israel's special operations community. By engineering a metamorphosis from wuss into warrior, he was determined to inspire respect where there had formerly been disregard.

Judge Zehava Levinson was even more astounded when her son defied the odds and made it through the unit's notoriously gruelling selection course. It seemed the boy had a reservoir of determination that had hitherto remained untapped. She was positively glowing with pride when, two years later, he stood with a handful of others to receive the wings of a fully fledged Shaldag operator. The highly classified nature of the unit's work meant that she never had any idea where Levinson was and what he was doing. But she assuaged her maternal anxieties with the knowledge it had to be important.

The auditorium doors swung open, propelled by two members of the military police detachment that had cordoned off the building. Levinson watched as a man attired in running gear made his way down the aisle, nodding in acknowledgement towards the Matkalistim, whose faces beamed with broad miles of happy recognition.

"Unit guy?" Levinson whispered to his neighbour, receiving a nod of affirmation in response.

There was something vaguely lupine about the way the man carried his athletic six-foot-plus frame as he clambered onto the stage at the front of the auditorium. Something that made Levinson understand instinctively that this would be someone you'd want on your side in a brawl.

Picking up a microphone, the man waited as the buzz of conversation dwindled into the quietude of hushed anticipation.

"Some of you already know me. For the benefit of those who don't, my name is Yossi Klein and, until a few months ago, I was Deputy Commander of the Unit. It should be obvious to all of you that this is a unique gathering. In fact, throughout my sixteen years of military service, I've never seen the entire special ops community gathered under one roof in this manner. While we might work together on the odd combined operation, our units usually stick to their separate zones and tribal specialties.

"But extraordinary problems require extraordinary solutions. That's why we have today summoned everyone from Matkal to Maglan and from the Yamam to Yahalom. What's on offer is the opportunity to take part in an operation unlike any conducted, not only by Tzahal, but by anyone, anywhere, at any time. You should have no doubt that this mission will incur extreme risk. You should also know that the advantages gained are proportionate to the dangers entailed. Those who join us will embark on an enterprise that has the potential to revolutionise Israel's strategic situation beyond measure. I can't tell you much more at this stage, except that all those who we select must have at least eighteen months remaining on active duty. This means anyone approaching his demobilisation date will have to sign on for an extra term of service. With that, I'll invite those who are interested, and who brought sports kit per instructions, to join me for a bit of PT. I'll see you out front in fifteen minutes."

'A bit of PT' turned out to be one of the most exacting physical training sessions Levinson had experienced during his entire army service. Klein set off towards the beach with a smooth, effortless loping pace that ate up the miles through painfully soft sand. Fifteen kilometres later, one hundred and sixty-six troopers gasped their way across the finish line within eighty minutes or less. The four-dozen laggards who arrived in dribs and drabs after the cut-off time were thanked for their efforts and summarily dismissed.

The remainder of that afternoon, and most of the following two days, were spent on Krav Maga, the brutal, 'no holds barred' unarmed combat system developed by the Israeli military.

"No mercy!" bellowed the senior instructor as the troopers lined up in two opposing rows. "I want to see real aggression! The guy opposite you is a terrorist who wants to slaughter your family and I want you to put him down! I want to see blood!"

The heavy padding and helmets worn by the combatants provided only partial protection against the barrage of punches, kicks, elbow and knee strikes that ensued. The object of the exercise was pain – inflicting it on your antagonist while enduring it yourself. Levinson had worked hard during his army service to enhance his upper body strength. All those hours spent in the weight room now came in useful.

Blocking a roundhouse left from his opposite number, Levinson moved in close, using a Judo osoto-gari move to drop his antagonist onto the mat. Following his stricken opponent down to the ground, Levinson pummelled his torso with a flurry of punches and elbow strikes until he heard the whistle signal the end of the bout.

The troopers soon moved from one-on-one fights to two-on-one and even three-on-one, with Klein observing closely from the sidelines. After each evolution, he consulted with the senior Krav Maga instructor and any troopers deemed deficient in fighting skills or raw aggression were informed that their services were no longer required. This winnowing process reduced the pool of candidates to one hundred and twenty-eight bruised and bloodied survivors. Attrition continued on the fourth day of the selection process, through tests of marksmanship on the range and personal interviews. At the end, only one hundred and eleven troopers were extended invitations to participate in the still nameless operation.

Once the initial selection process was complete, the chosen troopers queued up in typical army 'hurry-up-and-wait' style for processing by personnel clerks. They were then dispatched homewards, armed with a twelve-day pass and instructions to ruminate long and hard over the full implications of their decision. Anyone who chose to reconsider could return to his unit of origin with no questions asked. Klein clearly wanted only the most resolute and committed along with him on this most uncommon of enterprises.

By mid-afternoon, Levinson arrived at his home in the German Colony neighbourhood of Jerusalem. He had just settled down to enjoy a beer in front of the TV when his twenty-six-year-old sister appeared, her arms laden with books. A doctoral student in Jewish philosophy at the Hebrew University, Maya Levinson beamed in delight at the sight of her kid brother splayed on the living room couch.

"Shalom Baruch! I didn't expect to see you at home."

But Maya's smile transformed into a frown when she noticed the black and blue bruising that blotched her brother's forearms. "What did they do to you?"

"It's nothing. Just a bit of training."

"Barbarians!" she huffed. "Go put on a long-sleeved shirt. Ima will worry if she sees you this way."

Levinson nodded and walked down the hall to his bedroom, returning a few moments later clad in more modest attire. "I have a furlough. Almost two weeks."

"Ima will be very happy," said Maya. "Any plans?"

"I don't know. Perhaps I'll do a little trekking. The Golan maybe. Swim a bit in the Kinneret. You know how I love the North."

"I don't get it," replied Maya with a headshake of incomprehension. "You spend weeks at a time in the army navigating up hill and down dale, not to mention being beaten black and blue. Now you want to go trekking in your time off?"

Levinson grinned, "Without the fifty kilograms of weapons and equipment!"

"Still," she declared, "it's beyond me."

"And how are you?" enquired Levinson in a transparent gambit to shift the topic of conversation. "How's ... what's his face? I forget the name of the latest in your long series of male conquests."

"Hmph!" snorted Maya. "That's rich, coming from you, Mr never-had-a-girlfriend-in-his-life. In answer to your question, I'll have you know that Mr what's his face, AKA Nitzan, is just lovely. We've been seeing each other five months now and I think he might be the one."

"That's just what we need, another philosopher in the family," said Levinson with a theatrical roll of the eyes. "But seriously, sis. If you're happy, I'm happy. If not, I'll break his legs."

Maya giggled and administered a hug that was interrupted by the sound of a key in the front door. "That must be Ima. Ima, Baruch's home!" she yelled.

Zehava Levinson galloped up the stairs and enveloped her son in a fierce maternal embrace. "It's good to see you, sweetie! I thought you were closing Shabbat on base this weekend?"

"You know the army," Levinson replied with a shrug. "Every plan is a basis for change. I have twelve days off, so no complaints here."

"Nor here," said a beaming Zehava. "That's the sort of change I can endorse. What's on the agenda then?"

"I was just telling Maya that I might do a bit of trekking up north. I thought I might hike Nahal Zavitan and swim a bit in the Kinneret."

"Well, you have to spend at least a few days with us," Zehava chided.

"Of course, Ima," Levinson replied. "In fact, there's something I need to discuss with you."

"Hmm, sounds serious," said Maya with semi-mocking affection. "I have to run anyway. I'm meeting Nitzan and just came home to drop off some stuff." After planting another kiss on Levinson's cheek, she made a hasty exit out of the room.

Once he heard the front door close, Levinson turned to his mother. "Ima, I've been asked to take part in a special operation. They haven't disclosed many details, and even if I knew anything I wouldn't be in a position to say much more. We've been told that it will revolutionise Israel's strategic situation for the better. I'd have to sign on for another year, though."

"An extra year? What about your studies? You've been accepted into law at Hebrew for the next academic year. This would mean you'd have to defer."

"I know, Ima," Levinson replied. "But this is something really important that could change all our lives for the better."

"And really dangerous as well, no doubt," said Zehava, her head shaking in dismay. "You've already given four years. How much more do they want before allowing you to get on with your life? Besides, how do you really know it's so essential?"

Levinson simply smiled in response.

His mother threw up her hands in exasperation. "I know, I know! You can't tell me. At times like this, I regret signing your papers!"

"Don't worry, Ima," responded Levinson with a winning smile. "I'll be in very good hands. The mission commander is from Sayeret Matkal. He's put together a team of the best soldiers in the IDF. I'll be fine."

Zehava Levinson let out a hushed sigh. She then rose, took her son by the arm and led him towards the kitchen. "In the meantime, at least I can feed you. Come, I made knishes yesterday."

90

Twelve

"Emmaleh, have you seen my blue sweater?" called Dvorah Cohen from her upstairs bedroom. "I can't seem to find it anywhere."

"Just a minute, Mutti," replied Emma as she hastened towards the cellar door. "I think I saw it somewhere. Let me look."

Emma quietly descended into the bowels of the basement and pulled a large leather portmanteau from behind the boiler. Opening the suitcase, she rummaged within until she found the turquoise cardigan in question. Returning the suitcase to its hiding place, Emma hastened up the stairs to the kitchen. "I've found it, Mutti. It must have been in the laundry."

"Ah, thank you my dear," came Dvorah's voice from the second floor. "It's quite chilly and we really don't have the money to run the heater."

"I'm about to go out for groceries, so I'll leave it on the kitchen table."

"Be careful, darling."

"I will Mutti," replied Emma as she put on her coat and hat.

Emma pulled the front door shut behind her and made her way down the Hauptstrasse towards the Marketplatz in old town Heidelberg. Beyond the normal autumn victuals, the market was replete with the gastronomic spoils of Germany's military conquests. The vegetable stalls were overflowing with Jerusalem artichokes and asparagus from the Côte d'Azur. The cheese seller had stocks of Gouda from the Netherlands and Camembert from Normandy. But as enticing as those luxury items were, Emma was on the hunt for more basic, affordable and imperishable fare.

Stopping outside the butcher shop, she perused the sausages hanging in the window before stepping inside. "Guten Morgen, do you have any beef sausages?" she enquired.

"Let me ask," replied the young shop assistant with an apologetic smile. "I'm sorry, it's only my second day on the job."

Emma waited as the girl consulted with the mustachioed owner. "Who's asking for beef sausages?" the butcher demanded in a booming voice.

"I am sir," Emma responded with a bright smile.

The butcher strode to the other end of the counter to examine Emma more closely. After a few moments, he snapped his fingers and snorted triumphantly. "I know you! You're the Cohen girl. No wonder you only want to eat beef. You Jews think you're too good to eat pork like the rest of us."

"My money is as good as anyone's," snapped a bristling Emma. "If I want to buy beef sausages, there's no reason why you shouldn't sell them to me."

"The Führer says every pfennig of your money has been stolen from honest, hardworking Germans," replied the butcher in a tone of open contempt. "I don't need your business and I don't want you in my shop. Get out, you Jew bitch."

"I will not," Emma declared. She glanced at the shop's other patrons – three middle-aged women – in an implicit appeal for support. But the other shoppers shied away, looking in every direction but hers.

The butcher strode around the counter to confront Emma at close range. "This is your last chance. Get out or I'll throw you out."

Emma shook her head resolutely in silent refusal to budge, whereupon the butcher, a burly man in his early 40s, began to manhandle her out of the shop.

"Stop it, you barbarian! Leave me alone! Help! Somebody!"

The butcher pushed Emma through the door of his shop, straight into the arms of a Sturmabteilung patrol attracted by the hubbub.

"What's all this?" asked the Obersharführer in charge of the six-man brown-uniformed SA detachment.

The butcher spat contemptuously onto the cobblestoned roadway. "This damned Jewess refused to leave my store. I don't have to do business with her kind."

"Ausweis," the NCO barked at Emma. Reaching into her purse, Emma retrieved her ID booklet and handed it over to the stormtrooper.

"Hmmm," mused the Obersharführer as he studied the document carefully. "Emma Sara Cohen. You were quite correct," he said to the butcher with a respectful nod. "Well done. You ought to enlist in the SA. You seem to have a special talent for sniffing out kosher meat."

The butcher puffed up his chest like a peacock as the stormtroopers erupted with sadistic guffaws. "Thank you, sir. May I go now? I have customers waiting in the shop."

The NCO nodded affirmatively before turning his attention to Emma. "So what are we going to do with you?" he mused, his voice conveying a distinct undertone of menace. "Disturbing the peace, making a public nuisance, trying to pass as an Aryan. These are serious offences. I think we just might have to take you in."

Emma fell silent, frozen by a tide of raw physical fear.

"She's quite a looker," observed one of the SA troopers, eliciting a lascivious laugh from the NCO.

"That she is," replied the Obersharführer. "Almost pretty enough to make a fellow forget the rassenschänder laws."

The SA man's lascivious musings were interrupted by the arrival of an Ordnungspolizi constable. "What's going on here?" demanded the policeman.

"Just a Jewess making trouble," replied the Obersharführer defensively. "We were ensuring peace and order."

"That's a job for the police," barked the constable, "not the SA. I'll take over from here."

"But ..."

The policeman pulled himself up to his full 1.86 metres of height. Despite being of early middle-age, the constable's physical stature was impressive.

"I said I'll take over from here. If you're so keen to see action, why don't you enlist in the army?"

"I volunteered, but they turned me down for having flat feet," replied the stormtrooper in a tone of mixed embarrassment and self-righteousness. "So I'm doing my bit here at home."

"Doing your bit here at home," echoed the policeman in a tone of thinly veiled contempt. "We had plenty of flat feet with us in the trenches during the last war. We spent our time fighting real men, not harassing young women who are simply trying to buy food for their families. But alright, let's say you've done your duty to Volk und Vaterland. Now it's time for you to move on."

The Obersharführer took a backward step, intimidated by the constable's size and authoritative demeanor. "Sehr gut," he replied, handing Emma's ausweis to the policeman.

"Heil Hitler!" declared the SA NCO, raising his arm in an ostentatious Nazi salute.

The diffident wave that passed for a response from the constable elicited a sullen scowl from the Obersharführer.

The policeman glanced up from his examination of Emma's ID booklet.

"Was there anything else?" he asked with transparently contrived innocence, meeting the SA man's glower with a poker-faced countenance of utter impassivity.

Shaking his head in disgust, the Obersharführer turned to face his men. "Let's move. We have another three hours on duty and that means three more districts to patrol." The detachment of stormtroopers moved on through the Marketplatz and soon disappeared amongst the stalls.

The policeman's demeanour shifted to avuncular concern as he returned Emma's ausweis. "Are you alright, miss?"

Emma regained her composure and smiled in gratitude. "I've never been so frightened in my life."

"Pah," said the constable with a contemptuous wave. "I know his type. In another time he'd be petty street criminal or gang member. Only now he gets to strut around in a brown shirt and bully people under the auspices of the state." He shook his head disdainfully.

"I don't mean to be presumptuous," said Emma politely, "but shouldn't you be a little more discreet?"

The constable smiled wickedly. "It's quite alright. My reputation as a cynic is already well-established around the station and I gave up on promotion a long time ago. Besides, something tells me you can be trusted not to inform on me."

Emma smiled.

"My best friend in the last war was one of yours. Oskar Goldman. A little Jewish guy from Wuppertal. Wouldn't have weighed more than sixty kilos dripping wet, but what a fighter. Saved my life more times than I can recall. As I remember, he wouldn't eat pork either," said the constable said with a smile of fond reminiscence.

"What happened to him?" asked Emma.

"He didn't make it," the policeman replied with a cough that failed to hide his emotions. "He was killed fighting the Australians at Montbrehain just a month before the Armistice. That was a long time ago. Now, what was it were you looking to buy?"

"Beef sausages," Emma replied.

"And how much were you going to spend?"

"Thirty-five Reichsmarks."

The policeman grinned. "That's a lot of sausage, but I have a sudden hankering for Rindswurst myself."

Emma smiled in sudden comprehension and reached into her purse, extracting a wad of bills that she handed to the constable.

"Wait here," he said, while turning to enter the butcher shop.

Through the glass, Emma observed the owner remonstrating with the policeman, who was shaking his head insistently. The butcher ultimately threw up his hands and strode to the back of the shop, returning a few minutes later with a brown paper bundle tied with string.

She could see the policeman pick up the bundle and wag an admonitory finger at the butcher, who lifted his hands in protestation of his innocence against whatever accusation was being made.

The policeman exited the store and strode up to Emma. "I promised to make his life miserable if he snuck in any pork," he said with a conspiratorial wink.

Emma's eyes were wet with tears as she accepted the bundle. "Thank you. It's people like you who allow people like me to hope that better times lie ahead."

"There's no need for any of that," replied the constable in a tone of faux gruffness. "But you should probably get back home before we both get into any more trouble."

Emma nodded and mouthed one more silent thank you before turning to make her way across the Marketplatz.

Thirteen

Levinson took a knee upon reaching the end of the corridor. Cautiously peeking around the corner, he observed a couple of flashes and pulled his head back just in time for two 5.56 mm'Paintmunitions' training rounds to whizz past and hit the opposite wall with an audible splat. Levinson glanced at the yellow splotches left by the rounds on the wall before looking behind him at the men stacked up behind in urban combat formation. "Two, I think. At the far end of the corridor, behind an improvised barrier made by an overturned table and other furniture. Range thirty-five metres."

"Right," replied the Egoz lieutenant who was serving as team commander on this training evolution. "Let's flashbang 'em and then move in four-up formation with the second fire team covering from the corner. Gross and Levinson will be numbers one and two, while I'll be at number three and Cohen number four. Let's do it!"

Levinson opened a pouch on the right side of his tactical vest and extracted a flashbang grenade. Pulling the pin, he tossed it around the corner as far as possible without exposing himself to enemy fire. After two seconds, the grenade exploded with an incandescent flash and a deafening crack. Levinson immediately led the way around the corner, firing paintmunitions from his modified M4 carbine as he went. Keeping pace on his left was a trooper from the Parachute Brigade Palsar, who was generating a similar rain of suppressive fire.

But one third of the way down the corridor, the paratrooper suddenly dropped to one knee, yelling "stoppage!" as he feverishly worked the charging handle of his M4.

Levinson instinctively paused, waiting for the man behind to step around the kneeling trooper and close ranks. The momentary slackening of fire was an opportunity the defenders were ready to exploit. Popping up behind the overturned table were not two, but six defenders who dispatched a veritable hailstorm of return fire at the attacking force.

In a real combat situation, where ball ammunition was being used, the result would have been an absolute massacre. Levinson was pummelled to the floor by the impact of seven paintmunitions rounds on his head, arms and torso. Standard operating procedure required that all force-on-force training in the shoot-houses at the IDF's Mitkan Adam counter terrorism school be conducted wearing protective gear. But the padded vests, helmets and face masks worn by Gabi and his fellow troopers did nothing to shield their extremities from high-velocity paint rounds that hit home with painful force.

Looking around, Levinson saw the rest of his team in prone disarray, similarly covered with splashes of yellow paint.

"Cease fire, cease fire!" bellowed the loudspeaker bolted to the wall next to one of the ubiquitous CCTV cameras. "End exercise. Remain in place for debriefing."

With a sotto voce groan of pain, Levinson stood up and unstrapped the helmet–riot mask combination from his head. "Well, we fucked that one," he muttered.

His teammates nodded in glum agreement as the door to the shoot-house swung open and Chief Inspector Tzachi Dvir strode in. At age 33, Dvir was ten years older than most of those under his instruction. But the assembled troopers were aware of how well Dvir knew his business, not to mention the fact that he could PT them into the ground.

Yet the Chief Inspector wasn't a soldier in the strict sense of the term, hailing instead from the Yamam counter terrorism unit of the Israeli Border Police. The Yamam was unusual in the Israeli special forces firmament in that it was composed of long-service professionals, as opposed to conscripts.

Founded in 1974, after Sayeret Matkal botched a hostage rescue operation in the northern Israeli town of Ma'alot, the Yamam drew recruits largely from alumni of the IDF's elite units. Over the years, the special Border Police unit had refined a suite of precision tactics and techniques that encompassed every conceivable assault and hostage rescue scenario. As Dvir was a former Yamam squadron commander, it only made sense that he should be placed in command of the assault team on Operation Agag.

"Good job defenders," said Dvir to the team behind the overturned table. "You noticed a break in the enemy's momentum and exploited it. That reflects excellent situational awareness."

Dvir then turned to address Levinson and his assault team. "As for you gentlemen, that performance simply wasn't good enough. Who was the number two man?"

Levinson sheepishly raised his hand.

"Levinson, right?

"Yes."

"And what was your mistake?"

"I hesitated when my partner took a knee to clear his weapon," Levinson replied.

"Precisely," confirmed Dvir. "This evolution demonstrates how a minor error can disrupt the tide of battle and transform victory into defeat. All it takes is for someone to do the wrong thing at the wrong time and disaster can ensue. While this is true in any combat operation, it's a principle that applies with redoubled force to a take-down scenario like this one. Make no mistake, gentlemen: success on this mission will require us to maintain maximum offensive momentum at all times. We'll be conducting a decapitation assault against a dozen high-value targets at a location far behind enemy lines. That means going for HVT kills rather than prisoners."

Dvir paused for a moment, studying the faces of his audience to verify that he had their full attention.

"The target environment will be complex and varied – and this will require an effective combination of precision force and speed. By precision force, I mean matching our weaponry to the nature of each specific target environment so we bring accurate and effective fire to bear where needed, when needed. And by speed, I mean getting inside the enemy's OODA-loop and neutering their capacity to counterattack."

"But how are we supposed to make those decisions if we have no idea what the target is?" asked a burly sergeant from the Paratroop Brigade Palsar.

"You'll find that out in due time," Dvir responded. "Right now, we're here to find out what kind of raw talent I have at my disposal. By the end of the week, I should have enough insight to make the final decision who'll be joining me on the assault team."

"What about those not selected for assault?" enquired a trooper from Egoz.

"There'll be no hewers of wood or drawers of water on this operation," replied Dvir. "Those not on assault will be assigned to other roles essential to mission success. And believe me, there'll be more than enough action to go around. Let's not be dewy-eyed about the enemy. The people on the other side won't be wimps or pushovers. We'll be facing well-armed and determined fighters who'll be sure to take advantage of any mistakes we might make. So it's our job not to make any, or at least as few as possible. This means that once team assignments are complete, we'll be training more and more until we achieve a level of performance that's as close to perfection as humanly possible."

"You said that we'll be going for kills rather than prisoners. Does that mean everyone in the target area is to be considered hostile?" asked an Air Force pararescueman from Unit 669.

"There's a high probability we'll encounter a small number of non-combatants," replied Klein. "But there'll be no deviation from our clearing procedure, because the elimination of our HVTs takes precedence over everything. If the civilians can be spared without interfering with the mission, fine. We'll be taking no special measures to avoid collateral damage, though. This is an unfortunate tactical necessity of this particular mission. Are you okay with that?"

"All good," replied the pararescueman.

"All right then, let's get back to it. This time, roles will be reversed." Then turning to the Egoz lieutenant, Dvir shouted, "Moskovitz, your team is now defending. You'll be shooting blue and assaulters will be shooting red. Control will be changing the layout so we'll reconvene in twenty-five minutes. That'll give everyone time to restock with appropriately coloured ammo and defenders to come up with a deployment plan. Assaulters, after ammo reload you'll be running the obstacle course with me before coming back to mount your attack. That'll get your blood flowing. Move."

An audible groan arose from the newly anointed assault team.

"I don't want to hear any bitching and moaning," barked Dvir. "Remember, no-one is forcing you to be here. Say the word and you'll be sent back to your home units so fast the door won't hit your asses on the way out. Your choice."

The chastened assaulters fell silent and Dvir looked up at the closest CCTV camera and made a circular gesture with his right hand.

"Prepare for structural adjustment," the loudspeaker clamoured. "Vacate the building immediately. Adjustment to begin in sixty seconds."

"That's our cue," said Lieutenant Moskovitz as he led his troopers out of the shoot-house to the adjacent ammunition storage hut where they reloaded their M-4 magazines with paintmunitions. The hum of heavy-duty electrical motors could be heard from the kill house as control room operators rearranged the walls into one of the twenty-five possible layout permutations.

Ammo restocked, the assaulters trooped off to run the obstacle course while the defenders quietly waited for clearance to re-enter the building. Once back inside, they encountered an entirely new floor plan. A large conference room with two smaller offices on its periphery now stood where before there had been a series of corridors.

Moskovitz took a few moments to assess the new layout. "Okay, here's what we'll do. Pile up the furniture into a barricade over there," he said, pointing to the far corner of the conference room. "That'll draw their attention when they first enter. Then we'll take them from those two offices on the right. Let's get to it," he instructed with a clap of his hands. "We only have eight minutes before they attack."

The team members set about piling up the various items of furniture in the appointed corner. Once the barricade was complete, Moskovitz turned to address Levinson. "Just for the sake of precision, we didn't fuck up last time. You did. And that means you get to play decoy behind the table while the rest of us ambush them from the flank. Try not to get shot too often this time around."

Levinson stiffened to attention, delivering a parade-ground-perfect salute worthy of a Coldstream Guardsman. "As Roman gladiators used to say, we who are about to die, salute you," he announced theatrically. It was a perfect expression of sarcasm in a military noted for its inattention to pomp and circumstance.

"Don't be a smartass," growled Moskovitz, quashing the wave of guffaws that had erupted amongst his team. He gestured for Levinson to assume his position of sacrificial lamb behind the barricade and led the other troopers off to their ambush positions within the side rooms.

Levinson sighed softly in stoic resignation, settling down to make himself as comfortable as possible. Adjusting his face mask to ensure it was firmly in place, he chambered a paintmunition round in his M-4, opened the selector switch to semi-auto and awaited his inevitable fate.

Fourteen

Defense Minister Haim Bar'el hummed off key and drummed his fingers on the conference table as he sat waiting in the Pit.

Ever the urbane diplomat, Foreign Minister Hava Geffen cleared her throat in an oblique expression of annoyance.

"Sorry," Bar'el said with an apologetic smile. "Any idea why we've been summoned?"

Geffen shrugged. "No idea. Could be any one of a dozen issues we've currently got on the burner."

Bar'el nodded in agreement. Optimistic dreams unleashed by the Arab Spring of 2011 had long since dissolved into nightmares, as the brutal instincts of Middle East politics came to the fore with a terrible vengeance. For most of the past decade, the region had been awash with violent chaos that had redrawn national borders in a torrent of blood. Hopes of democracy, representative government and respect for individual liberty in the Arab world lay crushed beneath the treads of army tanks and the heels of jihadi boots.

The international border between Syria and Iraq had been erased by the rise of the Islamic State. The Hashemite monarchy in Jordan teetered on the brink of collapse, while the military regime in Cairo battled ISIS-aligned insurgents in the Sinai. A proxy war between a Sunni Egyptian–Saudi axis and Iranian-supported Shia insurgents had raged for years in Yemen. From Lebanon in the North to Eilat in the South, the entire Middle East was turning to shit right on Israel's doorstep.

Bar'el's gloomy ruminations were interrupted by the sound of the elevator descending from ground level. A minute later, the conference room door opened and Prime Minister Etzioni entered with Aaron Adivi in tow.

Taking his seat at the head of the table, he pushed the button that sealed the blast door to the situation room. "Thank you for attending on such short notice," the Prime Minister said. "You remember Professor Adivi?"

Adivi lifted his hand in greeting as Bar'el and Geffen smiled in welcome. "So I take it this has something to do with Operation Agag?" asked Geffen.

"Yes," replied the Prime Minister. "Why don't we begin with an update from Haim on where we stand on preparations for the mission?"

Bar'el nodded. "Things are progressing quite well. We have a twenty-man Shabak team on site in Göttingen providing security at Professor Hoffmann's lab. Lieutenant Colonel Klein put together a planning cell and made several recces to the target area. He's also had in-depth consultations with Hoffmann to acquire a layman's understanding of the technology involved. The end result has been an ops plan that has a very good chance of success. Klein has selected around one hundred of the best and brightest from our special ops community and they've been training non-stop for three months straight."

"And what about the Ramatkal? Is he over his fit of pique about the General Staff being kept out of the loop?"

"He calmed down after you had your talk with him," replied Bar'el. "He now thinks it's all some sort of super-secret foreign intelligence operation, which I suppose in a way is true. In any event, the generals are now reconciled to living with one of Don Rumsfeld's 'known unknowns.'"

"That's very good. What else is required before we're ready to launch?" asked the Prime Minister.

Bar'el shrugged. "As I said, the team is pretty much good to go. Current title deed records indicate our man on the ground in 1940 successfully acquired the property that will serve as the temporal transit point and forward operating base."

"Who owns it now?" asked Geffen.

"We do," replied Bar'el. "After purchasing the property, our agent filed a will with the local notary that bequeathed it to a foundation in Jerusalem ..."

"Let me guess," interposed Geffen. "It's a front for the Mossad."

Defense Minister Bar'el grinned. "Precisely. And that means the site is ready to receive and send."

"Very good," observed Prime Minister Etzioni. "Are there any other missing pieces?"

"The only piece of the puzzle still outstanding is the logistical task of delivering weapons and equipment to the launch location in France," replied Bar'el. "But because the shipping container we'll be using for that purpose will double in function as our time travel vehicle, that task is greatly simplified."

"So there's no need for a separate time machine?" asked Geffen.

"If you'll allow me," interjected Adivi with a questioning glance at Bar'el. The Defense Minister nodded in deference to Adivi's superior expertise. "The answer to that question is both yes and no. Hoffmann's helium device generates a temporal transit field that envelops any object in direct physical contact. All he has to do is bolt it to the wall of the shipping container and we're ready to go. But we'll need to build a customised container that will be quite a bit larger than any available standard size. Otherwise, we'll be bringing our boys back in too many waves, and that's a definite tactical risk."

"How big will this helium device have to be?" enquired Prime Minister Etzioni.

"That all depends on what you wish to transport," Adivi replied. "The larger the vehicle, the more helium is needed to generate an adequate temporal field. Our shipping container will measure twenty-by-four-by-three, so that will require a helium device with the rough dimensions of an old steamer trunk."

Foreign Minister Hava Geffen signified her desire to speak with a casual wave of her hand. "Prime Minister, I'm on record as a supporter of this operation – but I'm a little disturbed that we've already sent someone back through time. It seems to me that violated the protocol of what was agreed when we discussed this as a committee. And on that topic, I'd like to know where everyone else is. Why are only the four of us here?"

"All valid questions, Hava," said Etzioni, his palms raised in a placatory gesture. "Let me answer them in the order you asked. We dispatched an agent back in time to make the necessary logistical preparations for this mission's success. It was an extremely low-profile operation that involved moving Professor Hoffmann's two-person capsule by truck into a secluded spot in northern France where the transfer was made. Our agent is now in place and time, and ready to assist. Or, alternatively, he will be withdrawn from a prearranged date in early November 1940 if we do not proceed. Danger of exposure is minimal."

"That still doesn't explain why we're the only ones here," said Geffen. "Where are the other members of the committee? Where are Amiram and Tzvi?"

"Well," replied Etzioni, "therein lies the problem. I've been talking to Tzvi Kupperberg, trying to bring him around. He still has serious qualms about this entire enterprise."

"I don't understand," barked Bar'el in a tone of annoyance. "We explained the facts of life to him. We explained that, if we don't go through with this operation, we'll have to eliminate the German physicist or forcibly bring him to Israel. I thought his refined moral sensibilities said no to either of those two options."

"It's his grandchildren," said Etzioni. "He's spooked by the possibility, however unlikely, that we might be creating a world in which they'd never be born. Our Attorney General is adrift in a sea of raw emotion, which is quite remarkable for someone who's normally such a Yekke pedant. But he's obdurate. The last time we spoke, he was talking about keeping a security contingent permanently onsite in Göttingen."

"That's absurd," sneered Bar'el with a contemptuous shake of the head. "Even a battalion of Shabak wouldn't be able to help if the Americans, Germans or anyone else found out about this project. Typical head-in-the-clouds academic."

"Be that as it may," said the Prime Minister, "he remains firmly opposed to this operation."

"So why are we here?" asked Geffen.

"Because I want you to consider something unorthodox. Hell, something technically illegal."

"You want to proceed without full committee approval," declared Geffen. Etzioni nodded. "Yes, I do. Remember what's at stake here."

"I remember everything," rejoined Geffen, "the potential benefits as well as the probable risks." She turned to address Adivi, who had hitherto been sitting quietly next to the Prime Minister. "Professor Adivi, have you done any further analysis of the temporal probabilities involved in this enterprise?"

"Yes I have, Foreign Minister," Adivi replied. "Since our last meeting, I've gone over the numbers several additional times and the results confirm my previous assessment. The world will be substantially different in numerous respects, but it won't be unrecognisable. Changes will largely be for the better. Massive loss of life will be averted and the Jews will fare particularly well. I'm still quite confident that, as individuals, the consequences for us will be felt on the margins. The likelihood that our parents and grandparents will marry the same people and beget the same children is just over ninety-six per cent."

"Then there's the issue that what you're asking is a blatant deviation from the normal government protocol," Geffen said. "And you're right, it's likely illegal, but then there's a practical consideration as well. If we're bypassing the General Staff, how will the 'go' order be transmitted?"

"I'll deliver it personally to Klein," Bar'el replied. "It's highly unorthodox, but so is every other facet of this operation. It won't be a problem."

"I know Haim is a yes," said the Prime Minister. "But I'm looking for unanimity in this limited forum. If we can't achieve a consensus between the three of us, then I guess it just isn't meant to be. So that leaves it up to you, Hava."

Geffen lapsed into ruminative silence as her committee colleagues waited respectfully for her decision.

After a short period of reflection, she smiled. "I'm a yes as well. The issues are too weighty for us not to proceed. But I wonder ... if this is a success and I end up the Foreign Minister of a bigger and better Israel, will we be having a similar discussion about the use of Professor Hoffmann's device for other purposes?"

Adivi shrugged. "That I can't tell you. It's not a question I've subjected to quantitative analysis."

"In any event, we owe you a tremendous debt of gratitude, Aaron," said Etzioni in a tone of clear relief. "And thank you as well, Hava. I think that should conclude our business."

"Not entirely," interjected Hava Geffen as she turned to face Bar'el. "There's one more thing, Haim. Please convey my best wishes to Lieutenant Colonel Klein. Ask him to tell our boys how proud and how grateful we are for what they're about to do."

Fifteen

"That's a big ship," muttered Sous-Lieutenant Maurice Gilbert as he watched the unloading of the *ZIM Rosh Pina*. With a gross displacement of 150,000 tonnes, the Israeli container vessel towered over the quayside at Le Verdon-sur-Mer. It would take hours for a Post-Panamax crane to finish the task of unloading the twelve thousand containers aboard.

Gilbert and his seven gendarmes were there to guarantee the delivery of one particular item to one particular address. Riding shotgun in two Renault Mégane patrol cars, it was their job to ensure a forty-foot intermodal container would reach the Israeli embassy in Paris with its diplomatic seals intact.

"Mon Lieutenant," said Adjudant René Chandlier, the warrant officer who served as Gilbert's second-in-command. "I was just wondering what we're doing here in Le Verdon."

"You mean why a cargo destined for Paris would be off-loaded at the mouth of the Gironde in southwest France?"

"Yes, mon Lieutenant. We're over five hundred kilometres away. Why not Le Havre or even Saint-Nazaire?"

"You want the honest answer?" asked Gilbert as he looked at his subordinate with a cynical grin.

Chandlier nodded.

"I have no idea. And I have even less of an idea why the embassy insisted that we get off the A10 after Tours and travel through Vendôme. The Israelis tend to be paranoid about security and maybe they know something we don't. And it just doesn't make sense to deviate from an autoroute where you can do one-thirty onto crappy two lane country roads where the maximum speed limit is ninety," said Gilbert. "But those are our orders and that's what we'll be doing."

It took another forty-five minutes until the Israeli container was offloaded from the ship and transferred to a flatbed semi-trailer hitched behind a white Mercedes-Benz Actros 6x4 Prime Mover. Ten minutes later, all necessary documentation was signed and the convoy was on its way. The tractor-trailer was sandwiched between two police cars, with Sous-Lieutenant Gilbert in the lead and Adjudant Chandlier bringing up the rear. After exiting the port, the three-vehicle cavalcade turned onto the D1215 highway that paralleled the southern bank of the Gironde River. Taking the Castelnau-de-Medoc bypass, the convoy skirted Bordeaux on the A630 ring road, crossing the Garonne and Dordogne rivers and turning north onto the A10 autoroute towards Poitiers and then Tours. The trip was uneventful until the outskirts of Châtellerault, when the radio in Gilbert's car crackled.

"Hector One, this is Hector Two," called Adjudant Chandlier from the follow car.

Gilbert picked up the radio handset from its clip on the dashboard. "This is Hector One."

"There's a service area up ahead and we need a toilet break. Apparently, Leroux has a weak bladder along with everything else."

Gilbert grimaced at the sound of taunting laughter coming over the radio. Since his posting to the Quatrième Escadron the previous year, Leroux had acquired the reputation of a chronic fuck-up and was the butt of many a practical joke. There was no question that the man was a weak link in an operational unit of the Gendarmerie Mobile. In fact, the situation had reached the point where the sous-lieutenant was planning to talk with Leroux about a transfer to an administrative or logistical role. However, until then his welfare was Gilbert's responsibility and he moved to cut the bullying short.

"Enough horsing around. Let's keep our minds on the job. We've been on the road over four hours and we've earned a break. Twenty minutes for any food, drink and personal issues. We'll also refuel, out."

As the exit ramp approached, Gilbert instructed his driver, Gendarme Fabienne Bouvier, to trigger his indicator light. He lowered his window, sticking his arm out and gesturing to the tractor-trailer behind that they would be leaving the autoroute.

"I don't know why we can't have one of ours in the semi's cab with a radio," said Bouvier. "It would make things much simpler."

"No doubt," replied Gilbert. "But that truck is carrying the official property of a foreign embassy. It's like a giant diplomatic bag, and the seals on that super-sized container make the whole thing off limits."

The tractor-trailer responded by flashing its headlights to indicate message received, and it dutifully followed as the lead patrol car turned into the service area.

It was a typical highway truck stop, with banks of gasoline and diesel fuel pumps under a canopy roof high enough to accommodate semi-trailers, a restaurant, convenience store and even an automated carwash.

"There," said Gilbert, pointing to a vacant row of pumps in the middle of the fuelling station. The patrol car pulled up at the appointed spot and the sous-lieutenant handed his driver a fuel card. "Top it up and then give the card to Chandlier."

Bouvier nodded and set about the task of refuelling while his commander walked back to the cab of the tractor-trailer they were escorting. Gilbert was certain its tinted windows and windscreen were not compliant with the law, but diplomatic immunity meant there was nothing he could do about it. He motioned for the driver to lower his side window. A heavily bearded face gazed down at him from behind a pair of Ray Ban sunglasses.

"I'll fuel first and then you can pull up after me," Gilbert said to the trucker. "Once we're all topped up, you'll have the opportunity to grab something to eat and have a toilet break. I want to be back on the road within twenty minutes. Is that acceptable?"

The driver gave a perfunctory nod and rolled up the window.

What a rude bastard, thought Gilbert, shaking his head in disgust. And stupid as well. I'm surprised he can see anything through that tinting, much less with sunglasses on his head.

Gilbert walked around the truck towards Chandlier's follow car, intending to consult with his second-in-command. But the sous-lieutenant's attention was drawn to a fire engine red Jaguar XKRS convertible that pulled up to the same fuel pump on its opposite side.

The car was sexy enough, the sleek aesthetics of its elegant lines turning heads wherever it might appear. The woman at the wheel, though, was such an absolute stunner that she made her ride seem drab by comparison.

Gilbert couldn't help but stare as this vision of feminine pulchritude stepped from the sports coupé. With her flowing blonde tresses, green eyes, perfect facial features and a figure worthy of a *Vogue* front cover, she drew the attention of every male within eyesight. And when she spread a Michelin road map on the hood of the Jag and leaned over to study it, a horde of would-be Sir Galahads descended upon her, intent on rescuing a lady in obvious distress.

Gilbert straightened his tunic and pushed through the throng to her side. "Comment peut-je vous aider, Madame?"

The blonde looked up from the map, smiling demurely while batting a pair of heavily mascaraed eyelashes. "I'm sorreh," she replied in a deep South Carolina drawl, "but ah don' speak varah much Franch."

"That eez fine, Madame," Gilbert responded with a gallant smile. "I speak a bit of Ingleesh. 'Ow can I help?"

"Well ah'm tryin' to find the Chatoo du Paranay," she sighed. "But ah think ah missed the exit."

"I'm sorry, Madame. Where do you wish to go?"

"Chatoo du Paranay," she said in her southern drawl. "In Voolay near Pwahteeyay."

Gilbert shook his head in frustration and motioned for Chandlier to join him.

"Perhaps your English is better than mine," muttered the sous-lieutenant to his second-in-command. "But I have no idea what she's saying."

Chandlier saluted and turned solicitously to the woman to offer his assistance.

They'd all been so consumed by this ongoing drama that nobody had paid any attention to the man unobtrusively kneeling by the front right wheel of Chandlier's patrol car. Nor was any notice taken when this stranger lay on his back and reached up into the bowels of the Renault's engine block. Whatever business the man had to conduct was brief, and within twenty seconds he was up and walking towards a tan Peugeot 4008 SUV that waited nearby with its engine idling. Once this passenger was aboard, the Peugeot immediately pulled out of the service area and disappeared onto the autoroute.

"No, no, Madame," said Chandlier, pointing to the map with his index finger. "Zee Château de Perigny is here, just off the road from Poitiers to Vouillé."

"Ah think Ah understand now," declared the southern belle. "Vouz ate trez janteel," she said with a bright smile. Her serial offences against French elocution were instantly forgiven and forgotten, though, as she leaned over and planted a kiss on Chandlier's cheek. The adjutant turned bright red in a combination of pleasure and embarrassment.

With that, she folded the map and returned to the driver's seat of the Jag. Turning the ignition, she waved to Sous-Lieutenant Gilbert and roared away towards the on-ramp to the autoroute.

"Quelle femme," mused Chandlier as he wiped his cheek clean of lipstick residue.

"Vraiment," replied Gilbert. "Now it's back to work. I want the vehicles fuelled and ready to go in five. Anyone who needs a toilet break should move now. This is the last stop until Paris."

As Chandlier went off to ensure the prompt execution of his commander's orders, Gilbert again approached the tractor-trailer's cab and motioned for the driver to lower his side window.

"We'll be back on the road in five minutes," said the Gendarme officer. "If you need to take care of any personal issues, now's the time."

The driver nodded without a word and closed the window. He didn't emerge from the cab.

At the appointed time, the convoy pulled out of the service area northwards on to the autoroute. Within a few hundred metres, any lingering resentment Gilbert might have harboured towards the ill-mannered truck driver was eclipsed by a radio distress call from his NCO.

"Hector One, this is Hector Two, we have a problem."

Gilbert keyed his handset. "Hector Two, go."

"This is Hector Two. We have a serious mechanical malfunction. The auxiliary fan belt has snapped. We are immobile and there's no way we can continue."

"Merde," Gilbert muttered to no-one in particular. He lifted the handset to his mouth. "This is Hector One, message received. Notify the commandant de l'escadron and have him coordinate with Group IV/3 in Blois for the dispatch of a repair unit to your location. Also, request that IV/3 send an additional vehicle to reinforce me if one is available. Clear?"

"This is Hector Two, message received."

"This is Hector One, let me know if I can expect another car. If so, it should contact me on our escadron frequency and I'll liaise for a rendezvous."

"This is Hector Two, message received."

"This is Hector One, out."

For a moment, Gilbert mulled over his new situation before turning to

Bouvier. "Pull over to the passing lane, slow down until our truck pulls abreast and then keep pace."

Bouvier did as ordered and, once the Gendarmerie patrol car was neck-and-neck with the tractor-trailer, Gilbert lowered his window and waved. The bearded truck driver lowered his window and the sous-lieutenant gestured to indicate he'd now be assuming the trail car position. The truckie nodded to signify comprehension and rolled up his tinted window.

"Move us into position behind the truck," Gilbert instructed Bouvier. "We'll follow at one hundred metres."

Bouvier took his foot off the accelerator pedal, allowing the tractor-trailer to surge ahead, pulling the patrol car neatly into its wake.

The two-vehicle convoy progressed smoothly over the next one hundred kilometres until reaching their planned turn-off point, north of Tours.

"I still don't understand why we have to travel on these *putain* country roads," griped Bouvier.

"Nor do I," replied Gilbert. "But we're Gendarmerie and do as we're told."

The patrol car followed the semi-trailer into a warren of narrow rural byways that barely warranted classification as secondary. Then, at a crawling pace that speed-demon Bouvier found utterly annoying, the convoy made its tortuous way through a series of forgettable hamlets – Morand, Saint-Nicolas-des-Motets and Saint-Cyr-du-Gault.

Then it happened. On the northern outskirts of Gombergean, the left-rear tyre of the Mégane burst with an explosive bang. Bouvier struggled for control, wrestling the vehicle to a safe halt on the road shoulder. Gilbert looked on in helpless frustration as the tractor-trailer continued northwards without pause, soon disappearing from sight behind a wooded hill.

"Well don't sit there like blithering idiots!" the sous-lieutenant thundered. "Fix the *putain* tyre!"

The gendarmes spilled out of the car and extracted the spare, lug wrench and jack from the trunk while Gilbert pulled his cellphone from his pocket and began to dial. Then he suddenly paused before completing the call. Capitaine Vernot will have my guts for garters if I call in a second technical malfunction within the space of two hours, thought the sous-lieutenant. I have the route marked on the map, so we'll just change the tyre and floor it with lights and sirens. What the escadron doesn't know won't matter.

Gilbert exited the front passenger seat and walked around to supervise the tyre change operation. In his haste to get back on the move, the sous-lieutenant didn't notice a man discreetly observing the gendarmes' misfortune from the window of a nearby farmer's cottage. Nor had the young officer heard the faint report of the sound-suppressed rifle the onlooker had just used to dispatch a sub-sonic 0.22 calibre bullet to its destructive rendezvous with the patrol car's tyre.

Likewise, Gilbert was in no position to witness the rather curious incident that transpired a mere three kilometres down the road towards the hamlet of Pray. Just over the far side of that wooded hill, the tractor-trailer abruptly pulled off the road into a dirt driveway leading to a nearby complex of grain silos and storehouses for harvested agricultural produce. A pair of men loitered by a set of massive roller doors to the largest warehouse in the complex. The Israeli truck disappeared within and the men pulled the roller doors closed behind it. A second tractor-trailer, identical in every way to the first, then pulled out from behind the building and turned north onto the road leading to Pray and Vendôme.

The switch was carried out with such smooth precision that it was all over in less than forty-five seconds. But the gendarmes' tyre change took quite a bit longer. The doppelgänger vehicle was approaching Châteaudun before the clamor of Gilbert's siren was heard from behind. Two minutes later, the patrol car slipped into formation behind a white tractor-trailer that was making its way through the outskirts of that town. As a very relieved Sous-Lieutenant Gilbert travelled on towards his Paris destination, he remained none the wiser to the act of prestidigitation that had just taken place.

Sixteen

While the gendarmes were playing catch-up, the original tractor-trailer was undergoing a facelift within the confines of the warehouse where it had stopped. Licence plates were changed and colourful adhesive decals were affixed to the doors of the trailer cab on either side.

A man posted unobtrusively by the road watched as Gilbert's patrol car roared by in pursuit of its errant charge. Once the gendarmes disappeared from sight, the lookout spoke briefly into a handheld radio. Ninety seconds later, the tractor-trailer pulled out of the storehouse and retraced its path south on to D71 towards Gombergean. At the junction in the midst of that hamlet, the tractor-trailer turned northwest onto D108, making good time on the slightly better-quality road. On reaching the village of Sasnières, it turned onto a series of country lanes that ultimately led to la Hubardière clearing in the midst of the Forêt de Prunay.

The tractor-trailer pulled up beside a ramshackle packing shed that dominated the clearing. It was a large structure, measuring roughly eighty-by-twenty metres and flanked by two smaller outbuildings in close proximity. The rumble of the tractor-trailer's diesel engine lapsed into silence and the door to the cab swung open. The driver, now clean-shaven, jumped down, having discarded his costume beard and sunglasses on the tractor's passenger seat.

"Shalom Micha," hailed a heavyset man who materialised from the shed. "How did it go?"

"Smooth as silk," replied Micha with a smug smile. "It's been a long drive and I really need to take a dump. Something to eat would be nice too."

"No problem. There's a toilet over there," he said, pointing to the smaller of the two out-buildings. "When you're done, join me in the main shed. We have steak sandwiches."

"Sounds good."

After attending to his bodily functions, Micha walked back around the shed and entered through a side door. He paused for a moment, looking at the thirteen olive-coloured Oshkosh S-ATV all-terrain vehicles arrayed in serried rows along one wall of the shed. The seats of several S-ATVs were occupied by eight men who looked as though they were engaged in that classic military activity – 'hurry-up-and-wait'.

The heavyset man proffered a bottle of hand sanitiser that Micha accepted with a grateful nod.

"So," enquired Micha as he vigorously sanitised his hands, "when did the vehicles arrive?"

"Yesterday," replied Ze'ev. "We brought them in straight from the States via Le Havre. No fingerprints of a kosher conspiracy."

"Very good. Where will you want the semi?"

"Right over there next to the ramp," replied Ze'ev as indicated a five-by-three-metre steel plate that was leaning against the opposite wall. "You'll have to reverse your way in, but grab something to eat first. There's no rush."

"I don't see much by way of security," observed Micha.

"That's the whole point, but don't let your eyes deceive you," said Ze'ev with a grin. "There's food over there in the cooler. Pick up your sandwich and join me outside."

Micha walked over to the beer cooler, grabbed a steak sandwich and followed his host out of the shed.

"Watch this," said Ze'ev as he unclipped a walkie-talkie from his belt. "Security team, show yourselves."

A rustling sound was heard from the wood and, moments later, four ghillie suit-clad marksmen emerged from various points among the trees. Micha noted the M-4 carbines carried by two of the quartet, while the remaining pair were armed with scoped Remington 700 bolt-action rifles.

Micha shrugged. "I stand corrected. Well done."

"All good," Ze'ev instructed, speaking into the walkie-talkie. "Resume your positions."

The camouflaged quartet vanished into the forest foliage as silently as they had emerged.

"Once you've finished your sandwich, you can back the semi into the shed," Ze'ev instructed. "After you uncouple the tractor, your work here is done. The unloading is our job."

"Fair enough," Micha replied.

Some minutes later, his sandwich consumed, Micha clambered back into the cab and deftly backed the semi-trailer into its appointed spot. He then proceeded to uncouple the tractor and, with a wave, departed down the dirt road towards Sasnières, leaving a cloud of dust in his wake.

With the tractor's departure, the eight men rose from their repose and walked over to the steel plate, taking positions on either side of its long axis. The plate had three steel hooks welded to one of its narrow sides and, like pallbearers toting a coffin, they clipped the hooks into sockets located the end of the flatbed semi-trailer.

Wielding a pair of bolt-cutters, Ze'ev walked up the ramp and made short work of the diplomatic seals that secured the container. He swung open the doors to reveal a cornucopia of weapons and ammunition that ranged from anti-tank missiles to small arms of various types.

"Okay, guys," announced Ze'ev, "here's how it's going to work. We'll unload the container and distribute the weapons and equipment per the Pakal for this operation. Once that task is complete, you'll begin to kit out your assigned vehicles. You all have copies of the Pakal and I expect you to follow it verbatim. We've brought extras of almost everything so, if you have any problem, let me know. I want this to be picture perfect so that, when our guys get here, the only thing they'll have to do is press the ignition button and go. Vehicle inspection in three hours, so let's get to it."

Seventeen

Orli Wachtman noticed him almost from the moment he passed through the cemetery gates. Tuning out the rabbi's repetitive rendition of Psalm 91, she watched from the corner of her eye as the stranger approached along serried rows of sepulchers towards the opposite corner of the graveyard.

A lean 1.8 metres in height, he moved with the easy grace of a serious athlete. His pate was topped by a red beret with the infantry corps badge, and the twin oak leaf rank insignia of lieutenant colonel adorned each epaulette of his Class A uniform shirt. A paratroop officer. Then she noticed he was something more. The new-style square canopy wings on his left chest were those of a qualified free-fall parachutist, a skill found only among the elite troops of the army's top-tier special forces units.

As the stranger passed abreast of the funeral party, Orli got a close up of a face best described, not as classically handsome, but as interesting. Green eyes alight with intelligence were bracketed by crows' feet that bespoke years spent exposed to the elements. A strong mouth and flawless white teeth. No wedding ring in sight. All in all, a decidedly delicious distraction from the tedium of a funeral for an anonymous distant relative Orli was attending solely out of solidarity with her mother.

The officer surprised her by walking past the distinctive trapezoid-shaped headstones that marked the final resting places of Israel's military dead. He wasn't here to visit a fallen comrade.

Her interest piqued, Orli maintained a discreet surveillance as the special forces officer stopped on the far side of the cemetery and knelt before a large limestone stele. Most likely his parents. Of course, it would have been irredeemably tacky to make a flirtatious move at such a time and in such a place. Orli's mother would have been livid that her daughter might even be considering something so outré.

So Orli continued her quiet surveillance from afar as the stranger reached out to touch the gravestone and then brought those fingers to his lips. As if he were saying goodbye. The lieutenant colonel then stood up, straightened his beret and made his way out the cemetery, just as the burial service for the Wachtmans' first-cousin-once-removed came to an end.

With her mother deep in conversation with various family members, Orli slipped away towards the site of the special forces officer's obeisance. Perhaps she could find some sort of clue to his identity. Something that might enable an encounter to be orchestrated at some future point under a plausible guise of spontaneity.

Of course, Orli's girlfriends would affect scandalised shock at such a gambit; right up to the point where, through giggles, they would demand an in-depth recounting of every last detail. The mostly married members of her social circle loved to be briefed about the salacious ups and downs of the Tel Aviv dating scene that, in truth, entailed many more of the latter than the former.

Orli had tired of her role as a source for vicarious escapism from the mundanities of diaper changes and breastfeeding. With birthday number three-zero looming large on the horizon, she was beginning to feel a tad desperate. Desperate enough to push the bounds of propriety when a prime candidate like Colonel X happened across her path. With prospective pickings seemingly getting slimmer by the day, she was prepared to adopt some out-of-the-box thinking.

The inscriptions on the gravestone's limestone surface glistened under the sunlight as Orli approached, unworn and abraded by passage of the seasons. As the distance closed, she saw why. The first thing she noticed were the dates in Hebrew gematria and Gregorian calendar. Fourteen months ago. No wonder the lettering looked so fresh. The Jewish 'matzevah' custom of placing a permanent headstone after the first year of mourning meant the marker had only been in place around sixty days.

"Here interred are Shoshana Klein, aged 27, beloved wife and mother; and Anat Klein aged 2, beloved daughter, taken much too soon," read the epitaph. The inscription concluded with the traditional Hebrew acronymic invocation 'Tantzibah' taken from Chapter 25 of First Samuel: "May their souls be bound up in the bundle of life."

Not his parents. It was possible these were the graves of a sister and niece, but Orli's instincts told her otherwise. He was a widower. A widower and bereaved father mourning a tragedy that was far too fresh to allow for anything of the sort she had mooted.

Orli turned on her heel and returned to the funeral party, where her mother was chatting to another member of the extended family she didn't recognise.

"What were you doing over there?"

"Checking on someone I thought I knew," Orli replied enigmatically.

"And did you?"

"Mistaken identity. Can we go now?"

"In a moment, sweetie. Let me just say goodbye to Aunt Mazal."

"I'll wait in the car."

As Orli exited the cemetery, she cast a circumspect glance around the parking lot but he was gone. No point dwelling on maybes or might-have-beens. Settling into the front passenger seat of her mother's Toyota Camry, she pulled down the sun visor and examined her face in its mirror. Those laugh lines were becoming too pronounced for comfort. So perhaps it wasn't such a bad thing that their two ships passing in the night hadn't actually met until another round of Botox could be scheduled.

Eighteen

It's going to be chilly, thought Yiftach Beton while preparing for the night's coming excursion. He was all alone, having yesterday sent Lucille home to visit her parents in Blois with a couple of hundred francs in her purse. Clothing himself in a thick brown leather workman's jacket, knitted cap and gloves, he knelt by his bedside and prised a loose floorboard from its place. Reaching into the orifice, he extracted a Browning HP 9 mm pistol, a screw-on suppressor and four extra magazines of ammunition. Attaching the suppressor to the pistol's barrel, he shoved the weapon into his waistband and the magazines into his jacket pocket. Shouldering a small backpack, he walked out of the front door and paused for a moment to gauge the coldness of the autumn night air.

Just over twenty-six months had passed since Beton first took up residence in Prunay-Casserau. Located only one kilometre south of the Forêt de Prunay, the farming village counted a population of almost a thousand souls, a number sufficient to allow him some measure of anonymity. His quest to maintain a low profile was assisted by the fact that the home he purchased stood at the end of a secluded lane near the town's northern outskirts.

Deciding that his leather jacket would provide sufficient comfort, Beton threaded his way in cautious silence down a path leading towards the edge of the village. Three days earlier, a passing German platoon had posted curfew notices promising draconian punishment for anyone caught outdoors after dark. He wasn't particularly worried. Prunay-Casserau was far too modest a commune to warrant its own standing garrison of occupying troops. At most, the Wehrmacht made a sporadic appearance every few days with a daytime motorised presence patrol through the area.

Passing the last row of houses, Beton debouched onto a dirt road leading into wheatfields just recently reaped of their autumn harvest. As he worked his way northwards, the scent of fallen oak leaves and pine needles wafted through his nostrils, growing stronger as he approached the Forêt.

After six hundred and fifty metres, Beton hit the tree line and turned north. Skirting the woods for another two kilometres, he arrived at the dirt loggers' road that he knew led to the la Hubardière clearing. Ten minutes later he was standing in front of the packing shed.

Beton opened the padlock that secured the side door and entered, feeling his way along the wall to the nearest corner. Sitting down with his back to the wall, he pulled a small kerosene lantern and a box of matches from his backpack, lighting the wick to generate a dim yellowish light. Now the only thing left to do was wait.

In the silence of the deserted shed, his mind began to race with a long-dormant sense of excitement, newly awakened by the prospect of temporal redemption. Keep it together, Beton, he told himself. It's entirely possible no-one will come.

During the mission briefings that now seemed an eternity ago, a contingency plan had been developed in the event Agag turned out to be a no go. If that were the case, he was to present himself for extraction at this same location precisely ten days hence, at 01:00 on 3 November 1940.

If no secondary extraction were forthcoming, Beton had worked out a contingency plan to his contingency plan. He would make his way out of France via Spain to Lisbon, and from there back to Mandatory Palestine. It wouldn't even be all bad, he thought with a wry smile of self-consolation. The gift of foreknowledge should provide opportunities for a few strategic acquisitions. He should have more than enough money to snap up some choice Tel Aviv real estate at rock bottom prices. And some shares in a little-known company called International Business Machines wouldn't go amiss either.

But Beton's daydreams of becoming a 20th-century tycoon were interrupted by an apparition that materialised from naught at the far corner of the packing shed. Dimly visible through the gloom in its dark gray matte livery, a super-sized shipping container perched atop a flat-bed semi-trailer now stood in a space that had previously been unoccupied.

The doors to the container opened and a sextet of futuristic looking soldiers emerged, jumping onto the ground with weapons at the ready. Beton could see the men's heads bobbing about as they sought out possible threats with their 21st-century night vision gear. Within the space of two seconds, Beton was observed, and the bores of those six rifles all pointed directly at the agent's head.

Beton slowly raised his hands skyward and proclaimed "Agag" in a loud voice.

Rifle muzzles were immediately lowered and five of the soldiers moved off silently to cover the side door to the packing shed. The sixth man removed his helmet and extended a hand in greeting. "Shalom Yiftach. Long time no see."

"Shalom Yossi," Beton responded. "Longer for me than for you. I've been waiting over two years."

"True enough," replied a smiling Klein. "From my end, it was only around five months. Now we're all here in one place at one time, so let's get moving."

Klein beckoned towards one of the men posted at the shed door. Captain Benjamin Farkash, a 23-year-old Sayeret Golani officer of mixed Sephardic and Ashkenazi parentage, approached at a trot in response to the summons.

"All quiet?" asked Klein.

Farkash nodded. "Seems to be. But I'll feel better once I have my full team deployed."

"You and me both," replied Klein. "Let's set up the ramp and get your people into their 360-degree security perimeter."

With a nod of affirmation, Farkash clambered up through the open doors of the container and disappeared within.

Moments later, a scraping sound of metal on metal was heard as the edge of the heavy steel ramp appeared from within the container. Farkash reappeared, jumping down onto the ground with another dozen armed-to-the-teeth troopers who manhandled the ramp into place at the end of the container. Then, collecting the original five troopers who had emerged from the container with Klein, Farkash led his team through the side door to take up defensive positions in the woods around la Hubardière.

An S-ATV materialised in the doorway of the container, nosing its way carefully down the ramp with the low throaty rumble of a silenced diesel engine. With hand signals, Klein directed the vehicle to a point directly in front of the shed's main door. Two more S-ATVs followed suit and were guided to positions in column behind the first.

Klein and Beton walked over to the metal ramp, where they were joined by the three drivers of the S-ATVs.

"One, two, three!" said Klein, and the five men disconnected the ramp from its mooring to the semi-trailer, grunting under its weight. Moving several paces away, they carefully lowered the slab of metal to the ground.

Klein clambered up onto the semi-trailer, closing and sealing the container doors with the lock rod handles. Pounding on the container twice with his fist, he turned and jumped, hitting the floor of the shed with a parachute landing fall technique. Thirty seconds later, the semi-trailer with its container vanished as though they had never been.

"Ah, I almost forgot, this is for you," said Klein as he proffered a small brown paper bag just extracted from the bellows thigh pocket of his camouflage trousers. "A taste from tomorrow."

Beton took the bag and shook the contents into his palm. His face lit up with pleasure. "M&Ms!" He gobbled down a fistful, mumbling "Thanks Yossi" through a mouth half full of candy. "You're a mensch!"

Klein gave a smiling nod. "Okay, but finish stuffing your face and let's get ready for the second wave." He looked at his watch. "We have two minutes and fifteen seconds until arrival."

Like casket-bearers at a funeral, the men took their places on either side of the ramp, ready to lift and engage it when the semi-trailer reappeared.

HORMAH

Nineteen

At its essence, leadership is about persuasion; about convincing people to do things they would not otherwise be prepared to do. And the subtle art of animating human motivation may, at times, require no small measure of thespian talent.

Yossi Klein was in full showbiz mode as he passed among his men, stopping here and there for a brief chat. None of the troopers suspected their veteran commander was in the midst of the jitters that afflicted him without fail during the final countdown to contact with the enemy.

The la Hubardière packing shed that served as the forward staging base for Operation Agag had been transformed from its condition a few hours before. A daisy chain of LED camping lights was suspended from the rafters, powered by a sound-suppressed generator humming almost inaudibly in the far corner. The shed's interior walls had been covered with black plastic sheeting to prevent any leakage of light through the gaps in its clapboard siding. Every available bit of floor space was crammed with olive-coloured Oshkosh S-ATV off-road utility vehicles, parked bumper-to-bumper like planes on the deck of an aircraft carrier.

Swarming in and around the vehicles were several score men clad in camouflage uniforms and festooned with the impedimenta of 21st-century war. Most were busy inspecting their rifles, tactical vest loadouts and night vision gear for the umpteenth time. The drivers among them were doing yet another walk-around, testing tyres and checking cargoes were securely stowed. With every available centimetre of each S-ATV crammed with weapons, ammunition and equipment, there was much to inspect.

Klein clambered onto the hood of the lead Oshkosh and gained his men's attention with a few sharp claps. Gesturing them to approach, he was soon gazing upon a semicircle of young faces painted in greenish-brown hues.

"Just a few final words before we move. None of you is a tyro. If the collective combat experience of every soldier here was quantified and compiled, you'd end up with a tome the size of *War and Peace*. But this is a different category of mission. Different by orders of magnitude. There's no denying it's a lot more dangerous. We're farther behind enemy lines than ever before in a way we've never been before. Yet we all know what we're doing and why we're doing it."

"Yeah, we're here to make history … I mean, to change it," quipped Gavriel 'Gabi' Horman, the 23-year-old Shaldagist assigned as driver of Klein's command vehicle.

Klein paused until the spasm of guffaws subsided. "So speaketh the unit comedian," he said with a wicked grin. "Too bad the quality of your driving is even worse than the quality of your jokes."

Horman signalled touché by performing a ridiculously theatrical salute, which triggered a renewed wave of laughter among the troops.

"You can be certain of two things," continued Klein, his face now broadcasting a more serious mien. "Even the best of plans, and ours is very good, doesn't deliver a monopoly on events. The enemy also gets a say on how things unfold. That means somewhere, at some point, things will go to shit. It's inevitable and we've all seen it happen."

The mood amongst the assembled troopers was now fully transitioned from locker room to game day. Gone were the jibes and acts of horseplay as the men listened attentively to the words of their commander.

"Item number two is my solid guarantee that we'll overcome whatever fate throws our way. Remember the three principles that have been drummed into your heads since day one of recruit training – strive for contact, maintain mission tenacity and retain operational flexibility. We'll seize the battlefield initiative by striving to close with and assault the enemy whenever and wherever we encounter him. I expect each and every one of you to demonstrate adherence to our mission objectives, regardless of setbacks, fuckups or casualties incurred. And finally, we'll implement both those principles with a flexibility of mind that accommodates ever-changing circumstances. Am I clear so far?"

"Clear!" came a chorused response.

Klein's head bobbed in a nod of satisfaction. "There's no doubt the enemy will punch, but it's our job to adapt and counterpunch twice as hard. Resilience of mind and versatility will optimise our capacity to respond to whatever comes. So, while we do what it takes to achieve our objective, we'll also be creative in how we go about that task. This operation has been many months, and many decades, in the making. You've all been drawn from the army's most selective special units and you've rehearsed until every detail has been committed to memory. Each one of you is cross-trained on two other mission roles, so never question your professional readiness for this operation."

Klein reached into the tunic pocket of his battledress uniform and extracted a small bit of yellow felt cloth. Unfolding it, he held up for all to see. The cloth was cut in the shape of a six-pointed star with the word Jude in black letters inscribed across its centre.

"There's something much more important at play here than pure military skill. And that's the basic justice of what we've come here to do. It's good that you're better soldiers than the enemy, but never forget that you're also better men who are fighting in the most righteous cause imaginable. Questions?"

Klein paused, but after a few moments of silence he simply nodded. "Alright then, let's do what we came here to do." Looking at his watch, he counted down the seconds. "Departure will be precisely ... thirty-three minutes from now. Prepare to move."

Klein's words of dismissal galvanised his troops into a flurry of renewed activity. Team commanders assembled their men for one final inspection, passing from soldier to soldier to verify that nothing was out of order. Each man in turn, copped a slap of affirmation on the shoulder, then took his appointed place on one of the thirteen S-ATVs arrayed within the shed.

Meanwhile, Klein made his way over to the corner of the shed that was occupied by the flatbed semi-trailer. The shipping container/time travel vehicle was roped-off from the remainder of the shed by incandescent yellow crime-scene tape affixed to metal stakes extruding from the dirt floor.

Klein made his way through a gap in the tape cordon and walked up the metal ramp to the container's open doorway, halting for several heartbeats to observe the goings on within. A handful of men were calmly going about their own separate brand of business, divorced from the organised chaos that suffused the rest of the packing shed. The focus of their attention was an instrument-laden console that looked as though it had been pilfered from NASA Mission Control in Houston.

Two soldiers were seated in front of an array of technology that looked like an electronic gaming console on steroids. Soldier One was tapping away on a keyboard, while his partner maneuvered a joystick that featured a trigger mechanism at its top. This hi-tech array was complemented by two massive 150-centimetre LCD screens mounted on the container wall, one featuring a digital map and the other displaying aerial video imagery.

Klein walked over to Captain Benjamin Farkash, who was observing the video footage over the shoulder of the joystick operator. "Give me one final sit-rep before we move."

"All quiet in our immediate area," reported Farkash. "The UAV is doing 360s along a radius ten kilometres out. We're seeing substantial military activity within Objective Michal and at the AA sites around the town. The communications centre at Objective Yael is also pretty lively with sentries on patrol and a couple of Jeeps parked outside. Aside from that, the FLIR shows zero movement. The entire countryside appears to be in lockdown."

"That's because it is," volunteered Yiftach Beton, the only civvies-clad person in the packing shed. The grip of a Browning HP 9 mm pistol could be seen peeking from his waistband. "Three days ago, the Germans imposed a curfew on the entire area. Anyone venturing out between 19:00 and 07:30 can be summarily executed on sight. Two people have already been shot."

"Well, imagine the bastards' surprise when they find out we shoot back," Klein retorted, his teeth bared in a feral grin.

The topographical map on the left-hand display featured a small aircraft icon superimposed on its centre. Klein's practised eye discerned that the video imagery on the right-hand screen matched the placement of the icon on the neighbouring map.

The on-screen footage was a direct feed from a Shapo multi-sensor observation pod mounted on a Sparrow unmanned aircraft. The Shapo featured both CCD video and FLIR thermal cameras, but only the latter was of any real utility during the dark wee hours of this autumn night. Designed to detect the heat signatures of objects both animate and inanimate, the thermal imaging camera could pick up a moving vehicle at a range of four thousand metres. Higher temperature objects appeared in white, the warmer the brighter, against a dark grey background of colder material.

"You're right, Farkash," said Klein. "It seems nice and quiet out there. Now bring me up to speed on your security element. What's its status?"

"Team Four is in place and on task," replied Farkash. "BMNT is at 07:17 local. That's when I'll be doing a final circuit of the machine gun and AT positions. By then, there should be enough light to see whether any improvements or adjustments are required. Other than that, we just sit tight and provide overhead imagery throughout the operation."

"Very good," said Klein. "You heard my shtick to the boys about expecting the unexpected?"

"We've all heard it non-stop since day one," replied a smiling Farkash.

Klein bestowed an avuncular pat on the young captain's shoulder. "So now you can hear it again one last time. If things get really messy out there, it's likely we'll be pushing up against the Sparrow's endurance limit. I'll have the mini-UAV with me, but it doesn't have anything near the capabilities of your birds. So, if things get complicated, I'll want that second Sparrow up in the air well before you have to recall number one. We'll need seamless continuity of coverage. We can't afford to run around blindly out there."

"I'll make sure that doesn't happen," Farkash responded earnestly. "You know, it isn't that we don't get the importance of Team Four's role in all this. We do – every last one of us. But I'd be lying if I said we all didn't wish we were going with you."

"Understood, Farkash," said Klein. "But remember – you're the ones holding our ticket home."

"Yeah," said Beton. "And don't forget some of us have been here longer than others."

Farkash smiled empathetically. "Two years with no internet or TV. Must have been a real bummer."

"You have no idea," sighed Beton with a theatrical shake of the head. "I'll be quite content if I never have to hear Edith Piaf or Tino Rossi again."

Klein laughed, giving Beton a fraternal pat on the shoulder.

Beton responded with an outstretched hand. "Just in case I don't get another opportunity, I wanted to wish you good hunting and good luck."

"Thanks, Yiftach," replied Klein as he returned the courtesy. "But any success we enjoy will have a lot to do with you. Your contribution to this operation has been absolutely essential. Your time served has earned you a seat in the first wave of the return trip when we're done."

Beton nodded in silent acknowledgement and Klein turned his attention towards Aharon Adivi and Gerhard Hoffmann, who were unobtrusively observing the LCD screens from the far end of the container. As he approached the duo, Klein couldn't help but notice how incongruous they appeared among the physically fit, armed-to-the-teeth young soldiers swarming around them.

"Shalom to you both."

"Shalom u'vracha," Adivi replied with the traditional Hebrew salutation. "And how are you doing, Gerhard?"

"Fine, Colonel," replied Gerhard Hoffmann, with a self-conscious smile. "I'm very pleased we're finally all here and ready to go. To be entirely honest, I'm a bit nervous."

"That's understandable. These are uncharted waters for everyone. Just keep your eyes on the prize. I certainly don't have to convince you that it's worth the risk."

"True enough," replied Hoffmann. "After all, this was my idea. Don't worry about me, though, I'll be fine."

"All good," replied Klein in a back-to-business tone that indicated the time for repartee had passed. "I'll leave you to it then."

Bidding adieu to the academic twosome with a polite nod, Klein turned on his heel and exited the container. Making his way towards his S-ATV, he observed Baruch Levinson conducting a battery check on the Tadiran PRC9000 radio mounted in a special pouch of his RTO rucksack.

"How's it going, Baruch? All Okay?"

Levinson smiled. "Yep, Yossi, comms are good to go."

Klein nodded and climbed into the front passenger seat of the lead Oshkosh. Extracting a map from his tactical vest, he took another look at the route he and his men would be travelling to reach their objective. For self-evident reasons, there'd be no GPS-assisted navigation tonight, but Klein wasn't overly troubled by the absence of that particular piece of hi-tech gadgetry. He was old-school where land navigation was concerned, preferring to find his way by map, mind and compass. Truth be told, he considered GPS to be the last resort of the incompetent. Sure, the UAV shadowing the task force from above would be a major force multiplier once the battle was joined. Klein, however, was confident he could guide his troops to the target area unassisted.

The Israeli army's premier special ops unit, Sayeret Matkal, placed an absolute premium on land navigation. As a young recruit, Klein had spent month after month on training evolutions devoted to perfecting precisely that skill. By day he and his comrades would study maps and aerial photographs of their assigned routes, memorising every last detail of azimuth, distance and terrain. Then, by night, they'd each go their separate ways, orienteering solo from checkpoint to checkpoint over distances up to 50 kilometres until they all converged at a final rendezvous.

Maps were carried in sealed envelopes as an emergency measure, but the expectation was that all navigation would be done by rote memory. An open map was regarded as a mark of failure that usually ensured a one-way ticket out of the Unit. By the end of Matkal's twenty-month training course, Klein and the select few who'd survived the cut had been honed into consummate navigators. Finding his way tonight wasn't going to be a problem.

Klein looked at his watch and folded the map away, strapping on his Kevlar helmet as the oversized 'mitznefet' camouflage cover flopped untidily to one side. He picked up PRC9000 handset, holding it to his ear while keying the transmit button. "Vengeance stations, this is Kodkod. Start engines and comms check."

Almost immediately, Klein's handset began to crackle with incoming radio traffic.

"This is One, copy loud and clear. All One stations ready."

"Kodkod this is Two, good copy. Everyone's ready to move."

"Three, good copy. All ready."

Final confirmation came from Michael HarSinai, who was seated in the passenger seat of the rearmost vehicle in the convoy. "This is Mishneh Kodkod," said HarSinai, identifying himself by the IDF radio call sign for a unit second-in-command. "Confirming that the entire force has engines running and is ready to move."

The shed's interior was quickly filling with the exhaust fumes emitted by thirteen 600-horsepower turbocharged diesel engines.

Klein looked at his watch. "This is Kodkod to all Vengeance stations, comms check acknowledged. Moving now." He gave a hand signal to Farkash, who doused the lights and swung open the packing shed door.

Klein nodded to Horman and the Oshkosh lurched into motion. Within seconds it was enveloped by darkness. One by one, the other vehicles followed, each disappearing quietly into the night. Fitted with specially designed mufflers, the S-ATVs emitted no more than a low rumble that was inaudible to anyone over 100 metres distant. With each soldier mounting a Nivisys TAM-14 thermal vision monocular on his helmet, the column would be moving without lights as well.

The odds of premature discovery were diminished by the stealthy design of the vehicles, the lateness of the hour and the rurality of the area. But bitter operational experience had long ago taught Klein that the things you least expected were the things that ended up biting you on the ass. Disinclined to tempt fate, he plotted a circuitous route that gave the widest berth possible to the homes and hamlets dotting the countryside. If there were any local insomniacs in residence, Klein could only hope they'd taken this particular night off.

The chill of the late autumn air on his face exorcised the final vestiges of pre-mission angst from Klein's mind. Now on the move, his fretfulness dissolved into focus on the task ahead. Each facet of the operation had been analysed in detail and war-gamed multiple times. The end result was a mission plan that maximised every conceivable tactical advantage while minimising all foreseeable threats.

Now the time for cogitation was over. The issue would be decided the way it always was in battle – by the most effective application of kinetic force.

"Alea iacta est," Klein mused softly.

"Sorry, Yossi, I didn't get that," said Horman, his face reflecting puzzlement.

"Latin for 'the die is cast'," Klein said with an apologetic smile. "Something Julius Caesar said as he led his army across the Rubicon River in defiance of the Roman Senate. I wrote my staff college thesis on the conquest of Israel by Pompey the Great in 63 BCE. I've gotten in the habit of reciting that quote at the start of every operation. A bit of personal superstition, I guess."

Horman cast a cheeky grin back at his commander. "On a mission such as this, I think we need all the help we can get."

"True enough. Let me declare for the record that, as of 01:12 local, 25th October, the die is indeed cast. Operation Agag is finally underway."

Throughout the long months of mission preparation, Horman had acquired something of a waggish reputation among his comrades. He'd emerged as the unit's resident wit, whose irreverent humour and lighthearted talent for mimicry rarely failed to elicit a laugh. But there was something about Klein's Latinate pronouncement that triggered a metamorphosis in his demeanour. The trademark Horman irreverence evaporated as the trooper acknowledged his commander's words with nothing more than a tight-lipped nod.

This was the moment when the cosmic enormity of what they were doing registered on his psyche in the fullest emotional sense. As the convoy made its way in near-silence down a forested dirt road under the dim light of a waning moon, Horman whispered a sotto voce recitation of the Shehechiyanu – the ancient Jewish prayer of thanksgiving that he was alive to see this day.

Twenty

Oberleutnant Peter Koertig fastidiously examined his image in the mirror, careful to flick a small piece of lint off his tunic cuff. He was constantly reminding his soldiers that service in the Führer-Begleit-Bataillon was a tremendous privilege that required standards of performance well above those of regular Wehrmacht units. It simply wouldn't do for a soldier's appearance to be anything less than perfect in the presence of der Führer.

A low groan coming from the other end of the hall caused Koertig to smile. As a matter of course, he and his fellow officers had commandeered the largest bedrooms in the spacious villa where they were billeted. While Koenig had little doubt how uncomfortable it must be for a family of eight to be immured within the modest confines of the former maid's quarters, he wasn't particularly bothered. To the victors go the spoils and such are the wages of defeat. The French had proven themselves to be of debased racial stock during the previous summer's campaign. Now they were part of das Deutsches Reich and, over time, would become the better for it. Besides, the Beaulieus had only been forced to endure this moderate hardship for less than a week. Within a few hours, the Schnelle Kompanie of the Führer-Begleit-Bataillon would be gone from Montoire-sur-le-Loir and the family would once again have the run of their home.

Koertig glanced at his watch. 11:50 hours, which left ten minutes to go before the scheduled commanders' briefing. But the oberleutnant detested tardiness in others, and always liked to arrive at the appointed place well before the appointed hour. Feeling refreshed after a brief nap, he descended the stairs into the kitchen, where his company commander sat at a table sipping a cup of tea.

"Early as usual, Peter?" asked Rittmeister Freiherr Bruno von François rhetorically while flashing a comradely smile. "Not that there was much chance of a deep sleep with all those grunts and groans coming from the family."

The oberleutnant responded to von François' witticism with a perfunctory nod that, while remaining within the bounds of military propriety, nonetheless conveyed a palpable subtext of disdain. Koertig's barely concealed dislike for his company commander was not related to issues of competence or lack thereof. To the contrary, it was the very sprezzatura with which von François carried out his duties that Koertig found so profoundly annoying.

Freiherr Bruno von François hailed from Huguenot stock, part of the Protestant exodus from France that took place after Louis XIV revoked the Edict of Nantes in 1685. In 18th-century Prussia, the army offered the only route to socio-economic mobility for the scions of families without wealth or possessions. Through distinction on the battlefield and a couple of strategic marriages, the Françoises were able to add the nobiliary particle 'von' to their name. Bruno's great-grandfather was ennobled in 1760 by Friedrich der Große himself, as reward for his key role in storming den Süptitzer Höhen at Torgau. Along with that title came a twelve-thousand-acre estate in Silesia that firmly established the family within the Junker landowning nobility. The von François tradition of battlefield distinction continued during the campaign against France, with Bruno walking away from Dunkerque with both the Knight's Cross and a coveted posting to the Führer-Begleit-Bataillon.

But what really stuck in Koertig's craw was the natural charisma exuded by von Françoise that fostered a tremendous rapport with the men of the Schelle Kompanie. As a strict by-the-book disciplinarian, the Koertig disapproved of the easy noblesse oblige with which the Freiherr interacted with the rank and file. And, verdammt, to cap it all off, he even looked the part of a dashing cavalry officer, with lean blonde good looks that wouldn't be out of place on a recruiting poster.

Attributing his subordinate's poor humour to the earliness of the morning hour, von Françoise shrugged his shoulders and took another sip from his tea. A few moments later, the exterior door opened and Oberleutnant Richard Graber entered, clad in a long heavy leather trench coat.

Von Françoise nodded in greeting. "Well meine Herren, it's been a challenging week for the Schnell Kompanie. We've road marched thirteen hundred kilometres to provide the security screen for yesterday's summit meeting between the Führer and Pétain. All has gone well so far, but I don't want any screw-ups on this last leg of our mission. Let's review today's operation one more time."

The Freiherr paused, offering his subordinates an implicit invitation to pose questions or make comments. After a few moments, with no queries forthcoming, von Françoise resumed his oral briefing. "Von Ribbentrop's train leaves Montoire travelling northwards at 05:30, with Amerika following thirty minutes later. We're responsible for the Führer's external security during the initial stage of his journey. The Kompanie will deploy to Vendôme and Châteaudun, where we'll secure the most vulnerable points where the track passes through urban areas. Any questions so far?"

"No sir," replied Koertig.

"No sir," echoed Graber.

"Good. Koertig, you'll move your motorcycle platoon to Vendôme, while dropping off one combo team to cover the eastern end of the Saint-Rimay tunnel. The western end should be adequately secured by the communications platoon that set up shop in the signalman's house. The Wach Kompanie has also deployed men at fifty-metre intervals between Montoire and the western end of the tunnel. They'll be collected by the follow-on security train. I'll be joining you with my command element to help cover Vendôme. I want us to be in position to cover the key points along the track no later than 04:00, clear?"

"Clear, sir," Koertig barked, accompanied by a martial click of his heels.

"And is your platoon ready?" enquired von François.

"Yes sir," Koertig replied. "The men are briefed and I personally verified that all benzene tanks are full and all motorcycles operational with a full complement of ammunition. I also assigned Bäcker and his crew to cover the eastern end of the tunnel."

"Good choice," said von François. "Stabsfeldwebel Bäcker is a solid NCO."

The Freiherr turned to address his other platoon leader. "Graber, you'll move directly to Châteaudun with your armoured cars, where you'll cover the train's passage through the city. I want you to be in position no later than 05:30 hours. What's the condition of your vehicles?"

"Everything is in order, except for one of my 231s that developed an engine problem earlier tonight. The maintenance stabsfeldwebel now tells me it will remain unserviceable until he receives spare parts. The order will go through later this morning, but the vehicle will be immobilised for at least forty-eight hours."

"Why wasn't I informed of this?" asked von François, the dissatisfaction clear in his voice.

Graber blushed with embarrassment. "I was notified of the problem shortly after you turned in, sir. The stabsfeldwebel was confident it would be repaired by now so I saw no need to disturb you."

"And is it?"

"Sir?"

"Is it repaired? Is your entire platoon operational?"

"No sir," said an increasingly nervous Graber. "The malfunction has turned out to be more serious than originally anticipated. I have only five functioning vehicles."

"Only five functioning vehicles," echoed von François with pursed-lipped severity. "The question then becomes, 'whom should I punish?' The maintenance stabsfeldwebel for his recklessness in making commitments he can't keep, or you for being stupid enough to believe those promises?"

Graber stiffened. "The responsibility is mine, sir. I should bear the brunt of any disciplinary action you deem appropriate."

Von François looked sombrely at Graber, before administering a fraternal clap on the oberleutnant's shoulder. "Think of this as a learning experience, Peter. While you may hope for the best, always prepare for the worst. Always keep me abreast of every problem in my company, regardless of however trivial it may appear."

The Rittmeister's stern demeanour was suddenly wiped away by an avuncular smile. "Are we clear, Peter?"

"Absolutely sir. Very sorry, sir."

"May I assume there's no further need for me to enquire about the status of your remaining vehicles?"

"No sir," replied a chastened Graber. "They're fully fuelled and loaded with ammunition. The crews are conducting pre-movement maintenance as we speak."

Von Françoise dipped his head slightly in a seigneurial nod of acknowledgement. "Gentlemen, Châteaudun is the final town of any consequence before the greater Paris region, where security will be provided by the local garrison. By that point, the Führer's train will have outrun our capacity to keep pace on the roads and our primary mission will be complete. We'll rendezvous in Châteaudun and make our way home independently in convoy. Any last questions?"

Both oberleutnants shook their heads in unison.

"Koertig, is Bäcker aware of the rendezvous point?"

"Yes sir," replied the motorcycle platoon leader. "He's been fully briefed and will move on to Châteaudun once Amerika is safely through the tunnel."

Von Françoise stood up and clapped his hands in a spur to action. "Then let's get to it. I'll conduct a company commander's pre-movement inspection at 01:00 hours and I want us to be in motion no later than 02:00 hours."

The Freiherr straightened his tunic and led the way into the hall, where he and Koertig attired themselves with heavy ankle-length trench coats. Pausing for a moment to peruse the appearance of his subordinate officers, Françoise nodded in satisfaction. The Rittmeister then led them to the exterior door, through which they strode out into the night.

Twenty-one

The column of thirteen S-ATVs drove in near silence through the Forêt de Prunay. Their speed was slow, as the dirt track circa-1940 was much rougher and narrower than the 21st-century road they had walked at least a dozen times during mission rehearsals. As the wood's edge approached, Yossi Klein lifted the radio handset to his mouth. "Vengeance stations this is Kodkod. Halt, I repeat halt."

The Oshkosh shuddered to a stop as Horman hit the brakes. The rest of the vehicles came to a halt in column order.

"Vengeance Four from Kodkod," said Klein.

The handset crackled as the voice of Farkash came over the net. "Kodkod this is Four, send over."

"This is Kodkod, we're at woods' edge. Give me sitrep on the lay of the land beyond."

"This is Four. From on high everything looks all clear in your immediate vicinity. But the UAV shows a lot of activity going on within Meira," said Farkash, using the mission code name for Montoire-sur-le-Loir. "It looks as though the motorcycles and armoured cars are preparing to move."

"That will be the mobile company of the escort battalion," replied Klein. "Keep an eye on them and let me know when they're in motion."

"Four, good copy," replied Farkash.

"This is Kodkod, out."

An avid admirer of Ronald Reagan, Klein had long ago adopted the fortieth President's adage of "trust but verify." At the end of the day, there was no substitute for what they call at US Army Ranger School the 'Mark I human eyeball'. The UAV above was all well and good, but, before venturing forth from cover, he would have to see for himself with his own eyes.

Klein clambered down from the Oshkosh, took a few steps outside the tree line and went down on one knee. Flipping up the night vision monocular affixed to his helmet, he lifted a pair of FLIR Recon BN 10 thermal imaging binoculars to his eyes. He systematically scanned the territory ahead over a 180-degree arc. With their 4x magnification, his binoculars easily picked up the body heat of cattle asleep in their paddocks and non-migratory birds perched dormant in the naked trees. The farms and villages dotting the countryside also glowed brightly. But there was no movement to be seen.

Klein returned to his vehicle and motioned to Levinson, who once again handed over the handset.

"Vengeance Four from Kodkod."

The handset crackled as the voice of Farkash came over the net. "This is Four, send over."

"We're on the move into open terrain, so stay alert."

"This is Four, will do, out."

"Vengeance stations, this is Kodkod, continue movement."

Klein nodded to Horman, who drove the Oshkosh out of the woods on a dirt track through a wheatfield that lay barren after the autumn harvest. The column kept away from the beaten path, moving through orchards and fields in virtual silence. The low crunch of tyres over gravel was louder than the muffled throb of the S-ATVs' engines. Aside from the odd barking dog, nothing disturbed the quiescence of the crisp October night.

Until something did.

"Kodkod this is Four," came Farkash over the tactical network. "The UAV has picked up five vehicles approaching your position east to west along Route Churchill. ETA four minutes. Recommend you disperse into the field on your left and shut down. Repeat, pull off to your left and shut down."

"Kodkod, good copy. Vengeance stations this is Kodkod. Disperse into the field to our left and cut the engines. No-one fires without an explicit order from me. Move!"

The drivers of the S-ATVs responded quickly to the instruction, scattering into the barren field and shutting down their engines. With well-rehearsed precision, the soldiers debussed and deployed, going prone in a formation that provided security over 360 degrees.

Klein stepped around to the rear of the Oshkosh with Levinson as his shadow.

"Get me the Ness," instructed Klein.

Opening the lower rear pouch on his commander's tactical vest, Levinson withdrew something that looked like an iPad Mini on steroids.

While the Ness TSG Tactical C4I system wasn't fully functional without GPS, it retained the capability to live stream video footage from the UAV.

Klein draped a poncho liner over his head to prevent any breach of light discipline and switched on the Ness, bringing imagery from the UAV's thermal camera up on screen. He could see the hot engines of the enemy vehicles glow bright white against the cold dark tarmac of the road on which they drove. A kübelwagen led the convoy, with four trucks following in its wake. There was no way of knowing what or who these vehicles were carrying because canvas covers concealed their contents from the infrared spy in the sky.

"Vengeance stations, this is Kodkod," Klein broadcast over the tactical net, "enemy vehicles approaching – one Jeep and four trucks. They'll be passing from our right to left, from east to west. Arrival time one minute. Hold fire unless you hear otherwise from me."

The Israelis heard the enemy before they emerged into view. The trucks were particularly noisy, engines bellowing and gears crashing as they tooled down the Vendôme to Saint-Rimay highway, dubbed 'Route Churchill' by the Israelis, at about 50 km per hour. He could see that they'd be at least four hundred metres distant as they passed directly opposite. Their night vision ruined by headlights, his vehicles would be swallowed up against the dark-coloured earth of the harvested field.

Lucky we weren't caught on top of the ridge, Klein mused. As things stood, he assessed the danger of discovery as minimal. Nonetheless, he surveyed the deployment of his troopers and smiled with satisfaction. There were over four score rifle and machine-gun barrels silently tracking every movement of the hostile convoy. He had no doubt his men would make short work of the enemy if it came to a firefight. The first round fired, though, would signify mission failure because, at that point, the whole operation would become an abort.

It didn't come to that. The hostile convoy noisily clanked its way along until it disappeared over the crest of a hill. Klein gestured to Levinson, who on cue placed the PRC9000 handset in his commander's hand.

"Vengeance Four, this is Kodkod. Are we clear?"

"This is Four, that's affirmative in your current location. Route Churchill is clear of traffic, but be advised there's a lot of activity at the western end of Earthworm. Another two Jeeps just arrived at Yael and five personnel entered the building. Another two are standing about on what looks like sentry duty. Chain smokers too. Not recommended from a health perspective."

"All the better to shoot you with, my dear," quipped Klein, eliciting an amused smile from Levinson. "We appreciate the sitrep. Keep on keeping an eye out."

"This is Four, happy to be of service."

"Vengeance stations, this is Kodkod. Mount up. Movement in one." Klein returned the handset to Levinson and climbed back into the front passenger seat of his Oshkosh.

With all its complement back on board, Klein's vehicle returned to the dirt track and braked. Horman waited until the remaining dozen vehicles assembled behind in column and looked at his commander, who nodded in affirmation.

Horman hit the gas, with the other S-ATVs following suit. Until this point, the column had managed to steer clear of farmhouses and hamlets by taking a circuitous path along dirt farming tracks through fields and orchards. The 'scenic route', as it had humorously been labelled by the troopers.

But things were now going to get more complicated. The next leg of the journey took the Israeli raiders down Route Churchill – the same Highway N817 along which the enemy just passed. And, while this also meant passing in close proximity to several farmhouses, Klein could only hope their inhabitants practised the rule of early to bed, early to rise.

"Vengeance stations this is Kodkod, we're turning onto Churchill. Let's make it fast and quiet."

"This is One, good copy."

"Two, copy

"Three, affirmative."

"This is Mishneh, good copy. Fast and quiet."

Horman turned the lead Oshkosh onto the road, driving slowly at first until the radio crackled once again with HarSinai's voice, "This is Mishneh Kodkod, on asphalt."

Without prompting, Horman hit the gas and the S-ATV zoomed ahead. In reality, the force was exposed on the main road for less than three minutes. But to Klein those 1,500 metres passed with glacial slowness. He sighed silently in relief as his S-ATV turned off the highway into a narrow dirt track that passed through wheatfields standing deserted in the midnight stillness. The vehicles soon passed over a low hill onto its reverse slope, placing them in defilade from the highway. Another six hundred metres to the northwest brought them to a narrow asphalt road with a route atop the Saint-Rimay ridge that mirrored the rail tunnel burrowed through it.

Klein reached for the PRC9000 handset. "Vengeance stations, this is Kodkod. We've reached Route Patton. We'll be making a perpendicular crossing and moving on another three hundred metres to the dispersion point. Be advised we'll be passing directly over the top of Objective Earthworm as we go. Mishneh, notify me when everyone's across Patton."

The road crossing was completed without incident and, three football fields later, Klein again brought the radio handset to his mouth. "Vengeance stations, we're at the dispersion point. All stop and team leaders to me."

Horman hit the brakes and the other S-ATVs came to a halt in turn. One by one, engines were switched off, and for a brief moment the natural stillness of early morning was restored until breached by the muffled sounds of soldiers securing the perimeter.

When his subordinate officers had assembled around his Oshkosh, Klein addressed them in a low tone. "It's now 01:57 local. That gives us just over three hours to reach and prepare our fighting positions. Teams One, Two and Command will move their Oshkoshes in there," he said with a wave towards the wooded area to their north. Klein then turned to point in a southwesterly direction. "Michael, your VLUP is three hundred metres over there in that copse of trees on the far side of the ridge. I remind you to take the scenic route and stay on the dirt roads. We don't want farmers who're coming out early to work their fields wondering about mysterious tyre tracks."

Michael HarSinai nodded in affirmation.

"Guys, I've stressed this over and over, but I'm going to say it again – camouflage is key. The enemy will sweep the area before the target reaches the kill zone. It'll be a bust if they see anything at all, vehicles or personnel, and we'll be royally screwed in the bargain. Make sure everyone and everything is completely invisible."

Klein gave his officers a grin, his white teeth flashing against the contrast of his camo-painted face. "Now, let's do what we came here to do. Good luck."

143

His sub-commanders dispersed without a word. Once they had returned to their vehicles, Klein turned to his driver and nodded. "Yallah, Gabi, let's move."

Twenty-two

Bruno von François turned in the commander's cupola of the SdKfz 232 8-Rad armoured car to survey the disposition of his company one final time before movement commenced. The Freiherr and his lieutenants had spent most of the past two hours inspecting the vehicles, weapons and men of the company. For all his easy air of informality with the troops, von François was a demon on operational discipline. A soldier would be knocked back for reinspection for even the slightest fault or imperfection in his weapons or equipment. Peer pressure for excellence within a competitive unit like the Führer-Begleit-Bataillon made it very unusual that more than one reinspection was required.

When all was remedied to his satisfaction, von François gave the order to prepare for departure. Immediately behind the two armoured cars of the company command element were Koertig's twenty Zündapp KS 750 motorcycle-sidecar combinations arrayed in a double column, each seating three reconnaissance troopers. Bringing up the rear was Graber's five-vehicle platoon of Sdkfz 231 eight-wheeler armoured cars.

Von François glanced at his watch. 02:12 hours. Slightly behind schedule, but no matter. This was precisely why he allocated two-and-a-half hours for an eighteen-kilometre move that should have taken no longer than thirty minutes. Always better to have time and not need it, than to need time and not have it.

The Freiherr lifted his flashlight and whirled it in a circular motion above his head. He unclipped the intercom microphone from its mount inside the commander's cupola. "Ignition," he instructed, and was rewarded by the throaty roar of the eight-cylinder Büssing-NAG L8V-G gasoline engine. Looking once again to his rear, von François began to count the headlights that were blinking to life behind him. Satisfied that his entire complement was ready to move, he pointed his flashlight to the rear and waved it up and down.

Von François pulled a pair of dust goggles down over his eyes from the brim of his Knautschmütze 'crusher' field cap. "Horst, let's move. Straight ahead."

"Yes sir," came the voice of the armoured car's driver through the Freiherr's earphones.

As the 232 lurched into motion, von François glanced around once again to observe what was happening in his wake. He saw headlamps begin to move, singly in the case of the motorcycles, and in pairs on Graber's five Sdkfz 231s.

Returning his attention to the road ahead, he directed his driver through the streets of Montoire-sur-le-Loir onto Highway D24, leading northwards out of town. Another quick look behind revealed his entire command was in motion.

The Schnelle Kompanie of the Führer-Begleit-Bataillon was on the move.

Twenty-three

The four S-ATVs of Blocking West were midway through their move from dispersion point to their vehicle laying up position when the voice of Farkash was heard through the PRC9000 tactical network.

"All Vengeance stations, this is Four. Priority. I say again, priority. Enemy force on the move from Meira in your direction. I count twenty motorcycle combos seating three each, and seven eight-wheeler armoured cars. Force is proceeding north along Route Roosevelt. Estimate highly probable east turn onto Route Churchill towards Viola. If correct, ETA your location is ten minutes max."

"Four this is Kodkod, thanks for that," Klein replied. "Mishneh, what's Three's location?"

"150 metres north of VLUP," answered HarSinai.

"Halt immediately. If you've crested the ridge and are within eye contact of Churchill, I want you to backtrack northwards into defilade vis-a-vis the highway."

"This is Mishneh," replied HarSinai, "we've yet to pass the military crest and have negative eye contact with Route Churchill."

"Then hold in place," ordered Klein. "Deploy your vehicles in a line abreast along the crest, but be sure to remain in defilade. How copy?"

"This is Mishneh, good copy." HarSinai lowered the PRC9000 handset and switched to the PRC710 personal radio carried by each Israeli trooper in his tactical vest. HarSinai thumbed the transmit button on the Madonna boom mic attached to his headset and radioed over the Team Three frequency. "Three stations, this is Mishneh, you all heard Kodkod. Three Aleph and Gimmel on my left, and Three Bet on my right. Stay ready for action. A large enemy force will be crossing our front right-to-left on the far side of this ridge."

HarSinai deployed his S-ATVs as ordered and paused, the low rumble of their engines preternaturally loud against the stillness of night.

"All Vengeance stations this is Four, be advised enemy force has turned onto Route Churchill and will be crossing your front presently. Two, be aware one motorcycle combo has broken off from the main party and is moving along Route DeGaulle north of the ridge. It will arrive in the vicinity of Earthworm East within three."

"Kodkod, good copy," replied Yossi. "Good job, Four. Keep your eyes open, out."

HarSinai's S-ATVs waited at idle, weapons at the ready as the noise from twenty 751cc Zündapp engines passing just over the ridge grew from a rumble to a roar.

"Mishneh this is Four, column crossing your front now."

HarSinai signalled acknowledgement with two clicks of his handset transmission button. The Israelis remained quiet and motionless as the sound of their enemy crescendoed and gradually receded to the northeast.

HarSinai paused until the German engine noise dwindled. "Four, this is Mishneh," he asked over the tactical network. "Are we cleared to cross Route Churchill?"

"This is Four," replied Farkash, "enemy currently three-plus kilometres from your position moving east. Area otherwise clear. You're good to cross."

"Mishneh, good copy. Thanks, out," said HarSinai, then switching to the Blocking West Team net. "Three Stations this is Mishneh, same movement order: I lead, then Aleph and Bet with Gimmel bringing up the rear. Moving now."

It took less than a minute for HarSinai's three vehicles to travel the final two hundred metres to the wooded copse that adjoined Route Churchill on its northern side. In short order, the drivers of the four S-ATVs had reversed well back amongst the trees. Camouflage nets were quickly unfurled and adorned with foliage stripped from branches and bushes, rendering the Oshkoshes invisible from anything other than point-blank range. A perfect vehicle laying up point.

HarSinai's team then assembled for movement by foot to its assault position. Each man was loaded with more than his own body weight in equipment and ammunition. Klein once told HarSinai that Roman legionaries of the late Republican period were known as 'Marius' Mules'. Not much had changed over the intervening two millennia.

The twenty-two soldiers of Blocking West slipped across Route Churchill without incident. Once inside the woods, HarSinai directed them with whispers to establish a forward ammunition resupply point for the extra 7.62 mm machinegun rounds and the anti-tank missile reloads. Leaving Yosef Tzipori, the team medic, at the FARP to secure their six o'clock, the Israelis made their way down the slope. The troopers moved at an excruciatingly slow pace, using techniques honed by long hours of infiltration exercises to avoid the slightest crunch from fallen leaves or broken branches.

After progress of fifty metres, HarSinai raised a clenched fist as a signal for his soldiers to freeze in place. He was just inside the tree line, perched directly above the railroad cut that had been hewn into the steep southern slope of the Saint-Rimay ridge. Careful to avoid any sudden movements, he scanned the target area through his infrared binoculars and immediately recognised Objective Yael, the small two-storey signalman's house standing alongside the railroad track.

It was then that he caught the first real glimpse of his enemy – two figures only one hundred and fifty metres away, yet totally unaware of his presence. HarSinai gestured to Captain Erad Meshulam, the Shayetet officer tasked with taking down the house at the head of an eight-man assault element. Meshulam cautiously approached the tree line at a low crawl. Coming abreast of HarSinai, he lifted his own pair of IR binoculars from around his neck and turned them towards the Yael.

After a few moments of scrutinising the tactical situation around the signalman's house, Meshulam nodded and looked expectantly at his superior.

"Okay Erad," whispered HarSinai as he pointed down the slope to the East of the railroad cut. "Your assault position is just inside the trees over there, opposite Yael. Remind your people that stealth is the supreme virtue. I want you to take at least a full hour moving those seventy-three metres. Just like in training – slow, steady and silent."

Meshulam nodded.

"Remain in place after we hit the follow-on train with the Gomed. And wait until Boaz slots the two sentries before you break cover from the tree line. Then you take down the house and everyone in it. I'll be up here with the overwatch element to provide fire support as needed."

Meshluam responded with another silent nod and began a slow crawl back upslope to his assault squad. HarSinai spent the next hour silently positioning his crew-served weapons. The two NG7 7.62 mm machineguns took up their posts, one on either flank. He kept the Gomed anti-tank missile team in place directly above the tunnel entrance, ensuring a clear field of fire down the railroad tracks to the South.

Twenty-four

Sergeant Boaz Sheetrit set up shop twenty metres up the slope and offset to the West. Unfolding the bipod affixed to the front handguard of his Dan bolt-action sniper rifle, he switched on its Noga Systems Matisse M75 thermal sight. If it were daytime, he'd be using the Schmidt & Bender optic that did full justice to the 1,500-metre effective range of his .338 Lapua-calibre weapon. But Yael was close enough that the individual physical characteristics of the enemy sentries could clearly be seen through his thermal scope. They looked like something straight out of Laurel and Hardy, thought the sniper. One was short and fat while his partner was tall and thin. Hardly frontline combat material, but that wouldn't save them when the time came. The Kar98 rifles slung over their shoulders made them fair game.

It was in Palsar Giv'ati boot camp that Sheetrit came to be seen as something of a prodigy with a rifle. From the first, he impressed his commanders with his uncanny ability to score a ninety-five per cent hit rate with an X95 at three hundred metres over iron sights. After completing basic and advanced infantry training, he was dispatched to the IDF's sniping school at the Mitkan Adam base. With the Dan .338 in his hands, he became quite the artiste, consistently able to hit man-sized targets a kilometre-and-a-half distant.

Yet sniping was much more than just good shooting. The previous year, Sheetrit had been given the opportunity to hone his skills at the US Marine Corps Scout-Sniper Course in Quantico, Virginia. He'd been dispatched to Quantico as part of an effort to upgrade an IDF sniper program that was generally acknowledged as less than stellar. This mediocrity was the unintended by-product of a major factor in the Israeli army's battlefield excellence – the quality of its officer corps.

The human qualities required of good snipers – maturity, intelligence and a keen tactical eye – were also the stuff of superior small-unit combat leadership. The IDF had a policy of selecting officer candidates from the best of its enlisted ranks. As a result, many excellent soldiers who might otherwise have made outstanding snipers ended up as commissioned infantry platoon leaders.

Until one particular Israeli paratrooper lieutenant colonel was won over to the creed of sniping during a stint at the US Marine Corps War College. After his promotion some years later to the post of Chief Paratrooper and Infantry Officer, he was in a position to do something about that belief. With all the zeal of a convert, the now-Brigadier General incessantly advocated for the sniping cause with the IDF General Staff. Far better, he would say, that Israel's officer corps should lose a small number of high-quality personnel than the army forfeit the tremendous force multiplier that good snipers brought to the battlefield.

This is how a baker's dozen of especially selected Israeli infantrymen ultimately found themselves shooting at the Quantico range, sewing ghillie suits and stalking each other through the woods of northern Virginia. At the end of a gruelling twelve-and-a-half weeks, only Sheetrit and five other Israelis were still around to receive their 'HOGs Tooth', the bullet necklace worn by Marine Scout-Sniper 'Hunters of Gunmen'.

They jokingly called themselves the 'Kosher HOGs', but what these first Scout-Sniper course graduates did on their return to Israel was deadly serious business. With backing from the aforementioned Chief Paratroop and Infantry Officer, they revolutionised the craft of sniping in the IDF. Long-range precision musketry went from the status of a tactical afterthought to a central role in Israeli infantry doctrine. In the end, Sheetrit became something of an evangelist himself, putting his plans for university study on hold and signing on for an extra two years as a sniper instructor.

So it transpired that Boaz Sheetrit – one of the Kosher HOG originals – came to be lying prone on a forested slope above the Saint-Rimay rail tunnel in the midst of night, watching the men he was tasked to kill. He was warm and comfy, well-insulated from the chill of the French autumn night by two layers of tactical clothing, topped by a moisture-proof camouflage jacket.

Sheetrit looked up from his scope and adjusted the mottled ninja mask covering his head and face, glancing over at his spotter, Sergeant Gil'ad Reshef. Without a word Reshef nodded and Sheetrit keyed the button on the Madonna boom mic of the PRC710 radio headset he wore beneath his helmet. "Mishneh Kodkod Vengeance, this is Three Tzadik, in position and on target," the sniper whispered.

Moments later, the voice of Meshulam came over the Blocking West Team net, so hushed it was barely audible. "Mishneh, this is Three, we're at our assault point."

"Copy that," came HarSinai's muffled voice over the local Team Three network. "Vengeance Three stations, this is Mishneh. Overwatch elements are all in position. Good job. Now sit tight until further word, out."

There was nothing else to do but wait.

Twenty-five

Captain Azriel Weinstock went down on bended knee just short of the tree line, raising a clenched fist over his shoulder. Three other shadowy figures mimicked his movements, silently genuflecting in response to his unspoken order. Weinstock carefully uncoupled himself from his backpack, lowering the ninety-litre bergen to the ground. Liberated from that burden, he drew his Sig Sauer P227 Tactical from a thigh holster and verified with a quick twist that the suppressor was firmly affixed to the pistol's barrel.

When Weinstock wasn't wearing a helmet, you could see the black knitted kippa he wore pinned to his short blonde hair. The son of a prominent rabbi in the coastal Israeli town of Netanya, the 25-year-old former yeshiva student came from the Golani Brigade's elite reconnaissance company – Palsar 95. Like Michael HarSinai, he exemplified the new generation of modern orthodox officers who were rising to prominence throughout the Israeli army's special operations units. To this particular mission, Weinstock brought the added advantage of native fluency in French, his family having made Aliya from Toulouse when he was a child.

Glancing rearwards, Weinstock verified that his squad-mates had similarly lowered their packs and equipped themselves for silent action.

With an affirmative nod, Weinstock gave the tactical hand signal for column formation. Dropping to a prone position, he low-crawled out of the woods, through a muddy drainage ditch and up onto a dirt road named Route Dowding by the Israelis. Dowding was actually more of a farmer's lane that ran along the northern base of the Saint-Rimay ridge. On approaching the tunnel, for some reason the road's builders decided to dispense with a level crossing. They instead built the road on a crescent path up the slope of the ridge, over the tunnel entrance and down again on the other side. A handful of houses on the periphery of the Cherchenois hamlet were scattered along the lane.

Once atop the road, Weinstock hand-signalled his squad-mates to crawl forward into line abreast formation, facing upslope towards the apex of the crescent. He continued at a slow crawl up the sloping dirt lane, the gravel biting into his elbows.

Weinstock smelled the enemy before he saw them, a slight wind bearing the odour of burning tobacco in his direction. Looking left and right, he discerned nods of affirmation from his squad-mates that indicated they too smelled the enemy's cigarettes. The Golani officer rose into a low crouch that left both hands free to operate his pistol. Double checking at a glance that his men had assumed the same combat-ready posture, Weinstock led the way up the road. None of the Israeli special operators had to be instructed on the importance of tactical surprise, and they moved cautiously and quietly, minimising their footfalls like hunters stalking their prey.

As the Israelis crept forward, they began to pick up guttural snatches of German conversation. From the incessant chuckling coming from his squad-mates, one of the Wehrmacht soldiers appeared to have quite a talent for comedy. The shapes of the three Führer-Begleit-Bataillon troopers became progressively visible as the Israelis slowly crested the ridge. The Germans' body heat showed white against the dark grey background of their cold surroundings through the Nivisys TAM-14 thermal vision monocular-mounted Israeli helmets. Glowing even brighter was the engine of the Zündapp motorcycle-sidecar combo parked on the road shoulder.

"Shlomo," whispered Weinstock into the Madonna boom mike of his headset, "you're with me on the submachine gun. Tsuriel, you take rifle left and Meir you take rifle right. Fold your thermals and prepare to fire on my mark."

The Israelis folded the thermal vision monocular up onto their helmets and prepared to take down the still oblivious Germans standing thirty-five metres away.

"Ready, ready, fire!" said Weinstock in a normal voice.

As one, the four Israelis activated the Crimson Trace Grip LG617 lasers affixed to their pistols. Red dots materialised on the torsos of the German soldiers as they wheeled to confront this voice out of nowhere that spoke an incomprehensible tongue.

"Wehr ist ..." was all Stabsfeldwebel Bäcker managed to say before the Israelis opened fire.

While the noise emitted by four sound-suppressed P227s was minimal, the damage inflicted by their .45 calibre ACP bullets was maximal. The heavy-calibre rounds killed Stabsfeldwebel Bäcker outright and left his two crewmates mortally wounded.

First blood in Operation Agag had been drawn.

Flipping down his thermal vision binocular, Weinstock approached the wounded Germans and put an end to their groans with an additional round to each enemy chest.

As his squad-mates arrayed themselves to provide 360-degree security, Weinstock thumbed his PRC710 transmit button. "All Two stations, this is Two," he transmitted on the team network, "sentries eliminated. Rendezvous with me per the ops plan on Route Dowding at hash 21."

It took less than three minutes for the remaining sixteen troopers of Team Two to arrive from their staging position in the woods.

"Let's clean this up," instructed Weinstock. "Strip them of their weapons and drag the bodies into the trees. Meir and Tsuriel will play Purim dress up outside with German greatcoats and helmets while we set up in there." He pointed to a large house fifty metres down the road. "But first ... where's Ohad?"

The team commander's RTO trotted up bearing a PRC9000 in backpack mode. Sergeant Ohad Karmi handed the radio handset over to Weinstock.

"Kodkod Vengeance this is Two, enemy at Objective Rina has been eliminated without incident," Weinstock reported over the tactical net. "We will now take up our blocking position."

"Good work, Two," replied Klein from the ridge above. "One, you are cleared to move your team through Rina into your assault position."

"Two, good copy," came the voice of Team One leader Tzachi Dvir over the tac net. "Moving now."

"Keep me informed of your progress. Out," broadcast Klein.

Weinstock returned the handset to his RTO and turned to his deputy team leader. "Tamir, time to wake our new neighbours. Organise a fire team and let's make a house call. Ohad, you're with me. The rest of the team will spread out and establish a security perimeter. No firing without my explicit authorisation."

Weinstock led the designated quintet of troopers across the road to the nearest of the buildings scattered along the lane. It was a small complex composed of a farmhouse and barn with an open yard in between.

156

Approaching the front door of what was obviously the farmhouse, he raised his fist to deliver a knock.

Twenty-six

Les Allemands. Those two words surged through her mind with the first feeble blink of her eyelids.

A thudded hammering echoed through the house, pulling her from slumber's warm embrace. As she passed through the tipping point between insensibility and consciousness, a frisson of pure panic overwhelmed her.

An unexpected knock on the door in German-occupied France was a guaranteed generator of trepidation. When such a surprise visit arrived in the dark depths of night, that trepidation escalated into stomach-tightening dread.

Les Allemands ...

She shivered in the darkness beneath the heavy woollen quilt before steeling herself to the grim reality of her situation. The Germans were not noted for subtlety and would surely batter their way through the door if she failed to respond. Opening her eyes, she glanced by force of habit towards the far half of the king-sized bed. A second plump goose down pillow lay there, immaculate and undimpled by the weight of a human head. No salvation to be found there.

Tears of fear tinged with despair welled up in her eyes.

The pounding continued apace and she swung her feet out of bed, slipping them into a pair of tattered woollen slippers. Feeling her way to the light switch, she flicked it to the on position. Nothing. Since war's end, the supply of electric power had become a hit or miss proposition. In truth, much more of the latter than the former.

Lighting the kerosene lamp on the side table, she made her way towards the stairs.

"J'arrive! J'arrive!" she yelled while descending the staircase that led to the ground level foyer.

The pounding ceased.

"Qui est là?" she asked, her nervousness betrayed by a tremulous quiver in tone.

"Ouvrez la porte, s'il vous plaît, Madame," came a masculine voice muffled by passage through the heavy lacquered oak door.

She hesitated for a moment before turning the iron key of ancient provenance that protruded from the lock. With a metallic clank and groan of rusty hinges, the portal swung open to reveal a half-dozen men occupying her front yard.

They were soldiers, that much she could see in the arc of yellow light cast by her lamp. But not German. The exotic character of their uniforms and gear was apparent even to her untrained eye.

Mottled greenish brown smocks and pants with large bellows pockets, rather than rough woollen Wehrmacht trench coats. Hemispheric helmets topped by floppy camouflage netting with some sort of binocular-like device attached. Their weapons were stubby things that might be mistaken for child's toys, except for the casual menace with which they were wielded.

A tall slender figure approached the door. Clearly the one in charge.

"Good evening Madame," he said in Toulousain-accented French, his teeth white against the background of a face painted brownish-green hues. "I apologise for intruding at this time of night. Would you be so kind as to allow us in?"

Recognising the rhetorical nature of the request, she shrugged and stood aside as the man and two of his comrades passed through the foyer into her living room. She followed, watching silently as the commander took inventory of the room's contents and layout.

"First of all, Madame, is there anyone else in the house?"

"Only my daughter. She's asleep upstairs."

"And your husband?"

"Dead in the war. Killed last year by the Boche."

She examined the intruder for a moment as her brows curved in a quizzical arch. "You're not German."

"No Madame, we are English. And we're here on a very special mission. I have to ask you a few questions and it's important you tell me the truth."

She nodded.

"The next house over, the one on the outskirts of Cherchenois, who lives there?"

"The Sauveterres. But they've been gone since the Boche came. They moved south to live with family in the Vichy zone."

"So, there's no-one else other than you and your daughter between here and the edge of the commune?"

She again nodded in affirmation.

"Tres Bien, Madame ..." His mid-sentence halt was an obvious cue.

"Morency, Monsieur," she replied, brushing a stray wisp of hair from her face. "Danielle Morency."

The stranger nodded. "My name is Captain Azriel Weinstock. My men and I are here on an operation that could determine the outcome of the war. I can't say anything more."

"There's no need, Monsieur. The whole commune is buzzing with news about the meeting at Montoire between Hitler and the traitor Petain. You must be here to kill them."

For the briefest of instants, the young officer's aura of calm competence slipped as a startled look flashed across his face.

Danielle's lips curled in an impertinent grin as Weinstock struggled to regain his composure.

"Madame Morency, all speculation aside, please bring your child downstairs and we'll then discuss the situation further."

Danielle turned towards the stairs as Weinstock signalled with a sideways nod that one of his troopers should accompany her.

She climbed to the upper floor and paused at the doorway to Adele's room, tailed at a discrete distance by her escort. Placing the lantern on the floor, she raised an index finger to her lips and made a 'shush' sound. The soldier nodded. Slowly opening the door, she made her way through the darkened room towards the dim outline of a child's bed in the far corner. Danielle paused, listening to the soft breathing of her sleeping daughter coming at regular intervals like the lapping of the incoming tide on a sandy beach. Lifting the four-year-old in her arms with tender care, she returned to the hallway.

Danielle arrived at the ground floor as a procession of more armed-to-the-teeth men began trooping through her front door.

The soldiers dispersed through the house per directions issued by Captain Weinstock in a language she found incomprehensible, yet vaguely familiar.

The hustle and bustle woke Adele, who twisted in her mother's arms to stare, wide-eyed, at these face-painted interlopers. The young child's face contorted in that peculiar rictus signalling the onset of tears and, moments later, she began to wail.

Danielle gently stroked Adele's hair. "Chut, chut, mon coeur, n'ayez pas peur."

One of the soldiers pushed aside the sling of his fearsome machinegun and tentatively stepped forward with hand outstretched.

"Voulez-vous chocolate?" he said in an accent so atrocious that Danielle couldn't resist a slight laugh. The gunner, whose camouflage face paint could not hide a youthful visage that looked barely old enough to shave, responded with a sheepish smile.

"Merci, Monsieur," said Danielle. She broke off a piece of brown sweetness and placed it between Adele's lips. Ever so tentatively, the little girl bit down on the chocolate, at which point her face metamorphosed from distress to delight.

A collective chuckle that erupted among the onlooking troopers was brought to an abrupt end by Weinstock, who began barking orders in a back-to-business tone. As the soldiers scattered to their designated positions, Danielle pondered this vaguely familiar-sounding language and what it could tell her about the strangers who spoke it.

Suddenly it dawned on her where she'd heard those trilled 'r's and pharyngeal fricatives before. The High Holiday synagogue services that she'd attended as a child before her parents became completely estranged from Judaic observance.

"Vous n'êtes pas Anglais; vous êtes Juifs. C'est l'Hébreu dont vous parlez."

A moment of silence ensued as Weinstock recovered from another bout of flabbergast. "How do you know Hebrew?" he demanded.

"Sh'ma, Yisroel, Adonai Eloheynu, Adonai Ehad," she replied with a chuckle of roguish enjoyment at the wide-eyed surprise that materialised on the faces of the assembled troopers.

"But Morency isn't a Jewish name," challenged Weinstock.

"It's not. Nor was my husband. But my maiden name is Bernheim. Let's just say my parents weren't exactly thrilled by my marriage to Gaston. A shaygets veterinarian from the country wasn't exactly what they had in mind when they said I should marry a doctor."

A fleeting smile was the first hint that Weinstock might have a sense of humour after all. But the young officer's stern countenance then reasserted itself.

"Well, Madame ..."

"Danielle, please."

"Danielle, you are partially correct. We are Palestinian Jews serving in the British Army. But now I must ask whether you have a cellar."

"Yes, of course," she said with a gesture to her left.

"It is very important that you stay down there until I come to tell you it's safe."

Weinstock beckoned to a soldier who was in the midst of preparing a belt of machinegun ammunition for the bearer of chocolate to reload when the time came.

"Do you speak English, Danielle?"

"Yes, I do."

"Good. This is Shlomo Blumfeld. He speaks no French, but his English is fluent. He'll take you to the cellar and will make sure you're in a safe place. Do you understand?"

She nodded.

Weinstock turned to the soldier and spoke in English for Danielle's benefit. "Shlomo, take good care of them, they're of our people."

Blumfeld nodded and stuck his tongue out at Adele, a premeditatedly ridiculous sight that triggered a giggle from the sweets-happy child.

Danielle smiled at the young trooper, motioning with her head to the kerosene lantern. Blumfeld hastened to oblige.

"Capitaine Weinstock, one more thing," she said in French

She paused as he raised both palms. "If I can call you Danielle, you can surely call me Azriel."

She smiled in acknowledgement. "Alright, Azriel. Do you know how long we'll be down there?"

"Until the shooting stops, I suppose."

"And then?"

"Then what?"

"What happens to us?"

"We release you, of course. We don't wage war against women and children."

"And then?"

"I'm sorry, I don't understand."

"Capitaine … Azriel, you're going to launch an attack against Adolf Hitler from a house owned and occupied by a Jewish family. How do you think the Germans will respond to that fact?"

162

"I take your point, but I can't think about that now. I have to prepare my men."

"Then promise me that we'll discuss this before you leave."

Weinstock hesitated.

Danielle approached and looked directly into his eyes.

"Please, promise me." She placed a hand on his forearm.

Weinstock nodded. "I promise."

"Thank you."

Turning to Blumfeld, she beckoned that he should follow. Then, child in her arms, she led the way towards the kitchen and the cellar door.

"Do you know how long we'll be down there?"

"I can't tell you, Ma'am," Blumfeld replied in an accent that sounded almost British, but not quite.

"Then we will need more kerosene. There's a metal ... eh ... bidon..."

"Can?" prompted Blumfeld.

"Yes ... a metal can over there." She pointed to a door on the far side of the kitchen. "In the office."

The trooper acted on her direction and shortly reappeared, brandishing an ancient metal container.

She nodded and opened another door, revealing a staircase leading down into darkness. "This is the cellar."

After descending a few steps, she paused until Blumfeld joined her and the ambit of the lantern's light permitted the stairs to be negotiated safely.

The cellar was a dark, dank place, sub-divided by six thick pillars of cemented stone that supported the house above.

"I think we'll be safest in there," said Danielle as she pointed to a corner protected by the rearmost pillar and the stone staircase. "But we'll need blankets if we don't want to freeze. You can take them from my bedroom."

Blumfeld nodded and laid the lantern at her feet. He then produced a flashlight from one of the large pockets on his chest and disappeared up the stairs.

Danielle Morency settled Adele on her lap as she awaited the young trooper's return. The clumping of boots and equipment echoed through the ceiling, as the soldiers assumed firing positions in anticipation of a looming battle.

A thudding on the stairs soon announced Blumfeld's return. She stood to accept the goose down quilt he carried.

"Shlomo, do you know the word 'connard' in French?"

He shook his head.

"It means ... how you say it ... bottom hole?" She illustrated her question with a gesture that indicated her posterior.

Blumfeld laughed. "You mean asshole."

"Yes, asshole." She briefly smiled before her face assumed a more sombre mien. "Please make sure to kill that ... asshole ... Hitler."

"That's the plan," the Israeli replied with a cheeky grin.

Standing on tiptoe, she kissed Blumfeld's forehead. "Bon courage, mon brave. Good luck and be safe."

"Thank you," said the nonplussed young man before he turned and disappeared up the stairs.

And so, Danielle Morency settled back against the pillar and arranged Adele on her lap, spreading the quilt to cover them both against the chill of the autumn night.

How much of her home would be left standing by the end of tomorrow? Her lips pursed and shoulders shrugged. She harboured no particular affection for the place she'd lived over the past two years. A city girl by background and inclination, she had moved to the country like a proper wife in her husband's wake.

At this point, the whole question was entirely academic. If these Jewish soldiers failed in their mission, everyone in the house would soon be dead. If they succeeded, there was still no way she and Adele would be able to remain in this place. No matter how unlikely the circumstances that brought these strange Jewish warriors to her door, their lives and hers were now intertwined. Even if Azriel Weinstock didn't realise it yet.

Twenty-seven

Chief Inspector Tzachi Dvir heard the rumble of the locomotive as he lay prone on the narrow embankment looming above the eastern tunnel entrance. His watch showed 06:24 hours local. Amerika was running late. He keyed the transmit button on his PRC710 headset. "Hold your fire. This will be the advance escort train. Maintain concealment and let it pass. Team Two will take care of it from the houses above. Amerika will follow. Yoram and Mookie – you be ready with the Matadors to fire on my command. Just like in training."

The lead Führer-Begleit-Bataillon train passed peacefully through the ambush position and was four hundred metres down the track before the nose of Amerika's lead locomotive emerged from the tunnel's mouth.

"Wait for it ... wait ... ready ... ready," said Dvir over the Assault Team network.

When the coal tender of Amerika's second locomotive appeared from within the tunnel, Dvir issued the command to fire. The two Matador-armed troopers stepped from behind the railroad supply shed that stood fifty metres north of the tunnel entrance. As they'd determined by coin-toss months ago, Yoram targeted the foremost locomotive while Mookie aimed at number two. The Matador PZF90s they wielded were rocket launchers designed to knock out light armoured vehicles and bunkers. The BR50 steam locomotive was easy meat to the anti-structure version of the rocket.

The two tandem warheads tore through the outer casings of their respective targets' smokeboxes, exploding within and rupturing super-heaters and boiler tubes alike. The two locomotives slowly ground to a halt amid cacophonous screeching and clouds of steam, their forward inertia enough to pull the first third of the lead flakwagen railcar clear of the tunnel mouth. The engineers and firemen who crewed each locomotive jumped from the cabs of their incapacitated machines and fled across the fields as fast as their legs could carry them.

"Forward, follow me!" yelled Dvir as he rose from a prone position. He heard the whoosh of the Gill missile overhead, fired by Weinstock's Team Two from its position up the slope. Seconds later, the darkness was lit by an explosion marking the missile's impact against the tank turret on the lead escort train.

Two figures emerged from the flakwagen crew quarters onto the gun platform of the AA car, their body heat glowing a bright white through the Nivisys thermal monocular. Dvir raised his X95 and double tapped each of the Germans. The flaktruppen collapsed, slain by an enemy they never even knew was there. The locomotives' battery system continued to power the train's electric lighting and Dvir could see the bright glow from the open doorway to the flakwagen crew quarters. He tossed a pair of MK26 fragmentation grenades through the opening in quick succession and yelled "two grenades!" His teammates went to ground.

After the second grenade explosion, Dvir leaped up onto the gun platform, shouting, "Let's go!" Using the 20 mm Flackvierling 38 quad anti-aircraft gun as cover, he fired an entire X95 magazine through the doorway of flakwagen crew quarters.

Within seconds, Dvir was joined by the rest of his teammates, who rapidly sorted themselves into assault formation. On point were Rotem Greenspan and Sagiv Azoulai, each bearing an NG7 7.62 mm machine gun. At number three was Ira Maximoff, who was armed with an X95 and with a Crye12 twelve-gauge shotgun mounted beneath the rifle's 5.56 mm barrel. The Crye was loaded with solid shot, perfect for taking out door hinges.

Dvir himself was number four, followed by his RTO who, in addition to a PRC9000 radio, also carried two Bulldog Protective Systems bomb blankets for use if they had to blow things up. Following on came another five riflemen bearing rucksacks, each filled with four NG7 assault drums containing 125-round belts of 7.62 mm. Then came a trio of troopers armed with X95-Crye combos and another three toting X95s with under-slung GL40 grenade launchers. The team medic was next, followed by Yoram and Mookie, who were charged with bringing up the rear. The two Matador gunners were responsible for covering the team's six o'clock as the assaulters advanced through the train. They carried their now-empty launch tubes in compliance with Klein's 'nothing left behind' edict.

The lead fire team stacked up beside the doorway to the flakwagen crew quarters. Rotem pushed his NG7 around the door jamb and fired two fifteen-round bursts. Flipping up his Nivisys monocular into its stowage position on his helmet, the machine gunner led the team into the crew compartment.

As Dvir stepped through the door, his nostrils were assailed by the sour residual scent of the grenades' Comp-B explosive, seasoned by the rusty tang of human blood. Swallowing hard, he surveyed the devastation within. Bodies were strewn throughout the compartment, some sprawled on the floor and others half hanging from the bunk beds that were bolted to the compartment's walls. Some of the Germans were writhing with pain. Dvir watched impassively as Rotem and Greenspan fired a short two-to-three round burst into each German soldier to ensure any threat was neutralised. The Israelis had neither the time nor the inclination to deal with prisoners.

Reaching the end of the crew compartment, Rotem went down on one knee shouting "Drum change!" Sagiv slapped him on the shoulder and assumed the lead, moving onto the rear gun platform where he took up an overwatch position towards the next railcar in line

Now fully inside the tunnel, a reloaded Rotem slid over the bulkhead of the rear flakwagen gun platform onto the vestibule. He then affixed a pre-prepared 25-gram charge of Semtex plastique opposite each of the two door hinges. Yoram inserted a non-electric M18 blasting cap into each explosive charge, with a 30-centimetre length of M700 fuse attached. He then removed safety pins from the M81 fuse igniters affixed at the other end of the time fuses.

With a shout of "activated!" he tugged the M81 pull rings, pausing to verify that both time fuses were alight before clambering back over the flakwagen bulkhead. He joined his teammates sheltering behind the now-unfolded Bulldog bomb blankets, covering his ears and opening his mouth to minimise the overpressure effects from the impending blast.

Thirty-seven seconds later, the charges exploded, slicing through the aluminium wall of the railcar and blowing the inward-opening door off its hinges. Through the now-open threshold, Dvir could see rows of heavy shelving along both sides of the railcar's interior. Baggage car, he thought. Good to see our intel is spot on.

Covered by Dvir in overwatch, the two machine gunners clambered down onto the vestibule linking the rail carriages. The rest of the team followed, subdividing into two columns, with each half stacking up behind one of the machine gunners on point.

"Moving now!" yelled Rotem, who stepped over the threshold into the baggage car, bearing left while Sagiv bore right.

The two Israeli columns advanced past shelves piled high with suitcases secured in place by thick white cotton cargo netting. They were midway along the length of the railcar when the handle on the vestibule door ahead twisted downwards. The Israelis pazatzta'ed themselves prone and sighted their weapons. The doorway began swung inwards and the distinctive barrel of an MP38 became slowly visible.

Rotem and Sagiv opened fire almost simultaneously with their NG7s. Within seconds, the door's immaculate smoothness became a thing of memory, its surface perforated by a hail of 7.62 mm bullets that tore easily through soft aluminium. The MP38 submachinegun clattered to the carriage floor, followed by a man – obviously dead – who fell forward through the portal, his leather and canvas web gear strapped incongruously over pyjamas.

"Cover me," said Rotem, noting Sagiv's affirmative nod out of the corner of his eye. In deference to the closed confines of Amerika, both machine gunners were using the short-barrelled version of the NG7. At 1.93 metres, and eighty-two well-muscled kilograms, Rotem was easily able to aim his eleven-kilogram weapon from the shoulder as he advanced down the length of the carriage.

The vestibule door was half-open, jammed against the bloodied corpse that lay across the threshold. Rotem flattened himself against the end wall of the carriage and peeked through the door into the vestibule. He keyed the transmit button on his Madonna and announced, "Clear!"

Sagiv positioned himself on the other side of the doorway and Rotem glanced over his shoulder to see the remainder of his teammates stacking up along the rail carriage wall.

Dvir approached and clapped Rotem lightly on the shoulder. "Let's be extra careful." He nodded towards the dead German, "One of the Begleitkommando. I think we can expect more of them ahead, so let's keep it tight, just the way we trained. Establish fire superiority and then move."

Rotem nodded and proceeded into the vestibule of the next car in line, where he replicated the previous tactical door breaching technique: Semtex charges opposite the hinges; blasting caps and fuses; activate igniters; get the hell outta Dodge, and take shelter behind the bomb blanket deployed in the preceding carriage.

The blast sent the vestibule door careening forward into the next rail carriage, which should be the auxiliary power car if the intel continued to prove accurate.

Rotem leaned around the doorjamb and fired a few bursts through the opening, flinching as bullets ricocheted off the generator. The Motoren-Werke Mannheim diesel generator was the size of a sub-compact automobile and occupied the centre of the railcar. Arrayed along the sides of the car were barrels of diesel fuel to feed it.

"Moving now!" yelled Rotem as he ceased fire and took his first step over the threshold. He was caught almost immediately by a burst fired by an MP38-wielding German who popped out from behind the far end of the generator.

It wasn't the five 9 mm bullets hitting Rotem's torso that caused the real damage. Stopped by his Kevlar body-armour chest-plates, they caused bruising that would have been painful had the lead machine gunner been in a position to feel anything at all. But the two rounds that struck Rotem in the face were a different story. He fell backward and was dead before he hit the floor.

"Shit," muttered Dvir.

Sagiv opened up with his NG7 to suppress the Germans at the other end of the car, but the massive bulk of generator served as cover that rendered the enemy invulnerable to small arms fire.

Grasping Rotem by the drag handle on the back of his tactical vest, Dvir pulled the fallen trooper back into the baggage car. Out of the enemy's line of sight, he keyed the transmitter button on his PRC710. "Sagiv, fall back!"

Without the slightest slackening of the fire from his NG7, Sagiv got to his feet and crab-walked rearwards through the vestibule to the shelter of the baggage car.

Dvir glanced at the team medic, who shook his head in a mournful negative.

"Okay guys, change of tactics," Dvir barked. "Time to use the grenade launchers. I want Alef and Mesika to fire their 40 mms into the generator car. Make sure you aim for the far wall of the carriage. Otherwise, the grenades won't have enough range to arm themselves and the bastards behind the generator will stay unscathed. Clear?"

The Assault Team troopers nodded.

"Asher," Dvir said to the team medic. "You and Yoram are responsible for Rotem. I want to see his body with us when we reach the far end of the tunnel. Kelman, you take the NG7 and work with Sagiv from now on. Now, everyone except Alef, Mesika and Haim stack up behind the blanket and prepare for overpressure. Ears covered and mouths open. Move."

The two GL40 grenadiers posted themselves on either side of the baggage car vestibule doorway. On cue, Alef and Mesika leaned around their respective doorjambs and fired 40 mm fragmentation grenades that exploded in quick succession against the far wall of the generator car.

Sagiv and Kalman moved forward almost immediately, even before the smoke from the grenades had time to clear. The floor was covered by a treacly coating of diesel leaking from the now-perforated fuel drums. The troopers struggled to keep their footing as they advanced, weapons at the ready.

What the two machine gunners found behind the generator was gruesomely satisfying. Four more Germans, clad in a combination of pyjama pants and SS tunics, lay dead in a viscous pool of blood mixed with diesel. Sagiv signalled to those behind that the coast was clear and the remainder of the team slid their way across the car with more than a few slips and falls.

"Right, said Dvir. "Next up is Hitler's personal sleeping car. Let's be on our toes."

Sagiv nodded and prepared the door for demolition, with Kelman providing overwatch. It blew forward, revealing a narrow passageway with compartments on either side that occupied half the railcar's length. Alef and Messika immediately fired 40 mm grenades down the passageway into an open lounge area at the far end of the carriage.

With Kelman lying prone in the centre of the passageway providing overwatch, Sagiv and Maximoff, the Crye12 shotgunner, quickly ascertained that both sleeping compartments were empty. A quick peek into the lounge area revealed sumptuous leather chairs and a settee that were considerably worse for the wear after being peppered by grenade fragments. But the entire car was devoid of an enemy presence.

Examining the sleeping compartment on his right, Sagiv took note of the disarrayed bedding that hinted at its occupant's hasty departure. Placing his hand on the sheets, he called for Dvir to join him.

"Still warm," Sagiv said with a gesture towards the bed.

Dvir nodded. "They're moving Hitler towards the other end of the train."

Those five SS men were sacrificed to put some distance between us. It's the smart play. It's what I'd do."

"No big deal," chimed in the still prone Kelman, his cheek welded to the stock of his NG7. "HarSinai and Meshulam will take care of them at the far end."

"No doubt," replied Dvir. "But I don't want to give our Team Three colleagues the satisfaction of bagging the big prize. The bastards can't be that far ahead, so let's move. Next up should be the Begleitkommando car – so let's be careful. There may be other stay-behinds."

Sagiv nodded as he checked the assault drum that fed his NG7. He motioned for Kelman to join him in the vestibule, where the two machine gunners prepared to storm the next rail carriage in line: the Begleitkommandowagen, sleeping quarters for Hitler's close bodyguard force.

Twenty-eight

THEN

Obersturmbannführer Bruno Gesche was stone sober, an unusual state of affairs for a man whose fondness for schnapps was legendary throughout the SS. So notorious were his binge drinking habits that he'd attracted the wrath of the abstemious SS chief Heinrich Himmler, who twice tried to engineer Gesche's sacking from command of the Begleitkommando. The obersturmbannführer was always reprieved at the eleventh hour by Hitler, who harboured an enduring fondness for one of his oldest street-fighting comrades. The truth was that Bruno Gesche owed everything to his Führer. Tonight, that debt would come due.

Awoken by echoes of gunfire reverberating through the tunnel, Gesche had immediately recognised the threat those sounds portended. He quickly dispatched five Begleitkommando troopers forward through the train with instructions to fight a delaying action against whomever was attacking Amerika.

Gesche then proceeded to the Führer's personal Pullman car, where he knocked loudly on the door of Hitler's sleeping compartment. No response. Pulling a passkey from his tunic pocket, the Führer's chief bodyguard swung open the door and grimaced at the sight of his slumbering leader, utterly dead to the world.

Gesche turned on his heel and strode back out into the corridor, stopping opposite a compartment at the end of the carriage.

"Morell!" the obersturmbannführer bellowed as he pounded his fist against the door. "Morell, open up!"

The door opened to reveal a short, obese, middle-aged man peering back at Gesche through a pair of wire-rimmed glasses.

"What did you give him?" Gesche barked at Hitler's personal physician.

"Just the usual to help him sleep," replied Dr Theodore Morell defensively. "Why?"

"Why?" echoed Gesche sarcastically. "Because British commandos are attacking the train, that's why! I need him awake. Now!"

Morell disappeared into his compartment, returning moments later with a vial of liquid and a syringe.

"Arschloch Reichsspritzenmeister," muttered Gesche as Morell pushed his way into the corridor.

The doctor ignored the insult and made his way to Hitler's bedside, where he filled the syringe from the vial and administered an injection into the Führer's forearm.

"That should do it," Morell reported with an ingratiating smile. "He should be fully awake in about ten minutes."

"In ten minutes, the British will have put a bullet in his head, you idiot," groused Gesche with a disgusted shake of the head. "We'll just have to carry him."

The obersturmbannführer stuck his head out into the corridor and beckoned to a tough looking SS officer wielding an MP38 submachine gun.

"Franz, get in here!" barked Gesche to Sturmbannführer Franz Schädle, his second-in-command.

Schädle entered the compartment and noted his groggy Führer showing the first signs of a return to consciousness. The sturmbannführer simply nodded and the two SS bodyguards set about lifting their leader into a sitting position.

Taking Hitler by either arm, Gesche and Schädle half-dragged, half-walked the lethargic dictator out into the corridor, where they were immediately surrounded by the eleven remaining members of the Begleitkommando. The protectors then hustled their man away from the sound of the guns towards the train's rear.

As the party passed through the communications car, Gesche called a halt, motioning that the senior duty signaller, a paunchy, middle-aged stabsfeldwebel, should approach.

Gesche gestured over his shoulder towards the sounds of explosions and small arms fire. "We have enemy attacking the train. English commandos, I should think. I want you and your signallers to buy us some time. The Führer's safety must take precedence over all else."

The stabsfeldwebel gulped in tangible dismay. "But Herr Obersturmbannführer, we're not frontline troops. We're also unarmed in compliance with your security instructions."

"You wear the uniform of a soldier so you'll fight like a soldier!" snapped Gesche, before turning to face his Begleitkommando colleagues. "Kempa,

Dirr, Herzberger and Gildish, hand over your pistols to these men. You'll have to make do with your MPs."

The reluctance of the SS men to relinquish their secondary armament was only matched by the dearth of enthusiasm with which the Wehrmacht signallers received the weapons.

Gesche pulled his P38 from the leather holster he'd hastily belted around his waist, pointing the pistol at the stabsfeldwebel's chest. "Your only choice is which end of this weapon you want. Decide."

The stabsfeldwebel extended his hand and Gesche slapped his pistol into the man's palm.

Gesche pointed to the forward end of the car. "In a few minutes, the English will be coming through that door. I want you to make a barricade out of these desks, chairs and radio equipment. Then fight them off as long as you can. Good luck."

Having blithely consigned the hapless Wehrmacht signallers to almost certain death, Gesche turned once again to face Hitler. "Mein Führer, we should go on."

A dishevelled, pyjama-clad Adolf Hitler, still bleary-eyed and half-awake, yawned as he nodded in assent. Clustering around their Führer in a protective phalanx, the SS squad hustled him onward.

The party quickly made its way through the dining car, collecting four cooks who were in the midst of preparations for the breakfast meal. Next came two Pullman sleeper cars for junior staff, where their numbers were swelled by orderlies, aides-de-camp and a bevy of terrified amanuenses from the Führer's secretarial pool.

On reaching the first of two VIP cars, Gesche encountered three worried-looking senior officers – Heinrich Himmler, Wilhelm Keitel and Alfred Jodl, who had hastily pulled on their uniforms and were standing with pistols drawn.

Reichsführer-SS Himmler couldn't contain a fleeting grimace at the sight of his Begleitkommando nemesis. But the appearance of Hitler and the exigencies of the situation combined to put their internecine feuding on the back burner – for now.

"What's going on?" enquired Himmler.

"There are enemy working their way through the train," Gesche replied. "English commandos, I should think."

"They're also at the other end," said Generalfeldmarschall Keitel of the German supreme command.

"Yes," interjected Generaloberst Jodl, Keitel's Chief of Staff. "We've heard explosions and considerable small arms fire from outside."

"Have you done a recce to ascertain what's out there?" asked Gesche.

Jodl, Himmler and Keitel lapsed into embarrassed silence as the Begleitkommando chief pursed his lips in unspoken contempt.

Gesche turned to Sturmbannführer Franz Schädle, his deputy. "Franz, I want you to take the rest of the kommando and fight a delaying action from one of the cars we've passed. Where and how to deploy is your decision, but I need you to hold off the verdamnt Engländer for as long as possible. That'll give me time to figure out how we can get out of this damned mess."

"But if we're fighting back there," asked Schädle with a thumb-over-the-shoulder gesture towards Amerika's front, "who'll protect the Führer?"

"I'll use the flaktruppen," replied Gesche with a shrug. "Desperate times, desperate measures."

Schädle extended his hand.

"Good luck, kamerad," said Gesche, shaking the hand of his subordinate who was going off to play Leonidas at Thermopolye.

Gesche turned back to address the trio of Himmler, Keitel and Jodl. "Wait here," he said in a peremptory tone of command. The Begleitkommando chief then bulldozed his way towards the rear of the train, brusquely elbowing aside the senior staff officers who were milling around the corridors of the two VIP Pullman sleeper cars. Reaching the rear flakwagen, he clambered over the gun platform bulkhead and entered the crew quarters. Empty. Moving onto the rear gun platform, Gesche saw the flaktruppen arrayed to repel any attack from the western end of the tunnel.

"Well done, Hauptman," said Gesche while delivering a clap of approval to the shoulder of the railcar's commander. "What do we know?"

"The enemy are out there in force," replied the flak officer. "I went for a recce myself about ten minutes ago. It was still dark, but I was able to see that our rear escort train has been destroyed. The gun turret was alight and its ammunition was cooking off, which illuminated the immediate area. I saw many bodies. Twenty or thirty at least. The enemy has occupied a building that gives them a clear field of fire to the tunnel exit. I think they're also positioned on the slope above. They seem to have this uncanny ability to fire accurately in the dark."

"They've turned this place into the perfect kill zone," mused Gesche. "What about your flak guns?"

"I thought of that," said the flak commander. "But the curvature of the tunnel means we can't bring them to bear on any external targets."

"Well then," said Gesche with a wry smile. "It looks as though we're in a real shit sandwich. English commandos on either side and a Führer to protect."

"So it would appear," replied the flak officer with an equally wry grin. "What are your orders?"

Gesche glanced at his watch. 07:09. "It'll be dawn soon and that should even things up a bit. Except we won't be able to finesse our way out of this. There's no choice, but to push our way through the kill zone as quickly as possible and move back towards Montoire."

The Begleitkommando leader glanced around the gun platform, appraising the assembled flaktruppen, who were armed with Kar98s and pistols. "This is all you have by way of weapons? Nothing heavier? No MPs? Maybe a machine gun?"

"Sorry sir. The Flakvierling is our primary weapon. Aside from that, we only have side arms and rifles."

Gesche nodded. "Then that'll have to do. I want you to take your men far enough down the tunnel so there's enough room for every passenger to descend onto the tracks. Make sure you're not in the enemy's line of sight. Our only friend in this situation is the element of surprise, and I don't want the English to have any advance warning of our breakout."

The flak officer nodded.

"And leave me your best NCO."

"Feldwebel Kahler," said the Luftwaffe hauptman to a burly airman crouched on the other side of the platform. "You're with the Obersturmbannführer. Everyone else follow me."

The flaktruppen followed their officer over the gun platform bulkhead and down onto the tracks, where they cautiously advanced until the hauptman signalled a halt.

Observing that the flaktruppen were deploying per instructions, Gesche turned to Kahler. He was able to utter, "I want you to go forward ..." before a cacophony of small arms fire from the front of the train cut him off. Both men glanced momentarily toward the sound before returning to the business at hand. "I want you to go forward and send everyone you meet back to me here. Don't bother with the Begleitkommando, but keep going until there are no other passengers and then return yourself, keeping watch as rearguard. Move."

The NCO disappeared into the flakwagen crew compartment, just as the first passengers, two Wehrmacht colonels, arrived at Amerika's rear gun platform. Gesche directed them to take positions on the track between the flaktruppen and the train. A flow of people soon followed, quickly growing from trickle to a flood. From sixty-year-old jackbooted generals to young women clad in dressing gowns and slippers, they all clambered over the gun platform and down onto the track with greater or lesser ease. Gesche gazed upon the exodus with a cold indifference, until Reichsmarschall Hermann Göring and Reichsminister Joseph Goebbels appeared on the platform.

Efforts by the club-footed Nazi propaganda chief and morbidly obese Luftwaffe commander to negotiate a dignified descent ended badly, with both men in an ungainly sprawl on the tracks.

"That was a rough landing," japed an anonymous wag from among the onlooking Wehrmacht officers. "So high, yet now so low," jibed another unidentified satirist. A gale of malicious laughter swept through the throng, triggering an indignant glare from the corpulent Göring as he struggled to regain his footing.

Gesche shook his head in bemused contempt, but his mirth was cut short by the arrival of Hitler, with Himmler in tow.

"I apologise, Mein Führer," said Gesche, with a chastened expression on his face.

The now fully lucid Hitler glanced at the goings on below. "Well, he isn't known as 'der dicke' for nothing," quipped the Führer with a wry smile.

Gesche couldn't contain his laughter, which attracted an outraged glower from Göring that melted into pink-faced embarrassment at the sight of Hitler on the platform.

"Well let's get on with it, shall we?" Hitler instructed, and Gesche bestirred himself to assist his Fuhrer over the gun platform bulkhead. Himmler followed.

The flow of staff and passengers continued until, two minutes later, Feldwebel Kahler reappeared. "That's it, Herr Obersturmbannführer. I'm the last one, except for your Begleitkommando of course."

"Good work," said Gesche. He gazed down at the one hundred-odd people sandwiched between the rear of the train and the cordon of flaktruppen. They reminded him of a standing room crowd in a dingy theatre, their faces faintly illuminated by the dim light emanating from the flakwagen's crew quarters. Most were men attired in some variety of uniform, the sole exceptions being eight lachrymose female secretaries who clustered together, weeping tears of terror.

Gesche stood erect on the rear gun platform and tapped the barrel of his MP38 on the bulkhead to gain the crowd's attention. The cacophony of voices dwindled until only the muted sobbing of the secretaries could be heard.

"Meine Herren, here's the situation. We have a force of heavily armed enemy soldiers, probably English commandos, working their way along the train from the front. At our rear, they've established a close-to-perfect kill zone. So, there'll be no easy nor elegant way out of this."

Gesche paused for dramatic effect, ignoring the increased volume of secretarial keening generated by his words. "The plan is simple. We fight our way out of this rat trap and move back to Montoire. Surprise is our only friend and speed will be vital, so there can be no stopping to help the wounded. It will shortly be dawn, so you should be able to see. Just move like the wind and fire as you go. The flaktruppen will take the lead, followed by anyone else who is armed. The secretaries, those without weapons, the Führer and I will bring up the rear. Clear?"

Heads nodded, mostly among the flaktruppen and Wehrmacht officers. Majors, colonels and generals readied their sidearms for action, checking that magazines were correctly seated and chambering rounds.

Gesche tapped his MP38 barrel once again on the metal bulkhead to regain his audience's attention. "Meine Herren, the safety of our Führer is of paramount importance and we must all be prepared to die if that allows him to live."

Gesche raised an extended right arm to eye level. "Heil Hitler!"

"Heil Hitler!" chanted a chorus of male voices as a forest of rigid arms rose in the Hitlergruß.

"Khaler, you're with me," said Gesche, eliciting a nod from the NCO.

The two men clambered down from the flakwagen and set about chivvying the throng into a formation that complied with the obersturmbannführer's instructions.

178

Twenty-nine

From where Major Michael HarSinai was sitting, things were looking pretty good. The takedown of the signalman's house had been little short of flawless, with only one superficial wound incurred while sweeping the building. The bodies of the home's previous occupants, German signal troops, were now piled in an untidy heap outside the back door. The aftermath of the building's capture was almost equally one-sided, with the Israelis enjoying a veritable turkey shoot against German soldiers on the follow-on security train.

The train had been stopped dead in its tracks by a Gomed anti-tank missile that tore through the locomotive's steam box. Forty-five seconds later, a second Gomed destroyed the Panzer III turret atop the lead armoured railcar as its gun crew desperately sought targets in the gloom of night. The Führer-Begleit-Bataillon infantry fared little better as they poured out of the rail carriages where they had been dozing. Firing from windows on both storeys of the signalman's house, Mesulam's troopers exploited the 21st-century technologies of thermal-imaging and laser-sighting to wreak absolute havoc on their 20th-century foes. When fire from HarSinai's overwatch position on the ridge was added to the mix, a decimation of the German soldiery ensued.

The autumnal dawn creeping across central France revealed the full extent of the butchers' bill for the night. Over one hundred fallen Germans lay strewn around the escort train, some inert in death and others writhing in pain. Survivors, rendered leaderless after the careful culling of officers and NCOs by Sheetrit's sniper rifle, sought refuge in a cemetery two hundred metres south of the signalman's house. There they remained, huddled behind tombstones, afraid to move after Sheetrit achieved first-round headshots against two of the more adventurous among their number.

But this calm was suddenly disturbed by the distinctive sound of 5.56 mm fire. The gunfire was closely followed by a report over the Team Three network from a trooper stationed on the ground floor of the signalman's house

179

"We have movement in the tunnel. They're making a mad dash for it. Lots of them!"

The Israelis responded with characteristic initiative, marching immediately towards the sound of the guns in conformity with the IDF doctrine of 'Hatirah le Magah' – striving for contact. HarSinai watched from the ridge above as Meshulam emerged from the signalman's house at the head of a half-dozen troopers. The oncoming German mob was roughly 150 metres distant and closing fast. Meshulam raised his X95 and fired, dropping a pistol-wielding German before moving on to another target. The steep earthen banks of the railroad cut funnelled the fleeing Germans into a compact mass of humanity that was impossible to miss. Within fifteen seconds, he emptied his thirty-round magazine, killing or wounding over a dozen of the enemy.

"Guys!" shouted Meshulam as he reached for a new magazine. "Everyone downstairs and out the front door! I want you prone facing the tunnel! Don't let any of them pass!"

"Can I help from up top?" radioed HarSinai from his overwatch element's position.

"Negative, negative," came Meshulam's voice through HarSinai's PRC710 headset. "Hold your fire. Too much danger of a blue-on-blue from ricochets and fragments. How copy?"

"Mishneh, good copy," replied HarSinai. "We're holding fire."

There was no response forthcoming from Meshulam as the Team Three commander was busy positioning his troopers in a line formation. HarSinai watched as the Israelis commenced a withering fusillade that brought the attempted break-out to a halt under the sheer weight of its fire. A single pair of hands went up, triggering a Mexican wave of surrender gestures that swept through the dwindling ranks of still-ambulatory Germans. The gale of Israeli gunfire dwindled into silence as enemy pistols and rifles were cast on the ground.

Meshulam's troopers looked askance at their commander, who keyed the transmit button of his PRC710. "Mishneh Kodkod, this is Three Aleph, we've taken out many of them, but the survivors have raised their hands and surrendered. Request instructions."

"This is Mishneh," came Michael HarSinai's distinctive bass voice of over the team network. "Nicely done. Can you verify whether Target Agag is among the living?"

180

"Not from my current position," replied Meshulam. "Should I inform Kodkod Vengeance on the tactical net?"

"Negative," responded HarSinai. "I'm coming down and will be there in two. Wait for my arrival, out."

"Team Three be advised," broadcast Meshulam, "Mishneh Kodkod is on his way down from the ridge."

HarSinai emerged from the trees followed by his RTO and beckoned for Meshulam to approach. "Okay, let's have a closer look, but be extra careful. These are murderous bastards."

Meshulam turned to address his men, who had kept their weapons trained on the enemy throng. "Okay guys, you heard the word. Gabi, you take Sasson, Goldwasser and Kaplinsky to the left. I want you up on the embankment. Tzipori, you stay with Rafi and give me an update on his wound. The rest are with me on the right. Keep your weapons up and ready to fire. Drop anyone who poses a threat. Let's move."

The Israelis deployed per instructions, as HarSinai emerged from the tree line.

The crack of Sheetrit's Dan sniper rifle sounded from the slope above, followed by the thump of the MK47 as Team Three's overwatch element kept the Germans in the cemetery pinned.

HarSinai motioned for Meshulam to join him and the two Israeli officers strode into the railroad cut, stepping over bodies as they approached the gaggle of German survivors.

"Separate them into two groups," ordered HarSinai. "I want the HVTs and officers with the rank of general or above on their knees in a row over here," he said with a wave to the right. "Everyone else I want over there." HarSinai canted his head to the left.

Meshulam's perplexity at these instructions was written across his face. "What is it?" HarSinai asked.

"A word in private would be good," said Meshulam.

HarSinai shrugged and strode out of immediate earshot from the other Israeli troopers who were busy chivvying the Germans into two separate groups.

"Well?"

"I don't know what you're doing here," remonstrated Meshulam. "We're supposed to wipe them out and leave. There's nothing about an ... exhibition like this in the ops plan."

"Correct," replied HarSinai. "This is an unforeseen situation to which I'm adapting. Has it been that long since Bahad Echad? Have you forgotten the principle that every plan is a basis for change?"

"I haven't forgotten anything," snapped Meshulam. "I just think this is putting us all in unnecessary danger."

"What about Dvir and his assaulters? barked HarSinai. "They're still working their way through the tunnel. We need to wait for them before packing it in."

Meshulam shrugged. "Better to do that from cover in the signalman's house than out here exposed in the open. And I still think you should give Yossi a sit-rep before making any move."

HarSinai flashed a conciliatory smile. "Meshulam, relax. Everything's under control. The snipers, MK47 and machine guns on overwatch have our back. Think of this as a unique opportunity to send a message these bastards will never forget. We have a chance to demonstrate that their friggin' Führer was killed by none other than Jewish soldiers. It'll be over before you know it. Now, let's go and have a look at these assholes."

With that, HarSinai turned on his heel and strode back to the prisoners, leaving Meshulam little choice but to follow.

HarSinai approached the row of high-value targets, unsnapping his helmet chinstrap as he walked. A scruffy Joseph Goebbels stared in slack-jawed amazement at the sight of a knitted kippa perched atop the head of this face-painted futuristic warrior.

"Sie sind ein Jude?" uttered Goebbels in disbelief. "Unmöglich! Kann es nicht sein. Ein Jude?"

"Yah, Yoodeh," replied HarSinai, thus exhausting his command of the German language. He turned to address Kaplinsky. "I see Hitler, Himmler, Bormann, that little shit Goebbels, Jodl, Keitel and Raeder ... Göring, where's Göring?"

"Back there," said a grinning Kaplinski with a callous thumb-over-the-shoulder gesture. "Guess he was too big to miss."

Those Israelis within earshot erupted in laughter.

HarSinai briefly glanced at the rotund body of the fallen Göring, whose white uniform tunic was splotched with red stained bullet holes. He turned back to face his prisoners, switching to Israeli-accented King's own. "Who here speaks English?"

Three hesitant hands were raised among the non-high-value target group. HarSinai beckoned to a lanky man dressed in the dark blue uniform of a naval officer. "You ... come here."

The German got to his feet and came forward, nursing a bleeding left arm.

"What's your name?"

"Alois Hutmacher, Korvettenkapitän, Kreigsmarine. German navy."

"Listen to me very carefully, Korvettenkapitän Hutmacher. Your job is to translate what I say with word-for-word accuracy. By that, I mean one hundred per cent. It's also essential that you speak loudly enough so that everyone can hear. Do this and no harm will come to you. Clear?"

Hutmacher nodded. "But please, one of the women is seriously wounded. Will you do the decent thing and provide her with medical attention?"

"You arrogant bastard," barked HarSinai. "You dare talk to me about decency after the way the Germans have treated my people?"

"Not all of us are Nazis," replied Hutmacher in quiet voice.

"That didn't stop you from swearing allegiance to that turd over there," said HarSinai, gesturing contemptuously with his thumb towards Hitler.

Hutmacher just stood there, mute.

"Kus Emak," swore HarSinai with a disgusted shake of the head. He walked over to the cluster of frightened secretaries huddled among the lower-ranking prisoners. Three of the women were tending to another of their number who was bleeding from a bullet wound to her right thorax. A hissing sound emanated from her chest with every laboured breath.

"Tzipori!" HarSinai shouted to the team medic, who was treating the wounded Israeli on the stoop of the signalman's house. "How's Rafi?"

"Nothing serious," yelled the medic in reply. "Bullet grazed his shoulder. All under control."

"Then get over here. We have a female in her twenties with what looks like a sucking chest wound. See what you can do for her."

The medic gave Rafi a fraternal pat on the helmet and trotted over to the railroad cut, where he shooed aside the ministering women and cut open the stricken girl's blouse. Shucking off his backpack, Tzipori extracted a non-occlusive bandage and applied it to the wound. As her breathing eased, he began to prep the young woman's arm for an IV of saline solution.

Leaving the medic to his labours, HarSinai turned back to Hutmacher. "Okay, she's being treated. Now you and I have unfinished business."

183

HarSinai motioned for the German naval officer to accompany him back to the genuflecting high-value targets, stopping in front of the Reichsführer-SS.

"Remember, I want word-for-word translation."

"Yes, I understand. Word for word," echoed Hutmacher.

"Heinrich Himmler," announced HarSinai in a loud voice, "you are guilty of crimes against the Jewish people and the world's civilised nations. The punishment is death."

HarSinai looked expectantly at Hutmacher who, after a momentary hesitation, began to parrot the Israeli's words.

"Heinrich Himmler, Sie sind schuldig ..."

"Louder!" yelled HarSinai.

"Heinrich Himmler," shouted Hutmacher, "sie sind schuldig Verbrechen gegen das Jüdische Volk und den zivilisierten Nationen der Welt. Die Strafe ist der Tod."

Himmler looked on with dazed incomprehension, as if he were a disinterested third-party observer watching tragedy about to strike someone else. He remained strangely frozen as this strange spectre standing over him unholstered a pistol and brought its bore to bear.

Without further ceremony, HarSinai fired into the kneeling Himmler's forehead. The point-blank impact of a single heavy .45 calibre round was enough to cast the Reichsführer SS backward on his heels in a welter of blood, skull fragments and brain matter.

The secretaries renewed their weeping, this time accompanied by muffled sobbing from some of the terrified orderlies and cooks.

"Goebbels next," HarSinai instructed tersely as he strode over to face the Minister for Propaganda. "Same drill."

Hutmacher gulped. "Joseph Goebbels, sie sind schuldig, Verbrechen gegen das Jüdische Volk und den zivilisierten Nationen der Welt. Die Strafe ist der Tod."

"Nein, nein!" shrieked a panic-stricken Goebbels, raising his hands in supplication. "Bitte, meine Frau ist schwanger und wird jetzt jeden tag die Geburt erleben!"

"What was that?" asked HarSinai.

"He says his wife is about to give birth," reported Hutmacher.

"Tell him he should have thought about that before becoming such an asshole," replied HarSinai with a peremptory shake of the head.

"Sie hätten sich das überlegen müssen bevor Sei so ein Arschloch wurden."

"Nein!" pleaded Goebbels, his hands clasped before his face in a gesture of prayer. "Ich war es nicht, es war ..."

The Minister of Propaganda's lamentation was cut short by two .45 calibre bullets to the chest.

HarSinai noticed the glare being cast his way by the visibly fuming Hitler. Stepping over to stand directly in front of the kneeling Führer, he gazed down into the tyrant's face with a contemptuous smile. "Don't worry Schicklgruber, I'm leaving you for last," he said, glancing at Hutmacher as a cue for the German officer to translate.

"Mein Führer, er sagt sie warden der letzte sein."

Hitler struggled to his feet, his pyjama pants wet from the morning dew. The dictator puffed out his chest, pulling himself up to his full 1.76 metres Taking a deep breath, he spat in HarSinai's face, flashing a defiant grin at the sight of his sputum lodged on the Israeli's right cheek.

Slowly and deliberately, HarSinai wiped his face clean. Then, with the explosive speed of an accomplished Krav Maga fighter, he delivered a savage elbow strike to Hitler's jaw. Knocked unconscious, the dictator crumpled onto the track, eliciting a gasp of horrified astonishment from the Germans for whom the sight of their Führer enduring such indignity was unimaginable.

From the corner of his eye, HarSinai caught a flash of movement. He swivelled his head just in time to see a tall blonde man in his thirties draw a small pistol from a hidden calf-holster and jam the weapon's muzzle into Tzipori's temple.

The hostage-taker began bellowing in German, and HarSinai cast an inquisitive glance at Hutmacher. "Who is he and what's he saying?"

"His name is Gesche. He commands the Führer's personal guard. He's demanding that the Führer be allowed to go free."

HarSinai slowly returned his pistol to its holster, slowly raising both hands, palms outwards, in a 'just relax' gesture, pivoting slightly to the right so that the side of his head was hidden from Gesche's view. Discreetly keying the transmit button on his PRC710 headset, he said, "Sheetrit, do you have an angle?"

"Another twenty seconds," came the sniper's response over the team network.

"Tell him he's free to take Schicklgruber and go," HarSinai instructed Hutmacher.

"Sie sind frei und können den Führer mitnehmen," yelled Hutmacher.

Gesche began to advance towards the still unconscious Hitler, pushing Tzipori ahead of him as a human shield. But before he took his third step, the booming report of Sheetrit's unsuppressed Dan rifle echoed through the railroad cut. The 250 grain Lapua bullet ripped through the obersturmbannführer's skull, exiting from the back of his neck via the third and fourth cervical vertebrae.

Gesche collapsed like a marionette with severed strings, and Tzipori had the presence of mind to scoop up the little Sauer 38H the SS officer had been wielding.

An explosion suddenly reverberated from within the tunnel, followed by a staccato volley of small arms fire that sounded much closer than the muffled echoes the Israelis had previously heard.

"Dvir's team," HarSinai observed. "They're getting close. That means it's time to tidy up. So, who's next?"

The Israeli major did a quick count of the senior Nazis – fourteen remaining. He nodded towards a mustachioed army officer bearing Generalfeldmarschall insignia on his shoulder epaulets. "Keitel, you'll do for a start. Then Jodl, Bormann and Raeder. Too bad Doenitz isn't here as well."

HarSinai inserted a fresh magazine in his Jericho PSL pistol and set about completing the job at hand.

Thirty

"Scheisse!" muttered Oberleutnant Siegfried Franzman as he gazed northwards through his binoculars from his 88 mm flak batterie's position at Fosse Poudrière on the bluffs overlooking Montoire. It was less than an hour since he'd been pulled from slumber into wakefulness by the sounds of small arms fire and the explosive booms echoing across the valley. Pulling on his boots, he'd rushed to the battery command post in hope of finding out what the hell was going on. But all he'd been able to see in the early morning darkness were flashes of exploding ordinance and concatenations of bright red tracer rounds whipping across the sky. The uninterrupted line of sight he enjoyed northwards all the way to Saint-Rimay did nothing to help him make sense of unfolding events.

Nor did the advent of dawn bring clarity to his situational awareness. Beams of cold grey light peeking through an overcast autumn morning sky allowed him to see the smouldering escort train through his Zeiss BLC 7x50 field glasses. Yet, at 5,200 metres range, it remained impossible to distinguish between friend and foe.

The field telephone rang at battery fire direction centre and the signals NCO raised the handset above his head to signify the call was for his battery commander. Striding back to the communications desk, the oberleutnant raised the telephone to his ear.

"Flak Batterie 331, Franzman here."

"This is Oberstleutant Papp, 247th Signals Battalion in Montoire," came a nervous sounding voice through the handset. "I've had three soldiers from the Führer-Begleit-Bataillon show up at my hauptquartier with a report that the Führer's train has been ambushed. They say most of their comrades in the escort force have been killed. We've heard the sounds of firing from the North, but there are trees blocking our field of vision. Do you have any idea what's happening?"

"Barely," replied Franzman. "The follow-on escort train has been destroyed, that much I can clearly see. It's on fire and there are bodies all

187

around. I can also see people moving, but at this range I can't tell whether they're ours or the enemy."

"Can you hit them?" asked Papp.

"Say again?"

"Do your guns have the range to hit those people?" Papp repeated.

"Yes, of course," Franzman responded. "It's well within the capability of my 88s. But, as I told you before, from a distance of over five thousand metres I won't know who is friend and who is foe."

"Can you see Amerika? Is the Führer's train visible?"

"No, only the escort train, and it's on fire."

"That must mean the Führer is within the tunnel and the people you see are the enemy," said Papp in a definitive tone.

"I'm not so sure … "

"Hauptman Franzman," interjected Papp, "I'm the senior officer in this location and I'm giving you a direct order. I want you to open fire on those people. In the meantime, I've already notified Armee Oberkommando that the Führer is in trouble. I'll bring them up-to-date with your new information."

"It's Oberleutnant, actually," replied Franzman acidly. "And as you wish. But I'm formally noting, and there are witnesses here listening at my end, that the formal responsibility for this decision is yours."

"Yes, yes," replied Papp. "How soon can you open fire?"

"Within less than three minutes."

Franzman hung up the field telephone and walked over to the map table. "This is madness," he announced to nobody in particular. Using a military protractor, he measured the coordinates of the target area – the western mouth of the Saint-Rimay tunnel. Next, he stepped over to the battery's EM36 coincidence rangefinder, a one-metre-long tube with lenses either end. Looking through the eyepiece, he twirled the dial until the two images of the tunnel entrance were stereoscopically superimposed on one another. A glance at the range window showed 5,270 metres. Franzman strode back to the fire direction centre and picked up another field telephone, this one labelled "Batterie".

Cranking the handle, he waited until all of his gun captains were on the line. "Prepare to receive fire order." Pausing thirty seconds, he then continued, "Fire order, ground target, coordinates 343975 by 529255, azimuth 657 mils, range 5,270 metres, infantry in the open, high explosive, report when ready."

One by one, the barrels of the four 88s were depressed from anti-aircraft mode to ground target mode. The clank of shells being shoved into gun breeches could be heard as the crews scurried like worker ants around their weapons.

Within two minutes, all four gun captains stood with a red signal flag in hand, marking their readiness to fire.

"Number One alone will fire for adjustment," instructed Franzman. "Numbers Two, Three and Four will adjust accordingly once One is on target. Number One, ready?"

"Number One is ready to fire," came a gruff voice through the field telephone handset.

"Fire!" ordered Franzman and the distinctive bark of the 88 mm gun sounded over the roofs of Montoire-sur-le-Loir.

Thirty-one

The memoirs of any Allied infantryman who fought in Europe during WWII will tell you that the worst thing about being on the receiving end of an 88 was a complete lack of warning. A muzzle velocity over twice the speed of sound meant that an 88's shell arrived on target well before the sound of its firing was heard. Therefore, the Israelis had no advance notice when, over the space of an instant, their situation went to absolute shit. The first 88 mm shell arrived out of nowhere to explode against the concrete upper arch of the tunnel entrance. A spray of shrapnel and cement fragments wrought bloody havoc within the railroad cut among captors and captives alike.

"Kus Emak!" cursed Meshulam. He could see that HarSinai and Kaplinsky were both down. Of the high-value targets, only Hitler, Bormann and von Rundstedt were still alive by virtue of the fact that HarSinai had not yet reached their place in the queue. The junior-ranked German prisoners also suffered casualties from the incoming 88.

"Everyone back to the house!" yelled Meshulam as he raised his X95 and fired carefully aimed shots into the heads of the three remaining senior Nazis.

Meshulam ran over to HarSinai, hoisting the wounded officer on his shoulders in a fireman's carry. He turned to Hutmacher, waving his hand towards the non-high-value target German prisoners. "You can all go."

Meshulam then set out at a trot towards the signalman's house. The other Israelis were already within, having brought along the stricken Kaplinsky as a matter of course. No specific order to that effect was necessary because 'no man left behind' principle was an article of faith throughout the IDF.

"Wir sind frei zu gehen. Lauf um dein Leben!" shouted Hutmacher, triggering a mad rush as the surviving Germans scattered in search of safe haven.

Those who bolted eastwards were engulfed almost immediately by the concealing embrace of an adjacent wood. But those who chose to escape westwards suffered a much grimmer fate, attracting the notice of Oberleutnant Franzman as they stampeded in panic through an open field.

A well-trained 88 mm gun crew could fire fifteen rounds per minute – roughly one shell every four seconds. Hence, the hail of shellfire from the four-gun battery inflicted terrible punishment on the fleeing Germans.

Meshulam watched the slaughter with grim dispassion from the doorway of the signalman's house, until his RTO tapped him on the shoulder. "It's Dvir on the tactical net. They're done with the tunnel."

The captain turned and accepted the proffered PRC9000 handset. "One, this is Three, how copy?"

"This is One, good copy," replied Dvir. "Other than a few stay behinds, the tunnel was a dry hole. They must have tried to break out at your end. Did you take care of Agag?"

"Affirmative," said Meshulam. "They made a dash for it at our end, but we caught them in the railroad cut. You should be able to see the bodies from the tunnel entrance."

The bass voice of Yossi Klein suddenly materialised through the handset. "This is Kodkod Vengeance, can you confirm that Agag has been neutralised?"

"Kodkod, this is Three, I think so. He's lying in the railroad cut. I put two rounds into his head, but we were under artillery fire and had no opportunity to confirm the kill."

"This is Kodkod. 'I think so' isn't confirmation. I need absolute verification, otherwise, what are we doing here?"

"Kodkod, this is One," said Tzachi Dvir, "we're about to exit the tunnel through the cut. That'll put me into a position to confirm the kill on Agag."

"Very well," replied Klein. "But I want absolute certainty: one-hundred-and-one per cent. I want to hear that you saw brains, copy?"

"This is One, copy that you want brains. Three, what's the situation outside?"

"Be advised we've been taking artillery fire," replied Meshulam. "Get your people into the house with us quickly."

"Will do, but we have one harduf and three prachim" – the IDF radio procedure code words for KIA and WIA, respectively. "That will slow us down a bit," replied Dvir.

"This is Three, I copy that you'll be carrying casualties," said Meshulam. "When you come through, note that Agag is wearing blue pyjamas."

"Blue pyjamas?" echoed Dvir with an incredulous laugh. "You're joking."

"Dead serious, tartei mashma," replied Meshulam, using the Aramaic-derived Hebrew expression meaning 'in both senses of the term'. "You'll see him on the track about halfway down the cut. How copy?"

"This is One, good copy. We move in two mikes."

From the second floor of the signalman's house, Meshulam watched as Dvir and his Team One assaulters emerged from the tunnel mouth at a trot, carrying their casualties with them. "Kodkod One, this is Kodkod Three," he radioed, "the body in light blue thirty metres to your 12 o'clock."

"Copy light blue," replied Dvir, who paused to fire three rounds into the blue-clad body before sprinting to catch up with his teammates.

"He was already dead," Dvir reported as Meshulam descended via the stairs from the upper storey.

"Then he won't complain about another few holes in his head," replied Meshulam.

"More's the pity," said Dvir as he turned to his RTO, who approached with PRC9000 handset extended.

"Kodkod Vengeance, this is Kodkod One."

"This is Kodkod Vengeance," came the voice of Klein over the tactical net.

"This is One. The deed is done. Three rounds to the head. I saw brains."

"Well done," replied Klein. "Congratulations. Now give me a casualty count. What's your sit-rep?"

Dvir transferred the handset to Meshulam.

"This is Three, wait, over."

Meshulam approached the corner of the room where the medics were treating shrapnel wounds inflicted by the now-silent German 88s. "What do we have?"

Tzipori looked up his surgical gloves red with blood. "HarSinai is gone. In terms of wounded, we have five light and one moderate. I've stabilised the moderate. Two of the light wounds are in the lower limbs and will require assistance to move." The medic returned to his lifesaving labours.

Meshulam beckoned to his RTO. "Kodkod, this is Two. Mishneh Kodkod is harduf. In addition, between my team and Dvir's, we count another two hardufim and six prachim so far. Five light and one moderate. But I haven't been able to contact the overwatch element up the hill, so the casualty count is likely to increase, over"

"That fucking artillery?" asked Klein, the radio handset faithfully reproducing his embittered tone of voice.

"Affirmative," replied Meshulam. "We established complete fire dominance over the follow-on escort element, so it wasn't small arms. I'll update you when I reach their position."

"Copy that. Vengeance stations, this is Kodkod. Agag is down. I repeat Agag is down. We're now moving into the exfi … wait, wait, out."

The tactical net fell silent for half a minute until Klein's voice again was heard through the handset.

"Vengeance stations, this is Kodkod. All teams remain stationary and under cover. I repeat, all teams remain stationary under cover. We have imminent incoming enemy air and are deploying the Stingers. Out."

Thirty-two

Hauptman Sebastian Tanzer had only the vaguest idea where he was going, and was entirely clueless about what to do when he got there. He'd spent most of yesterday afternoon in the cockpit flying air cover over the conference with the Vichy leadership in Montoire. Then, just as the first light of dawn was breaking, he'd been roused from his slumber by a panicky stabsfeldwebel bearing a vague report that the Führer's train was under attack.

Half-dressed and unshaven, Tanzer stumbled into the Châteaudun airbase operations centre in pursuit of further clarification. But the frazzled oberstleutnant in command of the base did not take kindly to the young pilot's request for situational enlightenment.

"Your target area is the railroad tunnel here, three kilometres north of Montoire," said the oberstleutnant, his index finger pointing out Saint-Rimay on the map. "You're to take off immediately."

"What weapons will my aircraft be carrying? Do we know anything about the enemy?" asked Tanzer. "What about the location of the Führer? And what if I hit him by mistake?"

"You'll be armed with cannon and machine guns only. I've been explicitly informed that the Führer's train is safe within the tunnel," replied the oberstleutnant in a rising tone of annoyance. "Therefore, you're free to regard anyone you see in the target area as hostile."

Tanzer pondered these instructions for several moments. "I'd like those orders in writing please."

The base commander scowled indignantly at the impertinence of the young pilot. "This is direct from Luftflotte hauptquartier in Paris. In fact, it's straight from the mouth of Generalfeldmarschall Sperle who telephoned me less than twenty minutes ago."

Tanzer nodded. "That's all very impressive, but I'll still be needing written orders if you please."

The oberstleutnant's face turned beet red with vexation as he grabbed a piece of paper and inscribed a few furious lines.

The oberstleutnant thrust the foolscap in Tanzer's face in a gesture of unspoken belligerence.

The 24-year-old ace accepted possession of the paper with a dignified air, glanced briefly at its contents, and placed it in his tunic pocket. Tanzer then came to attention and delivered a parade-ground worthy salute. "Thank you, sir."

The oberstleutnant returned the courtesy, his anger somewhat mollified by Tanzer's display of deference. He glanced at his watch. "Get your schwärm of Emils airborne. A flight of Ju-88s is being armed and fuelled and should be ready to go within the hour. I'm also dispatching a company of flaktruppen to the area by road."

So at 07:44 hours local, Tanzer found himself leading a flight of four Me-109Es climbing southwestwards into a clear autumn morning sky. Beneath his port wing, he saw the glistening ribbon of the Loir snaking its way through the verdant French countryside like the coils of a giant silver serpent.

"Going level at 2,000 metres altitude," Tanzer transmitted to his three wingmen. Glancing behind him, he saw the other three 109s were maintaining formation. A moderately sized city soon appeared on their left, nestled along the bank of the Loir.

"That's Vendôme at my 10 o'clock," Tanzer transmitted. "Two minutes to the target area. We'll do a north-south pass at 1,000 metres directly over the tunnel to orient ourselves. Report anything relevant and I'll allocate targets as needed. Clear?"

His three wingmen affirmed receipt and comprehension of Tanzer's instructions.

"Begin descent now to 1,000 metres AGL. Stay in formation, and keep your eyes open."

Tanzer banked left and began a shallow dive. The first thing he noticed was a train stopped dead on the tracks several hundred metres north of the tunnel. He recognised it from yesterday's over-flights as one of the two escort trains that protected the Führer on his travels. A closer look revealed that the tank turret atop the lead railcar had been ripped open. Dead bodies lay scattered along the track.

A similar scene revealed itself on the far side of the tunnel ridge. The second escort train was even more badly damaged, with what remained of the turret resting upside down on the ground and two of its three passenger carriages alight.

Then, without warning, the formation's number two just exploded. Tanzer struggled with the controls against the shockwave that threatened to send his 109 inverted. Regaining control of the aircraft, he yelled "Break left!" into his throat mike, while slamming over the stick and stomping the rudder pedal.

Tanzer's eyes traversed the sky in search of the enemy fighters that were doubtless circling for another pass. "Does anyone see them? Where are they?"

"Nothing," said number three.

"Can't see anyth ..." was all number four was able to enunciate before he disintegrated in another violent ball of flame.

"Sheisse!" swore Tanzer. Altitude, he thought. I need altitude! Shoving the throttle forward, he hauled the stick back into his stomach and his 109 pitched upwards into a sharp climb. Swivelling his head from side to side, he searched desperately for a glimpse of his elusive assailants. But he never even saw the FIM92 Stinger missile streaking upwards from his four o'clock low.

The exhaust manifold of the 109's Daimler-Benz 601A1 engine generated more than enough heat to trigger interest from the Stinger's infra-red seeker. Like a bloodhound on the trail of a rabbit, the missile faithfully stalked every move of the German fighter, ultimately detonating against the right engine cowling. The annular blast fragmentation warhead propelled myriad shards of red-hot metal at supersonic speed, shearing off the aircraft's left wing and punching through the cockpit canopy into Tanzer's head. Death was instantaneous, a small mercy that spared him the helpless terror of being pinned in his seat by g-forces as he gyrated earthwards like a maple samara.

Thirty-three

"I'm telling you I saw it with my own eyes. They simply exploded in mid-air," expostulated Oberstleutnant Papp into the telephone. "All four of them. There were no enemy aircraft to be seen."

"Stand by," said the voice at the other end of the line.

A few seconds of silence ensued, before Papp heard someone new through his handset.

"This is Generalmajor Warlimont, Deputy Chief of Operations, Oberkommando der Wehrmacht. With whom am I speaking?"

"Oberstleutnant Helmut Papp, commanding the 247th Signals Battalion in Montoire, sir. We were posted here to provide communications support for the Führer during his conference with the Vichy French."

"Very well Papp, I need a situation report."

"Certainly sir," Papp replied. "At around 06:15 this morning, Amerika departed Montoire accompanied by two escort trains from the Führer-Begleit-Bataillon. Shortly afterward, intense firing erupted from the vicinity of the Saint-Rimay tunnel located three kilometres north of my location along the rail line travelled by the Führer's train. It was still dark at the time and our line of sight was blocked by trees, but we could see tracers and explosions from the tunnel area."

"What can you tell me about the Führer?"

"Nothing definitive, sir," replied Papp. "I've spoken to several wounded Begleit-Bataillon troops who managed to make their way back to Montoire. They tell of a very well-executed enemy ambush that has decimated their unit, but have no definitive information about the Führer, other than Amerika managed to reach the rail tunnel. So, I'm assuming he's safe."

"You're assuming?" echoed Warlimont, with a sarcasm-laden tone that was palpable even over 200 kilometres of copper telephone cable. "Beyond making assumptions that may or may not be correct, what other action have you taken?"

"Well sir, I immediately notified Armee Oberkommando hauptquartier in Fontainbleau that the Führer was under attack," Papp replied. "And, once it we had sufficient daylight, I ordered the 88 flakbatterie located on a hill above Montoire to open fire on the enemy. Around ten minutes ago, a flight of 109s flew over the area, but all four aircraft were blown out of the sky before they could take any action. We don't know precisely what happened, but none of my men spotted Spitfires."

"What else?"

Papp paused before responding with a note of respectful perplexity. "I'm not sure I understand, sir."

"Besides reporting to higher hauptquartier, activating the flakbatterie and summoning air cover, what else have you done? As a battalion commander, you have several hundred men under your direct control. It's now more than one hour after the assault on the Führer began and you've been in daylight for the past forty-five minutes. Why haven't you organised a counterattack? Where's your sense of initiative?"

"I ... I thought the appropriate place for me was here ... to coordinate and ..."

"Wrong answer," interjected Warlimont. "Papp, you are hereby relieved. Put your second-in-command on the telephone."

"But ..."

"Oberstleutnant," said the now audibly angry Warlimont, "let me clarify your situation. You've been relieved of your command and I have yet to decide whether you should face a court martial for dereliction of duty and cowardice in the face of the enemy. In fact, I'm half-inclined to order your summary execution by firing squad. So, the best thing you can do is slink off into a corner where I just might forget you ever existed. Am I clear?"

Papp meekly handed the telephone over to his deputy and walked out of the room without a word.

"This is Major Weiss."

"Weiss, this is Generalmajor Warlimont, OKW Deputy Chief of Operations, speaking from General von Stülpnagel's hauptquartier in Paris. Oberstleutnant Papp has been relieved and you now have command of the battalion. Do you understand?"

"Yes sir," Weiss replied in a tone that could not hide his bewilderment.

"I've been on an inspection tour of France and Belgium and have a Ju52 at Orly. I'll fly immediately to Châteaudun where a Storch will transport me on the final leg to Montoire. I should be there in around the hour, so you'll need to find a place in the vicinity of the tunnel where the Storch can land."

"Will do, sir," replied Weiss.

"In the meantime, your battalion will move to establish a cordon sanitaire around the entire tunnel area. By that, I mean a 360-degree perimeter that hermetically isolates the area. Your men should be deployed at a distance of at least two hundred metres from the Führer's train. No-one is to get in or out. No-one, is that clear?"

"Yes, sir," replied Weiss. "But what about survivors? Some may be in need of medical attention."

"All survivors are to be sequestered under guard until I arrive," said Warlimont. "Your battalion has a medical officer, doesn't it?"

"Yes, sir."

"He and his orderlies will be quarantined with the wounded. Just make sure he has all the medical supplies that are required. Do you have any questions?"

"No, Herr General," replied Weiss.

"Then I'll see you in about an hour."

"Jawohl, Herr General." Weiss lowered the phone and turned to the battalion operations officer, a bespectacled oberleutnant. "Saller, I want the entire battalion assembled under arms and ready to deploy in fifteen minutes."

"Everyone, sir?" asked Saller.

"Leave one platoon to guard the communications equipment. Aside from that, I want every last able-bodied man ready to go. We'll need the MG34s as well. Notify the motor pool to have every truck and kübelwagen up and running with drivers at the wheel. Then summon all company officers for a briefing here in five minutes. Move."

And move Saller did, racing out of his battalion commander's office, shouting orders as he went.

Thirty-four

"Yossi, it's Azriel for you," reported Levinson, proffering the handset attached to the PRC9000 he bore on his back.

"This is Kodkod, go."

"Kodkod, this is Two," came Weinstock's distinctive French-accented voice. "Incoming your position, Eye contact in two."

"Kodkod copies in two," confirmed Klein. He turned to address the soldiers in his command group. "Azriel and Team Two are about to arrive. Let's fold the netting and get the vehicles ready to move."

The troopers swarmed all over nine S-ATVs and set about the task of stripping the camouflage nets of their attached foliage, rolling up and stowing them in their appointed places. In the spirit of the IDF's sacrosanct principle of leadership by personal example, Klein leant his hand to the task.

They were halfway through the task of prepping the vehicles for movement when Weinstock emerged from amongst the trees, breathless and sweaty from the steep ascent up the ridge. The Francophone captain approached the S-ATV whose netting Klein was busily folding.

"Yossi, can I have a word?"

"Well done," said Klein, turning to face Weinstock and administering a congratulatory clap on the shoulder. "Outstanding execution with zero cas ..."

He paused in mid-sentence at the sight of an attractive young woman trudging up the hill bearing a large duffel bag. Walking directly behind her was Shlomo Blumfeld with a small child perched atop his shoulders. Klein's eyebrows arched. "What's all this?"

"What I wanted to discuss," replied Weinstock. "Her name is Danielle Morency and that's Adele, her daughter. They live in the house we used as our base of fire. They're also of our people and you can imagine what the Germans would make of that coincidence. Saving Jewish lives is the object of this entire mission, so I decided to start here and now. Leaving a Jewish

200

family to face the wrath of the Gestapo simply wasn't an option in my view."

Klein graced Danielle with a friendly smile. "Bienvenue, madame."

"Merci, mon Colonel," replied Danielle.

Klein turned back to face Weinstock. "I'm not going to criticise your judgement, although I'm also not sure we can take them with us the entire way. That depends on what our mad professors say about the temporal implications. But you made the right decision to get them out of immediate danger. Well done."

"Thank you," said Weinstock.

Klein reciprocated with a nod. "Put them on your vehicle and we'll talk to the professors when we get back to Open Window. In the meantime, we have to move." He stepped up onto the seat of his Oshkosh and bellowed, "Movement in exactly three minutes, so finish up and take your places."

Once all the camouflage nets were stowed and crew-served weapons reattached to their pintle-mounts, the troopers boarded their vehicles and the S-ATVs emerged from the tree line. They quickly settled into a column formation with Klein's Oshkosh in the lead

"Three, this is Kodkod," said Klein into his PRC9000 handset. "We're on the move and will be at your location momentarily. What's your status, over?"

"Three is loaded and ready to move," replied Meshulam from the South side of the ridge. "One is awaiting your arrival with its vehicles."

"This is Kodkod. Good copy," replied Klein.

"Kodkod, this is Four," came Farkash over the tactical network from Open Window, the mission's forward staging base at la Hubardière. "Be advised, UAV shows a large enemy force moving in your direction from Viola" – the mission code name for Vendôme. "I can see on screen twenty motorcycle sidecar combos with machine guns and two armoured cars. Looks like the same unit that passed us by earlier."

Klein gestured for Horman to hit the brakes and the column came to a halt. "Kodkod, good copy. Give me precise location and ETA while I have a look on the Ness."

"Lead elements have just crossed the Litani over the central bridge at Viola and are now passing reference marker 237 on Route Churchill, travelling west. ETA your location fifteen minutes max, maybe sooner."

"Kodkod, good copy," replied Klein, as he felt unseen hands open the rear upper pouch on his tactical vest. Turning his head, he saw the Ness TSG Tactical C4I system proffered by Levinson. Klein nodded in silent thanks and switched on the device. He glanced at the battery indicator. Sixty-four per cent. Good for another couple of hours.

The live feed from the circling UAV showed the enemy formation advancing apace, ten pairs of motorcycle-sidecar combos in the van followed by two eight-wheeler armoured cars. He reached for the PRC9000 handset.

"Vengeance stations, this is Kodkod, change of plan. Olar will transfer from my vehicle to Toren's and will lead Team One's S-ATVs to Three's VLUP location. After rendezvous, One's troopers will board their vehicles and Three will lead that composite column independently back to Open Window. Three, I'll leave the choice of route to you. Toren, you'll transfer the most serious prachim to your Oshkosh so you can work on them en route. Clear?"

Klein paused as his subordinate commanders acknowledged their new orders.

"In the meantime, Two and I will move east along Churchill where we'll establish a blocking position and engage the enemy," he continued. "Three, don't wait for us to take the first wave home. Put the wounded on the transporter and send them back, but I want Toren and the medics to stay behind in the event we have more casualties. Four, you will continue to maintain perimeter security until Two and I arrive."

Captain Gilad Sneh, the mission's operations officer – call sign 'Olar' in IDF radio voice procedure – jumped down from Klein's Oshkosh. He ran over to the S-ATV carrying the Agag Force medical officer, Major Yochai Lifshutz, call sign 'Toren' and clambered into the back.

The convoy then split, with the Oshkosh bearing Sneh and Lifshutz leading Team One's four vehicles southwest towards their rendezvous with Meshulam's blocking team and Dvir's assaulters.

The four remaining S-ATVs of Weinstock's Team Two fell in behind Klein as he made his way to highway D917, Route Churchill, turning eastwards towards Vendôme, pedal to the metal.

Klein watched on the screen of his Ness as the lead enemy motorcycles slowed to negotiate a ninety-degree turn while passing through a small hamlet on the Loir Valley floor. He consulted a laminated 1:50,000 topographical map with code names printed to signify various terrain features.

"Four, this is Kodkod, they're now passing through Varda, correct?"

"This is Four," replied Farkash. "That's affirmative, lead elements passing through Varda from the East."

The code word 'Varda' signified the hamlet of Villaria that stood some 1,500 metres southwest of Vendôme astride the highway to Saint-Rimay.

Shit, thought Klein. They're only ten minutes away.

Thirty-five

The handset of Weinstock's PRC9000 radio crackled as a precursor to an incoming broadcast.

"Two stations, this is Kodkod," came the voice of Klein. "Note the area just east of reference marker 244 on Churchill, where the road passes through a forest. The aerial photos show thick woods on both sides that create a natural choke point. That's where we're going to hit them. The key to the ambush will be the MK47. Two, how are you doing on 40 mm?"

Weinstock cast a questioning glance over his shoulder at Sholmo Blumfeld, who now manned the S-ATV's MK47 grenade launcher.

"Six boxes on the Oshkosh, plus another fifteen rounds left over from the train," Blumfeld volunteered in response to the unspoken enquiry. "Just over three hundred rounds all up."

"Three hundred rounds," Weinstock reported into his PRC9000 handset.

"That'll do," came Klein's reply. "We'll deploy the vehicles just north of Churchill along the tree line. Keep your engines running and be prepared to move on my command. Order of vehicle movement will be Two, Two Gimel, mine and Two Dalet. Two, I want your Oshkosh in position to rake the entire choke point from front to rear with the MK47. Bear in mind you'll be deploying just south of Churchill because the road curves mildly to the left as it enters the woods. Copy?"

Weinstock quickly studied his map and the 1940s-era aerial photos that covered the denoted area. "Kodkod Two, copies," he affirmed.

"They'll be canalised by the trees, with no room to maneuver except that narrow road that descends northwards back into the valley," Klein continued via the PRC9000. "Two Bet, take the Negev and your vehicle crew east-north-east through the trees and set an ambush along that road. I want maximum damage inflicted on this enemy force. We don't want any leakers getting away to haunt us. Copy?"

"This is Two Bet, good copy," came Staff Sergeant Gershon Halevy's

204

confirmation over the net. Halevy was a reliable red-headed kibbutznik from Sayeret Golani, who commanded one of Weinstock's two machine gun-equipped S-ATVs. Detaching the Negev from its pintle mount on the vehicle, he disappeared at the head of his five-man team into the woods.

"Two Gimel," continued Klein, "you move your Oshkosh alongside Two to deliver fire support with the other Negev. Those armoured cars may try to push straight ahead through the choke point or they may swing south. The woods south of Churchill extend only two hundred metres from the road, so their obvious move will be to try and outflank us. I'll be keeping watch on our right, but the Gill needs to be prepared for either possibility."

"This is Two Dalet, affirmative, we'll be ready for both options," broadcast Staff Sergeant Haim Zevulun, the Gill anti-tank missile crew commander.

Weinstock watched as Klein directed the disposition of forces for their hasty ambush. "Over there," said Klein to Horman, pointing to the tree line at his 10 o'clock. Horman turned the Oshkosh off the pavement towards the indicated direction.

In short order, the five S-ATVs were arranged in column formation in the field just north of the highway.

"Enemy ETA five minutes," came Klein's voice through the PRC9000 handset. "Two, now's the time to unload your passengers. How copy?"

"Two copy," confirmed Weinstock. He clambered out of the S-ATV's front passenger seat and walked around to the load bed where Danielle was sitting with her daughter. "Danielle, we're about to go into battle," he said in French. "You won't be safe with me. I want you to take Adele into those trees and wait."

Weinstock extended his hand to steady her as she descended from the Oshkosh. Taking the child from Blumfeld's hands, he gently placed the little one on the ground next to her mother. He opened a pouch on his tactical vest and extracted a small leather packet.

"I should be back for you in a little while. But if not, I want you to make your way back to your parents in Paris. Here are five thousand francs, just in case."

Danielle took the packet, her face betraying raw emotion. Weinstock was caught completely off-guard, albeit pleasantly, when she threw her arms around his neck and kissed him on the mouth.

"Good luck, Azriel. I fully intend to return your money. But for that I'll need to see you again. So please come back to us … please." Danielle then picked up Adele, turned on her heel and disappeared among the trees.

Most of Weinstock's beet red embarrassment was hidden by the camo paint that covered his face. Ignoring the salacious grins of his vehicle crew, he climbed back into the forward passenger seat.

Klein watched on the Ness as the enemy vanguard passed through the hamlet of Varennes and began the climb along Route Churchill out of the Loir Valley. "One minute. Make ready."

The unique 'thunk-thunk' of rounds being fed into the chambers of belt-fed automatic weapons erupted along the column.

Thirty-six

The bite of the cold autumn wind on Peter Koertig's face did nothing to cramp his enjoyment of the daydream that so thoroughly absorbed him. The scenario he envisaged from his seat in the Zündapp sidecar had him cast as the single-handed salvation of the Führer. That stuck-up bitch Magda Zinke will adjust her attitude when I come home wearing the Knight's Cross around my neck, he thought with a smile of lascivious anticipation. Instead of turning up that pert little nose of hers, she'll be begging for a spot in my bed.

This turn of events had been set in train just after dawn, when the Vendôme Kreiskommandant – a flustered, overweight, middle-aged major, appeared bearing a garbled message that the Führer was under attack. As for exactly where or precisely by whom, he had no idea. Neither additional information nor further instructions were forthcoming, and after thirty minutes of feckless frustration, Bruno von François decided to take the initiative.

Beckoning Koertig to approach, the Schnelle Kompanie commander said, "I don't know what's happening, but we're not going to keep on standing around here with our dicks in our hands. We'll head back towards Montoire with your motorcycles on point and my armoured cars following. Organise your people; movement in two minutes."

Then off they went, retracing their route westwards along highway N917. Koertig maintained a reasonable level of situational awareness as the column made its way along the Boulevard de Tremault and turned south into Rue Bretonnerie. By the time the column had passed over both branches of the Loir and the Isle de Vendôme, the oberleutnant had succumbed to wool-gathering fantasies of future grandeur and its opportunities for sexual conquest.

The progress of the Schnelle Kompanie into a wooded area bounded by thick forest scarcely registered on his consciousness. Koertig was completely oblivious to the trio of strange-looking vehicles that materialised at the far end of the woods ahead, until they opened fire.

A maelstrom of death suddenly engulfed the German column, jolting Koertig from reverie to horror in the space of an instant. He was still struggling to achieve situational awareness when his driver suddenly slumped over the handlebars and the motorcycle careened headlong into the roadside ditch.

The impact cast the oberleutnant face down into the mud, an indignity that saved his life. In his begrimed position, Koertig was sheltered from the machine gun fire and grenade explosions that tore his platoon to shreds. Watching in helpless, horrified fascination, the German officer noted the figure of a tall man wearing a strange floppy cloth helmet orchestrating this slaughter from the front passenger seat of the lead vehicle.

The German motorcycle troopers were cut down en-masse by scything shrapnel and lancinating bullets. Men were eviscerated, literally, their torsos rent open and glistening coils of intestines spilling out into scarlet pools of blood. Worse by far occurred when a tracer round hit the fuel tank of a Zündapp in the midst of the column. A stream of flaming gasoline spewed out like a giant flamethrower, igniting the skin and clothing of everyone it touched. The three riders aboard that motorcycle endured a particularly terrible death, screaming in agony as they were transformed into human torches.

Survivors of the initial onslaught sought shelter in the forests bordering the road. But those damned enemy gunners were alert and pursued the fugitives by fire, aiming their infernal explosive barrage into the woods, where tree bursts inflicted death from above.

From Koertig's perspective, this torment seemed to go on forever. Then, just as suddenly as they had appeared, the enemy vehicles vanished. The cacophony of explosions faded and all that could be heard were the moans of the wounded and the crackle of burning motorcycles.

Koertig rose from the ditch, dripping mud, and strode through the grisly detritus of what had once been his command. Ignoring pleas for help from the wounded, he moved from motorcycle to motorcycle and, in short order, found a Zündapp that worked.

Utilising the combo quick-release mechanism, Koertig detached the sidecar and pushed it aside. He mounted the Zündapp and turned the ignition key, kickstarting the ignition and gunning the engine. He then steered the motorcycle towards the enemy firing position that, just a few minutes before, had been generating so much terror and destruction.

Braking at the enemy's firing position, Koertig noticed large shell casings of a type he had never seen before littering the road. He nosed the motorcycle gingerly past the last trees, wary of the potential for another ambush. All he saw was a dust cloud hovering over a dirt track leading southwards through wheatfields recently shorn of their autumn harvest.

Turning in pursuit, he soon came to an abrupt halt, transfixed by the burning carcasses of two armoured cars. Von François must have been trying to outflank the ambush by swinging south of the wooded area. The correct tactical decision, thought Koertig, but enough of a 'school solution' to be easily foreseen by the enemy.

The weapons these Engländer are using, for they had to be Tommies, must be new, he mused, gazing at the conflagration. Lucky for us they didn't have them last summer in Belgium, or the whole campaign might have ended differently.

The armoured cars' 20 mm ammunition began to cook off, snapping like a mammoth popcorn-maker. The sound triggered a shift in Koertig's state of mind from shock to anger. He wanted payback. Putting the Zündapp into gear, he roared off, halting on the crest of a low ridge some six hundred metres to the South. From this vantage point he had his first real opportunity to assess the enemy. Raising his binoculars, Koertig saw five vehicles, of unknown type but heavily armed, travelling in convoy at surprising speed through open country. Extracting a topographical map from the leather case strapped to his belt, Koertig quickly oriented himself with the easy facility of an experienced armoured reconnaissance officer.

The Tommies were moving south between Villiersfaux to the East and Houssay to the West. Folding the map back into its case, Koertig set out in pursuit, shadowing the enemy from a distance of 1,000 to 1,200 metres, far enough that he hoped to remain unnoticed. The Engländer were swallowed up by a small hamlet perched on the edge of a narrow dell, reappearing a minute later as they ascended a road that climbed the far bank. He consulted his map – Sasnières.

The enemy column disappeared behind a row of trees flanking the southern bank of la Fontaine de Sasnières, the narrow creek flowing through the village. Koertig quickened his pace, snaking along the twisting laneways of Sasnières past slack-jawed peasants unaccustomed to such excitement.

Once across la Fontaine de Sasnières, he opened the throttle and shot up the hill, where he stopped to survey the lay of the land. A compound of farm buildings stood some two hundred metres ahead. Another 250 metres beyond the farm was a large wooded area identified by his map as the Forêt de Prunay.

The enemy was nowhere to be seen. The only place they could have gone was somewhere into the forest. Carefully examining the tree line with his binoculars, Koertig noted a gap where a dirt track led into the bowels of the woods.

So that was where he headed, circumnavigating the farm compound to the North. A near-miss burst of automatic weapons fire put paid to that plan, causing him to lose control of the Zündap and wipe-out into a furrow of freshly turned sod. For a few moments, Koertig lay motionless behind the motorcycle, stunned by his fall. Another burst of machine gun fire snapping overhead roused him from his state of stupefaction. Realising the vulnerability of his position, he leaped to his feet and dashed across the fifty metres separating him from a barn-like structure. Careful to keep the farm buildings between him and the estimated source of enemy fire, he ran northwards through the trees, across the dale and into Sasinières.

Breathless from his exertions, Koertig bent over, hands on knees. Looking up, he spied a 1920s-era Renault flatbed truck so run-down that the Wehrmacht hadn't bothered requisitioning it. Chest still heaving, he approached the house alongside the parked vehicle, unholstered his P38 and, pistol in hand, pounded on the front door. A bearded man who looked to be in his fifties opened the door.

"Ich muss Montoire sofort zu erreichen," said Koertig in a tone of command. "Sie werden mich in Ihrem LKW zu nehmen."

"Quoi?" rejoined the uncomprehending Frenchman.

"Ich muss Montoire sofort zu ..." repeated Koertig, before grunting a "sheisse" of frustration.

"Ich," said Koertig, pointing to himself. "Montoire. Sie," he continued with a finger pointed at the Frenchman. "LKW," he said pointing to the truck and making a steering gesture with both hands.

"Ah," said the Frenchman, "vous voulez que je pour vous emmener à Montoire. D'accord." The farmer raised his finger skyward to signify that the German officer should wait. "Un moment s'il vous plaît." The Frenchman took a coat from a rack on the wall and then turned to look at Koertig with an expressionless face that would have served him well at the poker table.

"Allons-y," the farmer announced, with the limp nod of someone steeling himself for a job that was unpleasant, yet unavoidable.

Pulling the door behind him, he brushed past Koertig on his way to the truck, climbing into the driver's seat. The oberleutnant holstered his pistol and joined the Frenchman in the cab. The farmer turned the ignition and the engine rattled to life. With screeching gears, the Renault lurched into motion, descending into the dell and turning northwest on a road that led along the bank of the stream.

On the outskirts of Sasnières, Koertig noted a sign with its arrowhead pointing in the direction of their travel. It read: "Montoire – 6 km."

Thirty-seven

THEN

Klein ran through the woods, swerving and ducking to avoid low-lying branches. Farkash and Levinson followed close behind.

"Kodkod, coming in," Klein yelled as he approached the Israeli machine gun position sited just within the tree line of the Forêt de Prunay. "Where?" he asked the young Negev gunner.

"Two hundred and fifty metres at your 11 o'clock," the machine gunner replied, pointing helpfully in the designated direction. "You can see the motorcycle lying there."

Klein examined the fallen motorbike through his binoculars, noting that it was painted in Wehrmacht grey. "And the rider?"

"Got away behind the farm buildings. I think I wounded him, but he ran like the wind."

Klein consulted his map, noting that the farm featured under the name la Racinière.

"Has there been any other activity?"

"Nothing," said the machine gunner with a shake of his head.

"Well done," said Klein with an avuncular pat on the gunner's shoulder. "We'll head back to Open Window. You keep a close eye out and let us know if anything changes."

The machine gunner's head bowed in a nod of comprehension and Klein indicated that Farkash and Levinson should follow.

Once the trio was out of the machine gunner's earshot, Klein cast a sombre glance in Farkash's direction. "This isn't good. I would guess that rider is a survivor from the column we ambushed on Route Churchill. Zevulun told me he caught glimpses of someone tailing us on our way here, but I didn't think we could afford the time to stop and take him down. Assuming I'm correct, this German now knows where to find us and is on his way to report. Not good at all."

"What are we going to do?" asked Farkash. "The device hasn't returned from transporting the first wave. We can't go home without it – and we're blind without the base station to operate the UAV."

"I need to have another talk with Hoffmann," said Klein. "In the event we're stuck here, I want you to organise us for movement. How many are we?"

"I have fifteen and Azriel has another seventeen – nineteen when you count his guests," Farkash said with a wry smile. "Another five from your command group, plus Dr Lifshutz and Professor Hoffmann who stayed behind. That brings us to a total of thirty-nine combatants and two civilian passengers."

Klein nodded. "Okay, I want you to remove the demo charges from my Oshkosh, Azriel's four and Meshulam's three. That'll give us eight vehicles if we have to exfil. I want you to take anything useful from the five we'd be leaving behind. Crew-served weapons, ammunition, fuel, radios, batteries, medical supplies, food – whatever we might need if we have to run. Strip them bare."

"You're talking as though it's certain we're here to stay," observed Farkash.

"I hope not," replied Klein. "But you know my motto: expect the worst and be pleasantly surprised."

"What about the micro-UAV?" asked Farkash. "Without the Sparrow, we're blind beyond line of sight from our outer perimeter along the forest's edge. It would really help if we could deploy the Skylark, especially in light of the fact that company may be coming."

"You're absolutely right," said Klein, "but the answer is no. I don't want to risk it. The Skylark is much smaller and more vulnerable to weather and wind. I want to keep that ISR capability in hand, in case we're forced to hightail it out of here. We'll just have to make do with the Mark I human eyeball."

"Right," came Farkash's laconic response.

"Beyond that, I'll let you know what Hoffmann says," said Klein. "That's all I can do."

The two Israelis exited the woods into la Hubardière clearing.

"In the meantime, you have work to do," Klein said. "Just make sure to pack explosives around the engine blocks of the S-ATVs we'll be leaving behind if we're stuck here. I don't want us giving the Germans a parting gift of revolutionary automotive technology."

"On it," said Farkash. He strode away in search of Roie Abargil, the unit's resident demolitions expert.

213

Klein turned to Levinson – his RTO. "Baruch, go find Azriel and bring him to me."

Levinson trotted off, returning less than a minute later with Azriel Weinstock in tow.

"Bad news," said Klein to Weinstock. "That guy on the motorcycle trailed us here. That means I'm expecting company soon, if we can't figure a way to get home."

Azriel simply nodded.

"I'm going to talk with Hoffmann," Klein continued, "but in the meantime, get your people ready to serve as a reaction force in case the Germans show up. Have them switch their comms to Team Four's frequency. I want everyone on the same network."

"Did you talk to Hoffmann about Danielle and her child?" asked Weinstock.

"Yes," replied Klein, "although the way things are looking, those temporal theory questions might be moot. In that case, they'll come with us, of course."

Klein went in search of Hoffmann and found the German physicist sitting on the ground with his back leaning against the packing shed wall. Hoffmann looked up with a disconsolate expression at the approaching Israeli officer.

"I'm sorry, Colonel," he pre-empted. "I have no idea what's gone wrong. Aaron should have returned for the second wave. I can't imagine what happened. It's all quite contrary to my calculations."

"Forget about that," said Klein with a dismissive wave. "I'm not interested in assigning blame. We're in a precarious situation and I need to make a decision. I need your guidance."

"Given how things have turned out, I'm not sure I'm qualified to provide any guidance on anything," replied a doleful Hoffmann.

Klein grabbed Hoffmann by the shirt collar, hauling the physicist to his feet. "Now listen to me, we don't have time for self-pity. Our ride home is overdue and I need your scientific recommendation on how long we should wait. Be aware that the Germans know where we are, so it's just a matter of time before they show up in force. There are forty other lives reliant on what you tell me right now, so man up and get a hold of yourself."

Hoffmann shook his head in bewilderment. "I ... I don't know."

"Your best guess, then," pressed Klein.

Hoffmann paused for a moment in thought. "I think Aaron would be here by now if he were coming. Something catastrophic must have happened at the other end of the transport cycle for him to be so far behind schedule. My guess and, mind you, that's all it is, would be that we're staying in 1940."

Klein nodded and turned to Levinson. "Round up all the officers. That means Farkash, Azriel and Roie. Bring the doctor as well."

Levinson trotted off to deliver the summons and, in short order, the officers of Agag Force were assembled around a map spread across the hood of the lead S-ATV.

Klein gazed sombrely at his subordinates. "Here's where we are. About thirty-five minutes ago, the transporter departed with the first returning wave consisting of casualties plus Teams One and Three. According to Professor Hoffmann's calculations, the interval at this end between departure and arrival should only be about four minutes. So, it's time to begin worrying."

"What does Hoffmann think?" asked Dr Lifshutz. "Does he have any idea what happened?"

"He's not sure, but the most likely explanation is that something damaged the device at the other end of the transport cycle. If that's correct, that means no return ticket. We're here to stay."

Klein paused, studying the faces of his officers to seek outwards indications of their internal state of mind. Benjamin Farkash, Roie Abargil and Azriel Weinstock sported stoic expressions, while Yochai Lifshutz stood there in gobsmacked shock.

"It can't be," Lifshutz said. "You don't understand. I have a wife and child. There has to be a way to get back home."

Klein put his hands on Lifshutz's shoulders. "Yochai, this is a bitter blow for all of us, but we all took this possibility into account when signing on for this operation. Just think about what we've accomplished. Consider the millions of lives we've saved. The here and now is our new reality, and we're just going to have to make the best of it. Can you do that, at least for now?"

After a moment's contemplation, Lifshutz nodded.

"Good," said Klein, while delivering a fraternal clap to the doctor's shoulder.

"What's our next move?" asked Abargil.

"Exfil. Cast your minds back to those contingency planning exercises we conducted during the prep phase of the mission."

"Excuse me, Yossi," interjected Lifshutz, "but I wasn't a party to any such thing."

"True enough," said Klein with an affirming nod. "My apologies, Yochai. I should have remembered you were a late addition to our enterprise. But a reiteration of what and why will benefit all of us, so everyone listen up. The Germans will be operating on the assumption we're British because it's the only logical conclusion they can reach. On that basis, they'll expect that our next move will be to the Channel or the Atlantic coast for extraction by the Royal Navy. We'll be doing the opposite – travelling south into Vichy territory and ultimately on to the Mediterranean, which isn't as simple as it sounds."

"What's the problem?" asked Lifshutz.

"The Loire River," answered Weinstock. "Most of its bridges were blown by the French Army last summer in an attempt to halt the German advance."

"Correct," added Klein. "The only bridges left intact are in the middle of major urban areas like Orléans, Blois and Tours. And big cities mean big German garrisons. So, we'll move cross-country to the East around the bend of the Loire, before turning southwards along the Saône and Rhône rivers to the Mediterranean coast."

Klein strode around to the load bed of his Oshkosh, returning moments later with an olive-coloured plastic storage tub sealed with bright orange cable ties.

"This is our exfil kit," Klein explained to Lifshutz. "It contains a set of maps for every vehicle commander and a library of 1940s-era aerial photos covering likely VLUP sites across central and southern France."

Snipping the ties, Klein removed the lid and extracted eight sealed packets. He piled seven on the passenger seat of the Oshkosh and ripped open the one remaining.

"Have a look here," said Klein as he spread a 1:100,000-scale topographical map sheet, a product of Le Service Géographique de l'Armée vintage 1938, across the S-ATV's hood.

"From this point in the Forêt de Prunay, we'll bypass Orléans to its north and east," said Klein, tracing a crescent-shaped path on the map with his index finger. "I'm operating on the assumption that the Germans know

216

we're here, so our first priority is breaking contact by moving out of this area. I don't like travelling by day, but we don't have any choice on this first leg. Are you with me so far?"

After a unanimous round of affirmative nods, Klein continued, "Our initial objective is fifty kilometres east-north-east of us in the Forêt de Marchenoir, where we'll establish a VLUP and wait for darkness. We'll be moving mostly over paved country roads so I'm thinking it should take us roughly two hours if all goes as planned."

"And if it doesn't?" enquired Farkash.

"We adapt and overcome," replied Klein. "We shoot our way through any roadblocks or other enemy force that might pop up in our path. But we do not stop. At this stage of the game, speed and surprise are the best friends we have. If we can establish a VLUP undetected in the Forêt de Marchenoir, we're halfway to safety. Then we move by night on successive legs to the Mediterranean coast where we find a ship and set course for Israel, with Malta as a fallback option. It won't be home as we know it, but it'll have to do."

"How many vehicles?" enquired Farkash.

"We're just over forty in number – so I think eight S-ATVs should suffice," answered Klein. "Also, I want everyone in the same network from now on. Make sure all PRC700s and PRC9000s are tuned to the Team Four frequency. Strip every bit of ammunition we can carry from the vehicles we'll be leaving behind. Siphon their fuel tanks as well. I want every one of our eight S-ATVs to be topped up and carrying at least two spare jerrycans of diesel."

"What about the troops?" asked Weinstock. "They deserve an explanation."

"They do, indeed," Klein agreed. "But it's imperative we move ASAP. So, let the boys know the basics and tell them I'll conduct a detailed briefing at the VLUP this afternoon. Hoffmann and I will take questions then."

"It might be worthwhile to take a closer look at that German motorcycle," said Farkash with a self-aggrandising grin. "I'm a pretty experienced rider and, if it's undamaged, it could come in handy."

"Good idea," Klein replied. "But I need you in the seat of your Oshkosh next to the PRC9000. I'm sure we have others who rode motorcycles back home."

"I'll do a recce to assess the motorbike's condition and make enquiries among the troops," replied a crestfallen Farkash.

"Do you want me to lay claymores?" asked Abargil. "It'd be a nice surprise to leave behind for our German friends."

"Tempting," said Klein with a rueful shake of the head, "but no. If I'm wrong about the Germans, we don't want some French mushroom hunter being blown to bits by accident." He glanced at his watch. "It's now 09:21 local. I want to be on the move no later than 10:20 local – 59 minutes from now. There's a lot to do and not a lot of time, so let's get to it. Don't forget your maps."

The officers filed by the front seat of Klein's Oshkosh, picking up their map packets and dispersing to their assigned duties.

Thirty-eight

Major Weiss squinted anxiously eastwards into the morning sun, watching for the Fieseler Storch that would be bearing Generalmajor Warlimont to Montoire. He heard it before he saw it, the growl of the Argus AS 10 engine becoming audible while the aircraft was still yet to be seen.

"There!" shouted Oberleutnant Saller, pointing in the direction of Vendôme as the Storch popped up over a row of trees that formed a dark silhouette against the brightening sky.

"Throw the smoke grenade," commanded Weiss. Saller dutifully cast a Nebelhandgranate 39 into the middle of the open field, west of the tunnel's western entrance. A gray plume billowed into the air, signalling to the Storch pilot both where he was to land and the easterly direction of prevailing winds.

The light plane flew over the field at an altitude of around 90 metres, turning sharply before coming in to land against the wind. The oil-and-spring shock absorbers in the Fieseler's main landing gear handled the furrowed field with ease and the plane came to a halt within one hundred metres of touchdown.

The right-hand door of the aircraft opened even before the pilot switched off his engine, and a slim figure with close-cropped greying hair jumped down onto the freshly harvested field.

At age 46, Generalmajor Walter Warlimont was young for the post he held – Deputy Chief of the Operations Staff at OKW. As he strode across the rotting stalks of wheat, leather briefcase in hand, he radiated an aura of authority that flowed naturally from the holder of such a senior position.

Flanked by a pair of oberleutnants, Weiss waited beside a Wehrmacht Opel Blitz three-tonne truck parked at the field's edge. He braced to attention and saluted. "Hello, sir. I am Major Weiss, Deputy Comm ... I mean Commander, Signal Battalion 247."

Casually returning the major's salute, Warlimont motioned with his head towards the two junior officers, one a model of rear-echelon smartness and the other hatless and begrimed, his uniform soiled by dried blood and mud.

"Who are these gentlemen?"

"This is Oberleutnant Saller," answered Weiss with a nod towards his neatly attired subordinate, "my Battalion Operations Officer." Warlimont doffed his head in acknowledgement as Saller clicked his heels and stiffened to attention.

"And this is Oberleutnant Koertig," said Weiss with a nod that indicated the disheveled officer. "He's the motorcycle platoon commander of the Führer-Begleit-Bataillon's Schnelle Kompanie. They were ambushed earlier this morning by the same enemy force that attacked the Führer's train. There were several survivors, all seriously wounded, but the oberleutnant was the only one to emerge unscathed. I thought you'd be eager to have a word with him."

"To what do you attribute your good fortune, Oberleutnant?" asked Warlimont, his attention now entirely focused on Koertig.

"Sheer happenstance, sir," replied Koertig, a tad defensively. "My driver was killed in the first fusillade and my motorcycle combo crashed into a ditch on the side of the road. I was thrown out of the sidecar and knocked unconscious."

"Any idea who the enemy were?" asked Warlimont.

"I think English commandos, sir. They drove very sophisticated vehicles and their weapons generated enough firepower to decimate my unit within the space of two or three minutes. These were definitely elite troops. Not partisans or francs-tireurs. I awoke as they were disengaging and was able to trail them until coming under heavy automatic weapons fire from what must be their base."

Warlimont turned to Weiss. "Do you know where these raiders are?"

"We think so, sir," replied Weiss nervously.

"And what have you done about it?"

"Sir, as a rear-echelon signal battalion assigned to an army group hauptquartier, we're armed only with personal weapons. We have no machine guns and fewer than fifteen maschinenpistolen have been issued to my NCOs. A company of flaktruppen from Châteaudun should be arriving soon with MG34s and mortars. In light of what happened to Oberleutnant Koertig and the Schnelle Kompanie, I deemed it prudent to await their arrival before taking any action. Since you and I spoke by telephone we've received additional information that complicates the picture somewhat."

"Go on," prompted Warlimont.

"Well, sir, three survivors from the Führer's train itself arrived at my battalion hauptquartier in Montoire about forty-five minutes ago. Two of them are young women from the Führer's secretarial pool and the third is an enlisted orderly to Feldmarschall Keitel. They report the definite deaths of Himmler, Goebbels and Göring and the likelihood – as yet unconfirmed – that the Führer was killed as well. They also say, and here the story becomes somewhat bizarre, that the enemy assault was carried out by Jews."

"Jews?" echoed Warlimont incredulously. "What kind of Jews?"

"The vengeful kind, sir," Weiss continued. "The survivors related that the enemy officer in command wore one of those special hats and made a speech about crimes against the Jewish people before executing Himmler and Goebbels. They also say that the attacking soldiers were speaking a language other than English among themselves."

"Where are these survivors?"

"I've quarantined them per your instructions," Weiss replied.

"Good," said Warlimont. "I'll want to debrief them at some point. But now there are more pressing matters that demand our attention. Koertig, can you drive a truck?"

"Sir?"

"A simple question, Oberleutnant. Can you drive a truck?"

"Y... yes sir."

Warlimont walked around to the drivers' side of the truck cab and opened the door to see an obergefreiter looking back at him with a deer-in-the-headlights expression.

"Out," said Warlimont, gesturing with his thumb.

That single word of command from a senior officer sent the driver scarpering.

"I'll sit up front with Koertig," said the general. "That way he can tell me more about these kosher commandos." Warlimont turned to address Weiss. "Major, you and your operations officer will ride in back. Did you bring what I asked?"

"Yes sir," replied Weiss. "There are thirty blankets and one hundred metres of rope in the cargo bed."

"Good, let's mount up and get moving." Warlimont walked around the truck to the passenger side and climbed into the cab.

With gears screeching, Koertig managed to get the Opel in motion, proceeding eastwards along the aptly named Rue de Tunnel.

The sight of Warlimont's red general officer collar tabs was enough to have the truck waved through the security cordon without delay. Soon afterward, Koertig brought the truck to a halt in the face of 88 mm shell holes pocking the road surface and human cadavers strewn atop it. The oberleutnant looked over to Warlimont, his glance posing an unspoken question.

The general nodded. "We'll walk from here." Alighting from the cab, he walked to the rear of the Opel, beckoning for Weiss and Saller to descend from the cargo bed. "This is what will happen next," said the general in a sharp tone of command. "We'll sweep the area, looking first and foremost for the Führer. Once he's been found, we'll focus on other senior officers and officials, such as Himmler, Goebbels and Göring. But the Führer is our priority. Are we clear?"

The three officers nodded.

"Then let's get to it. Saller and Weiss, start over on the left. Koertig, you'll be here with me on the right. We need to be quick but thorough."

The four officers began walking eastward in skirmish line fashion along the Rue de Tunnel, pausing for a brief inspection of each body in their path. Within the space of a few minutes, they arrived at the edge of the railroad cut, pausing in shock at the sight of the carnage within.

"I think that's Reischmarschall Göring," said Weiss, pointing to a body whose distinctive white uniform and corpulent girth lent themselves to easy identification.

"Saller, go check it out," instructed Warlimont. "The others will stay with me."

The general led the way down the slope towards a group of bodies that lay in a single serried rank.

"I've found him," announced Warlimont as he knelt beside the blue pyjama-clad corpse of the Führer. The rear of Hitler's skull had been blown out, leaving a slackness of skin that made the face droop like an ill-fitting Halloween mask. Without his trademark brush moustache, the corpse would have been rendered almost unrecognisable.

"Are you certain that's him?" asked Saller in a tremulous tone.

"Koertig, you've spent more time in the Führer's presence than almost anyone. What do you think?"

Koertig nodded, his face stained by tears of bereavement.

The general went through the motions of feeling the carotid artery for several moments before shaking his head. "I'm afraid he's gone."

Koertig stripped off his mud-spattered leather overcoat and draped it over Hitler's corpse, while Weiss and Saller looked on in open-mouthed shock.

Warlimont glanced up and down the row of senior officers. Goebbels, Himmler and Keitel. He looked over at Saller with a face that radiated stony-faced stoicism.

"Was that Göring over there?"

Saller nodded.

"Mein Herren," said Warlimont, his sharp tone of command cutting through the fog of grief enveloping his subordinates. "There'll be an appropriate time for mourning, but it's not now. The Reich has been left leaderless by an enemy attack, so we'll have to act quickly to prevent catastrophe. Oberleutnant Koertig?"

By force of habit, Koertig stiffened to attention, his cheeks still wet with tears.

"Herr General?"

"Fetch the truck."

"But, sir, what about the bodies blocking the road?"

"Take Saller with you. He can walk in front and move the dead. Or drive over them if you must. Either way, I want that vehicle right here where we're standing no later than five minutes from now. Weiss, you may go as well," Warlimont said.

As the three officers departed, the general noticed the shiny brass of freshly expended cartridge casings strewn about the bodies of the Nazi elite. He knelt to examine the casings more closely, noticing that some were short and fat while the others were much smaller and slender.

The short, fat casings were obviously from a pistol, and Warlimot turned one over in his hand to look at the headstamp markings on its base – 'M45-AUTO 10'. Something of a small arms expert, he knew that the numeral '10' on most headstamps would signify the year of manufacture. But that didn't make sense. The formal name of these cartridges was .45 ACP, the three-letter abbreviation standing for 'Automatic Colt Pistol'. Yet the weapon for which these rounds were designed only came into the US Army service the following year, hence its name – M1911. Perhaps these were rounds manufactured during the program's design and testing phase, Warlimont mused.

The slender brass casings told another story. They were clearly rifle rounds, but unlike any long gun cartridge the general had ever seen. They might have been suitable for small-game hunting, but these bullets were diminutive compared to the man-killing 30–06, .303 and 7.92 mm calibres in service with the militaries of America, England and Germany, respectively. He flipped the casing over in his hand to view its headstamp: 'LC 15' and a small circle symbol with an internal cross, like a miniature sniper scope.

Warlimont's musings on munitions were interrupted by the appearance of the Opel. The general pocketed four of the smaller rifle casings and several pistol casings as well.

On Warlimont's instructions, the officers wrapped Hitler, Göring, Goebbels, Himmler and Keitel in two blankets each, securing every individual bundle with lengths of rope. The bodies were then lifted onto the cargo bed of the Opel, the 130 kilograms of Hermann Göring requiring the combined exertions of all four officers.

"Our next stop is Châteaudun, where a pair of Ju-88s are waiting," said Warlimont. "After loading the bodies into the bomb bays, we'll take off for Berlin. There'll be vehicles waiting on the tarmac at Tempelhof and we'll move on directly to OKW. I'm deliberately using the pronoun 'we' because the three of you are coming along."

"To Berlin, sir?" echoed Weiss in a tone of incomprehension. "What about my battalion?"

"Who's your next most senior officer?"

"That would be the commander of the Wireless Company, sir. Hauptman Amsel."

"Right," said the general, walking to the cab of the Opel and returning moments later with a notepad and pencil. "We'll be moving directly to the airfield," said Warlimont while scribbling away. "These written orders will have to suffice. One of your NCOs on cordon duty will pass them on to Amsel."

"May I enquire as to their contents?" asked Weiss.

Warlimont finished writing, tearing the scribbled page from his notebook and folding it into his pocket.

"You may indeed," said the general. "Amsel will assume command of the battalion until your return. He's to maintain an inviolable 360-degree cordon sanitaire around the Saint-Rimay tunnel, with no-one, French or German, entering the quarantine zone on pain of summary execution. Montoire is also to be placed under a communications blackout, with all telephone and telegraph lines severed and the battalion's radios powered off. The town will be sealed and the local population placed under curfew. Finally, a building large enough to serve as a temporary morgue will be commandeered where all the dead are to be collected. These orders will be in force until further instructions from me are delivered by courier."

Weiss nodded. "Do you have any idea when that will be, sir?"

"At this point, all I know is that, the sooner we get to Berlin, the sooner your battalion can be taken out of deep freeze," Warlimont curtly replied. "Koertig, you're in the driver's seat again. Weiss and Saller, you'll be in the back with our cargo. Make sure you roll down the rear flap of the canvas cover. Let's move."

Once they were all aboard, Koertig performed a three-point turn, steering the Opel westwards along the Rue de Tunnel towards its junction with highway N817. He stopped at the cordon of signal troops securing that quadrant of the security perimeter and Warlimont descended.

The sudden sight of a general in their midst sent the entire complement of soldiers to rigid attention. Warlimont examined the troops and gestured for the feldwebel in command to approach.

"These are orders for Hauptman Amsel," he said, handing the folded notepaper to the NCO. "They're extremely urgent so I want you to take the Storch and deliver them immediately."

The feldwebel clicked his heels and braced to attention. "Jawohl, General." He then dashed through the field towards the Fieseler Storch.

Ensconced back in the cab, Warlimont nodded to Koertig, who engaged the gears. Looking out of the driver's side window, he saw the pilot and the NCO climbing into the aircraft.

Reaching the junction with highway N817, Koertig turned east towards Châteaudun. They were ten kilometres northeast of Vendôme when a column of military vehicles travelling in the opposite direction emerged from the hamlet of Pezou. Leading the convoy was a kübelwagen painted in Luftwaffe colours, followed by five Sd. Kfz. 231/8-rad armoured cars and ten Opel Blitz trucks.

"Those must be the reinforcements from Châteaudun airbase," said Koertig.

"Pull over here and follow me," ordered Warlimont. "But keep your mouth shut until otherwise instructed."

Koertig brought the truck to a halt and the general descended from the cab. The oberleutnant followed suit.

"Weiss, you and Saller stay inside with the cover closed," ordered Warlimont in a voice loud enough to penetrate the truck's canvas cover. "No noise."

"Yes, sir," came the muffled voice of Major Weiss from within the Opel's cargo bed.

The general strode onto the middle of the highway, waving his arms in an unmistakable signal that the oncoming column should halt.

The lead kübelwagen stopped several metres in front of Warlimont and a Luftwaffe major emerged out of the passenger seat.

"Good morning, sir. I'm Major Hugo Shriver from Châteadun," the air force officer said with an accompanying salute.

Warlimont returned the courtesy. "You're the relief column?"

"Yes sir," replied Shriver. "We received a message that the Führer's train is under attack somewhere near Montoire-sur-le-Loir. There were no specifics. I was simply told to make haste and provide whatever assistance I could."

"I'm pleased to inform you that the Führer is alive and well," said Warlimont with an easy smile. "The Fuhrer-Begleit-Bataillon was able to repel the assault."

Shriver smiled in turn at the glad tidings. "That's very good news, sir. Do we know anything about the attackers?"

"English commandos, we think," said Warlimont with a nod towards his younger companion. "But Oberleutnant Koertig here will be able to fill you in. He was heavily engaged during the battle to defend the Führer."

"Herr Major," said Koertig with a click of his heels.

"Koertig will not only be able to tell you about the Engländer weapons and tactics, but he knows where their base of operations is. Do you have a map of the area?"

"Certainly," Shriver replied. The major strode over to the kübelwagen and returned with a large sheet of topographical maps glued together. He then kneeled, and spread the map on the paved highway surface.

Koertig kneeled as well, extracting another map from the leather case hanging around his neck. After several moments of study, he oriented himself to Shriver's map, pointing with his index finger to the Forêt du Prunay.

"There," said Koertig. "They disappeared into this forest and I was fired upon by automatic weapons while trying to follow. That's where their base has to be."

Warlimont studied the map for a moment before looking up at Shriver.

"Major, you will continue on to Vendôme and then turn south towards Château-Renault," instructed the general. "And right here," indicating a point on the map with his finger, "you'll turn northwest on road GC8 to Sasnières. That will be your assembly area for an immediate assault on the enemy base camp. How many men do you have?"

"Almost two hundred, sir. The entire flak and security complement of the airbase."

"Weapons?"

"Four 80 mm mortars and nine MG34s, in addition to individual small arms. And, of course, the five armoured cars in direct support."

"That's very good," replied Warlimont, with a smile that exuded confidence he didn't really feel.

"Sir, would it be possible for Oberleutnant Koertig to be placed under my command? After all, he knows the local topography and is familiar with enemy weapons and tactics."

"I'm sorry, Major, but that's out of the question," replied Warlimont with a decisive shake of the head. "Koertig will be accompanying me back to Berlin. The intelligence people at OKW are eager to debrief him."

"What about the Begleit-Bataillon?" asked Shriver. "Would they be able to provide assistance?"

"I'm afraid not, Major," replied Warlimont. "They successfully saved the Führer, but took very serious casualties in the process. The Führer-Begleit-Bataillon has been rendered combat ineffective."

"Sir, might I have a word?" interjected Koertig. "In private?"

Warlimont responded with a sharp glance that conveyed annoyance at the oberleutnant's effrontery. But Koertig was unfazed, returning his superior's gaze with poker-faced nonchalance.

"Come with me," said Warlimont after a few awkward moments, leading the way to the far side of the truck, out of the Luftwaffe officer's earshot.

"I apologise for my presumption, sir," said Koertig. "But I don't understand what's going on. Why are you saying the Führer is alive when we both know he isn't?"

Warlimont exhaled with the exasperated sigh of a man being forced to explain something he thinks should be self-evident. "Oberleutnant, are you in favour of civil war?"

"Sir? said the young officer as his brow furrowed in surprise.

"Koertig, the Führer was a great man," Warlimont explained in a didactic tone. "Perhaps the most important visionary in all German history, wouldn't you agree?"

Koertig nodded.

"Because of that greatness, our Führer played an essential role in all major Reich policy decisions."

"You're saying that now there's a vacuum?" asked Koertig.

"Precisely," replied Warlimont, "and the last thing Germany needs is a mad scramble for the levers of power by every jumped-up party hack or storm trooper fanatic in Berlin. It's therefore vital to keep the Führer's death a secret until OKW can engineer a smooth transition of government. That's why I'm taking the bodies back with me to Berlin. They are proof positive that will forestall the otherwise inevitable ifs, maybes or buts."

"And we're still at war with England," volunteered Koertig.

"Indeed we are," rejoined Warlimont. "Particularly as evidenced by today's events."

"Yes sir, and that's precisely why I should be allowed to join Major Shriver."

"I've already ruled on that request, Oberleutnant. What is it you want, an opportunity for revenge?"

"To be honest, sir, yes, that's part of it. Those damned Jews killed my men and I'd like nothing more than to exact retribution. There's also a much more valid reason, a more objective reason why I should be allowed to go."

"That is?"

"Prisoners, sir. Wouldn't you welcome a chance to capture and interrogate some of the enemy troops? As I said before, these Jews are clearly elite troops and their weapons are extremely effective. That means Major Shriver will need every advantage he can get. Quite frankly I'm all that's available."

"Are you always this brash?" asked Warlimont with grudging, purse-lipped respect.

"Not really, sir," replied Koertig. "I'm normally much more deferential. But perhaps this is the sort of situation where normal rules don't apply."

"Perhaps not," agreed the general. "All right, you can go. With certain provisos."

"Yes, sir?"

"Number one: keep your mouth shut about the Führer. That much goes without saying. No mention of this Jewish hypothesis, either. As far as anyone is concerned, the enemy are British commandos. No more and no less. Do you foresee any problem complying with these instructions?"

"No sir," replied Koertig with a definitive headshake.

"And number two: try not to get yourself killed. I meant what I said about OKW wanting to debrief you. For that, I need you in one piece."

"Understood, sir," replied Koertig, coming to attention with a click of his heels.

Warlimont turned and walked back to the kübelwagen where Shriver was waiting.

"You may have Koertig on loan, but I want him back in good condition. Take care to keep him well clear of the front line. I also want you to bring me some prisoners."

"Yes sir, I'll do my best."

The general pulled out his notepad and jotted several lines, signing with a flourish of penmanship.

"In the event of an enemy retreat, your pursuit must be relentless," instructed Warlimont. "This is a written order that authorises you to commandeer any troops or equipment you require for that purpose."

Major Shriver examined the general's note, nodded and folded the paper into his pocket.

"One final thing. Under no circumstances are you to move west in the direction of Montoire-sur-le-Loir or Saint-Rimay. Those areas are strictly off limits. Do I make myself clear?"

"Yes sir," said Major Shriver.

"Then move."

Shriver saluted. "Koertig, you're with me in the kübelwagen."

Warlimont stood by, hands on hips, as the convoy lurched into motion.

When the last truck had passed, he walked around to the rear of his own Opel Blitz and pounded his palm on the rear cargo bed gate.

"Open up," he commanded. "It's me. Can either of you drive a truck?"

"I can, sir," came the voice of Major Weiss as the rear flap of the canvas cover opened.

"Good," replied Warlimont. "You can join me up front. Hop to it, we have a plane to catch."

ANABASIS

Thirty-nine

The kübelwagen carrying Oberleutnant Peter Koertig and Luftwaffe Major Hugo Shriver was just nosing its way out of la Fontaine de Sasnières stream bed when the Fôret de Prunay erupted in gouts of flame. The two officers stared in astonishment as chunks of debris soared above the trees, as if hurled aloft by a hidden giant. Then, as gravity reinstated its claim on this airborne detritus, the watching Germans saw twisting tendrils of black smoke rising towards the clouds above.

Instructing his driver to halt, Shriver hopped out of the jeep-like vehicle and strode back towards the lead Sdkfz 231 armoured car, where Oberleutnant Richard Graber occupied the commander's cupola.

"Join me at the kübel and send your gunner along the line with instructions for the men to dismount."

Graber nodded and spoke into his headset. The armoured car's engine shut down and the oberleutnant clambered out of the turret, followed by his gunner.

Graber joined Shriver and Koertig at the kübelwagen, while the gunner proceeded along the truck column conveying the major's orders.

Shriver gazed at the Fôret de Prunay through his binoculars and perused a map he had spread on the vehicle's hood. "Graber, your armoured cars will be of no use to us in that," he said with a gesture towards the thick woods 400 metres to their front. "I want you to deploy your vehicles along this line while we advance on foot." The Luftwaffe major glanced at the armoured car platoon commander, who nodded in acknowledgement.

"Koertig, you'll stay here with the armoured cars," Shriver ordered, raising his hand to silence any words of protest. "I have orders to ensure your safety and that's what I intend to do. So, no argument. You're here with Graber."

"Yes sir," replied a visibly crestfallen Koertig.

"Once we're inside the tree line, I want you to stay in this position until further notice from me," Shriver continued. "If we require close-range fire support, I'll let you know. But taking armoured cars blindly into those woods is asking for trouble."

"Jawol, Herr Major," said Graber with a quick salute.

In short order, Shriver had deployed his troops into three sixty-man reinforced platoons deployed in 'two-up' tactical order, like a pyramid with its base turned towards the enemy. His command team was positioned in the midst of the formation, behind the two leading platoons.

Weapons at the ready, the Germans advanced, passing by the farm buildings where Koertig had sought cover after being shot off his motorcycle several hours before. Despite Shriver's anxieties about the tactical deficiencies of maneuvering through open fields, the Germans reached the tree line without incident.

"All troops orient towards the smoke. Be careful!" yelled the major at the top of his lungs, just before he disappeared into the woods.

The cohesion of the German formation progressively degraded as the troopers moved through the thick forest. Although, the heavy black fumes swirling skyward served as a cynosure that faithfully guided the Luftwaffe airmen towards their objective.

Shriver cautiously emerged from the trees into the la Hubardière clearing, directing his troopers to assume covering positions. After a few moments of silence, he gestured for his airmen to continue their cautious advance. Alongside what appeared to be some sort of packing shed stood the twisted remains of five vehicles, their burning fuel tanks emitting foul-smelling thick black smoke.

The major dispatched an airman to summon Graber's armoured car platoon, while ordering a thorough search of the buildings in the clearing. Shriver walked toward the still-combusting vehicles, picking his way through the metallic detritus littering the clearing. One piece of debris caught his attention and he kneeled to examine a large jagged fragment of what appeared to be aluminium. It was still warm to the touch.

Shriver turned the fragment over in his hand. The letters '6.6L Turbo Dies ...' were embossed on its surface. Part of the engine no doubt, but unlike anything he'd ever seen before.

The major gestured to a nearby NCO. "Zultforter, take this and follow me."

Feldwebel Zultforter took possession of the aluminium fragment, shadowing his commander as Shriver continued his examination of the scattered debris. Upon the arrival of the armoured cars, Graber's men used their portable fire extinguishers to smother the flames belching from the blackened vehicle wreckage.

Shriver's second-in-command, Hauptman Laufen, approached and stiffened to attention.

"The buildings have been thoroughly searched, sir, but they're empty. Except for something rather strange."

Shriver arched an eyebrow. "What do you mean, strange?"

"Well, sir, the walls are draped with some type of film," explained Laufen. "Like a blackout curtain, but not made of cloth. The material is clearly not natural, but I have no idea what it is."

"Show me" instructed Shriver, and he followed the Hauptman into the shed.

"You're right," Shriver said as he felt the slick texture of the polyethylene between his thumb and forefinger. "This is definitely manmade. I want you to tear this down, roll it up and put it in the back of your Opel. Maybe the chemists at one of our universities will be able to identify it. Anything else of interest?"

"No, sir. Except for some indentations and heavy tyre tracks in the dirt over there."

"Show me."

Laufen led his commander to the corner of the packing shed where the time transportation device had once stood on its semi-trailer mount. Kneeling down, Shriver examined the grooves in the dirt left by the trailer's tyres and legs, and then shook his head in bemusement. "This is all very strange. These were obviously left by a large truck, but I can't for the life of me understand how they got it in here. I mean, look at the door. It's clearly not large enough to accommodate something of this size."

Hauptman Laufen nodded in agreement. "That much is obvious, sir."

Shriver shrugged. "All very irregular, but we'll leave it for others to ponder such mysteries." He turned to face his second-in-command. "Laufen, after you've loaded this sheeting, take a dozen men and get back to Châteaudun as fast as possible. Inform the oberst that we've pursued the enemy to their local base and found it abandoned. Tell him there's something very strange about this place and show him this sheeting as an example. Let him know I intend to secure the area until further orders are received."

"Jawohl, Herr Major," replied Laufen with a click of the heels. He exited the shed to organise a working party for the collection of the sheeting while Shriver walked over to join Koertig, who was examining one of the foam-speckled vehicle carcasses.

Leaning into the driver's compartment, Koertig noticed lettering embossed on the instrument panel. Wiping the surface clean with his hand, he stared at the writing. "Herr Major, sprechen sie Englisch?"

"Einige," replied Shriver.

"Können Sie das übersetzen?" asked Koenig as he gestured towards the wiped-clean portion of the dashboard.

Shriver perused the embossed lettering for a moment before sounding out the words in a heavy Teutonic accent. "Spetzial All-Teerayn Vehakle. Es ist irgendeine art der sondergeländewagen, ich denke."

"And what about the rest of it? What does 'Oshkosh, WI' mean?" pressed Koertig.

"Doesn't sound like any English word I know," said Shriver frowning. "The name of a place, perhaps? I have no idea, but surely someone will figure it out. In the meantime, our job is to secure this facility until further orders. Koertig, you have more experience in ground combat than we do, so I want you to command the inner cordon."

"Zu befehl, Herr Major," replied the oberleutnant with a smile of pleasant surprise.

"Take two platoons and deploy them in a 360-degree cordon around the clearing. Keep the men concealed inside the tree line. I'll keep the other platoon here with me in reserve. Graber will cover the outer approaches to the forest. His armoured cars will be next to useless in this," said Shriver with a gesture towards the thick woods surrounding the sawmill on all sides.

"Then with your permission, Herr Major, I'll attend to my assignment."

Shriver nodded his assent. "If you have any trouble from my officers, send them to me. I'll straighten them out."

Koertig came to attention and saluted. Once Shriver had returned the military courtesy, the oberleutnant strode away to organise his new command.

Forty

I shouldn't be having this much fun, Staff Sergeant Eldad Rivkin chided himself as he tooled northeastwards along the paved country byway marked on the map as IC64. But the throbbing of the Zündapp's 597cc engine between his legs, combined with the clear autumn sky, was enough to banish thoughts of his larger predicament from his mind for the moment at least. There would be time enough later to mourn the family he would never see again.

Passing through the hamlet of Villegomblain, he came to a stop at a T-junction.

"Turn right on the N817," came Klein's voice through Rivkin's PRC 710 headset. "The next village is named Oucques, about two thousand metres ahead. There you'll find another the T-junction where you'll go left past the market square and then turn right on N817 towards Saint-Leonard-en-Beauce."

"Through the village with the unpronounceable name, left at a T-junction and right on the N817 to Saint-Leonard," Rivkin echoed. "Moving now."

Less than two minutes later, he was moving through the outskirts of Oucques. Turning left on highway N824, he rounded a curve into the market square ... and suddenly slammed on the brakes.

It was difficult to tell who was more surprised, Rivkin or the two dozen German soldiers who had chosen Oucques as a pit stop on the route of their patrol through the area. The Germans were lounging around their vehicles, smoking, chatting and sipping bottles of lemonade when the motorcycle suddenly materialised at the end of the square. The Israeli rider was the first to react, turning the Zündapp on a dime and vanishing back around the bend before a single shot could be fired. The Germans quickly set out after the suspect motorbike with a kübelwagen and two Opel trucks.

Rivkin cast a glance over his shoulder at his closest pursuer – a German wearing an NCO's cap who stood in the passenger seat of a kübelwagen, trying to get a bead on the fleeing motorcycle with an MP38 submachinegun. Once the Germans hit a straight stretch of road on the western outskirts of the village, they opened fire.

The crack of 9 mm rounds flashing by at supersonic speed sent a paroxysm of terror coursing through Rivkin's body. He instinctively hunched low over the handlebars while sneaking another over the shoulder glance to his six o'clock. The German's mouth was moving like a silent film actor, his yells drowned out by the roar of the Zündapp's two-cycle engine. Then came a sledgehammer blow to Rivkin's back, and he lost consciousness in midair as the motorcycle careened off the pavement into the drainage ditch that ran parallel to the road.

Gravely wounded, the young Israeli sergeant didn't hear how his German's exultant laugh was cut short by the appearance of a strange-looking vehicle on the road beyond. Nor would he have the satisfaction of seeing how his assailant's short-lived triumph dissolved into tragedy.

Forty-one

From the front seat of the approaching S-ATV, Klein instantaneously took stock of the situation.

"Contact front, enemy Jeep!" he bellowed into his PRC710 Madonna boom mic. "Halevy will assault on my right. Rivkin is out there, so small arms only and watch where your rounds are going!"

Klein waited until Halevy's Oshkosh was abreast of his own vehicle. "Go!" he instructed Horman, who hit the gas as the colonel opened semiautomatic fire from his X95 bullpup assault rifle. The pintle-mounted NG7 on Halevy's S-ATV soon added its heavier staccato bark to the din.

The withering Israeli fusillade engulfed the kübelwagen with devastating results, its four occupants cut down before they were even able to react. Horman braked opposite the perforated Wehrmacht vehicle and Klein hopped out. After verifying that the Germans were neutralised, he rushed over to the unconscious Rivkin. The most obvious symptom of the trooper's wound was his laboured breathing.

"Doctor, I need you here now!" Klein radioed.

Klein gently carried Rivkin onto the paved road, just as the Oshkosh bearing Lifshutz and his medical team roared up to the scene of the firefight. The doctor and a medic clambered out and knelt by Rivkin, opening the medical packs they both carried.

"Yossi, we have movement," yelled Halevy.

Lifshutz nodded to signal that he had matters now in hand and Klein dashed back to his Oshkosh. Looking eastwards towards Oucques, the colonel could see two trucks rumbling out of the village towards the Israeli column.

"Contact front," Klein radioed over the team network. "Azriel, I want your MK47 and Halevy's Negev in line abreast with me, twenty metres beyond the enemy Jeep. Move."

Horman moved the Oshkosh past the perforated kübelwagen and was soon joined by Weinstock's MK47-armed and Halevy's Negev-armed S-

239

ATVs on either side. By this stage, the two German Opel Blitz trucks had approached to a range of four hundred metres and closing. The lead truck began to slow, as if in recognition of the menace exuded by the trio of strange looking vehicles blocking the road ahead.

Then death came calling.

A barrage of 40 mm grenades and 7.62 mm machine gun bullets shredded both trucks and passengers over the space of less than thirty seconds.

Observing that the German vehicles were now little more than burning wrecks, Klein yelled "ceasefire" at the top of his lungs. "Conserve your ammunition. We still have a long way to go. Remain in place while I go back to check on Rivkin. Keep your eyes open."

Klein clambered out of the S-ATV and strode back to where Lifshutz was treating the wounded trooper.

"So, Doctor, what's his condition?"

"Two bullet wounds, one to the right calf and the other to upper back. He also took a nasty spill off the motorbike that left him unconscious. But it's his back that's worrying me. There's no exit wound. I think he might have a pneumothorax."

"What does that mean in simple Hebrew?"

"It means the bullet entered his pleural space, and this resulted in a loss of negative pressure between the two pleural membranes. Pretty sure his lung has collapsed. That's why I put in the drain," said Lifshutz, pointing to the thoracic catheter protruding between Rivkin's ribs.

"He's breathing more easily," the doctor continued. "But I need to get in there to remove the bullet and see what other internal injuries might have been inflicted."

"Can we move him?"

"He's stable for now. But I need to operate. It's urgent."

"Only another fifteen kilometres to the VLUP," Klein said reassuringly. "You'll be able to do your work there."

"Then let's move, shall we?" urged Lifshuz. "The sooner I can see what's going on, the better."

"Noted," replied Klein. "Let me know once he's loaded onto your Oshkosh and we'll move."

Lifshutz nodded, gesturing that his medic should unfold the stretcher. The two men gently lifted the unconscious Rivkin onto the litter that was then secured to the cargo bed of the S-ATV. A drip delivering intravenous fluid through Rivkin's forearm was hung from a post affixed to a slot on the side of the Oshkosh.

"Kodkod Vengeance, this is Toren," Lifshutz radioed on his PRC710. "I'm good to go."

"Kodkod, good copy," came Klein's voice through the network. "Vengeance stations, this is Kodkod, I have the lead. Eldad is in serious need of surgery so we're going to pick up the pace. I want to be under camouflage at the VLUP in less than thirty so the doctor can begin to work. Moving now."

Klein's words imbued the vehicle commanders with a new sense of urgency that was manifest in their speed and tactical procedures. Previously, they paused to reconnoitre before traversing major highways. Now Klein simply led them through Oucques and across highway N824 without stopping. Any obstacle or opposition would be overcome through brute force and overwhelming firepower. They had the life of a friend to save.

Forty-two

SS Hauptsturmführer Helmut Wyzan sat quietly as SS Sturmbannführer August Belmann continued to peruse the documents on his desk, as if oblivious to the younger officer's presence. A petty power play typical of a rear-echelon bureaucrat who had never heard a shot fired in anger in either Poland or France, Wyzan thought.

But Wyzan kept his vexation to himself. Belmann's lack of combat experience hadn't prevented his appointment as security chief for the Orleans Feldkommandanturen and it was rumoured he had personal connections at the Prinz-Albrecht-Straße. So, it was wise to tread lightly.

When Belmann finally looked up, he affected a surprised expression, as though he had forgotten someone was seated across his desk. "Ah, yes, Wyzan. Are you familiar with the town of Montoire-sur-le-Loir?"

"No, sir."

"Come and have a look," said Belmann as he rose from his seat to peruse a large wall map hanging behind his desk.

Wyzan strode around to join him.

"It's right here," said Belmann as he pointed out Montoire's location, "about twenty kilometres southwest of Vendôme. I got a telephone call from Obersturmbannführer Knochen in Paris about some sort of partisan activity in that area."

"What kind of activity, sir?" asked Wyzan as he perused the map.

"Good question," replied Belmann. "The information that came down from Paris was very sketchy. As a matter of fact, I got the impression they're operating on rumour and snippets of information they've picked up from von Stüpnagel's Wehrmacht people. But no matter. I want you to organise a combat patrol from your kompanie and do a sweep of the Montoire area regardless. Even if these partisan stories turn out to be fables, it will still be a useful exercise. We haven't had much of a presence in that area, so I want you to instil a little fear among the locals."

"Very good, sir" replied Wyzan. "I think fifty men should be sufficient

242

for what you have in mind. Do you have any instructions about the duration of this mission?"

"I think four to five days should suffice. You should travel via Vendôme and liaise with the kreiskommandatur. They might have a better understanding of the local situation. In any event, I expect an initial report from you by 10:00 hours tomorrow."

"Zu befehl, Herr Sturmbannführer," replied Wyzan.

"How soon can you be on the road?"

"Within the hour, sir."

"Very good, Hauptsturmführer," said Belmann. "You're dismissed to your duties."

Wyzan stiffened to attention, his arm outstretched at a 35-degree upward angle. "Heil Hitler."

Belmann replied with a more casual version of the same salute. "Heil Hitler."

Wyzan walked next door to the school where his men were billeted, making his way to the former classrooms that were now serving as NCOs' quarters. The SS men braced to attention as he entered.

"Rührt euch," said Wyzan, and the NCOs relaxed at the order to stand at ease. "Oberscharführer Pruss, join me outside if you please?"

"Jahwohl, Herr Hauptsturmführer!" replied Pruss with the enthusiasm of a new recruit. Pulling on his great coat, he joined his commander in the entrance hall of the building.

"What's your platoon's current roster?"

"Only twenty-seven ready for duty, sir," replied Pruss. "We have two on sick call, four on home leave and three on training courses."

"I have orders to take a patrol and investigate partisan activity in a town a few hour's drive from here. We'll need fifty men, so you'll have to poach from the other platoons. If any of those platoon commanders give you trouble, tell them this is on my orders. Instruct the men you select to bring sleeping bags, shaving kit and a change of underclothes. We'll also need rations for five days. Tell the motor pool to prepare a kübelwagen and five trucks. And no duds. Tell them I'll personally be inspecting the vehicles to ensure they're fully fuelled and in operating condition. Am I clear thus far?"

"Perfectly sir," replied Pruss.

"We'll be leaving at 13:30 on the dot. When can you have the men ready for kit inspection?"

The SS NCO glanced at his watch. "13:15, sir."

Wyzan nodded curtly. "That only gives you fifteen minutes to correct any deficiencies. Cutting it a bit fine, aren't you Oberscharführer?"

"No, sir. My men will all be fully armed and equipped. I'll guarantee it."

"Very well, Oberscharführer. You'd best attend to your duties."

Pruss braced in a textbook fascist salute. "Heil Hitler."

"Heil Hitler," replied Wyzan with a Hitlergruß of his own.

Forty-three

Lieutenant Colonel Ralph Neville tapped his foot impatiently, eliciting a frown from the middle-aged amanuensis who sat before a pair of imposing oak doors. The 38-year-old grimaced in embarrassment, stilling his errant leg while mouthing an apology, sotto voce. Another fifteen minutes were spent perusing the portrait of Arthur Wellesley hanging on the opposing wall before the secretary's phone rang. She listened for a moment, before replacing the handset in its cradle and walking around to open the doors.

"The general will see you now."

"Thank you," replied Neville. Grasping the handle of the attaché case chained to his left wrist, he walked into the office and stiffened to attention before a large wooden desk manned by a thin grey-haired man wearing the insignia of a major general. As Neville was indoors and thus hatless, there was no salute.

"Stand at ease and have a seat," said Major General Francis Davidson, Britain's Director of Military Intelligence, motioning to a leather chair in front of the desk. "What's so important as to bring you down from Arkley View to the War Office?"

"Well, sir," replied Neville when he was seated, "there's some sort of major flap going on in France. I don't know precisely what's happening, but it's something substantial."

"What do you mean by 'major flap'?"

"Throughout the morning, our Y-network has been picking up very unusual voice radio transmissions. The Germans are employing code words, but at Arkley we've formed the distinct impression that the matters they're discussing would be restricted to transmission by Enigma in normal circumstances. It seems to us that whatever's happening is quite abnormal."

Neville placed the attaché on the desk and used a key on a chain around his neck to open the handcuff and unlock the case. Extracting a manila folder, he placed the file on the desk, sitting back quietly as the general began to peruse its contents.

After several minutes of silent study, Davidson looked up from the document. "All very interesting, colonel, but hardly conclusive."

"There's more, sir. Things don't appear in the report. Subjective impressions I didn't feel comfortable setting down in a formal document, and a supposition I didn't want to put in writing."

Davidson looked up from the file with an inquisitive expression on his face. "Go on," he prompted.

"It's not just what they say, but how they're saying it," reported Neville. "There's a real element of anxiety that's palpable in their voices. At times it even rises to the level of sheer panic. I've been listening to German radio traffic for over a year and I've never heard anything similar. Not even during the midst of last summer's fighting."

"Alright, so something has their Teutonic knickers in a twist. Very nice to hear, but still not enough to explain what brought you into town from Arkley."

"Location, sir."

"Location?" echoed Davidson.

"Yes, sir. Our DF people have triangulated the source of these transmissions to Montoire-sur-le-Loir, a small town about 150 miles southwest of Paris. It's home to a rail junction on one of the alternate lines leading northwards from Tours."

"I'm not following you, colonel," chided Davidson. "I'm time poor, so please get to the point."

Neville grimaced. "Sorry, sir. It's just that announcement last night on Berlin radio about Hitler meeting Pétain at an undisclosed location in France. We know Hitler travelled by train the day before to Henday on the Franco-Spanish border. And Montoire ..."

"Would be almost directly astride his route back to Germany," interjected Davidson as his face creased in an epiphanic smile. "A small country town situated on a rail line would be the perfect place to hold a summit. Are you thinking that something nasty might have happened to old Adolf?"

Neville shrugged. "It's just a theory, sir. There's no hard evidence."

"Colonel, we're intelligence officers, not barristers. We're in the business of gazing at dots and trying to connect them. Supposition, deduction and inference are the tools we use to assemble an intelligence mosaic. So informed theorising is not only acceptable, but downright desirable. Well done."

"Thank you, sir," said a relieved Neville.

Davidson walked over to a robust looking safe inset to his office wall. Twirling the combination dial back and forth, the general swung it open, extracting a leather binder.

Davidson perused the binder's contents before looking up with a nod. "As I thought, the SOE has no assets or operations ongoing in that sector. What about the air force?"

The lieutenant colonel shook his head. "I contacted both Bentley Priory and High Wycombe, sir. The RAF has had nothing in the air over the Montoire area during the past twenty-four hours."

"What about Admiral Keyes over at Combined Operations? Did you check with his people?"

"No, sir. I thought a commando raid would be highly unlikely in light of the fact that Montoire is so far inland."

"You're probably right," said Davidson with a nod of grudging concurrence. "But after we're done with our next appointment, I want you to make some discreet enquiries anyway."

"Certainly, sir," replied Neville a frown of perplexity etched across his face. "But I wasn't aware I'd be seeing anyone else today."

"Well, think again," said Davidson with a grin. "Your theory has just enough meat on the bone to warrant taking it up the food chain."

The general pushed the intercom button on his desk. "Mrs Crosswaite, call the JIC and Number 10. I need to see both Cavendish-Bentinck and the PM, together if possible. It's urgent."

"Yes General, I'll get right on it," warbled the voice through the intercom.

Davidson rose from his desk and walked over to a side table topped with glasses and a crystal decanter. Pouring out a finger's-worth of amber liquid into two glasses, he offered one to Neville.

"Gird your loins, colonel. You're going to see the Prime Minister."

Neville took a sip and nodded his approval.

"Royal Lochnager single malt," said Davidson with more than a hint of epicurean pride. "Queen Victoria's favourite – and mine"

"I can see why, sir. It's very fine stuff indeed."

"My supply is quite limited, but in the event you're correct, I thought a prospective celebratory drink would be in order."

"Indeed, sir," replied Neville.

Davidson raised his glass. "To the long overdue demise of the Führer.

May he be en route to hell, where an eternity of well-deserved torment awaits."

"Well-deserved torment," echoed Neville with his own glass raised.

The two officers sipped their whiskeys gingerly, savouring the precious spirit made so rare a commodity by the exigencies of wartime Britain.

The light on Davidson's intercom flashed, accompanied by a brief buzz.

The general sighed, placing his glass on the side table and returning to his desk. "Yes?"

"The Prime Minister will see you in fifteen minutes at the CWR. The service chiefs will also be there, as will the Chairman of the JIC."

"Thank you, Mrs Crosswaite."

Davidson opened the bottom drawer of his desk, extracting a Sam Browne belt with pistol holster attached. Flipping open the holster, he pulled out a venerable Webley-Fosbery revolver and checked that all chambers were loaded.

"I see you're armed Neville," observed the general as he slipped on his Sam Browne.

"Yes, sir, although by contrast with your .455 I feel almost naked."

Davidson laughed. "It's a lesson I learned the hard way, fighting the Pathan on the Northwest Frontier. Now, when I shoot someone, I want a round that will put my man down with one shot. Your .38 Enfield simply won't make a proper job of it."

"Very wise, sir," replied Neville. "I'll take that under advisement for future reference."

"Enough small arms small talk," said Davidson as he replaced the manila folder within Neville's open attaché. "Let's make tracks. We have a Prime Minister to meet."

Neville hastily closed the briefcase, reattaching the handcuff to his wrist while trailing his superior out the door.

The two officers made their way south along Whitehall, turning west into King Charles Street and entering the HM Treasury building through the rear doors. Walking along office-filled corridors, they came to a stairwell guarded by a quartet of tough-looking military policemen wielding M1921 Thompson submachine guns with 50-round drum magazines attached.

Fastidiously checking the officers' identity documents, the senior redcap – a sergeant – telephoned to request authorisation for entry to the subterranean Cabinet War Rooms.

After a few moments, the NCO nodded and hung up the phone. "You're cleared to enter, sir. You'll have to surrender your sidearms. You can pick them up on the way out."

"Of course, sergeant," Davidson replied. Both officers surrendered their pistols and the MPs braced to attention, the sergeant rendering an impeccable salute.

The general returned the courtesy and led the way down two flights of stairs into what once had been the basement of the New Public Offices Building. Turning right, their olfactory senses picked up the odour of burning tobacco, the source of which became clear as they entered the CWR map room. Winston Spencer Churchill was ensconced at the head of a large table, a trademark Romeo y Julieta clamped between his teeth. Also present were the service chiefs of staff – General Sir John Dill, Admiral of the Fleet Sir Dudley Pound and Air Chief Marshall Sir Charles Portal. Sir Victor Cavendish-Bentinck, Chairman of the Joint Intelligence Committee, was in attendance as well.

"Well Davidson, what do you have for us?" asked Cavendish-Bentinck.

"Let me begin by congratulating Sir Charles on his appointment today as Chief of the Air Staff," said Davidson, with the polished urbanity of a seasoned diplomat. "Very well deserved, sir."

Portal's head bowed in a modest nod.

"I have a war to run," said Dill sourly. "So, if the pleasantries are concluded, perhaps we can move on to the issue at hand?"

"Of course, sir," replied Davidson demurely. "Accompanying me is Lieutenant Colonel Neville, who is posted to Arkley View as a senior watch officer. He's taken the initiative to cobble together data from a set of disparate sources and the end result is an intelligence picture that could be extremely significant. In fact, if Colonel Neville is correct, the world as we know it is about to change radically for the better. As he's the one who did the work and is most au fait with the data, I'll now hand over to him."

"Thank you, sir," replied Neville, who strode to the foot of the table as Davidson took a seat against the wall. This second rendition of the colonel's thesis was much smoother in its retelling. When Neville concluded, all eyes in the room turned to the Prime Minister, who was busily engaged in a search through his pockets for a match to relight his cigar.

Once the Romeo y Julieta was combusting to his satisfaction, Churchill fixed Neville with an incisive stare. "Very interesting, colonel. And kudos to you for showing the courage of your convictions by taking this up the chain of command. But we also must concede that it's all very circumstantial."

"No question, Prime Minister," concurred Davidson.

"But nonetheless, we're obliged to take this contingency very seriously because of the potential consequences," Churchill continued. "If something along these lines has indeed happened, there's no question it would constitute an epochal event. Therefore, it's up to us to try and figure out what, if anything, is going on."

"We've made enquiries with the three services and are reasonably certain that our forces were not involved in whatever transpired," said Davidson. "Isn't that indeed the case, sirs?"

The service chiefs nodded their assent in unison.

"Very well then, but what about the French?" asked the Prime Minister. "Could it have been some sort of Resistance operation?"

"Not to our knowledge," replied Cavendish-Bentinck. "We have no active SOE cells in the Montoire vicinity. I don't suppose we can rule out the possibility of an independent operation conducted by parties unknown."

"We could make enquiries at Carlton Gardens," suggested Davidson, using the street address of General De Gaulle's London headquarters as a metonym for the Free French Forces. "They might know something."

"All right, but for god's sake be discreet," said Churchill. "Given half a chance, De Gaulle will take personal credit for whatever's going on, even if, as I strongly suspect, he's had absolutely nothing to do with it."

A gale of derisive laughter erupted among the officers in the room.

Churchill motioned for silence. "General Davidson, I assume you'll continue to keep a weather eye on this."

"Most assuredly, Prime Minister."

"And Victor, you'll keep your fingers on the pulse of the broader intelligence community?"

"Of course, Prime Minister," answered Cavendish-Bentinck.

"Before we disperse, might I make a suggestion?" enquired Portal.

"By all means, Chief Air Marshall," Churchill replied.

"I propose we dispatch one of our photo-reconnaissance Spits on a run over Montoire to see what we might see."

"Capital idea!" exclaimed Churchill. "How soon could you make this happen?"

"A sortie can be mounted later this afternoon," answered Portal. "We'll run the film through the photo-interpretation shop at Wembley on a priority basis and have a written report on your desk by 20:00 hours this evening."

"Very good, I'll look forward to receiving it," said the Prime Minister. "Anything else?" he asked, looking around the room, but no further comments were forthcoming. "So, we're done for now," said Churchill in summation. "I'd like to thank you all for coming, Particular kudos to Lieutenant Colonel Neville. Very impressive work, if you turn out to be right."

"Of course, sir. Thank you," Neville replied.

As the chiefs of staff departed in the wake of the Prime Minister, Cavendish-Bentinck beckoned for Neville and Davidson to approach.

"I want you both to keep me in the loop on this at all times," said the JIC chairman. "My office knows of my whereabouts 24 hours a day. If you catch a whiff of anything at all, I want to know about it. And Davidson, make sure you have one of your people at the Wembley PIU this afternoon to keep tabs on what's going on. In the event Portal's photo sortie turns up something interesting, we don't want the Brylcreem Boys hogging all the credit."

"Of course, sir," Davidson replied.

"And Neville, I'd like to echo the PM's words of praise," continued Cavendish-Bentinck. "Original thinkers with the intestinal fortitude to show the courage of their convictions are a rare commodity. So, once we're past this particular flap, I want you to come and see me. I'll book a table at the Savoy and we can discuss your future. I think you may have become destined for bigger things."

Forty-four

THEN

Yossi Klein weaved his way through the closely packed vehicles, towards the medical S-ATV where Doctor Yochai Lifshutz was reposed in the passenger seat, his eyes closed and face etched with utter exhaustion.

"Nu?"

Lifshutz looked up to see Klein standing with an expectant expression. The doctor pulled himself upright.

"Rivkin is stable. I managed to extract the bullet from his chest, which thankfully hadn't fragmented and was still intact. No vital organs were damaged, other than his lungs. That means we've been relatively lucky."

"And what about his lungs?"

"The pneumothorax?" asked the doctor, his sense of intellectual arrogance triumphing over his fatigue.

"Yes," replied Klein, ignoring the doctor's hauteur.

"Also doing not too badly," replied Lifshutz. "We drained the fluid and he's now breathing easily. There are 14 compatible blood donors among our group and I gave him a 250-cc transfusion for starters. I'm very concerned about the impact of travel, particularly along these crappy French roads. In any other circumstance, I'd want to keep him stationary for at least a week." Lifshutz said.

Klein clapped the doctor on the shoulder. "On the positive side of the ledger, we have another eight hours before our next leg of movement. We can keep him comfortable until then. I have a lot of faith in you, Yochai."

Lifshutz smiled in resignation as Farkash materialised, wending his way among the camouflaged S-ATVs.

"I've completed the inventory, Yossi," said the captain to his commander.

"I was about to do a circuit round the perimeter," said Klein with a nod of adieu to Lifshutz. "You can brief me as we walk. What's our supply situation?"

"Going from light to heavy, I'll start with pistols. We have seventeen Sig Sauers with 423 rounds of .45 ACP. Then there are thirty-four clean X95s, plus another one with the GL40 grenade launcher attachment. I didn't check every individual's pouches, but we're just shy of 31,000 rounds of boxed 5.56. We probably have another nine or ten thousand when we add what's in everyone's tactical vest. That's it for small arms."

"Not bad. What about crew-served?"

"We have one Dan sniper rifle with 147 rounds of .338 and four NG7s with 12,450 rounds of 7.62. There are three Stingers, one Gill launch module with seven rounds and three Matador launchers with eighteen rounds. We also have another six kilos of Semtex left over from the demolition job at la Hubardière. Combined, we have 96 M26 fragmentation grenades and 17 MK5 smoke grenades of various colours. On comms and ancillaries, we have PRC710s for everyone excepting the Professor and our two guests. Each vehicle has a PRC 9000, plus two additional backpack sets. The only item that really worries me is our supply of batteries for the NGVs and radios. We can recharge a few at a time with our solar kit, but that's a time-consuming process. The bottom line is we're likely to run short."

Klein acknowledged the report with a sombre nod. "What about food and medical supplies?"

"We have MREs for at least a week. Longer, if we ration them. As for medical supplies, I'll need to check with the doctor."

"You can do that later," said Klein. "In the meantime, I want to brief the troops at that open space in the middle of the VLUP. Let's assemble everyone who's not on perimeter guard duty. The boys deserve to know what's happening."

A quarter of an hour later, the entire complement, sans those on watch, was assembled at a clearing in the woodland. Weinstock sat off to the left with Adele on his lap and Danielle by his side.

"Okay everyone, I'll be speaking in English for the benefit of the two civilians among us," announced Klein, canting his head to indicate Gerhard Hoffmann and Danielle. "I wanted to conduct this briefing at the first opportunity, but earlier this morning our most important priority was to break contact with the enemy. Now that has been accomplished, we can discuss our situation. I know you must have many questions, so I'll turn things over to Professor Hoffmann who'll acquaint us with the basic facts of where we are and why."

Klein turned to Hoffmann. "Professor, would you please come up here and explain your theory of our current circumstance?"

Hoffmann stood up and dusted off his camouflage uniform. As he turned to address the troops, he had an uncharacteristically bashful expression on his face.

"Gentlemen, I just want to begin by saying how proud I am of you all." Tears appeared from the corner of the professor's eyes and began to course down his cheeks. "You've made this world a better place and I want to thank you."

"Professor, we're all very appreciative of your kind words," interjected Klein in a gentle tone. "But I think the men are expecting something a bit more scientific."

A silent chorus of nodding heads endorsed Klein's point and Hoffmann managed to compose himself, clearing his throat with a cough and wiping his cheeks clean of tears. "Yes of course. I apologise. And we Germans are supposed to be an unemotional lot."

Hoffman smiled sheepishly as a smattering of laughter swept through the troops.

"My working assumption is that something must have happened to the time transit vehicle at the other end of the cycle," Hoffmann continued. "You all remember that, on our outward leg, we carefully scheduled our arrival in waves separated by four minutes local time?"

Heads bobbed in affirmation.

"Of course, we had the same plan for our return. The transporter should have been back for the second wave well before the colonel and Team Two arrived at la Hubardière. So, the only logical conclusion I can draw is that the transporter was damaged or destroyed at the other end."

"Meaning we're stuck in 1940," said Levinson, more as a statement of fact than a question.

"I'm afraid so," replied Hoffmann. "We left la Hubardière at about twenty minutes past 10 o'clock local time. That's almost two hours after the first wave departed on their return leg. What should have been a reappearance after four minutes failed to materialise after one hundred and twenty."

"But what does this mean for our families?" Levinson persisted. "It can't be that they'll conceive additional versions of us because that would be impossible under the Novikov rule you mentioned during our pre-mission briefs."

"That's entirely correct, Mr Levinson," replied Hoffmann, his voice betraying a hint of pedagogical pride at a display of student excellence. "We spoke about all this before the operation, but ..."

"Yeah," interjected Gabi Horman, "but then it was just theory. Now it's our reality."

"Point taken, Mr Horman, so I shall reiterate. The only absolute certainty in all of this is that second versions of you will not be born during the 1990s. But the principle of Minimal Temporal Displacement, MTD, gives me great confidence that your grandparents and parents will find and marry each other just as in the world as we knew it. And, except for you, the same children will be born. That means your siblings will still be your siblings. Although, where you're concerned, I suspect your mothers are likely to conceive with a different sperm/egg combination during the same act of sex that brought you into this world. Remember your basic biology: there are millions of swimming sperm but only one fertilises the egg. Now it'll be another one among those millions. This shouldn't really matter because you'll be well into your 70s by the time an alternate you is born."

"What about our grandparents?" asked Levinson. "Will we be able to contact them when we get home?"

"That would be highly inadvisable," replied Hoffmann. "Besides, what are you going to tell them? Some crazy tale about travelling through time from the 21st century? How do you think they'll react to a stranger showing up on their doorstep with such a story?"

"They'd probably call the police," Levinson conceded reluctantly. "In the end, this just makes us into nothing more than historical extras. Who will we be able to marry without upsetting your MTD applecart?"

"The technical term for what you're saying is supernumerary, which means 'exceeding the usual number.' Remember that we've forestalled the Shoah, which means there'll be 5.8 million other Jewish supernumeraries out there, most of whom will end up in Israel. I think it's highly likely that you'll each end up marrying a Jewish girl who would have otherwise perished during the war."

"Look on the bright side," said Klein with an accompanying grin. "You'll be able to invest in Apple while Steve Jobs is still working out of his garage." His foray into humour did little to lift the sombre pall that had enveloped the troopers on full realisation of their predicament.

A glum-faced Ohad Karmi raised his hand. "So what's the tactical plan?"

"Thank you, Professor," said Klein in English. "I hope you'll excuse me if I switch to Hebrew for the benefit of my men."

Hoffmann nodded and reclaimed his seat.

"I'll begin with a story," Klein continued, addressing his men in their native tongue. "About 2,400 years ago, a force of 10,000 Greek mercenaries found themselves stranded in the middle of the Persian Empire near modern-day Baghdad. The rebellious prince who had employed them was dead and they were 1,500 kilometres from the nearest friendly outpost on the Black Sea. They had no food and were vastly outnumbered by the enemy. Yet, by means of superior tactics and discipline, these Greeks were able to overcome adversity and fight their way to safety."

"You're talking about Xenophon and the Anabasis," interjected Levinson.

"Ten out of ten for Baruch, although I'd appreciate it if he didn't steal my punchline," quipped Klein, his words of reproof emolliated by the smile with which they were delivered. "For those less conversant with ancient Greek history, Xenophon was one of those soldiers-for-hire whose written account of this expedition became one of the all-time classics of military literature – the *Anabasis*. Funnily enough, *Anabasis* translates from the Greek as 'the ascent', the same term we use to describe Aliya to the Land of Israel. I want you to know that there's a precedent in history for the situation in which we find ourselves. I'm confident that, whatever a bunch of Greek mercenaries could do in their Anabasis, we can do better in our Aliya. Any questions so far?"

Klein paused, his desultory glance moving across the faces of his assembled troopers, but no query was forthcoming.

"Okay then, our first priority is moving beyond the reach of German power. In October 1940, the only realistic options available are England, Switzerland or back to Eretz Yisrael via the Mediterranean. I ruled out England because northern France is heavily occupied by the Germans. Fighting our way through half the Wehrmacht and then finding a way across the Channel is not the smart way to go – and the Swiss border is much less heavily defended, but I'm not a big fan of mountain goats and yodellers."

Klein paused to canvas the faces of his troopers for any signs of disquiet or dissent. Finding none, he went on, "In my view, our best option is moving south to one of the French Mediterranean ports where we commandeer a ship. Eretz Yisrael is our primary objective, with British-held Malta as a fallback option. Although, even that's not as simple as it sounds."

"Why not?" asked Karmi.

"Last summer, the retreating French army blew most of the bridges over the Loire River. The only ones left standing are in big cities like Tours and Orléans. So that means we have to go around – east to the Saône River valley and then south along the Rhône to the Mediterranean. Which brings us to another matter entirely."

"Another surprise? Oh goody!" said Gabi Horman, his sarcasm triggering another round of guffaws from the young soldiers.

"I suppose you could say that," replied Klein, his face now cast in a solemn mien. "Bear in mind that we all accepted the possibility that something like this might happen while signing on to this operation. In that event, I proposed to the Defense Minister that we investigate options for supplementary missions. This is what I want to lay out for you now."

Klein gazed at his audience, assessing the extent to which he was holding its attention. The eyes of every Israeli trooper were riveted on their commander.

"Tomorrow morning, about 6,500 Jews in towns and cities across the Baden, Palatinate and Saar regions of western Germany will be taken from their homes by the Gestapo and SS. These people will be crammed into nine railroad trains and sent to a Vichy French detention camp in the foothills of the Pyrenees Mountains along the border with Spain. This event is known as the "Wagner-Bürckel Aktion" after the two piece-of-shit regional governors who initiated the whole thing. As it happens, the route of those trains will take them directly along the Saône and Rhône River valleys. Because we'll be in the same neighbourhood I propose that we liberate one of those trains and take our brothers and sisters home with us to Eretz Yisrael."

The silence was broken by gasps of surprise and chatter.

"Settle down," Klein instructed, and the noise gradually subsided. "We've accomplished our primary objective and, if I haven't said so before, it was an outstanding operation in every way. You should all be very proud of yourselves." Klein paused a few moments as the impact of his praise registered in proud smiles on the faces of his listeners. "Because we find ourselves in abnormal circumstances, I'm prepared to do something abnormal in response. On this question, and this question alone, I'm prepared to suspend military discipline and put this decision to a vote. Simple majority rule. We have two options. Option A is what I proposed before. These deportation trains are all scheduled to pass through the Mediterranean port city of Sète on their way to the Pyrenees. I say we liberate one of them and, on reaching Sète, we divert the train onto the docks where we commandeer a ship and sail home."

"How do we know there'll be a ship for us to take?" asked Karmi. "What happens if the harbour is empty? We'll be caught with our dicks hanging out."

Karmi's crudity triggered a spasm of sophomoric guffawing among the Israeli troopers that quickly dwindled into an expectant silence. Levity aside, it was a question that required an answer.

"Good question," replied Klein. "It just so happens that, after receiving the green light from the Defense Minister, I did some contingency research. The historical records show that, on 29 October 1940, there were three ships in Sète harbour that would meet our needs. There's no reason to think that our actions at Saint-Rimay would have changed this. If no ships are available, we simply continue south to the Spanish border where we destroy our kit and cross."

Klein paused, looking at Karmi, who acknowledged the sufficiency of his commander's answer with a nod of assent.

"That's Option A," Klein continued. "Option B would have us proceed directly to Sète with the identical objective of seizing a ship. From here that's a distance of around nine hundred kilometres. I estimate that would mean between five and seven nights of travel, allowing for an adequate hysteria margin."

"Yossi, if we go for Option A, what will we do with our S-ATVs?" asked Levinson.

"They'll be destroyed and left behind," answered Klein. "From that point on, we'll be moving by train."

"And that means giving up tactical flexibility," noted Karmi. "What if the Germans figure out what we're doing and block the track? It's a giant gamble."

"Yes, it's a gamble," replied Klein, "but a calculated one. Remember, this is October 1940. There's no email, no internet. Hell, the transistor hasn't even been invented. It's only four months since the end of a war that ravaged French infrastructure. In this world, we'll find that information moves very slowly by our standards. And remember that the train will be in Vichy territory, not the German-occupied zone. That means two completely different communications networks, not to mention language comprehension problems between the two zones. At the end of the day, I'm confident we can stay well ahead of their OODA loop and be out at sea by the time they catch on. Does that answer your question?"

Levinson and Karmi both nodded.

"Those are our choices," said Klein. "There's no denying the reality that Option A entails a higher level of risk. But to my mind, it's more than counterbalanced by the reward of bringing hundreds of Jews to safety. While I'll be opting for Option A, I want to stress that there'll be no recriminations against anyone who goes the other way. You've all performed above and beyond. This is an unprecedented situation and I want you to follow your conscience without any sense of pressure or compulsion. Now it's decision time. There are ten people on outpost duty whose votes we'll tally later. Of those present, raise your hands all who favour Option A."

Twenty-three hands shot up immediately from the group of 28 Israeli troopers, followed after a few moments' hesitation by four more.

Klein nodded. "And those for Option B?"

The lone hand of Dr Yochai Lifshutz was raised skyward.

"There it is," said Klein. "While I'll certainly be adding to the ledger the votes of our people now on outpost duty, it's clear that Option A prevails by an overwhelming margin. What the Americans call a 'landslide'. With that decision taken, there's a subsidiary issue to consider. The Wagner-Bürckel operation is under the command of none other than Adolf Eichman. History tells us that tomorrow night he will personally be present at the rail station at Chalons-sur-Saône to supervise the transit of those trains into Vichy territory."

"Does that put the asshole within range?" asked Karmi.

"It does," replied Klein. "And that's what we have to decide. Chalons is a city of 50,000 people on the Saône River where the demarcation line passes between the German-occupied zone and Vichy. Do we go after the asshole, as Karmi described him, in the middle of a small city with a German garrison? Or do we take the safer option of liberating one of these trains in a rural area, slightly farther south, in Vichy territory?"

Levinson raised his hand.

"Go ahead, Baruch," prompted Klein.

"The Professor might have something to say about this, so I'll speak in English. Adolf Eichmann has not yet become the man we know and hate from our history. We now have to hope he never will because of what we just accomplished earlier this morning. After all, preventing the Shoah was why we came here. There's no doubt Eichmann is an anti-Semitic bastard. It's also true that Germany in October 1940 is full of such people. Why take on extra danger to kill one bastard out of millions for something he'll never do?"

Klein turned to Hoffmann. "Professor, do you have anything to add on this topic?"

Hoffmann smiled sadly. "When I was first trying to enlist Professor Adivi in this enterprise, he kept telling me to stick with physics and leave military matters to the experts. I think this is an issue for you and the boys to decide."

"Fair enough," continued Klein. "On this one, I'll be pulling rank. I think Baruch is absolutely correct. We have more than enough trouble on our plate and there's no point tempting fate unnecessarily. We'll leave Eichmann to his own devices while taking down the train after it passes into Vichy territory. Do I hear any objections or dissent?"

Silence.

"Very good, and with that our temporary exercise in democracy has concluded. Normal military discipline is back in full force. We'll be establishing our next VLUP in a forest southeast of Epiry, a town about 265 kilometres from our present position. That means we have a long night ahead of us, so I now want everyone to get as much rest as possible. Return to your vehicles and get horizontal. I'll see you all this afternoon."

A low buzz broke out as the Israeli troopers conversed softly while they dispersed.

"Doctor," said Klein to Lifshutz, "I'm available if you feel the need to talk."

The doctor waved a hand in casual acknowledgement as he walked towards his S-ATV without a word.

Forty-five

Flying Officer Pierre Beauregard consciously forced the fear into what he called his 'mental box' and focused on the job at hand. Truth be told, these low-level trips scared the absolute hell out of him. His comfort zone lay at altitudes of 25,000 feet or higher, where the vast majority of photo-reconnaissance missions were flown. At that height, the Spitfire MKI PR Type A was well-nigh untouchable. Armed solely with an F24 camera in either wing, the Spits of the RAF Photographic Reconnaissance Unit were the fastest things in the sky.

Yet here he was, tooling over France at a mere two hundred feet above ground level. Easy pickings for any 109 that might happen upon him. At this height, it wasn't just purpose-made flak guns that worried him. He was flying low enough that a well-directed, or lucky, burst of machinegun fire might easily cast him earthwards in a ball of flame, with no opportunity to bail out.

Beauregard's angst was only accentuated by the fact that this had been such a panic job. Only thirty-seven minutes from mission tasking to wheels-up at Heston Aerodrome on the western outskirts of London. A quick stop at RAF Middle Wallop to top-up his fuel tanks, and then a straight shot across the Channel, bound for some place called Montoire-sur-le-Loir.

"Helluva way to fight a war," mumbled Beauregard in a deep Louisiana accent that invariably associated him with his namesake Confederate commander of the American Civil War.

In point of fact, General Pierre Gustave Toutant-Beauregard of Fort Sumter-fame, or infamy, depending on your point of view, was the Spitfire pilot's great-grandfather. It was his ancestor's military renown, combined with a love of flying and recognition that war was coming, that made Beauregard-the-younger decamp from Tulane University, in March 1939, to Britain. There he took a short-service commission in the RAF and, with a private pilot's licence and over 150 flight hours in his logbook, he breezed through pilot training with an 'above average' rating. Beauregard received his wings in April 1940, and hoped for a posting to a Spit squadron in Fighter Command, but ended up utilising his gifted navigational skills as a reconnaissance pilot.

The inherent danger of this low-level mission, and the sparse amount of time available to plan it, meant Beauregard would be drawing on every bit of expertise he had. Consulting maps and files maintained by the PRU's intelligence officer, he plotted a course that would thread his way through the web of Luftwaffe bases spread across northern France. The object of this particular exercise was avoiding the aerodromes' flak defences, but no-one really knew how up-to-date RAF intel really was. Today's the day I find out, he thought sourly.

Beauregard made landfall on the continent just west of a place that became synonymous with selfless courage in another historical circumstance – Pointe-du-Hoc on the Normandy coast. Skirting the city of Saint-Lo, he flew on the deck over the verdant countryside of Basse-Normandy. Despite the presence of three Me-109 bases within a ten-mile radius, his passage through the Luftwaffe's coastal defences was unmolested. The farther inland he progressed, the lower the risk of fighter interception.

Giving wide berth to the bomber base at Alençon, Beauregard steered southeast over the Forêt d'Écouvre, past Mamers and La Ferté-Bernard-Cheré. Picking up the Braye at Montdoubleau, he followed the river south until its confluence with the larger Loir, whereupon he turned east. Six miles and less than one minute later, he was over Montoire, where there was nothing much of interest to be seen.

However, the same could not be said for the rail line a short distance northeast of the town. On his left, Beauregard could see what appeared to be an armoured train, stationary with two of its three passenger carriages blackened by fire. An upended tank turret lay beside the lead car and bodies were strewn along the track on either side. Approaching a low ridge that lay perpendicular to his flight path, Beauregard spied another cluster of bodies in the railway cut leading to the entrance of a tunnel. On the far side of the ridge stood a second armoured train that also bore serious signs of battle damage.

This must be the 'something' they were talking about during mission tasking, thought Beauregard as he swivelled his neck, scanning the sky for signs of danger. Noting his fuel state, he quickly settled on a plan. Taking the Spit up to about 3,000 feet, he'd do a 180 and conduct two camera runs, northeast to southwest and then back again on a reciprocal course. Once his second pass was complete, he'd power climb to 27,000 feet and scoot back to Heston as fast as his Rolls Royce Merlin engine would carry him.

If all went well, he'd make it into town with time to spare for his hot date tonight with WAAF Flight Officer Sophie Willoughby de Eresby. Not only was she drop dead gorgeous, but as the Gallic nobiliary particle of her name indicated, she also hailed from one of those patrician families whose Norman lineage traced back to 1066. So tonight, he was pulling out all the stops. Hell, he'd even slipped a tenner to the maître d' at the Savoy Grill for the special table in the far corner. Even a blue blood like Soph should be impressed by the effort and expense, or so he hoped.

Now was not the time for romantic woolgathering. Beauregard reached down and flipped the switch that powered the brace of F24 cameras carried by his Spit. Pulling a tight 180-degree climbing turn to port over Thoré-la-Rochette, he levelled off and thumbed the trigger on the cockpit control column. Instead of firing a non-existent octet of .303 machineguns, the button activated the cameras in either wing.

Beauregard had finished his initial pass, and was turning back towards the northeast, when he spotted four specks above the horizon, approaching from the direction of Le Mans. Fighters? Bombers? They were too distant for positive ID, but Pierre wasn't inclined to stick around and discover which. It was definitely time to skedaddle for home.

Pushing the Spit's throttle into full emergency power, he pulled the stick to his stomach. The fighter leapt skywards like a thoroughbred stallion responding to the touch of spurs, clawing its way through the clouds at a two thousand feet per minute rate of climb.

Steering north-northeast to put distance between himself and those specks, Beauregard turned to port and set a direct course for home. Levelling off at a cruising altitude of 27,000 feet, he was far above the ceiling of German light flak. At 320 miles per hour, he was also moving far too swiftly for the heavier stuff to get an accurate bead. The only real danger he might encounter at this juncture would come from Me-109s or Me-110s lucky enough to position themselves precisely in his path. Even then, they'd only have one shot before he was gone with the wind.

But he didn't relax. Beauregard never forgot the words of his flight instructor back in Louisiana who'd flown Sopwith Camels over the Western Front in 1917–18.

"There are old fighter pilots and there are bold fighter pilots," intoned the crusty old WWI vet, "but there are no old, bold fighter pilots."

Hence, despite the statistical odds now leaning in his favour, Pierre Beauregard-the-younger continued to swivel his head hither and yon in a never-ending search of the sky around him. After all, it's always the thing you least expect that ends up taking a piece out of your ass.

Forty-six

Generalmajor Walter Warlimont tapped his foot restlessly as the Ju-88 taxied down the Tempelhof runway. On his instructions, the aircraft stopped in front of a hangar surrounded by a cordon of gorget-wearing feldgendarmen. A trio of senior Wehrmacht officers waited nearby.

The pilot toggled a switch and the bomb bay doors opened with a hydraulic whine. He then moved to open the hatch and lower the ladder, a role usually filled by one of the crew's two gunners.

But there were no other crewmen along for this trip. Just the pilot and Warlimont, who was gruff and in an obvious hurry. The pilot moved aside as Warlimont climbed down the ladder onto the tarmac, just as another Ju-88 taxied alongside. Weiss and Saller descended from the second bomber.

The major general beckoned to the oberleutnant in command of the feldgendarmerie contingent. The young military police officer approached and saluted smartly.

Warlimont returned the courtesy. "Oberleutnant, I am about to issue a series of orders you will follow to the letter. You and your men will perform your assigned duties with absolute precision. You will do no more and no less than I instruct and any deviation from this protocol will entail very harsh consequences. Do you understand?"

"Jawohl, Herr General," replied the feldgendarmerie officer.

Warlimont nodded. "Very well. There are items in the bomb bays of both aircraft that must be moved into that hangar. The items are secured in an improvised fashion, but in no instance should the ropes around the items themselves be cut or untied. Under no circumstances should the blankets wrapping these items come loose. Am I clear?"

"You are, sir," barked the oberleutnant.

"Good," replied Warlimont. "I'll give you a few moments to brief your troops. And one final thing, Herr Oberleutnant."

"Yes, General?" asked the young officer deferentially.

"Under no circumstances is there to be any speculation or gossip among your men about the contents of the items they're about to handle. I put you on notice that, after today, they will be under surveillance by the Geheime Feldpolizei to ensure compliance with my instructions. Please inform your troops accordingly."

The oberleutnant delivered another salute and summoned his platoon feldwebel who, in turn, assembled the thirty-strong detachment of feldgendarmen in ordered ranks.

Approaching the gaggle of senior officers, it was Warlimont's turn to salute.

"So," said Generalleutnant Friedrich Olbricht, Deputy Commander of the Home Army, "What's so important that it warrants dragging all of us out here in the middle of a work day?"

"Patience, Friedrich," said the second member of the trio, Generalmajor Hans Oster, deputy chief of the Abwehr, Germany military intelligence. "I'm sure General Warlimont will explain matters soon enough."

"Indeed, sir," said Warlimont. "All will become clear in a few minutes."

As per their orders, the feldgendarmarie unloaded the blanket wrapped bodies and laid them in a row on the hangar floor.

"Thank you, Oberleutnant," said Warlimont to the young military police officer. "You will now establish a perimeter around this building and allow no-one to enter without my direct order. Am I clear?"

"Certainly, sir."

"One more thing," said Warlimont as an afterthought. "I'll be needing to borrow a bayonet from one of your men."

A minute later, bayonet in hand, Warlimont led Weiss, Saller and the three generals into the hangar while the feldgendarmarie closed the door behind. Warlimont flipped the light switch and the interior of the windowless hangar was illuminated by yellow florescent lamps. Without uttering word, he proceeded to a bundle with a piece of light blue cloth attached, slicing the ropes that secured the blood-soaked blankets in place. Grimacing at the unavoidable messiness to come, he then proceeded to unwrap the gore-sodden shroud from around the misshapen corpse of Adolf Hitler.

The three generals stood in wordless shock, until Olbricht broke the silence.

"Is that ...?"

"It is," replied Warlimont in a business-like tone. "The others are Himmler, Goebbels, Göring and Keitel. The entire top echelon of the regime has been liquidated in one fell swoop."

Listening thoughtfully until now, Berlin city garrison commander Generalmajor Paule von Hase broke his silence with a one-word question. "How?"

"Ambush," replied Warlimont. "Hitler's train was attacked while passing through a rail tunnel just north of Montoire-sur-le-Loir."

"That's where the summit with Pétain was held," observed Oster.

"Correct. It was a very well-executed operation that would be far beyond the capabilities of any French resistance group. The Führer-Begleit-Bataillon was decimated."

"Then who?" pressed von Hase. "The British?"

"We don't know. Some of the survivors report that the enemy were non-English-speaking Jews."

"Non-English-speaking Jews?" parroted Olbricht in a tone of disbelief.

"That's what I was told," replied Warlimont. "There was no opportunity for confirmation because I made haste to get here."

"But from where? Russia?" pondered Oster. "They have millions of Jews."

"I seriously doubt it," opined Oster. "At present, Stalin is focused on extorting territory from the Finns. He has nothing to gain from picking a fight with us."

"Who then?" asked von Hase.

"Jews from British Palestine, perhaps?" suggested Warlimont. "Our intelligence indicates that they've developed quite an effective guerrilla force. Many of them enlisted in the British army once war was declared. It's likely some of them would be willing to participate in an operation so ... risky."

"God knows they have more than enough reason to hate us," mused von Hase. "Be that as it may, we have more important things to worry about."

"Indeed, sir," replied Oster, who then turned to address Warlimont. "Who else knows about the Führer's death?"

"These two officers here," replied Warlimont with a nod in the direction of Weiss and Saller. "They're from the signal battalion that provided communications support for the summit conference. I've deployed the battalion in a cordon around the ambush site with orders to prevent entry by anyone until further instructions are received from me personally."

"That's very good," replied Oster.

"But there is one other person who has seen Hitler's body," added Warlimont.

"Who is he and why isn't he here?" asked von Hase with an undertone of reproof. "It's vital this be kept under wraps until we can make the appropriate arrangements."

"I agree entirely, sir," replied Warlimont. "It's absolutely essential that we be in a position to forestall any mischief by the SS. But it's equally important to catch or kill these raiders before they escape. The oberleutnant in question is an officer from the Begleit-Bataillon. He's seen the enemy at close range and lived to talk about it. I thought he would be a useful addition to the force of flaktruppen from Châteaudun I've dispatched in pursuit of the raiding force. I've sworn young Koertig to silence and I'm confident he understands the larger issues at stake."

"Let's hope your character judgement is accurate," replied Oster with a rueful shake of the head. "If you're wrong and this gets out, we're likely to have a civil war on our hands."

"That's precisely why we have to move quickly and decisively," said von Hase with a glance at his watch. "It's now 15:48 hours. I'll schedule an emergency planning group for 18:00 hours at Wehrkreiss hauptquartier. Fellgiebel should definitely be there. Control of communications networks will play a key role. I'm inclined to invite Beck as well. Any other suggestions?

"What about Goerdeler, von Dohnányi and Popitz?" suggested Olbricht. "All three of them have protested the maltreatment of the Jews. That should provide some measure of credibility when it comes to negotiating peace with the English."

"And of course, Canaris should attend," said Oster.

"Indeed," replied von Hase, "Canaris should definitely be included in the planning group. Although, the others you mentioned are lawyers and diplomats. They'll have a role to play, but only later. We must bear in mind that, in the first instance, this will be an operational military matter, not a debating society. I intend to move against Prinz-Albrecht-Straße at 09:00 tomorrow morning, when our black-shirted friends are just sitting down to their morning coffee."

"What about the bodies, sir?" asked Oster. "We can't leave them here, even under feldgendarmerie guard."

"True," replied von Hase. "There's a bomb shelter beneath Wehrkreiss hauptquartier. We'll store the bodies there until we decide whether to destroy them quietly or hold some sort of state funeral."

"In that case, we'll need more rope, additional blankets and a truck," said Warlimont.

"I'll organise it with the feldgendarmie. They'll also provide an escort," said Oster.

"Very good, and make sure you bring those two signals officers along with you," said von Hase, indicating Saller and Weiss. "In the meantime, General Olbricht and I will go on ahead. Warlimont, why don't you join us? There are a few additional matters we need to discuss."

The three general officers exited the hangar and made their way to a Mercedes-Benz 770 staff car parked nearby. The driver opened the rear passenger door with all the obsequious deference of a snobby mâitre'd.

"Where to, Herr General?" enquired the driver.

"The Wehrkreiss hauptquartier in Grunwald," von Hase instructed.

The driver closed the glass partition between front and back seats and put the Mercedes into gear.

"So Warlimont, you're something of an enigma," observed Olbricht with a look of cool appraisal. "On one hand, your quickness of thought and clarity of situational analysis have been quite laudable. On the other, I always had you pegged as a true believer."

"Believer in what, sir?" asked Warlimont.

"In the Führerprinzip. The Nazi program. You always seemed so enthusiastic about Hitler's adventurism. Quite frankly, I find this display of pragmatism on your part to be somewhat surprising."

"It's really quite straightforward, sir," rejoined Warlimont. "I believe the Führer deserves great credit for lifting Germany from degradation to greatness, his unfortunate racial preoccupations notwithstanding. Nonetheless, now he's gone and the question of whether his positives outweighed his negatives will be one for debate by historians. At this juncture, we must focus on more practical matters. Our most compelling priority must be the seamless transition of authority to the only institution capable of providing the Reich with the leadership it requires at this critical hour."

"And that institution would be?" prompted von Hase.

"The army, of course, sir," replied Warlimont. "Germany must have sober and responsible men at the helm of government, not wild-eyed ideologues who'll drag the country down the path of irrelevant distractions. Above all, the last thing the nation needs is a violent power struggle to fill the void that has been created by the Führer's death. If that requires armed action against the SS, so be it."

"Very well said, Warlimont," said Olbricht with a nod of respect. "I confess to having harboured serious doubts about you, but I think you might be quite useful to our enterprise after all. Welcome aboard."

Forty-seven

Luftwaffe Major Hugo Shriver sat in the front passenger seat of his kübelwagen, smoking a cigarette and reading from a small leather-bound volume.

Koertig approached the vehicle and saluted. "Sir, I've completed my inspection and can report that the perimeter is secure."

"Thank you," replied Shriver. "What about rations? Did you dispatch a truck to Châteaudun for resupply as I requested?"

"Yes sir, it left ten minutes ago with a feldwebel and ten men."

"Very good. Now you can relax a little. It looks as though we'll be here a while."

"So it seems, sir. What are you reading, if you don't mind my asking?"

Shriver glanced at the book in his hand. "This? Just a bit of poetry. Nothing serious."

"Poetry, eh? I was very fond of von Arnim and Arndt at gymnasium."

Shriver hesitated a moment before answering, "Well, this is Heine."

"Heine? The Jew? Aren't his books banned?"

"Well technically, yes," conceded Shriver. "Still there's nothing political about his Nordsee poetry. I just think his phraseology is sublime. He had this uncanny ability to place just the right word in just the right …"

Shriver's literary exposition was cut short by the sound of approaching vehicles. Moments later, a kübelwagen debouched into the clearing, followed by five Opel Blitz trucks. The newly arrived vehicles had SS markings.

"I'd hide that if I were you," said Koertig, indicating the Luftwaffe major's leather-bound volume.

Shriver nodded and put the book away in his map case.

Helmut Wyzan exited the vehicle, dusting himself off before approaching the two Wehrmacht officers.

"Who is in command here?" barked Wyzan in an imperious tone.

Shriver slowly got to his feet. "That would be me. Major Hugo Shriver, commanding a force of flaktruppen from Châteaudun, at your service."

Wyzan stiffened to attention and delivered a Hitlergruß, frowning when Shriver reciprocated with a conventional military salute.

"Hauptsturmführer Wyzan from Orléans. Can you tell me what's going on at Montoir-sur-le-Loir? I was turned back by army troops who threatened to open fire if I proceeded towards the town. It made no difference to them when I told them of my orders, direct from SS hauptquartier in Paris. They just told us we should come here, instead."

"We were also given instructions to steer clear of Montoire at all costs," said Shriver.

"Instructions?" asked a still indignant Wyzan. "Instructions from whom?"

"From the Deputy Chief of Operations at OKW, Generalmajor Warlimont, delivered in person earlier today."

"Well, perhaps Generalmajor Warlimont has forgotten that the SS is not in the OKW chain of command," said Wyzan. "I'm sure Reichsführer Himmler will be very pleased to administer corrective measures when I inform the Prinz-Albrecht-Straße of this outrage. But that's for another time. Can you tell me what you're doing here?"

"Certainly," replied Shriver. "We were informed this morning that the Führer's train had been attacked."

"Attacked? The Führer!?" yelled Wyzan. "Is he safe!?"

"Yes, the Führer is fine," replied Shriver. "General Warlimont informed us that the Begleit-Bataillon managed to repel the attackers, albeit with heavy casualties." The Luftwaffe major gestured towards Koertig. "Oberleutnant Koertig took part in that battle. He serves in the Führer-Begleit-Bataillon."

Wyzan approached Koertig and extended his hand. "The German people will be forever in your debt."

Koertig flushed as he shook the SS officer's hand. "Thank you, sir."

"No need to be bashful," said Wyzan, turning once again to Shriver. "Please continue, Herr Major."

"As I was saying, earlier today we received word from Luftflotte hauptquartier that the Führer's train had been attacked. A flight of Me-109s was dispatched and I was ordered to organise a reaction force and move by road to Montoire. Just north of Vendôme, we encountered General Warlimont travelling in the opposite direction towards Châteaudun. He informed us that the attackers were English commandos and ordered me to move in pursuit. Because Koertig had the presence of mind to follow the British as they retreated, the general seconded him to me."

"This is all very strange," said Wyzan as he gazed at the row of burnt-out Oshkosh hulks. "They seem to have abandoned their vehicles, but are nowhere to be found. Could they have been evacuated by air?"

"Impossible," replied Shriver. "At the very least there were several dozen commandos involved in this operation. Evacuating that number of troops would require multiple transport aircraft accompanied by fighter escort. There's no way such an armada would escape Luftwaffe notice. Besides, where would they land?"

"That means they've gone to ground somewhere in this area," said Wyzan, his face furrowed with the smile of a hunter anticipating an impending kill.

But the SS officer's feral musings were interrupted by the arrival of another kübelwagen, this one with army markings. A portly army major climbed out and looked around with a flustered expression.

"I know him," volunteered Koertig. "He's the military governor at Vendôme. What's he doing here?"

Before Koertig could indulge in further speculation, the fleshy army officer noted Shriver's rank insignia and approached the Luftwaffe kübelwagen. "Would you be Major Shriver?"

"I am," answered Shriver as he clambered out of his own vehicle. "Who are you and how can I help?"

"I'm Major Trost, the Kreiskommandant in Vendôme. I've been instructed to inform you that one of our routine patrols made contact several hours ago with a heavily armed enemy force just outside the town of Oucques. Local French gendarmes reported that our troops were wiped out to the last man. We believe these are the same English commandos who attacked the Führer's train earlier today. Your orders, direct from General Stülpnagel himself, are to pursue, locate and destroy this enemy unit. Oucques is your initial objective. That's where you should be able to pick up the trail of these Engländers."

"Where exactly is this place?" asked Shriver as he unfolded a map on the hood of his kübelwagen.

"About twenty kilometres east of Vendôme," answered Trost while pointing to a spot on the Luftwaffe officer's map. "Here."

"So why didn't you proceed there directly?" asked a frowning Shriver. "You were much closer to the scene of this engagement than we are here."

273

Trost fidgeted nervously. "You have to understand, Herr Major, I'm in charge of the military administration of this region. Aside from a single platoon of feldgendarmen, my command is composed of clerks and civil affairs specialists. General Stüpnagel has dispatched two infantry battalions to this area, but they're coming from Calais and will only arrive at midday tomorrow. In the meantime, you're the only combat-ready force available."

"What about my orders from General Warlimont? He instructed me to secure this location until relieved."

"The English have clearly moved on, so I think a platoon might suffice for that purpose until our intelligence people arrive to analyse what the enemy left behind," said Trost. "In fact, given that this is now a security matter, I would think such a task might be well suited to our SS comrades."

"Out of the question!" bellowed Wyzan indignantly. "We are the Reich's elite, not gatekeepers. My men and I will not be relegated to guard duty while others go after the English gangsters who tried to kill the Führer. You're correct this is a matter of national security, and it falls directly within the province of SS authority. For that reason, not only will we be participating in the pursuit, but I will be in command of our joint force."

"Hauptsturmführer Wyzan," barked Shriver, "let me be absolutely clear about one thing. While I'm more than happy for you to accompany us, you will bear in mind that this is a Wehrmacht operation. You are junior to me in rank and will abide by my orders and my authority. Do you understand?"

After a few moments of sulky silence, Wyzan's head bowed ever-so-slightly in the most reluctant of nods. "Understood, sir."

"There's still something about this that bothers me," said Shriver as he refocused his attentions on the map. "If these raiders are indeed English, wouldn't their optimal escape route be west to the Atlantic for extraction by the Royal Navy?"

"Or northwest to the Channel," volunteered Koertig.

Shriver shook his head dismissively. "I doubt they'd go north because the entire Channel area is swarming with our troops. It's the most heavily occupied part of France. So no, I think the Atlantic coast around Saint-Nazaire would be their best choice. It's what I'd do in their place."

"It makes you wonder what these Englishmen were doing in a village fifty kilometres east of here," said Koertig. "Why would they be travelling away from the coast instead of directly towards it?"

"Perhaps they're trying to reach neutral territory in Switzerland," suggested Wyzan.

"I briefly considered that possibility until I calculated the distances," replied Shriver. "It's almost twice as far to the Swiss border than to St Nazaire."

"Could it be a feint?" pondered Koertig. "They go east and then double back to the coast, travelling at night?"

"Possible," replied Shriver with a shrug. "In fact, it's the only explanation that would make any sense at all. Major Trost, was there any mention of this paradox during your conversation with Paris?"

"None at all," replied Trost. "I was simply instructed to provide what little intelligence we have about the Oucques' incident and transmit your orders. It was a very short conversation."

"I see," replied Shriver. "Then may I make a suggestion?"

"Most certainly," replied Trost in a deferential tone.

"When you return to Vendôme, I would ask that you raise this question with someone in General Stüpnagel's hauptquartier who is senior enough to understand its significance."

"I can try. I spoke previously to Oberst Eiffler, the General's Chief-of-Staff. I suppose I can try to reach him, although I should also inform my superiors at the Feldkommandatur in Orléans."

"I would suggest you leave Orléans out of it at this stage," replied Shriver. "The assassination attempt on the Führer makes this an extraordinary situation that demands exceptional measures. It's essential that all possible escape routes be sealed in the event we end up on a wild goose chase. I would strongly urge that you convey this analysis to Eiffler, or even to General Stüpnagel, personally – and chain of command be damned."

Trost nodded. "I shall do that."

"Thank you," said Shriver while glancing at his watch. He turned to address Koertig and Wyzan. "The time is now 16:34, which leaves us just over four hours of daylight. I want us to be on the road by 16:50 at the latest. Our order of movement will be my kübelwagen, followed by the Luftwaffe trucks and the SS trucks, with Hauptsturmführer Wyzan's kübelwagen bringing up the rear. We have no radios, so make sure to keep the column tight. Wyzan, get your men organised while I detail a platoon to remain here. Koertig, you'll be with me. You can navigate."

Forty-eight

Emma looked at the pile of dirty dishes and sighed, recalling the days when the ranks of the Cohen household included a live-in maid to handle such drudgery. The employment by Jews of domestic servants had been outlawed these past five years since the enactment of the Nuremberg racial purity laws. Shrugging in resignation to current reality, she began to roll up her sleeves when a squeal of brakes and tyres was heard from the street in front.

Leaving the kitchen, she walked through the lounge room to the large picture window that looked out on the Lauerstraße. There she saw a feldgrau-hued Opel Blitz and a black Mercedes-Benz sedan had stopped in the middle of the street. A half-dozen green-uniformed ordnungspolizei clambered down from the cargo bed of the truck as a man clad in a leather trench coat and fedora emerged from the Benz.

Gestapo, concluded Emma as she watched the plain-clothes man consult a notebook binder and point to the Cohen home. Three of the ordnungspolizei peeled off from the group to the left. Securing the rear, she thought. Those who remained, uniformed and non-uniformed, approached the front steps of her house.

Emma rebuttoned her sleeves in anticipation of the pounding on the front door that immediately followed.

"I'll get it, Mutti!" she yelled.

Emma walked to mirror to check that her hair was in place and continued on through the front entry hall, where she opened the door.

"Is this the Cohen residence?" asked the notebook bearer, a middle-aged man with tobacco-stained teeth who spoke in an officious tone.

Emma nodded.

"I'm required to speak with the owner of this home," he intoned.

"My name is Emma Cohen and my parents are indisposed at present. You'll have to speak with me."

The man scowled and leafed through his binder until he found the correct page. After a throat-clearing cough, he spoke in a voice rich with the arrogance of someone endowed with life-or-death authority. "My name is Kriminalrat Portner of the Geheime Staatspolizei. How many Jews live here?"

"Myself and my parents," Emma replied.

Portner consulted his notebook and nodded. "Are there any firearms in the house?"

Emma shook her head. "My father did own some guns ... shotguns and rifles, I think. There was also a pistol he brought home from the war. He turned these all into the police when the law was changed a couple of years ago."

Portner again consulted his notebook. "Yes, that's consistent with our records. Three shotguns, two rifles and a pistol surrendered at Heidelberg Central Police Station on 21 November 1938."

"What's all this about?" Emma enquired, despite knowing the answer in her heart.

"Under provisions of the First Regulation to the Reich Citizenship Law of November 14, 1935, Jews are no longer eligible for the privileges of German citizenship," the Gestapo officer intoned didactically. "Under the authority of Robert Wagner, Gauleiter of Baden, I hereby inform you that your residency rights have been terminated as of today, 26 October, 1940. You are, therefore, subject to immediate removal from the Reich."

Mustering every ounce of available willpower, Emma submerged the raging torrent of fear beneath an outward façade of quiet dignity. "Where are we to be taken?" she asked.

"You'll be informed of your precise destination at the appropriate time," Portner replied in a tone of utter indifference. "Each Jew is entitled to take 100 reichsmarks and one suitcase filled with clothing, plus personal essentials. All other Jewish property is forfeited to the German people, including homes, businesses, motor vehicles, money, jewellery and other valuables. I would also advise you to bring a blanket and as much food as you can carry. You have thirty minutes to prepare." The Gestapo officer looked up from his notes. "Do you have any questions?"

The query was so obviously rhetorical, and posed with such infuriating blitheness that Emma failed to contain her anger. "Would it make any difference if I did?" she asked, contempt palpable in her voice.

Portner's face darkened at Emma's show of defiance, but then he simply sneered, revealing his nicotine-tarnished dentition in all its chestnut-hued ugliness. "Your thirty minutes begin now," he said with a glance at his watch.

Without another word, Emma turned on her heel, slamming the door behind her in the Gestapo officer's face. She descended into the basement and ferried up the suitcases pre-packed in anticipation of this event. She then climbed the stairs to her home's second storey and knocked on her parents' bedroom door.

"Come in," warbled Emma's mother in a reedy voice that betrayed her tenuous health.

Emma stepped through the door.

"Good morning leibling," said Dvora Cohen, while combing her hair at a cherry wood rococo vanity table.

"Good morning Mutti," said Emma. "Where's father?"

"In the library, dear," replied Dvorah.

"Mutti, we have to talk. Now."

"Can't it wait?" said Dvorah, frowning in disapproval at the ravages of age she saw gazing back from the mirror. "I'm about to get dressed."

"No, it can't." Emma took her mother by the shoulders, forcing Dvorah to turn away from the vanity.

"Liebling, you're hurting me," protested Dvorah. "Whatever has gotten into you?"

"Mother, the Gestapo are downstairs. They're here to take us away from Heidelberg and we only have thirty minutes to pack."

"Take us away?" said Dvora, her head shaking with disbelief. "Don't be ridiculous, child. This is our home."

Emma took Dvora by the arm, forcefully propelling her mother to the bedroom's large double window that faced out on to the Lauerstraße.

"Look, Mother," said Emma as she pointed at the uniformed police and plain-clothes Gestapo agent loitering on the street below. "They're here for us."

"But ..."

"Mutti!" interjected Emma. "There's no time to argue. I've packed suitcases for us all. I want you now to get dressed with as many layers of clothing as you can wear at one time. Can you do that?"

Dvorah Cohen nodded, her eyes widening with visceral fear.

"I'll go and tell father."

Twenty-seven minutes later, mere seconds before Portner's deadline,

278

the door to the Cohen residence opened and Emma walked onto the front step, followed by her mother and father. They each carried a medium-sized valise and had a blanket tied diagonally around their waist and shoulder like a Confederate soldier's bedroll.

Portner walked up the front steps, presenting a sheaf of documents and fountain pen to Manfred Cohen, Emma's father. "I'll need you to sign these, if you please."

"Let me have a look," replied Emma with extended hand. "I'm ... I was a lawyer."

The Gestapo officer shrugged, handing her the documents and pen.

Emma leafed through the paperwork for a few moments and proffered the documents with a definitive shake of her head. "This is obscene. My father will not sign."

Portner looked nonplussed. "You must. Those are my orders."

"We must?" replied Emma in a tone of open rebellion. "What will you do if we refuse? Deport us?"

Sensing possible trouble, the Orpos clustered behind Portner, ready to react with force if so instructed.

At a loss for words, Portner simply fell back on a reiteration of his previous demand. "Madame, your father simply must sign these documents."

Emma once again shook her head. "Mein Herr, you want us to sign a declaration stating that our property has been relinquished voluntarily. That is a lie. You know this as well as we do."

A now thoroughly terrified Dvora Cohen placed a hand on her daughter's arm. "Lielbling, pehaps we should ..."

"Mutti, be quiet," ordered Emma. She motioned with her head towards the waiting Orpos. "Herr Portner, you have the power to strip us of our possessions; that much is undeniable. You have no moral authority and we will not assist you in propagating the illusion that this is anything other than an act of thuggery. You can force us to go with you at the point of a gun. However, you cannot force us to legitimise this hoax by signing a fraudulent piece of paper that legalises your theft of our property."

Portner threw up his hands in frustration and snatched the documents from Emma's outstretched hand.

"You realise it'll make no difference in the end," said the Gestapo officer as he folded the documents into his notebook.

279

"My point precisely," Emma replied.

Portner gestured to an Orpo Wachtmeister. "Ebner, they're yours. Take one other man as escort. The rest of you, back on the truck and follow me. We have more house calls to make."

"Just a minute," protested Emma. "It's over three kilometres to the station. My parents are sick. There's no way they could make their way on foot, even if they weren't carrying luggage."

"Do you really expect the Reich to expend a single millilitre of benzene on the likes of you?" smirked Portner. "You're lucky we've laid on a train instead of making you walk your way out of the Reich."

Emma gazed at her mother and father, their frailty extinguishing the last embers of defiance in her soul. "Alright," said Emma, "you win. We'll sign. Just take us to the station in your truck. Please."

Portner extracted the sheaf of documents and offered them to Emma.

"A pen?"

The Gestapo officer reached into his jacket pocket and produced an expensive Orthos fountain pen.

Emma pointed out the signature line to her father, who duly autographed the document at the appointed place. She returned the signed document to Portner, who folded it into his notebook as he walked back to the Mercedez-Benz.

"But what about my parents?" remonstrated Emma in palpable desperation. "Herr Portner, we had a deal. My father's signature in return for transport to the station."

His hand on the open door of the Mercedes, the Gestapo man turned to face Emma with theatrical and deliberate slowness. He flashed a triumphal grin, savouring the utter deflation of the annoying Jew's arrogance.

"I don't recall any formal arrangement of the kind – and, even if I did, there's no real obligation to keep an agreement with such an untrustworthy race as yours. So ... what is it the French say on occasions like this? 'Bon voyage,' I believe."

With that, Portner climbed into the back seat of the car, which then drove off followed by the Orpo truck.

Ebner, whose rank of wachmeister was equivalent to a United States Army sergeancy, was all business, paying no heed to the tears of frustration coursing down Emma's cheeks. "It's time," he declared in a toneless voice.

Emma nodded soberly, focused now on the need to succour her

vulnerable parents during the impending ordeal. She picked up, not only her own valise, but her father's as well. "Mutti, papa, let's go. Don't worry, I'll be here to help."

They made for a quite pitiful procession, moving slowly westwards along the cobblestoned Lauerstraße. Every fifty metres or so, they paused as the Cohen seniors caught their breath. By the time they'd turned south into Große Mantelgasse, the streets were lined with residents who watched the expulsion of their neighbours in sombre silence. Only one intrepid soul, a woman, aged in her 50s, who they barely knew, gave public vent to her distress as she wept openly. She was even so bold as to give a wave of adieu, eliciting poisonous glances from her fellow onlookers, who remained silent out of prejudice or fear.

At the corner of the Hauptstraße, Emma and her parents were joined by Arthur Lilienthal, a fortysomething widower likewise proceeding under Orpo escort with his 12-year-old twin daughters, Sarah and Hanna, in tow. When this cavalcade of heartache emerged from residential streets onto one of Heidelberg's main commercial thoroughfares, the Hauptstraße, things went from very bad to even worse. It was there that the Hitlerjugend materialised like a pack of ravening hyenas, chivvying their prey. A dozen teenage boys, resplendent in red-white kerchiefs, brown uniforms and swastika armbands rounded on the hapless expellees.

First to fly were insults and imprecations – "sheissejude" and "saujude." A middle-aged businessman looking on from the sidewalk was a bit more creative, fancying himself as something of a wag. In stentorian tones he shouted, "Be happy Jews, now you'll have a chance to visit your promised land!", much to the amusement of his fellow passersby. Then came items of food, mostly eggs and tomatoes, and bags of rubbish. Only when stones were hurled did the Orpos finally put a stop to this gauntlet of harassment. Emma suspected the policemen's motives had less to do with compassion than with a desire to avoid carrying anyone who might be injured.

After a two-hour journey, both torturous and tortuous, the Cohens and Lilienthals finally arrived at the forecourt of the Heidelberg rail station. Still under guard, they were ushered through the red sandstone terminal building to platform two.

A wooden table had been placed astride the entrance to the railway platform, manned by two men clad in unofficial Gestapo uniform – leather trench coats and fedoras.

"Names?" asked Gestapo A in the humdrum tone of someone fed up by the tedium of his labours.

"Cohen. Emma, Devora and Manfred," Emma tonelessly replied.

"Cohen, Manfred; Cohen, Manfred," echoed Gestapo B, while he consulted his notebook, tracing lines of print with his index finger. "Yes," he said as he looked up at Emma. "A family of three living at 14 Lauerstraße?"

Emma nodded.

Gestapo B made a notation with his pen in the notebook. "And you?" he enquired of Arthur Lilienthal.

The same procedure ensued, with the Lilienthals' address being confirmed and appropriate notation made.

"You've been informed of your allowances for this journey," announced Gestapo A. "Currency in excess of 100 reichsmarks per person or any other type of valuable, including gold or jewellery, is contraband and subject to confiscation. You will shortly be searched, but I wish to offer you the opportunity to surrender any illicit material without penalty. Any prohibited items found afterwards will result in severe punishment."

The Cohens stood quietly while Arthur Lilienthal walked forward and placed a leather pouch on the table.

Gestapo man A opened the pouch, spilling diamonds across the table. The Nazi nodded knowingly. "Helmut, mark down Herr Lilienthal's diamonds. Anything else?" he asked of both families.

Lilienthal shook his head while the Cohens continued their silent vigil.

"Right," said Gestapo A, "empty your pockets and place your luggage on the table in front of me."

Emma ostentatiously turned out her pockets on to the table, making a small pile of their bread and cheese contents. She then heaved the Cohen's three suitcases up onto the table, opening them for inspection.

Gestapo A rummaged around, smiling in silent disdain at the ten kilograms of sausage he discovered in Emma's valise. Finding nothing of interest, he waved the Cohens through with the capricious arrogance of a powerbroker who can make or break people by whim. Emma quickly repocketed her food, closed her family's suitcases and walked past the checkpoint with averted eyes, exhaling in silent relief that her inspection had been so cursory.

The Lilienthals enjoyed no such luck, the interest of the Gestapo piqued by the trove of diamonds the accountant had previously surrendered.

As Emma made her way down the platform, she heard one of the Gestapo officers say, "Herr Lilienthal, your attempt to smuggle valuables out of the Reich was a typical act of Yid trickery. I'm curious what else you might be hiding."

She dared not turn around as she led her exhausted parents onto the station platform. Much of that space was already occupied by haggard people sitting in clusters of friends or family, casting fearful glances at the patrolling Orpos. At the far end, Emma spied a vacant bench and rushed forward in an attempt to beat several others competing for the same prize. She lost, only by a couple of metres, to a late-middle-aged man clad in an expensive overcoat and homberg hat. As the man turned in triumph to beckon his family forward, she immediately recognised Emanuel Goldberg, the obstetrician who had delivered her into this world.

"Dr Goldberg," said Emma, "my parents are exhausted. Could you please let them sit on the bench, at least until they regain some strength?"

Goldberg gazed back with eyes that reflected a fierce determination to promote his kin's interests against all comers. "Sorry Emma, but my grandchildren are with me. I have to look after my own."

Emma simply shrugged and turned back to her parents. "Papa, Mutti, come over here. There's a space where we can sit."

She guided her parents to an open spot on the platform, arranging their three leather valises in a row. She untied the blanket from around her shoulders, spreading it over the suitcases as a makeshift cushion.

"Papa, why don't you lie down and rest?" Emma urged. "After a while, Mutti can have a turn."

A fatigued Manfred Cohen gave a nod and gratefully sank onto the improvised bed his daughter had constructed. He was soon fast asleep.

The sound of hobnailed boots on cement caused Emma to cast a wary glance at an ordnungspolizei constable approaching along the platform. As the policeman wended his way through the clusters of dejected and desperate people, she noticed something vaguely familiar. Then it dawned on her – he was the kindly policeman who had proved such a lifesaver during that terrible incident at the butcher shop.

Reciprocal recognition on the policeman's part was almost simultaneous and he walked over to Emma. "Hello again, Miss."

Emma responded with a guarded nod.

"I just wanted you to know that I think this is wrong," he muttered.

Emma simply sighed.

"I have no choice. My family ... the Gestapo ... I'm sorry."

"So am I," countered Emma bitterly. "My father was an artillery officer in the last war. He doesn't deserve..."

"Jollenbeck, stop fraternising with the Yids and get back to your patrol!" came a drill sergeant-ish yell that echoed through the station.

Both Jollenbeck and Emma looked around towards the source of the shout, an Orpo NCO standing at the end of the platform, hands on hips.

"Jawohl, Herr Oberwachtmeister," replied Jollenbeck with a deferential wave. "I'm sorry," he murmured one final time before turning to resume his rounds.

Emma had no interest in the policeman's plea for moral absolution. It would be three years later when Professor Abraham Mazlow would introduce his 'hierarchy of needs' theory. The Brooklyn College psychologist might, nonetheless, have recognised Emma Cohen's instinctive focus on the most compelling necessity of that moment, which was shielding her mother from the biting chill of that late autumn morning.

Huddled beneath the family's sole remaining blanket, she embraced her mother in an effort to maximise the warming effect of their combined body heat. There they sat, shivering from a combination of cold and exhaustion, blindly awaiting the next twist of fate. Emma hoped for the best, but feared the worst.

Forty-nine

Danielle Morency smiled as Azriel Weinstock brought the surgical glove to his lips and blew, transforming the thin rubber gauntlet into a rotund, five-fingered balloon. Tying it off at the bottom, he handed the newly created toy to Adele.

"Maman, il est comme un coq!" the little girl proclaimed with giggly delight as she threw the balloon skywards and chased it across the forest clearing.

"Oui ma chérie," Danielle replied. "Don't go too far." She smiled at Weinstock. "You're very good with her."

Weinstock grinned. "How could I not be? I mean, look at her. She's cuter than the law allows."

"She's getting very tired," observed Danielle, exuding the inerrant authority of a mother with intimate knowledge of her child's habits. "Just you watch, she'll be ready for a nap within a couple of minutes."

And so it transpired. Adele's giggly pursuit of the glove balloon was suddenly interrupted by an acute bout of yawning. Danielle rose to her feet, enfolding the child in her arms. Ducking under the camouflage net stretched over Weinstock's S-ATV, she slid her daughter into a goose down sleeping bag and Adele fell asleep almost instantaneously.

"It's been an exhausting couple of days," said Danielle as she cast a loving gaze on the sleeping little girl.

"No doubt," replied Weinstock. "I'm sure you've had difficulty getting your head around all this and you're an adult. It must be totally mind-boggling to a four-year-old."

"Actually, I think it might be easier for her," replied Danielle. "At her age, things are far more basic. Besides, she's taken a real liking to you all. She's usually quite shy with strangers."

"Events of the past days have accelerated the flow of human emotion for everyone," observed Weinstock. "I think the boys have adopted Adele as their surrogate little sister. Remember, each of them has a family they'll never see again. It's really no surprise they've been doting on her."

"I suppose that makes sense," said Danielle. "From one perspective it's very sad, but in light of what you've accomplished, I hope you'd agree it was worthwhile."

"Our purpose in coming here was to forestall the Shoah. If we've succeeded at that task, there's no question it's worth the sacrifice. At least that's what I think."

"You all keep using that word. What does it mean?"

Weinstock cast a melancholy glance in her direction. "'Shoah' translates literally from the Hebrew as 'catastrophe'. Although, in our context we mean the unprecedented mass murder of European Jews that will take place over the next five years."

"Unprecedented how?" queried Danielle. "Jewish history is full of pogroms, expulsions and massacres. Also, over a million Armenians were killed by the Turks during the last war."

Weinstock shook his head. "No, this is something new. Something different, qualitatively and quantitatively. According to history as we knew it, Hitler invades Russia in June 1941. Behind the German frontline, there are special SS units tasked with killing Jews. They move from city to town to village shooting men, women and children without mercy. One-and-a-half million are killed this way, but firing squads prove much too slow and messy for what the Nazis have in mind. So, in 1942, the SS builds mechanised death camps – factories for killing people. By the time Germany is defeated in 1945, almost six million Jews from all over Europe are murdered, and millions of others as well. That's what we came through time to prevent."

Danielle sat in silence for a few moments, absorbing Weinstock's grim tidings.

"How ... how many French Jews?"

"I don't remember precisely, but if my recall of high school history is correct, I think about 70,000."

"It's very likely that you saved our lives, then," observed Danielle.

"Perhaps," mumbled Weinstock bashfully.

"Then a thank you is in order," said Danielle. At which point she leaned over and kissed the Israeli captain on the lips for the second time in so many days.

"So, Mister Future Man, did you have a girlfriend in the 21st century?" she asked as her lips curled in a coquettish smile.

Still flushed from her kiss, Weinstock smiled shyly, shaking his head. "Not really. I got to know a few girls at social events while I was studying at yeshiva. But then there was the army, and all-male combat units aren't very conducive to romance. My dad had someone in mind. Another rabbi's daughter. He tried to organise a shidduch, but nothing ever came of it. She was nice, but ..."

"No fireworks?" asked Danielle as her hands mimicked an explosion.

He shook his head. "What about you? How did you end up marrying a shaygetz cow doctor?"

Danielle smiled. "I met Gaston while we were both students. He was studying at l'École Nationale Vétérinaire d'Alfort while I was a Normalien reading classics."

"A what?"

"A Normalien is argot for a student at l'École Normale Supérieure. The university in Paris. I was studying Latin and Greek."

"Latin and Greek, eh?"

Danielle smiled self-effacingly. "I come from a family of socialists."

"Did you love him?"

"Love him?" Danielle echoed as her eyes glistened. "When I think about it now, I don't know whether it was really love. I was certainly infatuated. He was very handsome and charismatic. One of those brooding Marxists whose eyes shone with ideological fervour. Swept me completely off my feet. I became pregnant during the fourth year of my studies, so we eloped. I was absolutely enormous by the time I received my Diplôme. To the point where I literally waddled across the stage. It was quite the scandal! Adele came along about six weeks later – but enough about my unseemly past. Tell me about your family."

"Well, we're originally from France," said Weinstock. "Toulouse, to be precise."

"Ah, that explains your funny accent," Danielle quipped with a cheeky grin that defused any umbrage her comment might otherwise cause.

"Ha, ha," replied Weinstock with a smile that matched hers. "I really don't remember much of France because I was only five years old when my family settled in Netanya, a town north of Tel Aviv on the Mediterranean coast with a big Francophone community. My dad is a rabbi who works as the principal of a religious high school for girls."

"Brothers? Sisters?"

287

"Three brothers, two sisters. I'm the youngest."

"Ah, the baby of the family!" proclaimed Danielle with delight.

"Oh yes," answered Weinstock. "I was subject to a lot of swaddling and coddling when I was young. Although, I like to think I turned out alright."

"The jury's still out on that one," said Danielle with a disarming smile. "What about your mother?"

"A teacher at my father's school. Jewish philosophy and Hebrew literature."

Danielle nodded respectfully. "Ah, so you come from a family of scholars. Very much like me, but then very much unlike me. My parents are secular Jewish intellectuals who dabble in leftwing politics with infrequent visits to synagogue. They're big fans of Léon Blum."

"The former socialist prime minister?"

Danielle smiled. "Very good, you know your history, but I want to hear more about the future. Did you have flying cars in the 21st century?"

Weinstock laughed lightly and shook his head. "No flying cars, but air travel is quite routine and affordable. With a modern jetliner, you can get from New York to Paris in about eight hours."

"Eight hours!" she echoed. "Incroyable! What else?"

"Well, the world of the 21st century will surely be different because of what we've accomplished. I hope that change will be for the better, but we'll have to wait about eight decades to find out for sure."

"And what about Israel? Tell me about your Jewish state."

"The Israel we left had a population of just under nine million people, 75 per cent of whom were Jews. We had a very hi-tech economy that was at the forefront of computer science and online applications." Weinstock halted his exposition, picking up cues from the blank expression on Danielle's face. "You have no idea what I'm talking about, do you?"

She responded with a typically Gallic shrug.

"A computer is an electronic machine that can complete many thousands of calculations per second. The smaller ones we call 'laptops' because you can carry them in one hand. They can be used for everything from writing a novel through scientific equations to watching movies. Then there's the internet, which is going to be hard to live without."

"What's this internet?" asked Danielle.

"Well, imagine millions of these computers throughout the world all connected in one massive network. They can all communicate

288

instantaneously with each other through what we call 'email'. It's driving postal services throughout the world bankrupt. There's so much information in this network, the problem is finding the information you seek within a sea of data. There are also massive amounts of online pornography."

"Ah," said Danielle with an impish grin. "Now I know what you miss so much about this internet."

Weinstock's face turned beet red. "No, I didn't ... I would never ... " he hemmed and hawed.

Danielle looked down at the pine needle-strewn forest floor as she struggled to contain her laughter. After a few moments, her mirth under control, she looked up at the still-blushing Weinstock

"I apologise, chèrie. In future, I'll try to keep my risqué sense of humour under control."

Weinstock's face flushed anew in response to Danielle's term of endearment.

"Last night went pretty smoothly," he interjected in a rather transparent shift of topic. "I checked the odometer and we travelled 278 kilometres in just under eight hours without problems along the way."

Recalling the admonition of the Roman historian Seutonius to 'hasten slowly', Danielle adopted an innocent mien and embraced this transition back into Weinstock's comfort zone. It's a marathon, not a sprint, she thought, her mouth curling ever-so-slightly in a scarcely perceptible smile.

"I couldn't believe we were just cruising down the road as if we owned it," she said with a deliberate shake of the head to accentuate her amazement. "Unbelievable."

Weinstock responded with a smile that was two-parts modesty mixed with eight parts professional pride. "It's not so surprising. The Tanach tells us we should fight wars by subterfuge and deception. In our time, Israeli special forces have earned a global reputation for boldness. We've found that, when you act as though you belong somewhere, most people just accept your presence without challenge. Don't forget we were travelling at night under a waning moon. Let's just hope we've moved far enough to vanish off their radar."

"Weinstock, I have enough difficulty following your 21st-century patois without throwing in words that are completely foreign to me," said Danielle in mild reproof.

"Sorry," said Weinstock, "What did I say?"

"Le 'radar'. Qu'est-ce que c'est?"

"Ah. It transmits radio waves that bounce off ships or aircraft. Those returning waves are read by the radar receiver, showing the position of the objects. In 1940, it was ... is a very new and hush-hush technology that played a key role in the British victory over the German air force last summer."

"All very interesting," replied Danielle, "but what does that have to do with us?"

"It was just a turn of phrase. L'argot, ou une expression familière. Vanishing off the radar means disappearing from view. I was expressing the hope that the Germans have no idea where we are." Weinstock looked at his watch. "It's 16:45. Time to mark our route."

He stood up, ducked beneath the camouflage net and reappeared moments later bearing a roll of white plastic tape.

"What's that?" asked Danielle.

"We usually use it for marking paths through minefields. In this case, it'll guide us through the dark back to the dirt road."

"May I come with you?"

"That would be very nice," Weinstock replied with a shy smile. "What about Adele?"

"Shlomo?" asked Danielle in French-accented English. "Could you please watch Adele for a few minutes?"

"Happy to," answered Sergeant Shlomo Blumfeld. "But what if she wakes up?"

"A bonbon from your food and play with 'er until I come back. I won't be long. And she likes you."

Blumfeld smiled at the compliment and took a seat beside the sleeping bag within which Adele was cocooned.

As the pair made their way towards the trees, a wolf-whistle was heard behind them, triggering a spate of sophomoric guffawing that caused Weinstock's face to redden. He began to turn around in search of the offenders when Danielle took his hand.

"Never mind," she whispered. "They're just young boys being silly."

"They're jealous," he said.

"No doubt," she replied. "But come on, chèrie, ignore them. We have work to do."

Weinstock nodded and they continued on their way into the wood, her hand still encasing his.

Only now he seemed quite content for it to remain there.

Fifty

For the second time in twenty-four hours, Lieutenant Colonel Ralph Neville found himself within the subterranean reaches of the Cabinet War Rooms. He entered the same briefing theatre and noted the same complement of faces gazing back at him – with one exception. A bookish-looking RAF Flight Lieutenant stood next to a projector that was aimed towards a large screen at the front of the room.

"Well Neville, you must be feeling very pleased with yourself," said Winston Churchill.

"Yes sir," replied Neville. "I won't deny the news from Berlin was quite satisfying on a personal level. I'm also very happy about the broader implications."

"Of course, of course," replied the Prime Minister. "Nonetheless congratulations are in order, both over your outstanding piece of intelligence analysis and the personal consequences that have ensued."

"Personal consequences, sir?" replied Neville, his brow furrowed in puzzlement. "I'm not sure I understand."

Churchill flashed a roguish grin, proffering a small ring box to the Chief of the Imperial General Staff, General Sir John Dill. "He's one of yours, so you may as well do the honours."

"Certainly, Prime Minister," Dill replied.

"It appears you're out of uniform," the Prime Minister said to Neville, who opened the box to see a pair of Bath stars. When added to the crown and star already adorning each of his epaulets, he would be wearing the insignia of a full colonel.

"Thank you, sir," said Neville. "I don't quite know what to say."

"No need for thanks," said Churchill with an air of noblesse oblige. "Your promotion is very well deserved. Besides, Cavendish-Bentinck's new Chief of Staff must have the appropriate rank. Anything less would reflect ill on him."

"Of course, sir," said Neville in deadpan mode, unsure whether the Prime Minister was serious or speaking in jest.

292

"Now let's get back to les nouvelles de l'heure. Did you have a look at the aerial photos that came in last night?"

"I did, sir," replied Neville.

"Good," said Churchill. "Flight Lieutenant Horrigan is a photographic interpretation expert. Between the two of you, perhaps we can make some sense out of this. Flight Lieutenant, you may begin."

The lights dimmed and a black and white photograph materialised on screen.

"This is a German armoured train on the rail line south of the tunnel at Saint-Rimay," Horrigan intoned. "As you can see, it's been beaten up pretty badly. That upended object you see to the right of the lead car is a Panzer MK III tank turret that was blown off its mounting. There are dead bodies all about and the three passenger cars are burnt to a greater or lesser extent."

"General Davidson?" prompted Churchill.

"Well, sir, this particular tunnel is about two miles northeast of Montoire-sur-le-Loir, the town where we think Hitler held his conference with Pètain two days ago. As Colonel Neville noted yesterday, it's astride the most direct rail line from Montoire to Paris and, ultimately, Germany. We know that, whenever Hitler travels by rail, he's accompanied by a battalion-sized security unit. I think this train would be transporting that escort force."

"Next," instructed the Prime Minister.

A clunking sound was heard as Horrigan operated the projector's manual feed tray. A new photo popped up on the screen.

"This is the northeastern side of the tunnel. You can see a second armoured train that fared no better than its mate to the South. In this case, the panzer turret is still on its mounting, but if you look closely you can see that it's been ripped open like a tin of sardines. Note the signs of fire and the bodies strewn about here as well."

"So, whoever did this brought some serious firepower to bear," observed Air Marshall Charles Portal, Chief of the Air Staff. "It looks like something an aircraft would do, except we had nothing in that area yesterday."

"Sir," interjected Neville, "if I may?"

"Go ahead, Colonel," replied Churchill. "Please."

"Thank you, sir. To me, the most interesting thing is down at the bottom left of the photo. The area is partially in the shade, but if you look closely you can see two locomotives extruding from the eastern end of the tunnel. That raises the question of what's hidden within."

"What's your hypothesis?" prompted Churchill.

"Well, sir, I believe that what we're seeing here is evidence of a brilliant ambush. The tunnel is a perfect chokepoint. After destroying both escort trains, the attackers neutralised the two locomotives pulling Hitler's train just as they emerged from the tunnel. Then they sealed the tunnel at both ends, destroyed the escorts, and the Führer, along with his entire entourage, was caught like a rat in a trap."

"Ha!" exulted Churchill with a boisterous a slap on the table. "Rat in a trap! Quite descriptive, indeed! Are you buying the story that this was an SS operation? Some sort of coup attempt?"

"At present, we have no idea, sir," replied Cavendish-Bentinck. "The first announcement over Radio Berlin came in at 19:15 our time. While we do have certain assets in Berlin, we certainly won't be hearing anything for several days at the earliest."

"What size force would be required to execute such an operation?" asked Admiral Dudley Pound.

Neville and Davidson remained silent, deferring to General Dill as the senior army officer present.

"I wouldn't try it with anything less than a full battalion, and an anti-tank battery of 2-Pounders attached."

"So that means ... what, eight hundred men?" enquired Churchill.

"Just about," replied Dill.

"Wouldn't that lend credence to the story of SS culpability?", postulated the Prime Minister. "Himmler wouldn't have a problem moving eight hundred fully armed men plus support weapons around central France. Then there's the intelligence question. Who else would have enough prior information about Hitler's itinerary to allow adequate planning and preparation for what was clearly quite a sophisticated operation?"

"It would be well beyond the capabilities of the Resistance, such as it is," observed Cavendish-Bentinck.

"No doubt," concurred Churchill.

"Of course, we shouldn't discount the possibility that this was an army operation and the SS was framed," volunteered Davidson. "We know there's been considerable opposition to Hitler within the officer corps."

"Too Machiavellian, even for my twisted mind," replied Churchill. "But theories of culpability aside, at this stage I'm more concerned what this means for us. Colonel Neville, your thoughts?"

"Well, sir, I think we can infer a few things from the Radio Berlin news bulletin, cursory though it was. First and foremost, it's clear that the army is now in charge. Göring, Keitel, Raeder and Goebbels are dead, alongside Hitler, in what is being described as an attempted SS putsch. We've also been told that Himmler and Heydrich are under arrest and the SS is being disbanded. This removes the only source of a possible challenge against the army's seizure of power. The announcement of General Beck as provisional Chancellor is a very good sign. You may recall he resigned as Chief of Staff in August 1938, over his opposition to Hitler's designs on Czechoslovakia. In fact, the following year he made contact with our Foreign Office to solicit support for an anti-Nazi coup. All this would indicate that Germany is now governed by conservative military officers who've always been sceptical of what they considered Hitler's irresponsible adventurism."

"What can we expect going forward?" asked Admiral Pound.

"A policy of consolidation, sir," replied Davidson. "We believe they'll focus on cementing their rule over last summer's conquests. I doubt we'll see a serious move to mount a cross-Channel invasion of Britain next year. The Luftwaffe has only just begun the process of making good the losses it suffered over the past four months. We think it unlikely that the powers-that-be in Berlin will have much stomach for another tangle with a rested and replenished Fighter Command."

Davidson's analysis triggered a smile of proprietary pride from Air Marshall Portal.

"And the war at sea? Their U-Boat campaign?" pressed a much dourer Admiral Pound.

"In our view, likely to continue, sir," answered Cavendish-Bentinck. "Mostly as a means of exerting pressure they hope will make us more amenable to future peace feelers."

"What about the Italians?" asked Churchill. "We're in the midst of planning an operation to boot Graziani out of the areas of Egypt he invaded in September."

"Well, sir, in truth I'd advise in favour of a limited operation," replied Davidson. "By all means, we should give the Eyties a sound whipping that will send them packing back to Libya. But it might be wise to leave it at that. A more ambitious operation runs the risk of provoking German intervention in North Africa on the Italians' behalf. Our recommendation is to let sleeping Dobermans lie."

"Dobermans! Ha!" guffawed Churchill. "Very good, General, you're quite the wag. As much as I hate to admit it, your analysis is quite sound. We'll keep to our side of the border while giving il Duce a hiding he'll never forget. In the meantime, I'll propose to Cabinet that we prioritise our air and naval forces while making sure the army is gradually restored to full fighting power."

General Dill made no effort to conceal his chagrin at Churchill's determination that the army should be relegated to the proverbial resourcing back teat.

"Come, come, General," chided the Prime Minister. "Even you must admit that, in the absence of a credible invasion threat, the RAF and Royal Navy must take precedence."

Dill replied with a laconic, "Yes, sir."

"Well, if there's nothing else, I believe our business is concluded," said Churchill in a tone of imminent dismissal. "Thank you for a most informative briefing."

"General Dill wasn't very happy," said Davidson to Neville some minutes later, as the two intelligence officers made their way back to the War Office building.

"Yes, sir," Neville replied. "He was quite upset by the prospect of the army being at a funding disadvantage vis-à-vis the air force and navy. I only hope he's not the sort to shoot the messenger."

"Pah!" said Davidson with a dismissive wave of the hand. "Inter-service rivalry is a luxury we can't afford at this juncture of the war. The fact that I'm a career army officer doesn't blind me to strategic reality. Besides, the PM thinks very highly of you, which should insulate you from the wrath of the CIGS. Dill would look like an absolute fool taking action against an officer he himself just promoted."

"I hope so, sir," said Neville. "What about you?"

"Don't worry about me, Neville," scoffed Davidson. "I've been around too long and know where too many bodies are buried. You've done a remarkable job of analysis over the past few days, so let's not allow ourselves to become distracted by such pettifoggery."

"Of course, sir. Sorry, sir."

As they reached the arched entrance to the War Office inner courtyard, Davidson turned to Neville. "Colonel, I'm sending you home. I want you rested and sharp on the morrow, so have a relaxing evening and make sure to get a good night's sleep."

Before Neville could reply, the General disappeared through the archway with a familiar nod to the military policemen on duty.

Shaking his head in amazement, Neville turned southwards on Whitehall and began to make his way towards his home in Pimlico. It wasn't that he minded the walk. It wasn't even two kilometres, and the opportunity to clear his head would do him good. He made a mental note to talk with the admin people tomorrow about the car and driver he now rated as a full colonel. After all, if it's commonly said that rank hath its privileges, he might as well partake of his share.

Fifty-one

The VLUP was sited in a pine forest four kilometres southeast of Epiry, a hamlet perched at the edge of the Morvand Massif. The Massif was a hilly region with a thin population and thick woods spread across 450,000 acres of east-central France. Consulting his library of 1940s-era aerial photographs the previous day, Klein identified a perfect laying-up point – an interior clearing some 200 metres from the nearest firebreak trail. Under camouflage nets adorned with foliage judiciously stripped from the adjacent trees, the vehicles were nearly invisible from both air and ground. The Israelis had even taken pains to brush away the telltale signs of their tyre tracks leading off the dirt trail into the woods.

At 21:30 hours, the column decamped beneath a full moon masked by a gauze-like layer of a thin cloud. Wearing night vision goggles that amplified the ambient light by a factor of 50,000, Yossi Klein led the way on foot along the path marked earlier by Weinstock and Danielle. Verifying that all eight vehicles debouched from the woods in proper order, Klein climbed into the front passenger seat of the lead Oshkosh.

"Vengeance stations, this is Kodkod, we're on the move," he transmitted, nodding to Horman, who put the S-ATV into gear.

Klein's chosen route took the column through the sparsely populated foothills of the Massif. Driving boldly along country roads with full headlights on, no-one in the few villages or vehicles they passed thought to challenge their legitimacy. Until just short of an hour into their uneventful journey, as they approached the Burgundian hamlet of Sémelay, the voice of Yochai Lifshutz materialised over the tactical network. He sounded anxious.

"Kodkod, this is Toren."

"This is Kodkod, go," replied Klein.

"This is Toren. Rivkin is haemorrhaging internally and I need to operate immediately. That can't be done on the move so we'll have to stop. How copy?"

298

The network was silent, until Klein finally replied with a subtext of melancholy audible in his voice. "This is Kodkod, we're unable to stop. Do the best you can."

"This is Toren, do you understand that decision means Rivkin is going to bleed out?" asked Lifshutz, the bitterness of his intonation unmistakable. "Do you understand you've just handed down a death sentence?"

"I'm not here to argue," came Klein's curtly reply. "We won't be stopping. Do what you can, out."

On they drove.

The crossroads town of Luzy was the next commune of consequence along their route. Here, as before, the German-imposed curfew worked to their advantage. Deserted streets were lined by darkened homes with shuttered windows, the stillness of night violated only by the occasional barking dog. So far, so good.

But fortune is a fickle master – and, twenty kilometres further on, the Israelis ran face first into trouble.

Toulon-sur-Arroux was a small town built astride the Arroux River, its halves connected by a stone arch bridge built during the late 19th century. As Klein's Oshkosh negotiated a curve in the main road leading onto the bridge abutment, he was confronted by the sight of a roadblock erected midway across its span.

Switching on his NGVs, Klein counted six armed men manning the checkpoint.

"Go!" Klein ordered Horman as he keyed the transmit button on his Madonna boom mic. "Contact front! Contact front! We'll shoot our way through!" His hand dropped from the microphone to his X95 as he shouldered the weapon and opened fire.

The half-dozen gendarmes on duty that night stood no chance at all. In fact, they only managed to get off a total of nine rounds from their Berthier bolt-action carbines before being mown down by a hail of Israeli gunfire.

Klein spared the fallen Frenchmen hardly a glance as he led the column across the bridge and through the eastern half of Toulon-sur-Arroux. At a crossroads three kilometres beyond the town, he called a halt.

Walking back along the column, Klein approached the tail-end S-ATV, with a front passenger seat occupied by Captain Benjamin Farkash.

"Farkash, take a bit of Semtex and drop two telephone poles across the

299

road. While you're working, have your men cover the rear in case anyone has a mind to pursue."

"Fuse?"

"Three minutes should suffice," Klein instructed.

As Farkash moved off to commence his task, a shout emerged from an Oshkosh in the middle of the column. "Yossi, it's the Professor! He's been hit!"

"Shit," Klein cursed under his breath and then yelled in turn, "Doctor, we have another casualty! It's Professor Hoffmann."

Lifshutz materialised out of the darkness, directing an angry glare in Klein's direction.

"That's alright," said the doctor, his words tinged with morose sarcasm. "Rivkin just died so I won't have to multi-task."

Klein grabbed the medical officer by the collar, hustling him out of the troops' earshot to the opposite shoulder of the road. "Okay, I get it, you're upset about missing the boat home, but we can't afford this sort of bullshit. You and I are both responsible for the lives of everyone here, including a female civilian and an innocent four-year-old child. You can cry, moan or sit shiva once we're out of this, but now I need you to pull your head out of your ass and lose the attitude. Are we clear?"

Lifshutz nodded in chastened silence.

"Good, you have a casualty to treat. Go!"

As Lifshutz vanished into the darkness, Farkash reported in with a thumb's up gesture. "All set, Yossi."

Klein nodded and returned to his lead vehicle. "Doctor, are you ready?" he asked over the tactical net.

"This is Toren," came back Lifshutz in a flat, business-like voice, "I've transferred the Professor to my vehicle."

"Kodkod, good copy. Toren, keep me up to date as to his condition. All Vengeance stations, this is Kodkod. We move immediately once Four activates and is back in his seat. Four, you're up."

A half-minute of silence followed before the voice of Farkash came over the tactical net. "This is Four, activated and onboard vehicle."

"Vengeance stations, this is Kodkod, moving now."

They were well out of sight, four kilometres down a hilly twisting road, when a pair of explosions were heard in their wake.

A few minutes later, Lifshutz came onto the net and reported that

Hoffmann had taken a single bullet to the shoulder. "I think it may have fractured his right clavicle, otherwise known as collarbone."

"How would you categorise his condition?"

"It's a moderate wound. He's out of it now, but with the passage of time should be fine. Not life threatening, barring unforeseen circumstances."

"Good to hear," replied Klein, who refocused his attention on the task of navigating his little force along its anabasis. Turning south on the N485 to Perrecy-les-Forges, he led the column eastwards onto a secondary road marked as the GC60.

"Vichy demarcation line is five kilometres ahead," he announced. "Be alert!"

In October 1940, the Germans were still in the process of organising their occupation regime. There were far too many roads in far too many places to secure all of them all the time. Klein watched warily through his night-vision-goggles as a guard booth materialised on the left-hand shoulder of the road. The cold grey background that appeared in the lens remained unpunctuated by the glowing white that would indicate the live presence of man or beast. As luck would have it, this particular checkpoint was unmanned, and their passage out of German-occupied France was entirely anti-climactic.

So too was their progress through Vichy territory, as the column wended its way through the hilly terrain of southern Burgundy. Klein allowed himself a silent smile as they passed through the town of Cluny, home to the famed Benedictine monastery that spawned major clerical reforms during the 11th century.

Climbing eastwards along a hairpin mountain road through Donzy-le-Pertuis, the column crested the Mâconnaise range south of Mont Saint-Romaine and descended into the Saône Valley. This was the home stretch of their journey by S-ATV – and, just over thirty minutes later, Klein's Oshkosh slowed to a crawl along in the rail-stop town of Fleurville.

Klein tapped Horman on the shoulder and pointed to a driveway blocked by a low iron gate. "That's it. That's the station."

Horman hit the brakes and Klein clambered out of the passenger seat to inspect the obstacle in their path. "Baruch, get the bolt cutters. I think they're in Azriel's Oshkosh."

Levinson returned moments later with a pair of heavy-duty bolt cutters that made short work of the padlock sealing the gate. Three minutes later, the eight S-ATVs were lined up in the parking lot outside a three-storey building adjacent to a double north-south rail line.

"All officers except Toren assemble at my vehicle," Klein transmitted over the tactical net. Within less than a minute, Roie Abargil, Benjamin Farkash and Azriel Weinstock clustered around their commander's S-ATV.

"Okay, listen up," said Klein with a glance at his watch. "The time is now 01:14 hours on the morning of 27 October. According to the history books, we have just over two hours to prepare before the first train of deportees gets here. Roie, I want you to rig our vehicles for demolition. Same routine as before, but with one difference. People live around here and I want zero collateral damage from the blast. Can you do that?"

"We'll err on the side of caution," replied the combat engineer officer. "Smaller amounts of explosive and we'll use sandbags to tamp the charges around the engine blocks. Should be fine."

"Don't forget we'll need to keep a bit of Semtex on hand," Klein reminded him. "We'll want to blow the track behind us as we go.

Roie pursed his lips as he did some seat-of-the-pants estimation. "I think we'll have a couple of kilos left."

"That should be more than enough. Get to it then, and take Farkash along to help. I want everything ready to go within forty-five minutes."

As Roie and Farkash moved off, Klein turned to address Weinstock.

"According to SCNF records, the stationmaster is one Antoine Gladieux, age 32," said Klein. "He lives with his wife and two small children in the upper two storeys of the station building. Azriel, you'll translate for me. I want you to try and assess his political leanings by the way he reacts to our unexpected arrival. It'll be easier if he turns out to be a French patriot. But in the end, he's going to help us even if he's a rusted-on lover of Maréchal Pétain. Are we clear?"

"Got it," replied Weinstock.

"Gabi, Baruch, you're with us. Let's move."

As the Israelis approached the station building, they could just make out the words "Pont-de-Vaux – Fleurville" emblazoned on its side. Walking onto the verandah-covered platform, Klein pounded his fist on the double wooden doors of the passenger waiting room.

A head emerged from a second-storey window. "Qui est là?"

"Gendarmerie Nationale, monsieur," replied Weinstock. "Ouvrir, s'il vous plaît."

"Un moment."

The waiting room lights switched on and the doors opened to reveal a balding man in his mid-30s, who stared in consternation at the sight confronting him.

"Vous n'êtes pas les gendarmes," protested stationmaster Gladieux.

"No, we're not," replied Weinstock in French. "We are British soldiers here on a mission of vital importance to the cause of a Free France. My name is Capitaine Weinstock."

The stationmaster's facial expression metamorphosed from anxious suspicion into a reflection of pure joy. "Bienvenu, Monsieur," Gladieux exclaimed as he took Weinstock by both arms and planted a sloppy 'faire la bise' kiss on each of the young captain's cheeks.

Klein looked on with amusement. "I guess that answers the loyalty question."

Gladieux cast a quizzical glance at the strangely clad man speaking in an unintelligible language.

"This is my colonel," explained Weinstock. "He has no French, so I'll be translating on his behalf."

"Mon Colonel," Gladieux said, while bowing his head in a deferential nod.

"We're very pleased to find you're a French patriot," continued Weinstock. "There's much to do over the next few hours and we could use your help."

"À votre service, Mon Capitaine," the stationmaster proclaimed gravely. "But in return, I must insist that you shoot me when this is all over."

Weinstock responded with a look of shocked incomprehension, triggering a Gallic guffaw from Gladieux.

"Just a superficial wound, Monsieur, that's all," explained the stationmaster. "Otherwise, I would be placing myself and my family in jeopardy from the traitors and their Boche masters. An injury will allay their suspicions."

"What's that all about?" asked Klein.

"He wants us to give him a flesh wound alibi so he won't face retribution from the Germans," said Weinstock with a bemused grin.

Klein smiled diplomatically and nodded. "Say whatever's required to keep him onside and happy. At this stage, there's no need for him to know he and his family will be accompanying us."

"If we force him to come, he may not stay friendly," observed Weinstock. "Quite possibly," replied Klein. "He'll be joining us nonetheless. I won't leave anyone behind who might be a source of useful intelligence to the enemy. Plus, it'll be very useful to have a railwayman along for our ride to the coast. If he insists, we'll release him once aboard our ship in Sète. Until then he's ours."

"When are we going to tell him that he's about to take a trip?"

"At the last possible moment, of course. In the meantime, we have a train to liberate, so let's put Monsieur Gladieux to work."

Fifty-two

I can hardly feel my feet, thought Emma as she sat knees-to-chest amid the crush of a third-class passenger railcar packed far beyond capacity. There were eight or nine people crammed onto wooden benches intended for five, and the floor space between was filled to overflowing with people and their baggage. Only the main aisle was kept clear to facilitate the access of the truncheon-wielding SS guards who prowled up and down the carriage.

She shifted her legs slightly, purchasing slight relief at the cost of a toxic glare from the sour-faced man sitting immediately to her left. Emma fired back a tart look of her own, nodding towards the SS guards who had clustered by the carriage door in a vain attempt to escape the overwhelming stench of human sweat. Her circumspect attempt to assign blame where properly due only elicited a resentful snort from her irascible neighbour.

A pretty young auburn-haired girl sitting nearby shook her head in disgust at the man's boorishness, rolling her green eyes in silent solidarity.

Emma flashed a smile of gratitude. "Hi, I'm Emma Cohen from Heidelberg," she whispered.

"Miriam Shipperman from Mannheim. That's my oma," the girl replied sotto voce, nodding towards an elderly woman who sat on an adjacent bench looking exhausted.

"Where are your mother and father?"

"They died in a traffic accident when I was six. I was raised ..."

Emma put her finger to her lips and Miriam fell silent, just in time to avoid the malign attentions of an SS guard swaggering down the central aisle.

"I was raised by my grandparents," Miriam murmured once the coast was clear.

"Let's talk later when we don't have all these watchdogs around," murmured Emma in a soft undertone.

Miriam grinned conspiratorially.

Fatigue soon triumphed over discomfort, and the rhythmic swaying of the carriage transported both women into slumber. Emma was only jolted back into consciousness by an insistent tapping on her right shoulder. Opening her eyes, she saw her father gazing at her with a plaintive expression.

"I need to use the bathroom," he whispered.

A glance at her watch showed 2:57 in the morning. Emma realised she'd been asleep for an hour and they'd been stuffed sardine-style into this train for more than half a day. Where were they headed? With every window draped with heavy black cloth, none of the passengers had the slightest clue.

Emma shook her head in frustration. Infuriated at the sight of her father reduced to such a pitiful state, she made a decision. Helping Manfred to his feet, Emma guided him down the corridor towards the toilet at the end of the car. The Cohens were half way to their destination when a barrage of shouts erupted behind them. Emma feigned deafness, gently propelling her father forward with a hand to the small of his back. They were just short of the toilet door when a rough hand on her shoulder halted their progress. She turned to see the reddish face of an SS oberscharführer, literally frothing with rage.

"What are you doing in the corridor?" screamed the NCO, his spittle liberally spraying Emma's face.

"He's only going to the toilet!" she protested.

"Your old man can shit in his pants for all I care," blustered the oberscharführer. "In fact, it would only be fitting in view of how you Jews have been shitting all over Germany for years!"

"That 'old man', as you describe him, fought in France during the war and won the Iron Cross 2nd Class," rejoined Emma with barely suppressed fury. "Where were you in 1917? In a crib wearing diapers?"

"You Jew bitch!" yelled the furious obersharführer as he shoved his truncheon like a spear into Emma's solar plexus. She collapsed on to the carriage floor, dry retching and gasping in pain.

Manfred moved with surprising speed to succour his daughter, shielding her prostrate body as the Nazi moved in for another blow – but the SS man was suddenly thrown off balance by a violent lurch as the locomotive engineer hit the emergency brake. A cacophonous squeal of metal on metal and the hiss of high-pressure air were deafening as the train slowed, the clamour dying as it finally came to a halt.

Consumed by curiosity, the obersharführer left Emma curled in the foetal position and walked to the end of the carriage, where he met the fate of the proverbial cat. Opening the railcar's outer door, the SS NCO peered out into the external veil of darkness. Two seconds later, a red circle materialised on his forehead and the Nazi was cast back against the wall of the railcar as if thrown by some invisible hand.

Even more surprising were the dual apparitions that materialised through that same open doorway. Dressed in bizarrely mottled green-brown uniforms and festooned with weaponry, the two men held pistols with strange cylindrical protuberances attached. The duo exuded an unspoken menace as they moved silently through a carefully choreographed dance of death.

The first intruder knelt, extending his weapon towards the SS men at the other end of the car, while the second man aimed his pistol in the same direction over his genuflecting colleague's head. From her prone position on the floor, Emma could see the knuckles of the men's index fingers whiten as the two triggers were pulled.

Rather than the loud bark of a pistol being fired, only a muffled 'phutt' was heard. After several more 'phutts', Emma glanced towards the far end of the railcar. The bodies of the remaining four SS men were clustered on the floor in an untidy heap.

The lead gunman made a hand signal to his colleague and the pair silently advanced down the centre aisle, weapons extended. They stepped around the still-prostrate Emma and her kneeling father as if the Cohens simply weren't there. Not a word was spoken.

A quartet of new avengers entered the carriage to fill the space vacated by the original two. One of these arrivals cast a glance at the fallen obersharführer, shocking Emma by the casual manner in which he fired two additional 'phutts' to the Nazi's chest.

The deportees cowered in terrified silence along the sides of the carriage, uncertain whether these spectres promised salvation or damnation. The only sound to be heard was the sudden rattle of a lock being turned. The toilet door at the SS end of the carriage opened and an immaculately attired hauptsturmführer emerged.

Noting his subordinates lying dead in the corridor, the SS officer reached for his holster. But the business end of two large-bore pistols aimed at his head were enough to make him raise his hands in surrender.

The lead soldier, as that's what he had to be, issued instructions in a guttural language incomprehensible to Emma. The second man holstered his pistol and disarmed the SS officer, binding the Nazi's hands with a strange semi-rigid cord.

"Sprechen sie Englisch?" barked the man who was clearly the leader of these warriors.

The hauptsturmführer shook his head.

The leader of the pack turned to address the detainees, who were observing events with rapt fascination. "Does anyone here speak English?"

After a long silence, Emma got to her feet. "I do," she said with raised hand.

The commander strode back along the aisle, passing the four soldiers who moved forward to provide overwatch towards the vestibule connecting their carriage to the next.

"My name is Yosef Klein. May I ask who you are?"

"Emma Cohen," she replied in fluent German-accented English.

"We don't have much time and I need someone who can translate for me. Can you do that?"

Emma nodded.

"Excellent," said Klein, his smile revealing radiant white teeth that contrasted sharply against his greenish-brown painted face. He gestured that Emma should move forward and they both returned to stand over the plasticuffed SS officer.

"Emma, please tell this piece of shit that I'd like nothing more than to put a bullet through his head. Just like his friends over there," said Klein, indicating the pile of SS bodies with a sharp nod.

"Dieser Offizier sagt, es gibt nichts, was er möchte mehr als Sie zu töten," Emma translated.

"The only thing keeping him alive is that he might be useful to me," Klein continued.

"Die einzige sache die ihn lebendig behält besteht darin, dass ich ihn möglicherweise nützlich finden konnte," she echoed.

"His usefulness depends on him following my instructions completely and exactly."

"Dein Nützlichkeit hängt von folgenden die Anweisungen dieses Offiziers."

"Now ask him if he understands," Klein instructed.

"Verstehen sie?"

The SS officer nodded.

"I want to hear him say it," Klein barked.

Emma nodded. "Er möchte von dir hören."

"Ich verstehe," said the hauptsturmführer in a poisonous tone.

"Good," said Klein to Emma. "So, here's what's going to happen. We're going to walk through this train with Mr SS in the lead. As we enter each car, he'll call on his men to surrender. If they do, they live. If they don't, they die. Very simple. You'll be with me to make sure he doesn't try to be a smartass."

"I don't know what a … 'smartass' is," said Emma.

"Let me put it another way. Your job is to ensure he doesn't try any tricks," Klein explained. "That he follows my commands."

As Emma conveyed Klein's instructions to the SS officer, another half a dozen of these otherworldly liberators entered the carriage. One of them approached Klein and began to speak in the guttural language she didn't understand. Then one of the deportees within earshot, an elderly Orthodox rabbi from Mannheim, suddenly broke down in sobs.

"Sie werden sprechen hebräisch! Sie sind jüdische Soldaten hier, um uns zu retten!" the rabbi exclaimed with tears of happiness coursing down the lines of his bearded cheeks. Rising from his seat, he enveloped the next passing soldier in a hug, kissing the thoroughly abashed Levinson on both cheeks.

"What's he saying?" asked Klein, his voice betraying impatience at the interruption.

"He says you're speaking Hebrew and this means you're Jewish soldiers who've come to save us," answered Emma as her eyebrows arched inquisitively.

"All true, but we'll talk about that later. Now we have a train full of SS bastards to kill or capture. Does he understand what he's supposed to do?" asked Klein, with a nod towards the manacled hauptsturmführer.

"I've explained his role to him," replied Emma.

"Did you tell him you'll be right there, listening to every word out of his mouth?"

Emma nodded.

"Okay, then," replied Klein. "Let's get this show on the road."

Emma gazed back in blank incomprehension.

"Sorry," said Klein with a sheepish smile. "Another bit of slang. It means let's begin."

Klein yanked the hauptsturmführer to his feet, taking a position immediately behind the plasticuffed SS officer. Another six of the Jewish avengers queued up behind Klein, each man holding a pistol in one hand and grasping a thick fabric handle sewn onto the rear of the strange-looking vest of the soldier immediately in front.

Klein gestured that Emma should take her position at the end of the line. "Keep your hands on the vest of the man in front of you and let me know if this sheisskopf deviates from the script."

Once again, Emma was at a loss to understand the specifics of Klein's cinematic turn of phrase. But his meaning was clear enough from its context. She took hold of the handle on the back of the lanky soldier in front of her and waited for the order to advance.

"For Emma's benefit, we'll be working in English. Moving now," Klein announced as he shoved the suppressor attached to his Sig Sauer P227 Tactical pistol into the small of the Nazi's back.

The SS officer took his cue and began to walk forward at a pace controlled by the pressure of Klein's left hand on the German's shoulder. The conga-line of assaulters shuffled back along the train into the connecting vestibule between the railcars. Another hard jab of Klein's pistol into the hauptsturmführer's kidney signalled the SS officer to pull open the door into the next carriage.

As it turned out, the process of clearing the train turned out to be an entirely one-sided affair. As they were in hostage rescue mode, Klein and his troopers were disinclined to provide any benefit of the doubt to their SS adversaries. The slightest hint of Aryan hesitation or resistance elicited an immediate bullet to the head. By the time the final car was cleared, the tally was 36 dead and 15 captive SS, with zero IDF casualties. Even more impressive was that, during the takedown of seven grossly overcrowded carriages, not a single Jewish deportee suffered collateral injury.

The dead SS were stripped of their weapons and their bodies unceremoniously dumped off the train. The prisoners were trussed hand and foot with plasticuffs, while Antoine Gladieux was dispatched forward to the locomotive with a trio of Israelis to serve as firemen. Within minutes of its liberation, the train was once again in motion, southward bound towards Lyon, Avignon and the Mediterranean coast.

Fifty-three

Peter Koertig ignored the curious stares directed his way as he passed through the corridors of Wehrkreiss hauptquartier. It was true that his mud-stained overcoat and grungy tunic made him stand out from the cleanly shaven, well-tailored, rear-echelon desk jockeys. Perhaps his appearance might serve as a useful reminder to these 'papiersoldaten' that some people were still fighting a real war.

His NCO escort led the way to a pair of closed doors on which he knocked.

"It's Oberleutnant Koertig," the stabsfeldwebel announced through the now open portal.

"Yes, yes, send him in," a familiar voice said from within.

Koertig nodded perfunctory thanks to the NCO and walked across the threshold.

The first thing he noticed was the massive topographical map hanging at the front of the room that covered all France and the Low Countries from Marseille to Amsterdam. Generalmajor Walter Warlimont stood in consultation with three field-grade officers, one from each of the armed services.

"Koertig, come over and join us," invited Warlimont with a wave. "Gentlemen, this is Oberleutnant Koertig of the Führer-Begleit-Bataillon."

Koertig clicked his heels and bowed.

"These officers are Oberst Augustin of the Luftwaffe, Oberst Clemens of the Heer and Kapitän zur See Unger."

"Very pleased to meet you, sirs," said Koertig, his back ramrod straight as he braced to attention.

"At ease, Leutnant," Warlimont instructed. "When did you arrive in Berlin?"

"At 02:30 this morning, sir. It was all very efficient. I was airborne within fifteen minutes of my arrival at Châteaudun and went directly into a debriefing session with the Abwehr upon landing."

"Are you finished with Oster's people?"

"For now, sir, but they did say I should keep myself available in the event they require me further."

Warlimont nodded. "Fair enough. First, I have a few questions of my own. You visited the scene of the battle that took place the day before yesterday in a French village south of Châteaudun, correct?"

"Yes, sir. Oucques, sir."

"That's the one. So, what can you tell me beyond the sketchy information contained in the incident report?

Koertig hesitated, glancing at the Army and Luftwaffe obersts and the Kriegsmarine kapitän zur see. "Herr General, how much ... detail would you prefer?"

Warlimont smiled paternally. "Very good, Oberleutnant. Your discretion is commendable, but these officers are fully briefed on the situation. You may speak freely."

Koertig nodded. "Well, sir, a platoon-sized patrol of around twenty-five men was attacked and annihilated. There were no survivors. We arrived well after the incident and I was able to question a number of villagers, but they went to ground when the firing started and didn't see much of anything. At least so they claimed."

"What about those unusual cartridge cases?" prompted Warlimont. "The report states you found more of those."

"Yes, and something else as well." Reaching into his map case, Koertig produced a 40 mm casing from a Mk47 grenade.

Warlimont took the proffered cartridge casing, observing it from several angles before turning it base upwards to read the headstamp. He noted that '40 mm x 53' was engraved along the top and 'AE' along the bottom. He'd never heard of a weapon firing such a large calibre shell that could be mounted on a vehicle the size of a kübelwagen.

"All in all, there's little doubt the Oucques incident involved the same enemy commandos who killed the Führer, sir."

"No doubt. Of course, for the record, the conspirators involved in that terrible crime have already been punished," said Warlimont, his mouth curling in a cynical smile. "The SS and SA have been abolished and Heydrich has been executed along with his chief lieutenants. Off the record, though, I very much want to have a talk with these elusive English raiders of ours. And while on that subject, I have some news."

312

"Yes, sir?"

Warlimont picked up a large wooden pointer and indicated a point on the map marked by a small red pin. "Last night, a checkpoint of the French gendarmerie was destroyed here at Toulon-sur-Arroux."

The general moved the tip of his pointer to a second pin affixed southeast of the first. "About twenty minutes ago, I received word that early this morning a train was hijacked about fifty kilometres south of Chalons-sur-Saône. A section of track was also destroyed to inhibit the possibility of pursuit by rail."

"A train, sir?" asked Koertig in disbelief. "With all due respect, that makes no sense. These people have been very smart so far. Why would they give up the tactical flexibility provided by their vehicles in order to travel by rail?"

"That was precisely my reaction," replied Warlimont. "Then I discovered what this particular train was doing, and the picture began to make some sense."

"Sir?"

"It seems the Gauleiters of Baden and Rheinpfaltz came up with the bright idea to get rid of their Jews. So, yesterday, they arrested over five thousand people and packed them off by rail to some God-forsaken Vichy detention camp in the Pyrenees."

"The hijacked train was part of this expulsion operation," said Oberst Wilhelm Clemens, "thus confirming the account of those who survived the attack on the Führer."

"Precisely," replied Warlimont. "These Jewish commandos are clearly heading southward. But where? And why?"

"Spain, sir?" volunteered the Luftwaffe Oberst Gunter Augustin.

"I doubt it," responded Warlimont, his head shaking decisively. "There must be hundreds of people on that train, including children and the elderly. That would rule out a covert trek through the mountains. I can't imagine the ultra-Catholic Franco rolling out the welcome mat for a trainload of Christ-killers showing up at a Spanish border crossing."

"Then it has to be one of the Mediterranean ports, sir," suggested Unger. "They'll be trying to seize a ship and escape by sea. It's the only other option available to them."

Warlimont pondered this thesis for a moment, before breaking out in a broad smile of concurrence. "I think you're right, Unger. Of course, it's audacious enough to be completely absurd. Yet, as you rightly state, what other choice do they have? As Oberleutnant Koertig can attest, these Jews suffer from no lack of courage or daring. How do we stop them? Clemens?"

"With some difficulty sir," replied Clemens. "The fact is, we have no ground forces of any consequence in the Vichy zone. The closest army units would be along the Atlantic at Bayonne, a distance of more than five hundred kilometres. Even then, those are occupation troops, not the first-class combat soldiers required to tangle with such a dangerous enemy."

"What about the Kriegsmarine?" asked Warlimont. "Surely we have naval assets in the Mediterranean?"

"Not really, sir," replied Unger. "Gibraltar is heavily defended and Großadmiral Raeder has felt that any attempt to force the Straits would be a very costly endeavour for very little gain. We've basically left the Mediterranean to the Italians, sir."

Warlimont nodded and focused his attention on Augustin. "Then there's the Luftwaffe, which I hope will be a case of last but not least. What can the air arm do to help?"

"Well, sir, our closest air units would be a gruppe of Ju-88s at Orléans-Bricy and a gruppe of Me-110s at Chaumont."

"What are you proposing, that we bomb the train?"

"That would be one option, sir," replied Luftwaffe Oberst Augustin. "But, in view of your desire to ensure prisoners are taken, I would recommend airborne assault."

"Airborne assault?"

"Yes, sir. 1-Fallschirmjäger-Regiment is based at Orly, outside Paris, along with its assigned transport aircraft. I'm confident we could put two or three companies in the air within ninety minutes at the latest. Not only will they reach the area more quickly, but their deployment by parachute gives them the utmost flexibility once we discover the enemy's final destination. They're elite troops and the best we have. If anyone can beat these super-Jews, it will be our fallschirmjäger."

Warlimont picked up a manila folder from a nearby desk, perusing its contents for a moment and then glancing at his watch.

"Our report says the train was seized at around 03:00 this morning, which would give our Jews a head start of five hours. We can assume they've already stopped at least once to replenish the locomotive's water supply. On that basis, I would place them somewhere between Valence and Montélimar."

The room fell silent as Warlimont perused the wall map. "Avignon is key," he said after several moments of study. "That's where we learn whether they'll be going east to Marseilles or west towards Montpelier. If my calculations are correct, they'll arrive there in about one hour. Oberst Augustin, what's the speed of a Ju-52?"

"Around two hundred kilometres per hour, sir."

"The Mediterranean coast is roughly eight hundred kilometres from Paris," Warlimont mused. "We're talking five hours minimum before the fallschirmjäger would arrive in the area, correct?"

"Yes, sir," affirmed Augustin. "You should be aware the Ju-52s would also be on their last legs in terms of fuel."

"Sir, if there are no German troops immediately available, perhaps we should lodge a request with the Vichy authorities to stop the train," suggested Unger.

Warlimont shook his head sharply. "Out of the question. This is an extremely sensitive matter that directly involves the death of the Führer. Not something we'll be sharing with our new Gallic allies. Besides, their battlefield performance hasn't exactly been inspirational. We're dealing with a highly competent enemy who had no problem cutting the Führer-Begleit-Bataillon to shreds. How do you think the French would fare in a fight with these Jewish raiders?"

"I understand, sir," said the naval officer in a chastened tone. "My apologies."

"No matter," said Warlimont with a dismissive wave. "But tell me this: which ports would be available if they went west?"

Eager to redeem himself from his tactical faux pas, the Unger made a great show of studying the map. "Sète and La Nouvelle south of Narbonne, sir. But Sète has three times as much wharf space and lies directly along the rail line leading south from Montpelier. If they go west, it's highly likely that'll be their objective."

"Agreed," said Warlimont. "Gentlemen, I think the commander of our little Jewish army will want to avoid a major city such as Marseilles like the plague. So, from this point, we'll be operating on the assumption that Sète is the destination of our kosher quarry."

Warlimont paused for a few moments as he perused the map. "Sète is another one hundred and twenty kilometres from Avignon, meaning their estimated time of arrival is between three and four hours from now. Unger, how long does it take to make a docked ship ready for sea?"

"That depends, sir," the naval officer replied. "Starting a cold steam turbine engine takes at least four hours if all the safety protocols are followed. But, if the ship has only docked to offload or take on cargo, the boilers would be kept pressurised and she could get underway in around thirty minutes."

"There's no time to waste then," said Warlimont. "Oberst Augustine, I want a full battalion of fallschirmjäger airborne within the hour. Their orders are to conduct a direct parachute assault on the docks of Sète port with the objective of catching our Jews before they sail."

"Yes, sir."

"I also want you to stage those Ju-88s and Me-110s to airfields in the Sète area in case we miss the boat, so to speak. Sinking them will be an option of last resort, but under no circumstances am I prepared to let those people escape."

"Yes, sir," replied Augustine as he braced to attention and delivered a salute. "With your permission, I'll proceed to issue the appropriate orders."

Warlimont returned the salute with a nod of assent and the Luftwaffe officer departed.

"Unger," Warlimont continued, "you'll be going to La Spezia. If we have no naval forces in the Mediterranean, we'll just have to rely on the good offices of our Italian friends. How many destroyers do they have?"

"At La Spezia, around fifteen. I can't cite the precise number from memory, but it's certainly over a dozen. Six or seven cruisers as well. They have an even larger fleet farther south at Taranto."

"A single merchant vessel shouldn't constitute much of a challenge, even for them."

"One should hope not, sir," Unger agreed.

"Very well. Go to your quarters, pack some essentials and get yourself to Tempelhof within the hour. By the time you arrive in Italy, I will have coordinated your mission with their Comando Supremo. You will accompany any Italian naval force that sails to intercept our fugitives. As my direct representative, you will speak with the full authority of OKW vis-à-vis our allies. Your orders are to secure any prisoners for immediate transfer to German custody. Under no circumstances is anyone to be interrogated by the Italians. Have I made myself clear?"

"Yes sir," replied Unger.

"And Oberst Clemens, you may continue with your duties, although I'd appreciate it if you would remain available in the event further assistance is required."

"Of course, sir," replied the army officer.

Once the remaining two field grade officers left the room, Warlimont exhaled and opened the collar button of his tunic.

"So, Koertig, it's been a very eventful forty-eight hours."

"You might say so, sir"

"I've been very impressed by your circumspection and your ability to see the bigger picture. I'm pleased to announce your promotion to hauptman and to offer you the position of my aide-de-camp. The former is not contingent on the latter, of course, but I would be very grateful if you joined my staff."

"Of course, sir," replied Koertig. "It would be an honour to serve with you. As my first assignment, I would ask your permission to accompany Kapitän zur See Unger to Italy."

"Why?" asked Warlimont in a tone of surprise. "Still bent on vengeance?"

"There is that, sir," admitted Koertig. "I can't deny my desire to look these Jew bastards in the face once they're captured. On a more practical level, though, I think my language skills might be put to some use. You see, sir, I lived in Milan as a child and am reasonably fluent in Italian."

"Milan?" countered an incredulous Warlimont. "What on earth were you doing in Milan?"

"My father was the Lighting Director for the Leipzig Opera," replied Koertig. "He lost that position when things got bad in 1930, and was offered a job at La Scala. We were there four years."

"Where is your father now?"

"In Munich with the Bavarian State Opera. Also Lighting Director. It's a very specialised craft, sir."

"Koertig, you never cease to surprise me," said Warlimont with a bemused smile. "In light of your knowledge of Italian, I agree to your proposal. I've already arranged quarters for you here and transferred your personal possessions from the Begleit-Bataillon barracks. My stabsfeldwebel will show the way. Go clean yourself up and report back

317

here in thirty minutes. In the meantime, I'll lay on a car for you to Tempelhof. You can catch up on sleep during the flight."

"Thank you, sir," said Koertig. He braced to attention and delivered a stiff-armed Hitlergruß salute.

"There's no need for that," said Warlimont in a tone of mild reproof.

"Sir?"

"A general order was issued yesterday, instructing all Wehrmacht personnel henceforth to employ traditional military courtesies. No more of that Nazi straight-armed rubbish."

Koertig again braced to attention, raising his hand in a classic military salute. "I'm sorry, sir. I wasn't informed."

"No matter," said Warlimont as he acknowledged the oberleutnant's courtesy in kind. "Far more important that you comprehend the full complexity of my plans for you."

"Yes, sir?"

"While on the face of things you'll be Kapitän zur See Unger's junior aide-de-camp, in reality you'll be my eyes and, more importantly, my ears down there. Make sure your Italian hosts are none the wiser about the fact you speak their language."

"You want me to spy, sir?"

"Not exactly," countered Warlimont. "Just listen to what's being said. People tend to be looser of tongue if they think no-one can understand them. Are my instructions clear?"

"Yes, sir. Completely."

"Excellent. Well, be off with you, then. Good luck and good hunting."

Fifty-four

Baruch Levinson gazed down at himself and snorted in disgust. In his wildest imagination he never would have envisaged himself wearing a Nazi uniform. Yet here he was, clad in the black garb of a Rottenführer, the SS equivalent of a lance corporal. He felt filthy, and not merely because the previous owner's level of personal hygiene left much to be desired.

"Okay men, we're about to stop for another water refill," said Klein, who was dressed for the occasion in the uniform of an SS obertruppführer. "The SOP will be the same as Lyon. Two men on either side of every railcar. No talking. Just stand there looking like brutal SS assholes, and hopefully you'll scare the hell out of anyone who comes along. If someone insists on making conversation, summon me and Azriel. Three toots of the whistle will be the signal to board."

"It's the Purim from hell," quipped Gabi Horman, triggering a bout of laughter from the counterfeit SS men.

"Quite true," smiled Klein. "There's only one more water stop after this and then we can change out of these black monkey suits."

Azriel Weinstock was playing the lead role in this masquerade, dressed in a uniform expropriated from the hauptsturmmführer who had previously commanded the train. The now not-so-dapper SS officer sat in his underwear at the end of the carriage, along with his similarly disrobed troopers. The Germans remained plasticuffed hand and foot, with two Israelis standing close guard.

A slight jolt accompanied by a metallic squeal signalled that the train's brakes had been activated. Levinson reached for a nearby handrail to steady himself against the railcar's deceleration. The locomotive slid to a halt with much hissing of vented steam, and the make-believe SS troops filed off the railcars to their appointed positions along the flanks of the train.

Levinson could see that they had pulled onto a side track leading past a massive water tank emblazoned with the names La Tiel–Montélimar. From his position opposite the lead door of the first passenger car, he watched as Gladieux laboured alongside a local railway worker to replenish the train's water supply. The two men wrestled a large rubberised hose up to a lid atop the tender. The rail yardsman then ignited a gasoline generator, powering the pump that propelled a flow of water into the tank.

The Fleurville stationmaster had turned out to be quite a find. Not only did he jump at the chance to liberate his family from the clutches of Vichy tyranny, but he was also a competent locomotive driver who had taken a desk job to spend more time with his wife and kids. The Israelis were thus able to dispense with the dubious services of the original German locomotive crew. Now they were bound and shackled along with the skivvy-clad SS.

Within the space of twenty minutes, the tender's water tank was filled to the brim and they were ready to roll. With a handshake of thanks to the local railroad man, Gladieux clambered back into the cab of the locomotive. Three blasts of the steam whistle followed and the faux-SS men began to clamber back aboard their respective rail carriages.

Levinson was about to do likewise when he saw his commanding officer beckoning him to approach.

"From this point onwards, I'll be riding in the cab with Azriel," Klein instructed. "Inform Farkash that he'll be in command of the carriages. I'll be available on the 710, but try to minimise radio traffic. Our batteries are almost flat."

"Will do, Yossi," Levinson replied.

"Tell him to cut no slack with the prisoners," continued Klein. "If they cause any trouble, he has my authorisation to shoot those SS bastards out of hand."

Levinson nodded and began to negotiate a path along the now crowded centre aisle of the railway car. Midway along the length of the carriage, his knee inadvertently bumped against a shoulder covered by cascading ringlets of auburn hair.

"Slicha," apologised Levinson, as the head to which that hair was attached swivelled to peruse him. He paused, rendered momentarily speechless by the puzzled expression etched across a beautiful oval-shaped face. "Sorry," he repeated in English, his face blushing bright red in embarrassment as he summarily continued on his task.

Levinson found Farkash in the second car and faithfully transmitted

Klein's instructions. As he returned, the young Israeli trooper stole another glance at the redheaded stunner, noticing for the first time that she was seated alongside a slightly older, but no less gorgeous, raven-haired woman. Sisters, perhaps? The raven-haired woman looked up as Levinson passed and their eyes met, triggering a mischievous smile on her part and an embarrassed blush on his.

Stepping gingerly over the stretcher upon which the bandaged Gerhard Hoffmann lay sleeping, Levinson took his place among his friends, next to the mound of weapons and equipment. From the corner of his eye, he could see late twentysomething raven-haired woman whispering something to the early twentysomething auburn-haired woman. Despite his ignorance of the German language, the import of her hushed protestations and crimson-flushed face was clear enough. Whatever the older of the pair was saying, her younger sister clearly found it cringeworthy.

But the raven-haired woman clearly wasn't about to take no for an answer. Ignoring all protestations and dissent, she stood up and approached Levinson with the confidence of a good-looking woman who knows she can command male attention whenever and wherever.

"Hello," she said in English with a bright smile. "My name is Emma Cohen."

"Baruch Levinson," the young Israeli soldier countered, shyly.

"I noticed you've been admiring my friend."

"Ah," said Levinson, his cheeks again reddening with a new flush of bashfulness. "It's just … I thought you might be sisters."

"Actually, we just met. She's from Mannheim while I'm from Heidelberg. Why don't you join us? We can offer you something to eat."

"I don't … " was all Levinson managed to say before Emma bent down and took his hand. "Bring your weapon and sit with us. It shouldn't make any difference if you're sitting a few metres over there as opposed to over here."

Choosing to ignore the envious looks of his comrades, Levinson allowed himself to be ushered down the aisle, where he took a seat in the space indicated by Emma.

"Baruch Levinson, this is Miriam Shipperman," said Emma with a hand wave of voilà. "Given the way you two have been sneaking glances at each other, I thought I should put you both out of your misery and arrange introductions."

One would be hard-pressed to decide who was most flustered as the cheeks of both Miriam and Levinson took on reddish hues.

"Your English is excellent," said Levinson in a flustered gambit to change the subject.

"Thank you," replied Emma. "I spent eighteen months at the Middle Temple in London while researching my doctorate. It was a comparative analysis between English common law and the Prussian Civil Code on the principle of consideration in contracts."

"You'd enjoy meeting my mother," said Levinson. "She's a district court judge."

"A judge?" echoed Emma with pursed lips that conveyed scepticism. "I didn't realise British rule in Palestine was so ... avant-garde. There were no women on the Queens Bench or at the Old Bailey when I was in London."

Levinson responded with a simple shrug, reduced to silence by the realisation his off-the-cuff comment had ventured into dangerous territory.

"Let's eat," said Emma with the bright smile of a conversationalist seeking to overcome an awkward silence. "Baruch, can you get that suitcase? The black one?"

Levinson 's gaze followed the line of her outstretched arm and he grabbed the indicated valise from the baggage rack above.

Emma opened it and produced a brown-paper bundle wrapped in string. She gently awakened her parents with soft nudges to their shoulders.

"Mutti, Papa, es ist Essenszeit."

Dvora Cohen awoke, recoiling in terror at the sight of an SS trooper seated just inches away.

"Don't worry, Mutti," said Emma soothingly. "He's not really a Nazi. He's one of our Jewish heroes in disguise."

Dvora flashed Levinson a wan smile and turned her attention to Manfred, who had yet to show signs of a return to consciousness. "Emma, I'm worried about papa. I think he needs water."

Levinson was able to pick out the word "wasser," amid this mother–daughter exchange. "Does your father need water?" he asked.

"Yes," replied Emma in English. "What little I brought was finished hours ago."

"I'll be back in a second.'"

Levinson got to his feet and walked back to the equipment pile, returning with his Agilite tactical vest. Unzipping the Modular Assault Pack attached to the vest's rear, he produced a three-litre hydration bladder. Opening the velcro straps that secured the bladder's drinking tube to the vest, Levinson returned to his former seat and poised the drinking valve over Manfred's mouth.

"Ask your mother to open his mouth, please."

"Offene Papas mund, Mutti."

Dvora complied and water began to flow into Manfred's mouth as Levinson slowly squeezed the hydration bladder. He desisted once the elder Cohen's cough signified he was somewhat revived.

"May I have some?" asked Emma.

"Sure," replied Levinson, and soon the bladder was empty after making the rounds of thirsty people.

"Don't worry," said Levinson with a cheerful smile. "It has a filtration system so I can refill it anywhere."

"I've never seen anything like it," said Emma as she offered Levinson a piece of Rindswurst. "You should know it's beef, but not fully kosher."

The young Israeli simply shrugged and took a ravenous bite out of his sausage. "It's good," he said with a mouth full of sausage.

"I'm no military expert," said Emma, "but I've never seen equipment like yours. That drinking device is quite ingenious."

"We call it a 'shluker' after the sucking sound it makes when you drink," said Levinson as he illustrated the point with a slurping sound that elicited an appreciative laugh from Miriam. He smiled shyly. "It's pretty cool. It lets you drink and fight at the same time."

"Cool? Does your … shluker refrigerate the water as well?" asked Emma.

"No, no," replied Levinson with a shake of the head. "I meant 'cool' in the sense that it's good."

"Then why not just say good?"

"It's a slang expression," replied Levinson with an apologetic shrug.

Emma pointed to the prone figure lying on the stretcher at the front end of the carriage. "Who's your injured man? He looks a bit old and fat to be a soldier."

Levinson grinned. "He's our technical adviser. Thankfully he's not badly wounded. Our doctor says he'll be fine."

"And them?" Emma asked, now pointing towards the dozen-plus fettered SS-men. "Will they be fine? Has anyone bothered to give them food or water?"

"Don't know and don't care," Levinson replied with a callous shrug.

"I suppose I'll have to take that matter up with Mr Klein," replied Emma huffily as she glanced around the carriage. "I don't see him."

"That's because Colonel Klein is riding up front in the locomotive," said Levinson, enunciating his commander's formal rank with deliberate emphasis.

"Well, who's the man in charge here?"

"That would be Captain Benjamin Farkash. He should be in the next car."

Emma nodded, arose and began to thread her way through the crowded aisle in the indicated direction.

The silence that ensued was ultimately broken when Levinson mustered up sufficient courage to meet Miriam's gaze "Do you speak English? Nein sprechen Deutch," he said shyly, pointing to his own chest.

Miriam smiled in amusement at his fractured German. "You mean 'ich nicht sprechen Deutch'. And yes, I speak a little English. We learn it in our schools."

"Right. Sorry," Levinson countered. "I'm afraid my languages are Hebrew, English and some schoolboy French."

"Don't worry," said Miriam. "My Hebrew is from bat mitzvah. Not so good. My English is better."

Baruch nodded. "Are these your parents?" he asked with a gesture towards the sleeping Dvora and Manfred Cohen.

Miriam opened her palms in a universal gesture of incomprehension.

"Mother and father ... mamma and papa?"

"No, no," replied Miriam with a negative headshake. "Mamma and papa of Emma. My mamma and papa are dead. This is my oma, my großmutter," she continued with a gesture towards her slumbering grandmother.

"I'm sorry ... about your momma and papa," said Levinson in soft empathetic voice.

Miriam again shook her head. "Long time before. Auto ..." She complemented her words by clapping her hands sharply together and producing an onomatopoetic "bang" with her mouth.

"Ah," said Levinson. "An auto accident."

"Ja, ein autounfall. I very little and my Zaydie take care of me after. What about you? Where do you come?"

"I'm from Palestine," answered Levinson, sticking to the script every Israeli had been instructed to follow. "From Jerusalem."

Miriam's face broke into a beaming smile. "Ah, Yerushalayim!"

"Yes, Yerushalayim," he confirmed.

"Why did you come for us?" she asked, her hand moving in an expansive gesture that encompassed the entirety of the railcar. "From Palästina?"

"Yes, we came to help you, and do a few other things as well."

Miriam brushed an errant tear from her eye. "I heard the rabbi say you are like Engel."

"Engels? The communist?"

"No, no, no," said Miriam as she pointed her index finger skywards. "Engel from Gan Eden, like Gavriel."

"Ah, you mean angels."

"Yes, angels," echoed Miriam, "but very strange angel dressed like devil."

"We're certainly not angels," said Levinson. "Have you heard of the saying 'kol Yisrael arayvim zeh, lehzeh'?"

"My Hebrew is very bad," said Miriam with an apologetic smile.

"It comes from the Talmud. It means all Jews are responsible for one another."

"Our HauptSynagoge in Mannheim was Reform. No Talmud and not much Hebrew."

"I'd be happy to teach you," volunteered Levinson. "Hebrew, I mean."

"That would be nice. Are you … orthodox?" Miriam asked, making a circular motion around the top of her head.

"No, not at all," laughed Levinson. "But we study Talmud in high school. At gymnasium."

Their conversation was interrupted by the return of Emma, her matchmaker's smile replaced by a sourpuss frown.

"Was is los?" enquired Miriam, her face creased in a frown of concern.

"I don't think much of your Mr Farkash," Emma said edgily in English for Levinson 's benefit.

"Why?" he asked

"The prisoners have been tied up for hours and are doing their … personal needs in their underwear. It's unnecessary and cruel."

"I'm surprised you care about them at all, seeing what they've just done to you," rejoined Levinson with a shrug of indifference.

"I don't care about them," countered Emma with a taint of huffiness. "I care about us. I don't want to see us acting like them in any way, shape or form."

"With all respect, Emma, we're nothing like them," pronounced Levinson in an indignant tone of his own. "They're the animals who threw you out of your homes. Not for anything you did, but just because of who you are. Now the tables have turned and the predators have become the prisoners. They can shit in their pants for all I care."

"Ah," said Emma with a grim smile, "that's precisely what one of them said to my father just before you arrived. 'You can shit in your pants.'"

"Emma, you have no idea who these people really are. What kind of crimes they're prepared to commit."

"Oh really, Mr Levinson from Palästina? You forget I was there when the synagogues of Heidelberg burned in November '38. You forget I have lived with the daily humiliation and deprivation of being a Jew in Germany these past seven years. Yet you have the hutzpah to tell me I don't know the evil of the Nazis?"

Levinson shook his head in frustration. "Emma, I'm not trying to minimise the extent of your suffering, but there are things you don't know. Things I can't tell you. Things that mean these bastards are not worth an ounce of your concern or pity. Anyway, we have explicit orders from Yossi that the SS are to remain shackled until we arrive at our final destination. You can bring it up with him then. In the meantime, we won't be taking any chances."

Fifty-five

"To be a good soldier one must love the army, but to be a good commander, one must be prepared to order the death of the very thing you love."

Major Karl-Lothar Schultz had little knowledge of the American Civil War and even less of the Confederate general to whom those sentiments were attributed. Nevertheless, the words of Robert Edward Lee were quite an accurate expression of the German officer's conflicting emotions as he rode with his men into battle.

The burly commander of III Bataillon, Fallschirmjäger-Regiment 1, gazed fondly at the dozen paratroopers of his command group who were dozing on benches running along either flank of the Ju-52's fuselage. Mostly still in their teens, they were all volunteers, the few successful applicants from the many who competed for a spot in one of the Wehrmacht's most glamorous units. At age 33, Schultz often felt like their father and, as Robert E Lee's so aptly described, the dilemma of command meant that, in addition to acting in loco parentis to his troopers, he also functioned as their executioner.

Just over two-and-a-half hours had passed since regimental commander Oberst Bruno Bräuer summoned his subordinate commanders to an urgent briefing.

"Gentlemen, I've just received mission orders direct from OKW for Operation Tilphousia," declaimed Bräuer. "The information I have is sparse and the intelligence even sparser. All I have to tell you is that we are instructed to mount a battalion-scale parachute assault at the port of Sète on the Mediterranean."

The assembled officers studied the 1:500,000 Luftwaffe navigation maps they were issued at the commencement of the briefing.

The objective of this operation is to seal the harbour," continued Bräuer, "and prevent the escape by sea of a British commando force. I want the chosen unit to be airborne by 10:00 hours, 68 minutes from now."

"But sir," protested Major Erich Walther, who commanded the

regiment's I Bataillon. "Half of my equipment has been loaded onto freight cars in preparation for our redeployment back to Stendahl."

"I'm fully aware of the regiment's logistical situation, Major," countered Bräuer. "By now, all of you are fully aware of my firm belief in the merits of competition. Therefore, the first battalion commander who notifies me that he's ready to go will get the green light for this mission."

"Sir, as fallschirmjäger, we're trained to achieve surprise by doing the unexpected," observed the III Bataillon intelligence officer, a tall, slender former law student by the name of Günter Weiselbladd. "But this is out of the ordinary, even by our standards. I wonder about the urgency of this operation. Would these fugitive Engländer have anything to do with the killing of the Führer?"

"Unknown at this time, leutnant," replied Bräuer, "although I must admit that the same hypothesis did occur to me as well. Let's leave such speculation to others and focus on our role, which is fighting Germany's battles. On that topic, I've been explicitly warned that these Britishers are heavily armed and very well-trained. So, make sure to prepare your men for a tough fight and don't skimp on your ammunition load. Better to have and not need than need and not have."

"What about maps, sir?" persisted Weiselbladd, holding up the Luftwaffe chart. "These are useless for tactical purposes and I'd like to convene a battalion planning group as soon as possible."

"We make do with what we have," declared Bräuer. "That means the mission commander will have to improvise an operations plan from the air, and there'll be no mucking about. Sète is at the outer limit of a Tante Ju's range, so you should have enough fuel to make one reconnaissance pass before coming around again for the drop. Meine Herren, as with all our operations, speed and violence of action are essential. I strongly suggest you should jump as close to wharfside as possible without unduly endangering your men. The end result should have that port sealed, no later than thirty minutes after the last man hits the ground. Any further questions?"

None were forthcoming.

Bräuer nodded. "Very well. I dismiss you to your preparations. See to your men."

The entire regiment worked like men possessed, with riggers giving a perfunctory once-over to 600 RZ16 parachutes hastily pulled from shipping pallets. The troopers packed their jump smocks with extra pistol magazines, while para-containers were loaded with rifles, crew-served weapons and ammunition.

It was a close-run thing but, in the end, Schultz notified Oberst Bräuer of III Bataillon's readiness a mere four minutes before the runners-up from I Bataillon announced the same. Shortly afterwards, the first of the 52 Ju-52s bearing the battalion's 579 men began lumbering down the runway on their take-off sprints.

The monotonous roar of the tri-motor transport's BMW engines had a soporific effect that overcame the discomfort inflicted on the paratroopers by the heavy gear they bore. Most dozed off, with heads lolling to one side and chins resting on chests. They deserved a rest after their mad scramble to prepare the battalion for this rush mission, thought Schultz. But the mantle of command afforded him no such luxury.

The battalion commander spent most of his first hour aloft in frustration, trying to envisage an adequate assault plan on the basis of a patently inadequate map. Struggling to his feet, Schultz waddled down the centre aisle towards the nose of the aircraft, burdened by the bulky parachute strapped to his back. Entering the cockpit, he tapped the pilot on the shoulder.

"What's our current position?"

"That's Nevers at our 11 o'clock," replied the Luftwaffe major, who occupied the left-hand seat.

Schultz peered over the pilot's shoulder, directing desultory glances between the town ahead and the map in his hand. "Then we're one third of the way."

"Just about," confirmed the pilot. "We have a sweet tailwind that's giving us an extra push. As of now, our estimated time of arrival over the target area is 13:25 hours."

"What about our fuel state?"

The pilot examined one of the gauges on the cockpit instrument panel. "Just under 70 per cent remaining."

"Hand over to your copilot and have a look at the map with me."

Once the transfer of control was complete, Schultz continued his exposition, using a stubby pencil as a pointer to illustrate his instructions.

"I want you to steer for this point on the coast," the pencil indicating the town of Agde, ten kilometres southwest of Sète. "Then you'll turn north along this spit of land between the lake and sea, taking us directly over the port area where I'll select the drop zone."

"Then we circle back to rendezvous with the formation for the drop?" asked the pilot.

Shultz shook his head. "Too complicated. Too much opportunity for friction and confusion. We'll jump on the first pass from an altitude of two hundred metres. It'll be a small drop zone, so I want aircraft to assume column formation. All following aircraft will jump over our position, using our canopies as a marker. Understood?"

"Understood," affirmed the pilot. "I'm glad we're only making one pass. By that point, we'll be flying on fumes with the closest airfield at Montpellier. We'll be lucky to make it without having to use our own parachutes."

Schultz grinned and clapped the pilot on the shoulder. "We all have our problems, eh? Mine is conducting a combat airborne assault against elite enemy commandos with zero intelligence. Yours is getting this crate down in one piece."

The transport pilot responded with a fatalistic smile of his own.

Schultz checked his watch. "I'll be going aft. Pass on the plan to the other aircraft and report to me when confirmation is received."

The pilot nodded and turned around in his seat to face forward, motioning his copilot to relinquish the control column.

On the way back to his seat, Schultz checked his pistol and the 12 magazines of 9 mm ammunition attached to his load-bearing harness. Like his troopers, he'd be jumping armed solely with a handgun. Per fallshirmjäger doctrine, the paratroopers' rifles, submachine-guns and crew-served weapons would be dropped in para-containers mounted beneath the fuselage of the aircraft.

The tactical flaws of this arrangement had been driven home with brutal force the previous May during the battalion's assault against the Waalhaven airfield in the Netherlands. Jumping just after dawn, the pistol-armed fallschirmjäger had been ravaged by Dutch gunfire as they raced to reach the para-containers holding their heavier weapons.

This immediate post-landing vulnerability had been the subject of much discussion at the 7 Flieger-Division's after-action debrief held last July in Brussels. Schultz and several other battalion commanders had called for the urgent development of methods and equipment that would enable fallschirmjäger to jump with their personal weapons. The assembled paratroop officers were dismayed to learn that the design of the RZ16 parachute currently in use by German airborne troops was thought to make such a solution impossible.

The problem stemmed from the manner in which the RZ16's suspension lines descended from the parachute canopy to D-rings on the parachute harness located between the jumper's shoulder blades. Not only did this design deny German paratroopers the ability to exercise any directional control over their descent, it also enhanced the parachute's tendency to oscillate. The risk of injury on landing was further increased by the face-forward position in which fallschirmjäger hit the ground.

Therefore, the powers-that-be at Oberkommando der Luftwaffe had decided that jumping the RZ16 with attached weapons or equipment would be unacceptably hazardous. Of course, none of those papeirsoldaten geniuses safe behind their desks in Berlin had ever conducted an opposed airborne assault armed only with a pop-gun. Schultz found this triumph of bureaucratic stupidity to be all the more infuriating in light of the fact that German aircrews were already equipped with conventional parachutes that allowed canopy control.

Schultz allowed himself a discreet headshake of disgust. Such doctrinal matters would have to wait. In the meantime, his boys had a battle to fight, and it might be wise to follow their example by getting a bit of rest while he still could.

The paratroop battalion commander unstrapped his distinctive Model 1938 rimless fallschirmjäger helmet and placed the headpiece on his lap. Closing his eyes, Schultz tried to relax, but sleep proved elusive. He couldn't help but worry that, if the vague intelligence on the calibre of their enemy contained any measure of truth, they might be in for a very rough afternoon indeed.

Fifty-six

Behind his deadpan mien, the mood of Yossi Klein fluctuated between hope and anxiety. The rail portion of their journey had gone well. Far better than expected, in fact. Not only did they manage to take down the train with zero casualties – dead Nazis didn't count – but the SS uniform subterfuge worked flawlessly as well. Three water stops passed without incident, and the appearance of a French-fluent hauptshturmführer – Azriel Weinstock-in-mufti – was enough to induce fawning subservience from the switchman at the Sète marshalling yard. With the pull of a few levers, the train was rerouted from the main Montpeilier–Narbonne line into the Sète harbour area, no questions asked. The gendarmes manning a security checkpoint at the port perimeter fence simply waved them through.

Minutes later, the train screeched to a halt on the wharfside at the Bassin Orsetti.

"Thálatta," murmured Klein to no-one in particular.

"Sorry, say again?" queried Weinstock.

"Thálatta means 'the Sea' in classical Greek. It's what the Ten Thousand yelled in celebration once they came within sight of the Black Sea. At least that's how Xenophon tells it."

"So that's our ticket out of here?" asked Weinstock, his head canting towards a nearby merchant ship.

The *Mauritz van Nassau* was moored at the Quai Est, just as Klein's pre-mission research had indicated. From his 21st-century vantage point, he had managed to glean basic information about the ship's size (5,724 gross tonnes), age (christened in May 1913) propulsion system (fuel oil triple-expansion steam) and homeport (Rotterdam). Yet none of the records he had accessed almost eight decades after the fact shed much light on the Dutch freighter's status and condition. Now, the words 'shabby' and 'dilapidated' sprang to mind as Klein stood on the quay examining the rust and peeling paint scarring the vessel's hull. The past twenty-seven years spent hauling miscellaneous dry cargo around Europe from the Baltic to

332

the Mediterranean had taken their toll. Yet beggars are in no position to be choosers. The *Mauritz* was the most suitable ride in town.

Klein issued instructions for his faux-SS troopers to discard their black uniforms and don their IDF camouflage battledress. Then, with his men now suitably attired, he organised a boarding party, instructing the rest of his troopers and deportees to remain aboard the train.

Klein led Weinstock, Levinson, Horman and two other Israeli soldiers up the gangplank, where they quickly discovered a caretaker crew of five sailors at lunch in the mess. If any resentment was generated by the interruption of their meal by strange intruders armed with exotic weaponry, the French seamen kept it to themselves.

In fact, the crew were so complaisant that just a few questions from Weinstock sufficed to fill in the blanks regarding the ship's circumstance. As it turned out, the *Mauritz van Nassau* had been unloading a cargo of Algerian wheat as the phony war erupted into the real thing the previous May. News then arrived that her owner had been killed during the Luftwaffe bombing of Rotterdam, casting the question of ownership into an abeyant Dutch judicial system. Matters were further complicated by the escape to England of the owner's only son and sole heir, where he now flew Spitfires for the RAF. With the Dutch courts not yet fully functional under the new regime of German occupation, the *Mauritz van Nassau* remained docked in legal limbo, its paint continuing to flake and its rust continuing to spread.

As fortune would have it, counted among the caretaker crew that day was the ship's fourth engineer, who had come aboard to conduct routine engine maintenance.

"Ask how long it will take to get her moving," Klein instructed Weinstock, who dutifully translated his commander's question.

"La chaudière est froide, donc trois, peut-être quatre heures si toutes les procédures sont suivies," the engineer replied with a shrug.

"Too long," replied the dismayed Klein after the Frenchman's answer had been rendered into Hebrew. "Ask him what's the bare minimum he'll need to get us underway."

"Rien de moins que deux heures se risquer la rupture de la chaudière," replied the engineer.

"He said at least two hours," translated Weinstock. "Otherwise the boiler might burst."

"The sooner we begin, the sooner we can get the hell out of here. Head down to the train and collect a couple of the boys and Antoine."

"The stationmaster?" asked Weinstock.

"Yeah," replied Klein. "He used to be a locomotive driver. He should know enough about steam engines to keep our new friend honest. Once you've returned, I want you to escort this gentleman to the engine room and get things rolling. While you're down at the train, also tell Farkash to start loading passengers and our equipment. Ms Cohen will serve as our liaison to the deportees and work with Farkash to allocate sleeping space. Have him organise a five-man QRF with weapons and equipment on deck and ready to go."

"Where will you be?"

Klein glanced at his watch. "Plotting our course. It's now 12:42 hours. I want a status update on the engine situation at 13:15. Move."

Weinstock disappeared down the gangplank as Klein made his way to the captain's cabin, just off the ship's bridge. The Israeli colonel tossed the small duffle he was carrying on to the bed, unzipping the bag and extracting a sealed plastic packet and a small well-worn wooden box.

The packet contained a series of 1938-vintage UK Hydrographic Office charts. Selecting a map featuring a '1' in big blue marker ink on its underside, he unfolded it on the triangular desk fitted to the 90-degree corner formed by two bulkheads. The chart encompassed the entire western Mediterranean, from Marseilles to Tunis and Spain to Sardinia. Next, he opened the wooden box to reveal a sextant within its padded velvet interior. Finally, from the Cordura bag, he pulled a leather-bound tome with a title embossed in gold letters on its front and spine: *Simplified Celestial Navigation* by P.V.H Weems and E.A. Link Jr.

Klein gazed at the sextant and sighed. While sublimely confident of his abilities in land navigation, the prospect of doing the same at sea filled him with anxiety. True, he'd spent a week at the Israeli Naval Academy in Haifa learning the basics of sextant use, but he wasn't exactly overflowing with confidence in his ability. This happened to be a sentiment to which Yossi Klein was rather unaccustomed.

Nonetheless, he busied himself with laying out a prospective course across the Mediterranean until, thirty minutes later, his concentration was broken by a knock on the cabin door.

"Come."

The door opened to reveal Weinstock and Farkash.

"What's the engine situation?" enquired Klein.

"We're gradually building up steam pressure," Weinstock replied. "But it'll take time if we don't want to destroy the boiler."

"And how are we doing on fuel?"

"I didn't think to ask," replied Weinstock. "I'll get you an answer right away."

Weinstock disappeared, leaving Farkash alone in the doorway.

"What's the loading situation?"

"Going well," replied Farkash. "Our weapons, equipment and ammunition are aboard, as are all the deportees. I can't say I like working with that Cohen woman. She acts as though she's running the show. Giving orders here and there. A real pain in the ass, she is."

Klein grinned. "Yeah, I heard about your spat on the train. Don't worry, she's already complained to me about the prisoners. She's quite ... outspoken, shall we say?"

Farkash shrugged. "A politer way of putting it, I suppose."

"On that pleasant note, I'm due to check in with the ever-delightful Madame Cohen to get a sit-rep on how our passengers are getting along."

"Well, she's taken that bull by the horns as well," said Farkash with a shake of the head. "She's strutting around like queen bee, assigning people to sleeping quarters and talking about food rationing. I'll happily leave her to you."

"Yeah, that's why they pay me the big bucks," said Klein with a droll smile that elicited an empathetic chuckle of empathy from Farkash. "In the meantime, you take over as duty officer while I go below, and don't forget to hydrate the prisoners. That'll be one less thing for her to complain about."

Slinging his X95 across his chest, Klein made his way towards the companionway that led down into the bowels of the ship's cargo space. He found Emma in the forward hold, a dank cavernous place that assaulted his nose with the stench of so many unwashed humans crammed together.

Spying his arrival, she bustled towards him on an interception course, her beautiful face furrowed by frown lines. "Colonel Klein, this is most unsatisfactory. People are certain to become ill if we keep them down here."

"Sorry I wasn't able to commandeer the Queen Mary, but this was the only ride in town."

The overt sarcasm in Klein's voice brought a reddish blush to Emma's cheeks.

"I ... I'm sorry," she stuttered.

"Ms Cohen, this is a thirty-year-old cargo ship with cabin space for two dozen crew. It goes without saying that the best accommodation will be reserved for children and the infirm. If it's any consolation, my boys and I will be roughing it down here with you. We'll be happy to donate our sleeping bags to any children or the elderly who won't have a cabin spot."

Emma nodded, her equanimity recovered. "Again, I apologise for my previous tone. I just wanted to point out that we'll have massive health problems if we're not careful."

"Once we're underway, people should be able to spend a lot of their time up on the top deck, assuming this good weather holds. Besides, one of my people is an excellent doctor. I'd be very surprised if there aren't a few more to be found among eight hundred German Jews."

"I know of one," replied Emma, "but I'm sure there are others."

"Good. So, once you've finished organising everyone's sleeping arrangements, you can talk to Dr Lifshutz about putting together a medical team. Now, shifting to another topic, Farkash told me you've done a provisional inventory of food supplies. What's our situation?"

Emma grimaced and shook her head. "Dire. The ship's kitchen is almost empty. Along with what our people brought, we have enough for a couple of days. Maybe four or five if we implement rationing."

"Right. It'll be another couple of hours before the ship will be able to move, so we might as well take advantage of that time. I want you to organise five parties of ten able-bodied men each for a search of the warehouses along the docks. I want no-one under the age of sixteen or over the age of forty, and I'll assign some of my guys to escort each team. Any food we find, we take."

"You mean steal," rejoined Emma.

Klein gazed back at her with an undiplomatically caustic smile. "I believe the technical military terms are foraging and requisitioning. Or didn't they teach you that at law school in London?"

Emma simply blushed – again.

"I'll be up in the captain's cabin getting the aerial photographs that we'll use to brief the teams. How long will it take you to conscript our foraging parties?"

"Fifteen minutes?" proposed Emma.

"Make it ten," replied Klein as he turned on his heel, leaving a thoroughly discomfited Emma Cohen in his wake.

She proved as good as her word and almost as good as his, with the required fifty physically fit Jewish men assembling on the quarterdeck almost precisely twelve minutes later.

With Emma translating, Klein used a 1937 vintage French Armée de L'Air aerial photograph of the port to assign each team to a particular warehouse. He then attached an escort squad of four Israeli troopers per team and sent them on their way. As the foragers made their way down the gangplank, Klein turned to Emma.

"Would you please accompany me to the bridge? There are a few additional matters we should discuss."

Klein led the way along companionways and up ladders to the captain's sea cabin, where he motioned for Emma to sit on the chair while he took a seat on the bunk.

"I'm going to need your assistance on another matter," said Klein with a gesture towards the charts and sextant. "I would like you to enquire among the deportees as to whether any of them have experience with navigation at sea."

"Well, Colonel Klein, perhaps now would be a good time to reveal where you're planning on taking us. You haven't said anything and the people are beginning to wonder. I hear them talking."

Klein nodded. "I apologise, Ms Cohen. You're quite correct. In mitigation, I can only plead to being rather busy over the past few hours. The answer to your question is home, of course. We're taking you to Eretz Yisrael. To Palestine."

"I thought so," replied Emma. "While I don't dispute that Palestine is our only logical destination, you should be aware that not everyone shares that view. In fact, I overheard a few people talking about going back to Germany. Only a handful, mind you, but I thought you should know."

Frown lines traced their way across Klein's forehead as he cogitated for several moments until a purse-lipped nod reflected a decision made.

"Ms Cohen ..."

"You may call me Emma," she interrupted in the noblesse oblige tone of a blue-blood granting the extraordinary privilege of familiarity to a social inferior.

Klein bit his tongue. Now was not the time to inflame matters by giving vent to his annoyance though another retort. "Emma, there are a few things I haven't yet told you about our situation. The simple fact is that the liberation of your train was only our secondary objective. The primary reason we came to France was the assassination of Hitler and the senior leadership of the Nazi government."

Emma pondered this news for a few moments. "I see. Were you successful?"

Klein flashed a feral grin. "Completely. And not only Hitler, but Himmler, Goebbels, Göring and senior Wehrmacht commanders as well. They're all dead. We cut off the entire head of the snake."

Emma sat in silence, a contemplative look etched across her face.

"You look underwhelmed," observed Klein with a bemused grin. "Not exactly the reaction I expected. Aren't you pleased?"

"No, no," protested Emma with an exculpatory wave of her hands. "Please don't misunderstand me. They were evil and I'm glad they're gone."

"I was wondering for a moment there. In light of the fuss you made about those SS men, I was beginning to think you might be one of those 'make love, not war' pacifists."

"I'm not a pacifist," she snorted indignantly, "but I assume you know the difference between killing the enemy and abusing prisoners."

"Thanks for the instruction in military ethics," replied Klein, his annoyance again on full display. "But allow me to clarify the reality of our situation. We're about as deep in enemy country as it's possible to go, and I have forty trained soldiers at my disposal. With those odds, the only advantage I have is surprise. That means hitting hard and moving quickly to keep the enemy guessing. Yet, here I am, in charge of eight hundred civilians including women, children and the elderly. Given the circumstances, you should cut me a little slack when it comes to those SS assholes."

"Point taken," conceded Emma, her palms rising in a gesture of surrender. "But you have to admit that this news will complicate matters considerably. Once word gets out that Hitler is dead, it's likely that more people will want to try for home."

"Have you ever read any Orwell?" Klein enquired.

"The English journalist? Not really."

"In 1939, he wrote a book titled *Coming Up for Air*. It's about a middle-aged man who plans a trip to his childhood home, only to find it unrecognisably changed for the worse. The pond where he planned to go fishing has been turned into a garbage dump and an old girlfriend has aged very badly."

"What's your point?"

"My point is that you can't go home again because home doesn't exist anymore. Anyone who thinks they can just ride back into Mannheim and reclaim their confiscated property is dreaming. Besides, how are they going to get there? They won't be able to cross into Occupied France, much less into Germany. It's crazy."

"Quite right," agreed Emma. "Therefore, I suggest we keep this news under wraps for now. You can fill everyone in once we're at sea."

Their deliberations were interrupted by a knock on the cabin door, which opened to reveal Farkash sporting a broad grin across his face and a can in either hand.

"One of the search parties has found food … and lots of it."

"What sort?" asked Klein, gesturing that Farkash should hand over the cans.

"Tinned meat and vegetables, mostly. Stuff we can definitely use."

Klein examined the cans of beef stew for a brief moment. "That's good. Start loading as soon as possible."

"Already done," Farkash replied. "I've summoned the other four teams to assemble at the warehouse. Although, you should be aware that some of it is pork and shellfish."

"Get it aboard anyway," said Klein. "If any situation justifies pikuach nefesh, it's this one. We've had a dream run until now, but things can turn to shit in the blink of an eye. So better get moving. I'll finish up here with Ms Cohen and join you on deck shortly."

Farkash disappeared as Emma arched an inquisitive eyebrow in Klein's direction.

"What was that all about?" she asked.

"One of the search parties has found food," Klein explained. "I should go and supervise the loading process. As Ronald Reagan said, 'trust but verify.'"

"I've never heard of this Reagan."

"Of course not," said Klein, his mouth betraying the faintest hint of a smile.

"I should come along, in case there are problems in translation," Emma said.

They both made their way through the bridge and onto the quarterdeck, where Farkash had things well under control. The search teams had converged on a warehouse some two hundred metres from the jetty, and were supported by additional volunteers from among the deportees.

Like worker ants provisioning their nest, a queue of men shouldering cartons snaked its way up the gangplank and vanished into the ship's hold. Faced with a cordon of heavily armed Israeli troopers standing guard on either flank, the French warehouse workers had deemed discretion the better part of valour and made themselves scarce. Likewise, the gendarmes responsible for policing the port were notable by their absence from the scene.

Klein stood quietly at the gunwale for several minutes, observing the loading process. Concluding that things were ticking along nicely without his direct supervision, he cast a sideways glance at Emma. "I'm going to need your help with something ..."

Klein halted mid-sentence and turned his gaze towards a distant throbbing sound that was faintly audible.

"Binoculars!" ordered Klein with hand outstretched. Farkash hastened to transfer the optic from around his neck into his commander's grasp.

"Bombers?" suggested Farkash.

For several moments, Klein remained silent as he studied the oncoming specks dotting the sky to the southwest. Then he lowered the binoculars and returned them to his subordinate. "Three engines. That means Ju-52 transports. It seems we really pissed them off."

Klein turned to face Emma. "Okay, listen up," he said in English to make himself universally understood. "Those are transport planes full of German paratroopers who are about to mount an airborne assault against the port. I presume their mission is to stop us from leaving. Emma, I need you to get anyone not engaged in loading food below deck. Farkash, send someone down to the engine room to let Azriel know we'll have to get the ship underway sooner than planned. I don't care if we're moving at a crawl, as long as we're pulling away from the quay."

"Got it," replied Farkash.

"In the meantime, I'll take the guys on the wharf along with a Negev team to buy us some time," Klein continued. He glanced around the ship, his eyes finally settling on Horman, who was dozing by the ladder leading to the bridge. "Gabi, over here now!" barked Klein in English.

Horman's eyes snapped open and he sprang up like a coiled spring, trotting over to Klein's location along the ship's wharfside rail.

"How long to get the UAV up?" Klein asked his driver, who doubled as a drone operator.

"Standard time is eight minutes," replied Horman, taking the lead from Klein and rendering his response in the Queen's. "Plus another few to bring it from the bridge."

"I'll need it airborne in five," instructed Klein as he gestured towards the approaching objects, now readily identifiable by the unaided Mark 1 human eyeball as aircraft. "That's about how long we have before those German paratroopers begin their drop onto our doorstep. I'll take a squad to fight a delaying action, but it'll be vital that I know where the enemy landed and what their movements are. We're going to be outnumbered, so accurate intel will be our only advantage. While you're up on the bridge, bring my tactical vest, helmet and the carry bag with the maps. Move."

Horman dashed off on his assigned task.

"Now where's Baruch?" Klein enquired.

"I saw him with Miriam a while ago," said Emma who, despite the approaching menace, couldn't resist a proud smile at her matchmaking handiwork. She pointed towards the bow where Levinson was sitting tête-a-tête with Miriam Shipperman, saying something that made her burst into happy laughter. The mutual body language made it obvious that the pair were well on their way to becoming a couple.

Emma smiled. "They're very ... süß. Very sweet."

"No time for romance," said Klein before bellowing, "Baruch, to me!"

Baruch Levinson planted a kiss on Miriam's cheek, rose to his feet and approached his commander at a trot.

"Okay, Romeo, what's the situation with the PRC9000s?"

"Batteries are flat," replied a blushing Baruch. "I've set up the recharger, but in this weather, that'll take a while." He gestured towards the cloudy sky.

Klein nodded. "Alright, we'll use the 710s on the Team Four frequency for comms. I'll need Halevy with one of the Negevs and you'll be his number two. I want an ammo load of at least 1,200 rounds between the pair of you. Questions?

Levinson shook his head.

"Move."

As Levinson went off in search of Gershon Halevy, Klein turned to address Farkash and Emma. "I'm going to need seamless cooperation from the two of you," he continued in English. "Things are likely to get very messy, very fast and coordination will be vital. We'll be at sea at least a week and will need as much food as we can get. So Farkash, keep the loading parties working until you see my red flare. Then get them back to the ship on the double. Put the MK47 on the roof of the wheelhouse and find a good spot for the sniper team. Position the remaining three Negevs as you see fit. I think we can safely assume that the Germans will be right on our tail as we fall back to the ship. It's likely we'll need all the suppressive fire we can get. Clear?"

Horman appeared with Haim Zvulun, lugging heavy backpacks along with Klein's tactical gear. Extracting a tripod from the pack he was carrying, Horman extended it to its full 1.2 metres of height. Atop the tri-legged stand he affixed something that resembled, to a 21st-century observer, an oversize wi-fi router from which dual antennae extruded.

In the meantime, Zvulun was assembling what looked like a model-aeroplane on steroids, snapping wings, tail assembly and an electric-motor-powered propeller to a video-camera bearing fuselage. Emma watched with unalloyed fascination as the Skylark I-LE aerial drone took shape. Then, as the UAV was in the throes of the assembly process, Baruch opened a control console that resembled something familiar to the Israelis, but entirely beyond Emma's imagination – a ruggedised laptop computer.

Connecting the console into the router by cable, Horman nodded to Zvulun, who switched on the electric motor. A high-pitched whine assaulted their ears. The UAV's propeller metamorphosed into an orb of blurry movement as Horman threw the Skylark into the air like a large paper aeroplane. The UAV clawed its way upwards, just as the sky began to fill with the first parachute canopies of German fallshirmjäger.

"Who are you people?" asked Emma in an astonished tone. "I'm no military expert, but I've never seen anything like your weapons and equipment. Are you from another world?"

"A conversation for another time," replied Klein with an enigmatic smile. "Now, you'll excuse me if I switch to Hebrew."

The roar of passing German aircraft waxed and waned, with each departing plane leaving a dozen fallshirmjäger bobbing through the air in its wake.

Strapping on his tactical vest, Klein rummaged around the carry bag until he pulled out a 1937-vintage aerial photograph of the port. Peering over Horman's shoulder at the Skylark console screen, he quickly identified the German drop-zone – the rail marshalling yard east of the Bassin de la Sète du Midi.

"They're landing in the switchyard here," said Klein, pointing on the aerial photo to a series of railroad tracks spreading towards the dockside like the teeth of a pik-comb. "That puts the Rhône-Sète Canal squarely between them and us," Klein continued, his index finger tracing the manmade watercourse that separated the port into north and south halves. "That's where we stop them if we get there in time."

Klein paused to read the handwritten notation scrawled on the photo in marker ink. "There are two bridges across the canal. This big one to the West is the Pont du Mas Coulet, but this one here is almost directly opposite their drop zone," said Klein, his finger pointing to a narrow footbridge across the canal. "This is where they'll try to get across, so this is our vital ground. This is a race we can't afford to lose. If they get to that bridge first we're going to be in a world of shit."

The impromptu planning group was interrupted by the arrival of Halevy, toting the NG7 machine gun, and Levinson, who was laden with a backpack full of 7.62 mm linked ammunition.

"Time to move," Klein instructed while glancing skywards as yet another plane disgorged its load of German paratroopers. "Farkash, you know the drill if anything happens to me. Get these people to safety. Get them home to Eretz Yisrael. I've laid out a course on the charts in the captain's cabin. You'll just have to do a little on-the-job training with the sextant. Who knows, maybe one of the deportees has some sailing experience. Good luck!"

Farkash responded with a sober nod and moved off to organise the ship's defence.

As Klein approached the gangplank, his progress was interrupted by a feminine voice calling from behind him. "Colonel Klein."

He turned to observe Emma gazing up at him with an unfamiliar expression. The hauteur to which he had become accustomed was gone, replaced by something else. Feelings of concern, perhaps?

"If I can call you Emma, you should reciprocate," Klein replied in English with an amicable smile. "My first name is Yossi."

Emma nodded. "Alright, Yossi. It's just ... We've had more than our share of disagreements and you must think I'm a terrible prima donna. I've never thanked you ... for what you and your men did. I didn't want you to leave before ..."

"Not necessary," interrupted Klein with a dismissive wave. "It was our duty and our privilege."

In retrospect, Emma's next move surprised her as much as it startled Klein. In an act entirely out of character, she lifted herself on tiptoes and planted a kiss on the Israeli officer's left cheek. The anomalous display of emotion quickly faded into self-conscious embarrassment as Emma awkwardly disengaged, the rose-coloured tint suffusing her face matched by the flushed hue of his.

As Emma and Klein exchanged goodbyes, a more maudlin scene was transpiring a few metres away between Levinson and Miriam Shipperman.

Miriam had come from her seat at the bow to join Levinson and had been keenly listening to the conversation. The tears welling up in her eyes were a clear indication that she understood the gist of what was said, despite her limited English.

Miriam looked up at Levinson, taking both of his hands in hers. "I don't want you to go."

Levinson smiled, detaching his right hand and gently wiping the tears off her cheeks with his thumb. "Don't worry, I'll be fine. Yossi will look after me."

Levinson leaned down to kiss her chastely on the forehead.

"Come on Baruch, time to move," said Klein as he put on his PRC710 headset. He keyed the transmit button on his Madonna. "This is Kodkod, comms check?"

"Kodkod, this is Four, I hear you five-by-five," came the voice of Farkash through Klein's earphones.

Without further ado, Klein strapped on his helmet and strode down the gangplank, Halevy and Levinson rushing to keep pace. Once atop the jetty, the trio set off northwards at a quick trot, joined by the ten troopers who had been standing security along the flanks of the loading party.

Emma watched from the gunwale as the Israeli fighting patrol jogged northwards into the Place Mangeol, the clanking rustle of jostled weapons fading with distance. She was joined by Miriam, who enveloped the older woman in a hug as they watched those Jewish warriors sallying forth to do battle on their behalf.

Passing through la Place, Klein and his men bore northeast into Route 108, the main highway to Montpellier, where they disappeared from view.

"We need to get everyone below deck, just in case there's shooting," Emma related to Miriam. "If I pass the word at the rear of the ship, will you let people know up here?"

Miriam nodded and the two women turned themselves to the task of chivvying the deportees below deck. Now, there was nothing else they could do but work, wait and hope.

Fifty-seven

Karl-Lothar Schultz glanced around at the hundreds of deflated parachute canopies that littered the railroad switchyard like supersized milk-coloured rose petals. The seamstresses of this town are going to do a booming business in silk wedding dresses, he thought.

All things considered, the Luftwaffe battalion commander was reasonably content. The jump itself had been uneventful, with neither flack nor small arms fire to plague his troopers' descent. While a handful of fallshirmjäger suffered injury from landing on the cement crossties or steel rails crisscrossing the switchyard, the vast majority of men were hale, hearty and eager for a fight.

On hitting the ground, the paratroopers hit the quick release buttons on their harnesses and scrambled to tear open the weapons containers littering the drop zone. As the minutes passed, this milling mob gradually coalesced into coherent units, as company commanders set about rallying their men.

A hasty reconnaissance conducted through the cockpit windows of the lead Ju-52 had given Schultz a general grasp of the local terrain. There were over a dozen merchant ships and trawlers moored at various points along the Sète quayside, but he had no intention of frittering away his battalion in penny packet searches. The key to the entire port complex was the bottleneck formed by two artificial breakwaters constructed at the entry to the harbour. Once either of them was seized by his fallshirmjäger, the Engländers would have nowhere to go – at least not by sea.

After a quick consultation with his company commanders, Schultz deployed his battalion in classic 'two-up' tactical formation – a triangle with 7 and 9 Kompanien as its base and 8 Kompanie following as the apex. A series of loud whistle blasts swept through the German ranks as officers signalled their men to kick off the battalion's advance.

Schultz watched as his lead elements disappeared from view among the industrial buildings adjoining the railyard to the South. So far, so good.

Mere minutes later, the preternatural peace was broken by sporadic automatic gunfire that immediately swelled into a sustained fusillade.

Sprinting to the sound of the guns, Schultz soon arrived at a row of brick warehouses abutting a fifteen-metre-wide canal where his men were exchanging fire with an unseen enemy on the opposite bank.

Seeking the highest rank in his immediate field of vision, Schultz's glance settled on Oberleutnant Ulbrecht Lannon, the senior platoon leader in Kompanie 9. "What's the situation, Lannon?"

The oberleutnant glanced up to see who was addressing him, before returning his attention to the far side of the canal and firing a long burst from his MP38. Shultz observed the impact of Lannon's 9 mm rounds, but could not identify their intended target.

"We're in contact with enemy elements on the other side of the canal," Lannon reported, his cheek still welded to the stock of his submachine gun and his eyes still fixed downrange. "Strength unknown at this time, but there were enough of them to cut down the platoon that tried to cross the canal." He gestured towards the pedestrian bridge to their left. "Including Hauptman Eichel," he continued, naming his company commander.

"Eichel is down?"

"Yes, sir. I've assumed command of the kompanie."

Schultz lifted his binoculars and examined the bridge, a weatherworn iron and concrete structure arched in the middle to allow the passage of barges beneath. Fallen paratroopers were piled one upon the other in an unruly pile at the apex of the arch. The desperate writhing of the wounded caused the heap of bodies to twitch ever so slightly, as though this mass of death breathed with a grotesque new collective life.

"You should be careful about being seen with those binoculars, sir," warned Lannon. "They seem to be ..."

A burst of automatic weapons fire stitched a line of holes along an adjacent wall, spraying brick fragments in all directions. As Shultz hit the deck and crawled into cover, he grinned at Lannon. "What was that you were saying about them targeting officers deliberately?"

Lannon cast a grim smile in the direction of his battalion commander. "NCOs and machine gun crews as well. Giving the devils their due, they definitely know how to shoot."

"From the air, I saw a larger bridge about five hundred metres to our west," said Schultz. "Has anyone tried to exploit that crossing?"

Lannon shrugged. "Not to my knowledge, but we've been rather busy here and Kompanie 7 is engaged on our left. I don't know what Kompanie 8 is doing."

"Well let's find out," replied Schultz, swivelling to address one of his command group runners, Obergefreiter Hans Wiesling. "Wiesling, Kompanie 8 should be positioned one hundred metres to our rear. I want you to find Hauptman Scherer and instruct him to move his company west until he finds a road bridge across this damned canal. His orders are to take the bridge and press on to the mouth of the port. Tell him that we'll soon be attempting another crossing here. If all goes well, he can expect to see us on his left flank. Do you understand?"

"Jawohl, Herr Major," replied Weisling, who took off towards the rear at a quick trot.

"Günter, I have a job for you as well," said Schultz to Weiselbladd, his battalion intelligence officer. "Swing around to our left and find Hauptman Candler. Tell him that he's to move Kompanie 7 to positions in our immediate rear and report to me with all his machine guns plus crews."

Weiselbladd nodded and set off on his appointed task.

A slackening of the small arms cacophony drew the battalion commander's attention to a high-pitched drone that sounded from above. "What on earth is that thing?" asked Schultz, his arm pointing towards what appeared to be a toy aeroplane flying directly overhead.

"No idea," replied Lannon. "It's been buzzing around for a while now, but it doesn't seem to be dangerous. It doesn't shoot and I have other things to worry about."

"Fair point," Schultz conceded. "Let's get your machine guns up and your men ready to assault the bridge." He turned to address Flieger Johann Zirkel, his seventeen-year-old runner who reminded him of an over-enthused puppy. "Zirkel, load the flare pistol with a red."

Schultz accepted the flare pistol with a regal nod and cast another glance skywards at that bizarre flying ... whatever it is. He couldn't fault Lannon's tactical logic. His company was currently engaged with a very deadly enemy and this airborne enigma hadn't fired a single shot. In his current circumstance, the oberleutnant was correct to triage this unknown aerial object as a non-immediate threat.

Yet logic wasn't enough to allay a nagging sense of disquiet that plagued the mind of Karl-Lothar Shultz. When it came to battlefield surprises, he much preferred to give rather than to receive.

Kompanie 7's six remaining machine gun teams arrived with all the usual clanking and rattling of weapons, ammunition cans and belts. As they deployed, the battle settled into a desultory rhythm, with lengthy lulls interspersed by the occasional burst fired from the German bank of the canal. No answer in kind was forthcoming from the southern side, which largely frustrated the attempt to identify the enemy's positions.

Give the bastards credit for excellent fire discipline, mused Schultz but, in the end, he settled on the most likely enemy location: a two-storey stone building thirty metres westwards of the bridge. Solely guesswork, he thought, but that's where I'd put my people if I were the English commander.

The sound of multiple footfalls caused Schultz to turn rearwards, where he saw the men of Kompanie 7 in the process of deploying as ordered. Red-faced from exertion, Hauptman Candler, the company commander, trotted forward, accompanied by Weiselbladd, the battalion intelligence officer.

"Listen up," Schultz instructed once the two officers arrived, "here's what is going to happen. Lannon, you'll establish a base of fire from this position. You'll have Candler's nine machineguns to augment your six. Do you see that two-storey building over there to the right of the bridge?"

"The stone one with the red-tiled roof?"

"That's the one," replied Schultz. "I think it's the primary enemy position, so there's where you'll concentrate your fire. Be prepared to engage any alternative targets that might appear. Are we clear?"

"Yes sir, but shouldn't I be leading the assault?" Lannon asked.

"Negative," replied Schultz in a firm tone of command. "I'll be taking the men across."

"Do you think that's wise, sir?" queried Weiselbladd. "I mean ..." The intelligence officer's voice tapered off mid-sentence, but his glance at the stricken fallschirmjäger on the bridge made his meaning clear.

"I'm touched, Günter," said Schultz with an avuncular smile. "But a commander can't lead from behind."

The battalion commander swivelled to address Lannon. "The success of this assault will be contingent on the establishment of fire superiority over the enemy. Your job will be to suppress the Engländers so we don't end up like poor Eichel. And I don't want any friendly fire accidents. Make sure to shift your fire in accordance with our movements. Am I making myself clear?"

"Yes, sir," replied Lannon, flashing a frown of disappointment. "Although I'd still prefer to be with my men."

Shultz smiled proudly. "I wouldn't expect any less, but those are my orders. Candler, have your men ready to cross once my two platoons have established a bridgehead on the other bank. We go in three minutes. The signal to commence the assault will be a red flare."

Fifty-eight

"Kodkod Vengeance, this is Four," came the voice of Farkash through the PRC710 headpieces worn by Klein and his rearguard detachment.

"This is Kodkod, go," replied Klein.

"We can see them massing behind that row of warehouses just opposite the footbridge. It looks as though they're about mount a major assault."

"How many?"

"At least 250," Farkash replied. "Say two-plus rifle companies. Another company-sized force is moving to your west towards the road bridge."

"You're just full of good news today."

"Don't shoot the messenger."

"Won't have the time, or the ammunition," Klein quipped. "I'll be too busy dealing with our German friends to worry about the sorry likes of you. On a more serious note, what's the situation with the ship? How much more time until we can get her underway?"

"Another forty minutes as of two minutes ago."

"Copy," replied Klein. "We'll just have to buy you that much time. Thanks for the heads up. Kodkod, out."

Klein peeked through the lower left corner of a second-storey window facing onto the canal. Nothing visible yet. Ducking beneath sill-level, he moved at a crouch over to the stairs.

"Uziel, can you hear me?"

Staff Sergeant Uziel Buzaglo appeared in the stairwell. "Loud and clear," replied the swarthy Sayeret Givati NCO of Moroccan-Jewish descent who led the fireteam on the ground floor.

"You heard Farkash's sitrep," Klein continued. "So, here's the plan. We wait until they're midway across the bridge. Then we deliver a salvo that stops them in their tracks. We all empty one mag and then scarper. We should be able to break contact cleanly if we move quickly enough. If we have to disengage under pressure, I'll provide overwatch with Gershon and the Negev while you make your ..."

351

"Yossi, they've fired a red flare," interjected Halevy from his position at the second-floor window on the right. "I think ..."

The Negev gunner collapsed backward as a massive fusillade suddenly engulfed the front façade of the stone building. Nine MG34s firing at a cyclic rate of 900 rounds per-minute spewed around 130 bullets per second at the structure, triggering a cascade of sparks and clouds of dust.

The fraction of those projectiles finding their way through the windows transformed the room into a deadly nightmare. The Israeli troopers instinctively pazatzta'ed onto the floor as myriad bullets snapped overhead, filling the room with fine plaster dust as they thudded into the interior walls.

"Stay down!" yelled Klein. He crawled past Levinson, who was lying prone next to the fallen Halevy. A simple glance at the gaping entry wound that had replaced the bridge of Halevy's nose made further examination unnecessary.

"Ilan's hit!" yelled Levinson over the snap and thump of incoming bullets. Klein scanned the room until he saw another one of his men, rifleman Ilan Simcha, splayed in an utterly unnatural pose atop a growing pool of blood.

Slipping the sling of the NG7 from over Halevey's head, Klein unstrapped the Negev gunner's tactical vest. He then crawled over to Ilan, subjecting the trooper to a perfunctory examination that yielded the same conclusion.

"This is much too hot!" Klein shouted over the din. "We move now! Gershon and Ilan are gone, but we leave no-one behind. They come with us. I've picked up the machine gun and Gershon's vest. Let's move with our casualties at a low crawl to the stairwell. Baruch and I will bring Gershon. The rest of you bring Ilan. The Germans will be here in less than five minutes and I want to be out the back in less than one."

Slithering on their stomachs to the stairs with their dead in tow, Klein and his troopers made their way to the ground floor, where they joined Buzaglo and his fire team. The Israelis exited the building through the rear, emerging into an alleyway that led southwards through an industrial precinct towards the Sète railway lines and the coast. The alley was bounded on the West by a high stone wall, and to the East by a two-storey concrete building that looked like some sort of factory.

The distinctive 'buzzsaw' sound of rapid-firing MG34s suddenly tapered off, followed by the voice of Farkash coming over the net.

"Kodkod, this is Four," reported Farkash, "their lead elements are across the bridge and approaching your previous position at the house. They're showing a high degree of caution and advancing in bounding overwatch, which should grant you a bit of a head start."

"Understood," replied Klein. "Appreciate the sitrep. Keep it coming, out."

The troops were moving much too slowly for Klein's comfort, encumbered as they were by the deadweight of the inert bodies carried, fireman-style, across their shoulders.

"Men, we need to hustle," he urged. "The Germans are just about to knock on our former front door. This lane is a natural kill zone and I want to be well away before they show up."

The Israelis quickened their pace, with grunts of exertion sounding from the two troopers burdened with the unit's dead. Once past the factory building, they found themselves in an open storage area piled high with track, gravel and sleeper ties – all maintenance supplies for the adjacent rail switchyard.

Klein motioned for the group to halt and beckoned Buzaglo to approach.

"Baruch and I will stay behind for a bit to play rearguard. You can see the railroad tracks up ahead. Turn right and follow them westwards. They'll lead you straight to the ship."

"I can join you," offered Buzaglo. "After all, three barrels are better than two."

"I appreciate the idea, but that's a definite negative," said Klein, his head shaking sharply. "Get the troops back to the ship. Don't worry, we'll be right behind you."

"Okay, Yossi, understood," replied Buzaglo. "We won't sail without you. If necessary, I'll come and get you myself."

"No need for melodrama. We'll just rough them up a bit and then be along presently. End of discussion. Move."

Buzaglo and his contingent disappeared as Klein led Levinson behind an untidy stack of heavy wooden railroad ties, stained brown with creosote oil preservative.

Klein knelt and opened the Negev's bi-pod. "Get me another assault drum and have the extra barrel ready for a quick change."

Levinson dropped to his knees, shucking the pack off his back and extracting the requested items.

Klein found a gap in the pile of ties that provided hidden observation over the laneway. The two Israeli stay-behinds watched and waited.

Not for long.

After no more than three minutes, one of those distinctive rimless fallschirmjäger helmets bobbed out from the doorway of the building formerly occupied by the Israelis.

With the coast apparently clear, the German paratroopers made their way cautiously into the lane, more and more of them entering until they constituted a reinforced platoon. The fallschirmjäger deployed in two columns, one strung out along the stone wall and the other arrayed along the side of the factory.

"Ready?" Klein asked in a low voice as the German point men approached to within thirty metres.

Levinson nodded.

"Now!" Klein yelled, shouldering the Negev as he rose to a standing position, while Levinson followed suit with his X95. The two Israelis opened fire simultaneously, lashing the narrow alleyway with a volley of death and dismemberment.

Caught between the stone wall and the factory, the Germans had nowhere to hide. Within seconds, the lane was transformed into a charnel house. By the time Klein had emptied his 125-round assault drum and Levinson had fired two 30-round magazines, every single one of those forty-odd German paratroopers was down, dead or wounded.

"Reloading!" shouted Klein as he went down on one knee. Pushing the magazine release button, he removed the assault pack from the housing at the bottom of the weapon that served as its secondary feed mechanism. Slamming a new assault pack into place, he flipped up the tray cover and slipped the spare barrel into place in one easy motion. He then drew back the charging handle and the machine gun was once again ready to fire.

Klein peered through the gap in the ties. "That seems to have sucked the wind out of their sails for the moment. That's our cue. We don't want to be here when they bring up those machine guns from the other side of the canal. You fully loaded?"

Levinson nodded.

"Okay, you first. Run to the railroad tracks and go right. You can cover me from the corner of that shed when I make my move. Ready?"

Another nod from Levinson.

"Go!" yelled Klein, rising to his feet and firing several short bursts as Levinson dashed across the yard.

"Ready!" yelled Levinson, as he began to lay down suppressive fire from overwatch at the storage shed, fifty metres to the rear.

"Moving now!" shouted Klein in response.

The familiar high-pitched bark of outgoing 5.56 mm rounds was suddenly supplemented by the sharp cracks of incoming bullets breaking the sound barrier overhead. That meant the fallschirmjäger weren't wasting any time. A new wave of paratroopers was entering the alley.

Klein sprinted across the yard and around the corner of the shed as the thud of German rounds slamming into the planking increased in volume and frequency.

"Bastards don't lack guts," gasped Klein as he knelt to regain his breath. "Lucky they only have bolt actions."

"I think they're working up the courage for another try," said Levinson as he fired again towards the enemy.

"A couple of claymores would come in handy right now."

"Why go small?" asked Levinson, his mouth spreading in a wry grin. "As long as you're in wish list mode, why not ask for an Apache attack helicopter or Merkava?"

Klein laughed. "A Merkava would be nice, but ..."

His words were drowned out by the sudden pounding crescendo of German bullets striking the shed. The distinctive MG34 buzzsaw sound could be heard over the din.

"Shit, they've brought up their guns," said Klein. "Time to go."

The two Israelis scarpered into the railyard, turning west towards the haven of Sète harbour quayside and the sanctuary of the *Mauritz van Nassau*.

As they ran, Klein engaged in a hasty tactical assessment of their situation. His conclusions were less than pleasing. The railyard was completely devoid of rolling stock, rendering it bare as a billiard table without balls or rack. To their left, the waves of the Mediterranean lapping on the shoreline precluded any chance of escape in a southward direction. A series of railroad tracks stretched ahead, their crossties like so many rungs on giant ladders laid carefully on the ground in serried rows.

It was a race. And the sharp snap of bullets scarcely missing his head informed Klein that they'd lost. The sanctuary offered by the warehouses might as well have been half a world away.

Klein paused his retreat to fire a long 25-round burst from the Negev.

But in the midst of his half-pirouette, back towards his route of retreat, he was pummelled to the ground by a massive blow to the thigh. Within seconds, the initial numbness caused by the shock of the bullet strike metamorphosed into a white-hot spasm of agony.

Glancing down at his leg, Klein saw a flow of garnet-hued blood seeping into the gravel of the trackbed upon which he lay. No spurting. That was a good sign. At least the femoral artery was still intact. Lucky, because he couldn't spare the half-minute it would take to slap a field dressing on the wound. There were more pressing matters demanding his attention.

Gritting his teeth against the pain, Klein rolled onto his stomach and snapped open the NG7's bipod. Moving the machine gun's selector switch to full-auto, he began to lay down a curtain of suppressive fire against the helmeted enemy heads bobbing out from behind cover to take shots at him. At present, they appeared to have only bolt-action Kar98s and a handful of MP38 submachine guns, but when they brought up their MG34s, his goose would be well and truly cooked.

A sudden slap on Klein's shoulder was immediately followed by the distinctive sound of outgoing 5.56 mm rounds over his head, seemingly next to his ear. He looked around to see Levinson kneeling at his five o'clock, emptying a magazine down range at the fallschirmjäger.

"What are you doing here?" growled Klein. "Get back to the ship. I'll provide overwatch."

"With all due respect, that's bullshit. We have to move. Over there!" Levinson cocked his head to his left.

Klein glanced in the designated direction and saw a small, two-storey brick building adjacent to the railyard's northernmost track some thirty metres away. "Don't think I can walk," he said, as he fired another seven-round burst at their pursuers.

The tempo of German fire increased in direct proportion to the growing number of fallschirmjäger materialising from behind the shed.

"Come on!" barked Levinson as he seized the drag handle on the back of Klein's tactical vest and yanked his commander upright.

In what was little short of a miracle, the fugitive Israelis made it into the brick building without additional injury.

Fifty-nine

Levinson bolted the door behind him and gently laid Klein on the floor before making a quick visual survey of their surroundings. Arrays of floor-to-ceiling industrial shelving piled high with spikes, fasteners, bolts and other tools of the railroad trade revealed the building's function as an equipment storehouse. Then Levinson noticed an iron quarter-landing staircase in the far-left corner that led upwards to a second level.

"We need to get up those stairs," muttered Levinson. "When the Germans get here, their first move will be to chuck a couple of grenades through the door. Defending from here is not an option."

Klein said nothing, signifying his comprehension by a weak nod of the head. With a loud grunt of effort, Levinson pulled Klein erect and provided auxiliary propulsion to his rapidly fading commander as the duo made slow and painful progress to, and up, the stairs.

Gently depositing Klein on a bare space of floor, Levinson turned his attention to the industrial shelving that also lined the walls of the second level. With considerable effort, attended by loud grunting, he managed to overturn the heavy metallic rack closest to the stairwell, pushing it down onto the landing. Anyone trying to ascend from the ground floor would now be utterly exposed while negotiating this improvised obstacle. Levinson then upended a second shelf, manhandling it to the top of the stairs in the hope it would provide some measure of cover against enemy fire from below.

His ad hoc combat engineering tasks complete, Levinson returned to the side of Klein.

"Time to look at that wound. You've been bleeding steadily for a while."

Klein just lay there, his wan face betraying injury-induced fatigue. Levinson used his fighting knife to cut away his commander's battledress trouser leg. He then removed an Israeli combat dressing from a pouch on Klein's tactical vest. Tearing open its airtight packaging, he placed the dressing's primary sterile pad over the bullet exit wound on the front of Klein's thigh. Next, he applied

357

the detachable secondary sterile pad to the entry wound about 15 centimetres below his commander's right buttock and began to wrap the four-metre elasticised bandage around the wound area. Threading the bandage through its integral plastic 'pressure applicator', he pulled tight to exert a tourniquet effect and secured it in place with the closure bar.

Pausing for a moment to peruse his handiwork, Levinson nodded in satisfaction. "I think I should take the Negev."

Klein mustered just enough strength to respond with a weak nod of assent and Levinson slipped the sling over his commander's head to take possession of the weapon. Dropping his backpack on the floor, he extracted a fresh assault drum and reloaded the machinegun, cycling the charging handle to chamber the first round.

Levinson moved to the east-facing window and cast a discreet glance outside. Two dozen German paratroopers were approaching warily. "Fuck, they're closing fast," he muttered.

Shattering the windowpane with a blow from the Negev's butt, Levinson squeezed off a 10-round burst. The oncoming fallschirmjäger immediately went to ground and returned fire.

The single shots from Kar98s were soon joined by the sheet-ripping sound of an MG34 and a hailstorm of bullets hitting the brick wall.

"They'll be coming through the door soon," yelled Levinson as he crawled over to the stairwell. "How many grenades do you have?"

No response. Levinson cast a glance over his shoulder and saw Klein, now semiconscious, his head lolling on his left shoulder.

"Double fuck." He keyed the transmit button on his PRC710 Madonna boom mic. "Four, this is Kaspit Kodkod," referring to himself by the IDF call sign for a commander's radioman. He then realised that the button failed to emit the 'click' sound that attended a radio transmission. Opening the radio pouch on his tactical vest, he extracted the PRC710. The backlit window that normally showed the frequency was dark. He twisted the off-on button back and forth several times. No joy.

"Triple fuck," he grunted. "Dead battery."

Levinson liberated two additional MK26IM fragmentation grenades from Klein's tactical vest, doubling his explosive arsenal. He had just returned to his position atop the stairwell when the sounds of the front door being kicked open came from below. The thumps of two objects hitting the earthen floor quickly followed.

Levinson covered his ears and opened his mouth to protect against the concussive blast he knew was imminent. A pair of explosions in quick succession rattled the heavy timber floor and raised a massive cloud of dust that swirled through both floors of the storehouse. Placing Klein's two requisitioned grenades within easy reach, he shouldered the Negev, aiming the weapon at the stairs.

A brief smattering of rifle fire announced the Germans' entry into the ground floor of the storehouse. A guttural colloquy ensued among the fallschirmjäger, but the only word Levinson recognised was "handgranate". This could only mean another salvo of potato masher grenades would soon be coming his way up the stairs.

Time for a little pre-emption. Levinson pulled the pin from the nearest M26IM and released the safety lever, waiting two seconds before throwing it hard at the wall opposite the mid-storey landing, where the stairwell turned ninety degrees. The grenade bounced off the wall and disappeared below, triggering a loud chorus of guttural alarm from the Germans below. One second later, an explosion ensued and the guttural shouts were replaced by glottal cries of pain.

"Hitler sucks dick!" barked Levinson in English, more as a tension release than out of any expectation his imprecation would be understood.

At least one of the fallschirmjäger below spoke sufficient English to pick up on the defamatory intent of Levinson's shout. "Und Churchill ist ein schwein!" came the indignant rejoinder from the floor below.

Levinson cast another M26IM down the stairwell by way of reply, followed by a long burst from the Negev just to show he meant business.

A preternatural stillness settled on the storehouse, with the Israelis trapped on the second floor and the German paratroopers loath to mount what would clearly be a very costly assault up the stairs. Each combatant party remained ensconced in its positions, waiting for its enemy to make the next move.

The awkward silence was broken, some minutes later, by a German-accented voice whose vocabulary and elocution bespoke an excellent education.

"Engländer, you have fought well, but your position is now hopeless. We have hundreds of troops while you only have a handful. I urge you to put down your weapons and surrender. I guarantee you will be treated honourably in accordance with the Hague Convention and the laws of war."

"Did you ever study the Greek classics? Herodotus, perhaps?" yelled Levinson.

"Yes, of course. At gymnasium."

"Then do you remember the Battle of Thermopylae? Where the Persians demanded that the Spartans give up their weapons?"

"I am not here for the history lesson," replied the now clearly exasperated voice. "I am here to say you must surrender or die."

"I'll answer with the words of Leonidas to Xerxes, 'molon labe!' If you want our weapons, come and take them!"

"This is your final chance, Engländer. Surrender now or die."

"I have a better idea," yelled Levinson. "Why don't you surrender to me?"

The German response to Levinson's retort was delivered in the form of two potato-masher grenades, one of which bounced off the improvised barrier erected at the top of the stairwell. The second grenade landed in Levinson's lap, making it a simple enough matter to hurl it back from whence it had come.

"You'll have to do better than that, you fucking pussy!" Levinson shouted, once the echo of the explosions subsided.

Before the Germans could respond, a series of explosions accompanied by small arms fire was heard from outside the building. Cocking his head as he listened, Levinson was able to discern the sharp-pitched reports of 5.56 mm fire amid the din from without. He looked towards Klein with a smile etched from ear to ear.

"Yossi, do you hear that? The guys are here! It's going to be Okay!"

"Grenade!" came the cry in Hebrew from a voice outside the building. The ensuing explosion was followed by an intense barrage of 5.56 mm fire that suffused the ground floor of the storeroom.

"Yossi?" came the shouted question below.

"Up here! Yossi's wounded and unconscious. I'm going to need help with him!"

Farkash appeared, vaulting over the upended shelving unit. Buzaglo followed, with a septet of Israeli troopers in his wake. The sounds of the firefight ongoing outside the storehouse continued unabated.

"Told you I'd be back," said a grinning Buzaglo.

"How is he?" asked Farkash as he strode over and knelt to examine Klein.

"Gunshot wound to the right thigh. No damage to the artery, but he lost a fair bit of blood before I was able to apply a bandage."

360

"And you?"

"I'm fine," said Levinson. "Not a scratch."

"Right, then let's get the litter," Farkash directed.

The Team Four medic, a staff sergeant named Yedidia Gluska, produced a FlatEvac fabric litter that had the added advantage of enabling stretcher-bearers to operate their weapons while evacuating a wounded man.

Gluska briefly examined the field dressing applied previously by Levinson, nodding his approval. Shortly thereafter, the litter-bearing Klein was carefully manoeuvred past the overturned shelving units to ground level.

A gruesome sight greeted Levinson as he reached the landing midway down the stairwell. The earthen floor of the storehouse was littered with over a dozen dead fallshirmjäger, their jump smocks smeared red with blood. This was the first time he had encountered the butcher's bill of battle at close range, and his stomach churned. There was no way of knowing which of the Germans had been killed by his grenades and which by Farkash's relief force. At the end of the day, that distinction was irrelevant. Getting Klein back to the ship was the only thing that mattered.

Another two Israeli troopers had remained on the ground floor, tasked with keeping the Germans at bay outside with rifle fire. This brought the size of the rescue party to eleven, including Farkash.

"We'll go on my smoke," instructed Farkash as he extracted an MK5 blue smoke grenade from his tactical vest, pulling the pin and casting it out the door. After a hiatus of four seconds, the grenade began to spew a thick blue cloud.

"Move!" Farkash commanded, standing aside so that the four litter-bearers could take the lead, accompanied by Gluska.

Levinson and the unencumbered troopers assembled in a rough rearguard formation, keeping pace with the litter-bearers as a protective screen. The distinctive report of an outgoing Lapua .338 round signified that Staff Sergeant Maor Tzur was at work, providing overwatch on the Dan bolt-action sniper rifle. Each 'boom-crack' marked another bullet directed to its target by the Noga Systems Matisse M75 thermal sight that enabled Tzur to see through the smoke with X-ray vision.

"I have more smoke grenades in my backpack," said Farkash with a glance towards Levinson. "Get me a couple now and keep feeding me as we go."

Keeping one hand on the trigger assembly of the Negev and his eyes fixed towards the enemy, Levinson unzipped the assault pack affixed to the back of Farkash's tactical vest.

Reaching inside, Levinson felt the cylindrical shapes of multiple smoke grenades. Extracting two, he handed them to Farkash while leaving the assault pack unzipped at the top for easy access.

Their withdrawal proceeded with Levinson feeding Farkash one grenade per minute to create a constant smokescreen in their wake. With Tzur administering inflicting headshots on any German who showed himself for more than a second, the fallschirmjäger were soon disinclined to pursue.

After four hundred metres, the Israelis approached the cover of two long rectangular warehouses built astride the main rail track leading to the quayside. As they came abreast of the buildings, they passed the prone Tzur, who had taken up his firing position behind a heavy wooden crate on the loading platform. Without a word, Tzur rose from his sniper hide, folded the bipod of his Dan rifle and joined the withdrawal.

The thump of the MK47 grenade launcher and crack of machinegun fire was now clearly audible ahead. As Farkash reached the wharf end of the warehouses, he signalled for the column to halt and gingerly peeked around the building's corner towards the Quai de Orient.

"Okay, here's the situation. The troops on the ship have engaged a company-size force attacking along the quayside from the North. If the enemy commander has any sense at all, he'll conduct a flanking movement to the East – which puts us directly in the Germans' path. They're likely to show up on our doorstep at any moment, so we'll have to move quickly. I'll throw smoke to cover the final one hundred metres of open quayside separating us from the gangplank."

"Only two left," reported Levinson.

"That means we'll just have to hustle. Stretcher-bearers in the lead. Be ready to move on my word."

From the lee side of the warehouse, Farkash hurled an MK5 onto the wharfside area between him from the *Mauritz*'s gangplank. After a four-second delay, the grenade began to sputter and hiss, releasing a cloud of bright yellow smoke. Recognising what this meant, the Israelis providing overwatch from the ship increased the tempo of their machinegun and automatic grenade fire against the pursuing fallschirmjäger.

"Go!" Farkash yelled two seconds later, when he deemed the smokescreen thick enough to conceal his men.

The stretcher-bearers were first to move, grunting and panting as they transported their burden across the open wharf and up the gangway to the *Mauritz*'s quarterdeck.

"Now it's our turn," said Farkash as he tossed the last remaining smoke grenade onto the quay.

The wharfside was now alive with the crack and whizz of German rounds being fired blindly into the smoke. The seven remaining Israelis hunched over and ran for their lives.

Levinson was halfway up the gangway when he heard that now familiar sickening thwack, so akin to the sound made by a butcher's cleaver hacking its way through a slab of beef ribs. He turned to see Buzaglo slumped over the rail, blood streaming from beneath his helmet, down his slack-jawed face.

Propelled by a fear-driven jolt of adrenalin, Levinson hefted Buzaglo in a fireman's carry and lurched his way up the gangway. Moments after the last trooper's feet hit the quarterdeck, he heard a pair of sharp cracks in rapid succession. Levinson glanced towards the forecastle of the ship, just in time to see the thick hemp hawser vanish through the gunwale hawsehole, severed from its knot around the deck bollard by a tiny pre-prepared charge of Semtex plastique.

Levinson saw Roie Abargil standing in the main hatch to the superstructure of the *Mauritz*, radio detonator in one hand while beckoning with the other. As he trotted those last few metres to the safe haven of the ship's interior, Levinson felt the deck plates begin to vibrate. The vessel slowly pulled away from the quay.

"Follow me," instructed Abargil as he strode along a dank passageway, illuminated by an ugly yellow light emanating from bulbs ensconced in metal light cages. The combat engineer officer turned into a compartment that Levinson recognised as the ship's mess. Entering in turn, he saw Lifshutz administering a saline solution IV to the forearm of an unconscious Klein, who was lying supine atop one of two dining tables in the compartment. A quartet of middle-aged men watched the ministrations of the Israeli medical officer with expressions of rapt professional interest. Doctors from among the deportees, Levinson surmised.

Lifshutz glanced up at the new arrivals at this makeshift casualty clearing station and motioned for Levinson to lay Buzaglo on the second dining table.

"Can you continue here, Doctor?" asked Lifshutz, posing the question in English to a bearded man who looked to be in his 60s.

The German doctor nodded and the Israeli physician turned his attention to the inert Buzaglo. Ever so gingerly removing the injured man's helmet, Lifshutz bent over to examine the head wound that was generating such copious bleeding. Flicking on a penlight, he appraised the wound, then picked up Buzaglo's discarded helmet and perused its exterior and interior. The doctor then startled everyone in the room by breaking out in a raucous spate of laughter.

"What the fuck?" expostulated Levinson.

"Sorry," guffawed Lifshutz as he proffered Buzaglo's blood sodden helmet. "Take a look for yourself."

The smoothness of the headgear's interior shell was marred by the blunted tip of a bullet that extruded roughly 2 mm. Flipping it over, he saw the base of a German 7.92 mm bullet that had lodged in the helmet, stopped by its aramid ballistic fibre construction.

"Does this mean he'll be alright?"

"Indeed, it does," said Lifshutz in a voice that betrayed his relief. "He may have a small fracture of the skull and probably a concussion. Aside from a monster headache, he'll ..."

The doctor's prognosis was interrupted by the sound of running feet from the outer passageway that presaged the arrival, moments later, of Emma Cohen and Miriam Shipperman.

Emma rushed to Klein's side, her face creased with concern as she gently took the hand of his free arm.

Miriam stood frozen in shock at the sight of Levinson's blood-soaked uniform. Tears began to course down her cheeks.

"Miriam, it's not mine," Levinson said soothingly.

Miriam sobbed audibly in relief, racing to him and entwining her arms around his neck while delivering a kiss to his mouth that was anything but chaste. When Levinson's rising tumescence made itself felt, she took a step back and smiled.

"We go now, yes?" she said in stilted English. Her smile conveyed unmistakable intent that transcended all linguistic limitations.

With a happy nod, Levinson led the way to the only place onboard that might promise them privacy – the captain's sea cabin. Thus, Baruch Levinson and Miriam Shipperman were utterly oblivious as the *Mauritz van Nassau* made its way through the Nouveau Bassin, past the inner breakwater of Jetée Quatre-Cinq, and into the Avant Port.

As the ship passed the Phare lighthouse into the Rade Exterieur roadstead, the couple was engaged in their own private expedition of discovery. A journey in which a superabundance of enthusiasm more than compensated for a scarcity of experience.

By the time they were done, the *Mauritz* was well out to sea on the first leg of its Mediterranean anabasis, and the minds of Levinson and Miriam were elsewhere entirely. They lay intertwined on the captain's bunk, luxuriating in a post-coital bliss that was far in excess of anything their prior sexual naiveté had equipped them to imagine.

"Wow," said Levinson in a voice tinged with awe, triggering a spate of delightfully feminine giggles from Miriam. He smiled in his turn and the two of them united in that particularly intimate variant of laughter that marked co-conspirators in an affaire de cœur.

There they lay, heartbeats gradually subsiding into a more normal syncopated tempo, just as the vibrating hum of the ship's engines settled into a rhythm that sounded routine. After a time – they couldn't tell how long – their idyll was interrupted by the sound of the locked door handle being tried, followed by an insistent knocking.

"Just a minute!" shouted Levinson in English as he and Miriam leapt up from the bunk and scrambled to clothe themselves. Pulling on his filthy camouflage battledress, he waited a few additional moments until his girlfriend – a fair description of her new status – was minimally decent, before unlocking and opening the door.

Sixty

"Sorry to interrupt," said Emma, her eyes bright with amusement at the déshabillé young squatters, "but Colonel Klein requires the bed."

"Right ... right," replied Levinson, the fire engine tint of his cheeks a true reflection of his embarrassment. "How is he?"

"The doctors say he'll be fine with a bit of rest." Emma stepped aside, her back flush with the bulkhead, to make way for the four Israeli stretcher-bearers carrying the still unconscious Klein. Medic Yedidia Gluska kept pace with the litter, holding aloft the IV bag of saline solution connected to the needle in Klein's forearm.

"Yes, well ... I have things to do," Levinson stuttered. Gathering up his weapon and tactical gear, the young Israeli trooper disappeared into the corridor without another word.

"Over there," instructed Emma, her arm pointing to the bunk.

The litter-bearers gently lifted their commander onto the captain's bed. Gluska tied the IV bag to a vent on the bulkhead with a length of 550 paracord.

"Doctor Lifshutz will be up in a while to check on him, but for now he needs to rest" said the medic. "Let me know if anything changes."

"Thank you, Yedidia," said Emma. She planted a kiss on the medic's cheek and dispatched the Israeli to his other duties, while taking a seat in the vacant chair at the chart table.

"I'll stay," volunteered Miriam as the door to the sea cabin swung shut.

"Thank you, liebschen. That would give us an opportunity to have a talk," said Emma, her lips curling into the knowing smile of an elder sibling enquiring into the assignations of a younger sister. "I suspect you might have some news to share."

"No regrets Emma," replied Miriam, her matter-of-fact tone belied by the sudden strawberry hue that suffused her cheeks. "He's the one. I know it sounds crazy because we met only yesterday, but he will be the father of my babies. I know this."

"Are your sentiments reciprocated?"

"Not in so many words, but there was no need," Miriam replied. "I don't expect you to understand, but when you know, you know."

"I'm not that much of an old maid," Emma protested as she enveloped Miriam in a sisterly embrace. "Also, I'm not being critical. In fact, I'm very happy for you both."

Behind the veneer of bubbly felicitation, a mammoth struggle was underway between Emma's head and heart. Every rational synapse between her ears was screaming that Miriam's profession of undying passion was patently ridiculous. Le coup de foudre, as the French called love at first sight, was the stuff of cinema fantasy, not real life. Or so she told herself.

Yet, like metal to a magnet, Emma's eyes were drawn to the unconscious figure of Klein at rest in the captain's bunk. There was no denying that she found him fascinating and infuriating in equal measure. Her mood was in constant flux, like a psychic metronome. One moment, she'd be ruing her public display of affection on the ship's upper deck, while the next she'd be struggling to contain feelings of raw sexual attraction so powerful they terrified her.

These fluctuations of mood were instantly banished from her thoughts when Klein suddenly stirred, his eyes flickering open as he regained consciousness. He painfully raised himself on an elbow as Emma disentangled herself from Miriam and knelt at his side. "How do you feel?"

"Like someone took a hammer and nail to my leg," groaned Klein.

"I can have Doctor Lifshutz get you something for the pain," Emma volunteered in a honeyed tone of solicitude.

"No. No drugs. I need a clear head. Where are we? Have we left port?"

"Yes, a couple of hours ago. We're well out to sea."

"Who's at the helm? Who's navigating?"

"Captain Farkash is on the bridge. As you requested, we managed to identify someone who served as a naval officer during the last war. His sextant skills are a bit rusty, but he's confident all will be well with a bit of practice."

"That's very good," said Klein as he lowered himself back onto his pillow with a painful sigh. "There's something else. I need you to recruit the most talented seamstresses and graphic artists on board and bring them to me."

"You're welcome," replied Emma dryly. "But before I embark on this new quest, it's time for you to come good on your promise."

Klein's pain and fatigue didn't stop him from arching an eyebrow. "What promise?"

"Your promise to tell me things as yet unsaid. The truth that dare not speak its name."

"Ah ... yes," mumbled Klein, as he cast the subtlest of momentary eye flickers towards Miriam.

"I think she can be trusted," replied Emma in response to Klein's unspoken cue. She turned to address her younger companion in German. "Miriam, has Baruch told you any more about his background ... about who he is really is?"

Miriam shrugged. "Only that he comes from Jerusalem, where his mother is a judge, but you were party to that conversation as well."

"Of course, more recently you've been focused on ... other matters," said Emma, her words accompanied by the coyest of smiles that caused the younger woman's cheeks to blush anew.

"English please," protested Klein.

"Very well," replied Emma. "Miriam, Colonel Klein is about to provide us with answers. Although, first need a commitment that what you're about to hear will never be repeated in any form outside this cabin. Not to your grandmother, or anyone else. Can you agree to that?

"Yes, surely so."

Emma turned back to Klein in unspoken anticipation.

"Okay. Now we're at sea, there's no reason why you shouldn't know it all. Just promise not to throw something at me when what I'm about to say sounds absurd."

"Promise," said Emma, with a glance towards Miriam that triggered a nod of assent.

With that, Klein began to relate a story that, despite its implausibility, Emma instinctively believed. The non-sequiturs and incongruities that attended the miraculous arrival of these Jewish super-warriors suddenly made a certain sense that, while bizarre, had a coherent logic. The pieces finally fitted.

The revelations did not stop there. Emma's passage through the threshold of belief on the topic of time travel triggered something else, as well. The emotional callus she had built as protection against an ugly world began to crack and then crumble.

She fell quickly and she fell hard. Miriam was right. As Emma looked into Yossi Klein's eyes she just knew, and she immediately set her mind to the task of winning her newly beloved's affection. She didn't know whether he might have a wife or lover in his other time and place, but it didn't matter. That was then and there, while this was here and now. She would afford him due time and space to mourn, if this was what he required. But the end result was never in question. Now that she had decided to love him, he would be hers. The possibility of any other outcome never entered her mind.

Unaware that his future was being mapped out by Emma, Klein suddenly felt the shock and stress of injury draining the last dregs of his energy. "I have to rest," he murmured as his eyes flickered with fatigue.

Emma glanced at Klein's IV, its bag now near empty. "Your infusion needs changing. I'll have Dr Lifshutz bring up a new bag. In the meantime, I'll start to organise your team of artists and seamstresses. I'm sure Miriam will be happy to stay and look after you."

"Yes, of course," said Miriam, while Klein was able to manage only a weak nod by way of response.

"I'll see you later, darling," said Emma as she bent over and kissed Klein on the lips. She shrugged as she caught sight of Miriam's Cheshire cat grin through the corner of her eye. "I suppose this makes us just a couple of romantic idiots," she said in German.

"Romantics, yes; idiots, no," Miriam archly replied. "I remain convinced that we'll be attending the brises and bar mitzvahs of each other's children in the Land of Israel."

"Well, I suppose the events of the past twenty-four hours should be enough to make a believer out of the most hardened atheist," observed Emma. "So Be'ezrat Hashem, as the rabbis say."

With that appeal to divine intercession, the now thoroughly discombobulated former secularist set out to track down Doctor Lifshutz.

Sixty-one

The worst thing about exercising command from Berlin was the inability to control events at the pointy end of the very operation you just set in motion. Once plans were conceived and orders cut, the tyranny of distance intervened to place tactical implementation firmly in the hands of others. To the perennial frustration of Generalmajor Walter Warlimont, those others were invariably less intelligent and less talented than he, in his not-so-humble self-estimation.

Warlimont reached for the packet of Players Medium Navy Cut lying on his desk. "Sheisse," he cursed under his breath. Only one left.

Extracting this last cigarette, Warlimont applied its tip to the flame of his silver-plated Dunhill Bijou lighter and settled back to savour the 'finest Virginia tobacco'.

As he idly watched the smoke from his cigarette swirl towards the ceiling, Warlimont felt sufficiently at leisure to reflect on the madness of the preceding three days. The lightning trip to smuggle high-ranking bodies out of France could have been taken from the pages of a modernised *Scarlet Pimpernel* – his favourite book as an adolescent. Then came the orchestration of a coup d'état that entailed the coordinated defenestration of SS and Nazi officials throughout the country. To describe these events as hectic would be quite an understatement.

As Warlimont's mind moved to musings on Germany's strategic situation, he felt cause for considerable satisfaction. Stability of governance and a restoration of political sanity was now ensured by the Wehrmacht's seamless seizure of power. This brought hope that a new Germany, free of Nazi fanaticism and excess, might finally shed its pariah status among the nations of the world.

Militarily, there was no great cause for immediate concern. It was true that the RAF had managed to wrest a close-run victory from the Luftwaffe over the summer. Yet, with its maritime supply lines under constant U-Boat assault, and no help forthcoming from an isolationist America, Great

Britain was still very much on the defensive. There would be no danger emanating from the West for the foreseeable future.

To the East, the debilitating impact of Stalin's purges was manifest in the woeful performance of the Red Army during the Winter War against Finland. After 35,000 of its senior commanders were dispatched to gulags or the execution cellars of the Lubyanka, the Soviet officer corps was oversupplied with political sycophancy and undersupplied with military talent. The Russians were a paper tiger, even after their forced annexation of the Baltic States and Bessarabia.

The only real fly in the strategic ointment came courtesy of Germany's idiot ally Mussolini. Just yesterday, without so much as a word of warning, il Duce sent his troops across the border from Italian-occupied Albania into Greece. Now, less than two days later, the fascist offensive has ground to a halt in the face of fierce Greek resistance amidst the mountaintops and valleys of Epirus.

Warlimont shook his head in disgust. The sheer incompetence of the Italians irritated him. The next thing you knew, Mussolini would be asking for German assistance to extricate himself from this quagmire of his own making. Not for the first time, he wondered whether the Pact of Steel was more trouble than it was worth.

His ruminations were interrupted by a knock on the door.

"Come in!" bellowed Warlimont, and Luftwaffe Oberst Günter Augustin appeared in the doorway bearing a manila hemp folder.

"It's Tilphousia, sir," Augustin reported. "The after-action debrief."

"Ah, a bit of unfinished business. Tell me, how did the Luftwaffe fare in its effort to tie up this last loose end?"

"Not well, sir. The Englishmen successfully made their escape, but, as the casualty figures indicate, not for want of effort on the part of our fallshirmjäger."

"Let me see," said Warlimont, accompanied by an impatient 'bring-it-here' flick of his wrist. Opening the folder, he perused its contents for a few moments before looking up at the Luftwaffe officer with a grim expression. "There were 57 dead and another 138 wounded from an original complement of 576."

"Almost 35 per cent, sir," volunteered Augustin. "It includes fifteen of the battalion's officers killed or wounded, among them the battalion commander who died of mortal injuries. It was a very serious fight, sir."

"It appears so, and it only strengthens my determination that these Engländer must not escape. I want to know who these bastards are, and how they so easily triumph over the best we have. They have some sort of secret up their sleeve, and I want to know what it is. When will our air units be ready for action?"

"Not before dawn tomorrow, sir. Our bombers should be arriving shortly at the airfield outside Montpellier, but it'll be dark by the time they're refuelled. Tomorrow morning is the earliest the search could commence, but you should be aware our operational window is likely to be constrained by oncoming weather issues."

Warlimont sighed. "What are the meteorologists saying?"

"That there's a fast-moving storm front moving west-to-east across the Iberian Peninsula. Predictions indicate it will reach our search area in the Mediterranean sometime tomorrow evening."

"Then we'll just have to mount a maximum effort while the skies are still clear," Warlimont commanded. "That means every serviceable plane in the air at dawn. What about lines of communication with the Italians?"

"We're working on it, sir," Augustine reported. "A Luftwaffe signals unit is en route to Montpellier by Ju-52, and our naval attaché in Rome is in the process of obtaining access to Italian naval frequencies. Once that information is received, the signallers should be able to liaise between our forces."

"Coordination is essential. Bear in mind that I want prisoners for questioning at the end of this, if possible. That means we're reliant on the Italians for the actual interception and boarding of the English ship."

"Understood, sir," replied Augustin.

"Have you taken steps to update Unger on his arrival in La Spezia?"

"That is also being handled by our naval attaché in Rome, sir. Kapitän zur See Unger will receive a briefing document once he lands in Pisa."

"Thank you very much, Oberst. Please keep me informed of any developments," said Warlimont in a tone of dismissal. "On your way out, can you ask my staff feldwebel to fetch me another packet of Players? He should still have a few from the stocks we captured in France."

"Happy to, sir," Augustin replied.

The Luftwaffe oberst departed as Warlimont took one final drag from his cigarette and stubbed it out in the cut-down 88 mm shell casing that served as an ashtray. The pieces were all in motion, but there were many

372

hours yet to pass before any of them would clash. At this juncture, there was little to do except wait – his least favourite part of high command.

Reaching down, he opened the lower-right cupboard of his desk, extracting a precious bottle of Glenfiddich and shot glass from within. Say what you wish about the British, but there was no question the finest schnapps in the world came from Scotland. Truth be told, Warlimont had developed a similar grudging respect for these elusive English raiders. Jews or not, they were tremendously impressive. While he resolved to pursue them without respite, the German general hoped that at least some of these enemy commandos would survive the process. Not only was he personally curious to gauge their mettle face-to-face, but there were serious questions still outstanding about the events at Montoire. Questions to which he was determined to find answers.

Sixty-two

Peter Koertig watched through the window of the Ju-52 transport as the bright orange orb of the sun descended to its daily rendezvous with the zaffre-hued Ligurian Sea. Moments later, the aircraft touched down on the main runway of Pisa's San Giusto Airport and taxied towards a column of three black staff cars parked adjacent to a nearby hangar. The pilot cut the engines as the Luftwaffe crew chief opened the passenger door, lowering a set of steps to bridge the gap between fuselage and tarmac.

Once they were on terra firma, the Germans were approached by a group of Italian naval officers, led by a man in his early 40s bearing the rank insignia of Capitano de Frigata – equivalent to a Royal Navy commander.

"Kapitän zur See Unger, I presume?" enquired the officer in Italian-accented German.

"That is correct," replied Unger with a polite nod. "And this is my aide-de-camp, Hauptman Koertig."

"Capitano de Frigata Giuseppe Buonarota at your service," the Italian declared with the accompaniment of a salute that Unger returned. "Welcome to Italy. I've been assigned as your liaison officer and am here to translate or provide any other assistance you may require. First and foremost, I've been asked to give you this." He bowed slightly while extending a white envelope.

Without a word Unger opened the envelope and perused its contents. He then handed the document to Koertig, who read and returned it to his superior.

"Thank you, Capitano," said Unger. "We're ready."

"Would you like any refreshment before we begin the drive to La Spezia? The journey will last just under two hours."

"We'll be fine," replied Unger. "Our mission is rather urgent."

"Understood," said Buonarota. "We'll leave immediately. Kapitän, you may ride with me in the lead car. Hauptman, you will probably find it more comfortable in the second."

Koertig saluted and was midway through a turn towards the designated vehicle before an interjection by Unger. "Thank you for your consideration, Capitano, but I think it would be better if Hauptman Koertig comes with us. He can sit in front next to the driver."

The only tic betraying Buonarota's poker-faced suavity was an ever-so-slight arch of his right eyebrow. "Of course," said the Italian with a diplomatic bow. "Shall we go, Mein Herren?"

The staff cars made their way out of the airport, turning north on Route No 1. Crossing the Arno River, they brushed past the eastern outskirts of Pisa, making excellent time due to the deference paid by other vehicles to what was clearly a convoy of high-ranking officials. It was just after 18:00 hours when the car carrying Unger and Koertig pulled up in front of an imposing three-storey stone building with a Doric colonnade that made it look more like a courthouse than a military headquarters.

"Please follow me," asked the ever-urbane Buonarota, his arm sweeping in a gesture of invitation. The Italian led the way up a sweeping marble staircase to the third floor, where they walked through a massive set of oak doors at the end of the corridor. Ignoring several yeomen and amanuenses busily pecking away at typewriters in an outer office, he knocked on a second pair of doors, only slightly less impressive than the first.

Buonarota entered what appeared to be an inner sanctum, only to reappear moments later. "Gentlemen, the admiral will see you now," he said with a slight bow and beckoning gesture of welcome.

Koertig followed Unger through the doors, where he saw a panoply of a half-dozen senior naval officers in attendance.

"Kapitän zur See Unger," announced Buonarota in a loud voice, "I would like to introduce Ammiraglio de Squadra Sansonetti, commander of our Second Fleet here in La Spezia."

Unger and Koertig both braced to attention, rendering salutes almost in unison.

Switching to his native tongue, Buonarota introduced Unger and Koertig, describing them to his admiral as special emissaries of the new German government.

"Tell these gentlemen how shocked we were to hear of their Führer's assassination," intoned the admiral. "It was a disgraceful act of treachery and a great loss to us all. They probably didn't see it in the darkness, but

375

we have lowered our flags to half-mast out of respect for our great German ally."

Koertig listened impassively as Buonarota translated his commander's words into German. He found no fault with their accuracy. So far, so good.

"Please inform the admiral that his sympathy and respect are profoundly appreciated," replied Unger. "It is in our hour of need that we come to you with a request for assistance." The German naval officer paused, allowing his Italian counterpart to translate.

Receiving a nod from the admiral, Unger continued, "A force of English commandos conducted a raid on a target of considerable strategic significance in southern France. They escaped from the port of Sète in a merchant vessel and are en route, we believe, to Gibraltar. Given that our Kriegsmarine has no combat assets in the Mediterranean, we have come to seek the aid of the Regia Marina."

"I received a message from Comando Supremo conveying a request to that effect from your OKW," replied Ammiraglio Sansonetti, once the German's words had been rendered into Italian. "I agree that the Englishmen will most likely make for Gibraltar, using the coast of neutral Spain as a bolthole if they run into trouble. Their only other option would be Malta, but that would entail running the gauntlet of our naval and air bases in Sardinia and Sicily. They'd have to be mad."

"Our tactical analysis yielded the same conclusion," agreed Unger. "That's why it's imperative that we deploy forces to prevent that scenario from becoming reality."

The Italian admiral strode back and forth behind his desk for a few moments, before turning to face the Germans. "Gentlemen, we're eager to provide whatever assistance we can, but we find ourselves constrained by the operational demands of providing naval support to our ground troops in Greece. Add to that the threat posed by the recent reinforcement by the Royal Navy of its forces in the Mediterranean Theatre."

"Of course, we wish your Greek endeavour every success," replied Unger diplomatically. "And there's no doubt the arrival of so-called 'Force H' at Gibraltar gives the enemy a formidable combat capability. Yet these factors notwithstanding, the capture of these English commandos remains an issue of the highest priority to the German government. Any assistance you might provide will earn il Duce considerable gratitude from my superiors in Berlin."

"I appreciate your concerns," replied Sansonetti. "I am prepared to put one of our most modern destroyers at your disposal. The *Ascari* was launched only two years ago and can make 38 knots at flank speed. This will be a joint operation with Regia Aeronautica, which will conduct an air search for your elusive freighter. Once the vessel is spotted by one of our aircraft, the *Ascari* will chase it down and bring it to heel. Is this acceptable?"

If Unger was underwhelmed by the offer of a single destroyer, he hid his disappointment beneath an urbane façade. "I thank you on behalf of the Deutsches Wehrmacht. You may rest assured that my report will note your cooperative attitude."

Roughly an hour later, at 19:48 hours, the Italian destroyer, *Ascari*, pulled away from the Prima Darsena dock, moving through the breakwater into La Spezia's outer harbour. With the headland of the Isola de Tino receding in its wake to starboard, the open waters of the Ligurian Sea beckoned and the destroyer picked up speed. Landlubber that he was, this was Koertig's first time on anything larger than a rowboat, and he couldn't help but be impressed by the feeling of raw power imparted by the throb of the destroyer's engines.

Stowing personal gear in his junior officers' billet, Koertig climbed the ladder to the main deck. He was jolted by the chill of the autumn night, which was intensified by the biting wind from the destroyer's 30-knot speed. Glancing around to orient himself, Koertig saw the ship's wake shining effervescent in the moonlight like a trail of giant gossamer unspooling from the stern. He found his way to the bridge, where he joined Unger and Buonarota at a large chart table.

"Ah, Hauptman, I hope you found your quarters satisfactory?" Buonarota enquired with all the solicitude of a high-end hotel concierge.

"Quite so. Danke."

"I was just explaining our intended course to Kapitän zur See Unger," Buonarota continued, his arm outstretched towards the map. "As you can see from the markings on the map, we'll proceed southwest past Corsica to a point south of the Balearic Isles. Then we'll swing west of Ibiza and sail north along the Spanish coast. If the Englishmen's destination is Gibraltar, we'll be perfectly positioned to intercept."

"How long will it take us to reach the Balearics?" enquired Unger.

"The captain intends to maintain a speed of 32 knots," replied

Buonarota, "which gives us an arrival time off Minorca of about 08:00 hours tomorrow morning."

Koertig glanced at his watch. "Twelve hours. How far will the British be able to travel in their commandeered freighter?"

"Good question," conceded Buonarota. "And one we've fully considered. It is highly unlikely that any merchant vessel they've managed to commandeer will have a speed greater than fifteen knots. By the time they're off Barcelona, we'll have reached the Balearics and begun our northward sweep. There's no way they'll be able to slip past us."

"Our Italian colleague's calculations are quite correct," confirmed Unger. "That means nothing of consequence will be happening until tomorrow morning. Koertig, I want you to get some rest so you'll be fresh and alert when things get interesting. You're dismissed."

Koertig arrived back at his compartment after only one minor incident of misdirection. After undressing and clambering into his allotted bunk, the fatigue of the past 48 hours hit home with a vengeance. Moments later, he fell into a deep sleep that left him insensible to the later arrival of his compartment-mate, an Italian gunnery officer who was coming off watch.

Sixty-three

Colonel Ralph Neville tapped on the glass partition separating the passenger compartment of the staff car from his driver, ATS Section Leader Emily Marshall. As the 1937 Humber Snipe MK II was stationary, caught on Watling Street in a long line of army lorries, the pretty brunette seated at the wheel turned around and slid open the partition window.

"Very sorry, sir," she reported in the cultivated tone of the British upper-middle class. "There seems to be some sort of major obstruction ahead. I think it must be bomb damage from last night's raid."

"Yes, by all accounts Stanmore was hit pretty hard," replied Neville.

"Do you think they were going after Fighter Command, sir?" asked Marshall. "Revenge for the Battle of Britain, perhaps?"

"I doubt it," said Neville. "Their night navigation isn't that good. This was the first major Luftwaffe attack since Hitler's death, so I think they were sending us a rather pointed reminder that Germany is still in the war."

"That's a rather depressing thought, sir," said Marshall, with a forwardness that bespoke her social class rather than her formal rank.

"No doubt, but as there's still a war on, we should get about fighting it. I think that will require an alternate route. We left Station X over an hour ago and have been stuck here for twenty minutes. This isn't doing anyone any good except the Germans."

"Righty oh, sir," replied Marshall. She performed a deft three-point turn that headed the Humber back towards St Albans, then west to Harrow, past the playing fields of the famous school that was Winston Churchill's alma mater. Turning south through Wembley, Neville watched the twin towers of Empire Stadium slip away in the distance. On to Paddington and Edgeware Road they came, around Hyde Park and past Buckingham Palace to Whitehall.

"Well done, Section Leader," said Neville as the Humber came to a halt opposite the arched entrance to the War Office inner courtyard. As he emerged from the passenger seat, he adjusted the pistol holster attached to his Sam Browne and the attaché case chained to his left wrist.

Carefully comparing the photograph on the colonel's ID to his actual visage, the military policeman saluted and granted Neville entry to the building. His next destination was the office of General Davison, where Ms Crosswaite now graced him with a familiar smile.

"Is he available?"

"Yes Colonel," she replied. "He gave instructions that you're to go straight in."

Neville nodded his thanks and knocked twice before entering the inner sanctum. Then he removed his No. 2 Service Dress hat beneath his left arm and braced to attention.

"I'm back, sir."

"So, I see," said Davidson. "Stand at ease, Colonel, and please tell me what was so damnably urgent to require a sudden trip all the way out to X?"

"Well, sir, in light of events, I thought it advisable to lodge a special request with the JIC to be notified personally if anything out of the ordinary was reported from France. Then last night, I received word of some very unusual Boniface intercepts that just might be related to the incident at Montoire. I thought it best to work directly with the German linguists so nothing would be lost in translation, so to speak. That's why I thought it worth the trip."

The mention of Montoire caused a visible uptick in Davidson's interest level. "And?" the general prompted.

"Well, sir, the message in question emanated from the Kriegsmarine liaison station at the French naval base in Toulon addressed to OKW. It's an after-action report on a battalion-sized Luftwaffe parachute assault mounted yesterday at a place called Sète, a medium-sized deep-water port about 130 miles west of Marseilles."

"Does this Sète have any strategic significance? Naval assets? Coastal fortifications?"

"Not really, sir," replied Neville. "It has primarily been used for the importation of Algerian wheat into metropolitan France."

"So why on earth would Jerry conduct an airborne operation against a facility of no military importance within the territory of their Vichy allies?"

Neville unlocked his briefcase and extracted a manila folder that he passed to Davidson. "Well, sir, that's where things become interesting. At the top of page one, you'll see the mission objective defined as 'seizure of the port area in order to prevent the escape by sea of an English commando raiding party'. Then, towards the bottom of page three, the enemy are also described as 'Palestinian Jews serving in the British Army.'"

Davidson turned to page three and grunted upon finding the referenced passage. He read silently for several moments, before glancing up from the document to transfix Neville with a piercing gaze. "Are you certain this is an accurate translation of the original Boniface?"

"Absolutely, sir," replied Neville. "I double-checked with the cryptographers and linguists. I'm completely confident it's a true rendition of the original."

"I know that chap Ben Gurion declared support for the war effort. Still, has his statement translated into any real collaboration with that armed underground of theirs … what's it called?"

"The Haganah, sir," supplied Neville.

"Yes, yes, the Haganah," echoed Davidson.

"Not to my knowledge. Although, back in 1938, some of their units were trained in irregular warfare tactics under the tutelage of Major Wingate."

"Wingate?" grimaced Davidson. "Isn't he that onion-eating, Bible-quoting eccentric who went native during his posting over there? As I recall, he became more of a Zionist than the Zionists themselves."

"He's the one, sir. By all accounts, he created a very effective counter-guerrilla force that played a major role in putting down the Arab revolt."

"Be that as it may, I remain a sceptic," opined Davidson. "There's a world of difference between a reprisal action against a rebel Bedouin village and an operation to kill Adolf Hitler in the midst of occupied France. Of all people, I wouldn't expect Jews to be the ones who could carry out something this audacious."

Neville willed his face to maintain its deadpan expression. "Be that as it may, sir, these raiders, whoever they are, gave a very good account of themselves."

"True enough," Davidson conceded as he continued to peruse the report. "They certainly appear to have administered a sound thrashing to those German parachutists."

"Sir, if I may, I'd like to suggest that a low-key visit to Palestine might be useful. I know that, over recent months, certain lines of communications have been opened with the Haganah. I might be able to arrange a few meetings that could allow me to suss out what, if anything, they know."

Davidson frowned. "Do you think it's really necessary for you to travel all that way? Isn't there anyone over there who could do the job?"

"I'm not sure that would be desirable, sir," replied Neville in a tone of polite dissent. "The obvious sensitivities of this matter mandate keeping the circle of knowledge as small as possible. I'd really be loath to bring in anyone else if it's not absolutely necessary."

"Makes sense," Davidson conceded. "How long will you be gone?"

"No more than three weeks, sir. There's a BOAC flight leaving Southampton for Lisbon this evening. If all goes well, I should arrive in Cairo via the West African route in three days. Once in Egypt, I'll brief Admiral Cunningham about the possibility that our ship of fugitives might be coming his way. If these raiders are genuinely Palestinian Jews who've managed to commandeer a merchant vessel, they'll likely be trying for home. It will be very helpful to have the Mediterranean Fleet ready to intercept if they show up anywhere east of Malta."

"I see," said Davidson. "But per your concerns about compartmentalisation, I presume you'll disclose only the bare minimum information required."

"Oh, absolutely sir. I'll speak to the Admiral of the hows, but without the whys."

"Then on to Palestine?"

"Yes, sir."

"Very well, Colonel," said Davidson as he rose from behind the desk with an extended hand. "You have a plane to catch, so I should let you go. Good luck and hurry back."

"Thank you, sir," replied Neville. Placing his No. 2 Service Dress cap atop his head, he rendered a farewell salute that his hatless general did not return.

Executing a precision about turn, that would have brought a smile to the face of the toughest Brigade of Guards regimental sergeant major, Neville took his leave. He had places to go and people to see.

Sixty-four

Utter frustration.

The peals of Shoshi's laughter echoed as she ran along serried rows of orange trees with Anat clasped in her arms. She paused to cast a smiling glance over her shoulder, beckoning for him to join them on their journey through the citrus grove.

Follow he did, right on her tail in hot pursuit. But no matter how fast he ran, no matter how hard he tried, his outstretched arms always just fell short. His wife and daughter remained just out of reach.

A gentle weight on Klein's shoulder pierced the veil of his slumber, drawing him against his will into wakefulness. Opening his eyes, he saw a hand belonging to Farkash, with Emma Cohen standing in the cabin doorway holding a glass of water.

"Sorry to wake you, Yossi," reported Farkash in English, "but we have something of a situation."

"How long have I been out?" croaked Klein as he rubbed his eyes.

"Just over 25 hours. The time is 9:17 on the evening of 28 October," replied Emma.

"What's our position?" asked Klein as he raised himself on one elbow from his supine position on the bunk. Emma handed him the glass of water and he chugged it in one long gulp.

"We're about sixty nautical miles south of the Balearic Islands," said Farkash. "Bearing south-south-east towards the Algerian coast."

"Can you show me on the chart?"

Emma stood aside as Farkash vanished through the door, only to reappear with rolled-up charts in hand and a middle-aged man in tow.

"Allow me to introduce Alois von Stockhausen, formerly of the Imperial German Navy during the first war," said Emma. "He served upon *SMS Stettin* at the Battle of Jutland and knows his way around a sextant."

"Von Stockhausen?" echoed Klein.

"Alois' wife is Jewish," replied Emma, a tad defensively.

"Yes," said von Stockhausen in a heavily accented English. "My Hanna insisted on accompanying her mother. I could not let my children lose their mother, or myself lose my wife."

"Are your children with us as well?" asked Klein.

"Yes," replied von Stockhausen. "Two boys aged 16 and 13, and my baby girl aged 11."

Klein smiled and nodded his approval. "Lovely. I look forward to meeting them. In the meantime, can you show me our course and position?"

"Certainly, sir," the former German naval officer replied as he unrolled the maritime chart. With his index finger, he indicated a spot two-thirds of the way between the Balearic Isles and the Algerian coast. "I took my last sextant reading at dusk about four hours ago. Moving at an average speed of around twelve knots per hour would put us at 38.17 degrees latitude and 5.51 degrees longitude. I'll have our precise position when I take another reading at midnight."

"How long before we turn east along the African coastline?"

Von Stockhausen paused to consult the map and his notes. "Just under five hours from now, sir. At around 02:00 on the morning of 29 October."

"Very nice," smiled Klein as he turned to address Farkash. "What's our situation with the flag and paint job?" he continued in English for the sake of the two non-Hebrew-speakers.

"All done, Yossi," replied Farkash in the same language. "The lettering across our stern now proclaims us to be the Turkish cargo ship *Manzikert*. The artists did a quality piece of work, especially when you consider that they were struggling with stencils and paint while hanging over the side on a bit of scaffolding. The flag looks realistic as well. Enough to pass muster when a Spanish coast guard boat came sniffing around as we were passing between Majorca and Minorca."

"Sounds good. Now, what's this situation you mentioned?"

"It's the prisoners," interjected Emma. "The SS men. Our people are very angry. Some want to throw them overboard."

Klein shrugged. "To be honest, it doesn't particularly matter to me one way or the other. The only question in my mind is why do you care?"

Emma's audible sigh bespoke her exasperation. "I've already had this conversation with Baruch Levinson ... and with Benjamin Farkash, here. As I told them both, if we claim to be nothing like the Nazis, we need to act nothing like the Nazis. This means no lynching."

"Benny, why don't you and Alois return to the bridge and recalculate our course and speed?" Klein instructed, his canting head indicating the door.

Once the cabin door closed, Klein turned and addressed her in a steely tone. "I resent the implication that we are in any way similar to the SS. We aren't in the habit of deliberately killing civilians; whereas, shooting innocents is a Nazi specialty. Those SS bastards are all guilty as sin."

"So now you hold yourself up to be judge, jury and executioner?" fired back Emma.

"What do you want to do?" asked Klein, not bothering to gild his sarcasm. "Hold a trial?"

"Not a bad idea," replied Emma. "There are more than a few lawyers in our group and we have one retired judge who served on the Reichsgericht – our highest court."

"You can't possibly be serious," spat Klein.

"Think about it," urged Emma. "It would provide some measure of closure to our people, while providing some measure of fairness to all concerned – including the SS."

"Which is more than they were prepared to afford you," Klein observed.

"That's beside the point. If you despise those men so much, you could serve as prosecutor. As a colonel, you surely have some experience in military law."

"Lieutenant Colonel, and I've only dealt with minor disciplinary issues. What you're proposing is more along the lines of a drumhead court-martial."

"A what?"

"Drumhead court-martial. It's an old British Army term used to describe a summary trial for battlefield misconduct. A drum served as an improvised writing table on which the proceedings were recorded. There were few procedural protections for the accused and a guilty verdict was almost always a foregone conclusion."

"I want a fair and proper trial, not a military kangaroo court!"

"How do you propose to accomplish that? Under what legal code would this court of yours operate? Where would you find an unbiased jury? You yourself said our people want to lynch them."

"We don't have jury trials in the German court system," Emma noted archly.

"Ah, so you want to subject the SS to German justice?" challenged Klein.

385

"Which version? I know from history that the Nazis fastidiously amended German law to ensure that everything they did was entirely legal. What do you want to do, arbitrarily revert to Weimar law?"

"What's your alternative?" Emma snapped.

"To shoot the bastards and dump their bodies over the side in the middle of the night," replied Klein in a tone of matter-of-fact aplomb.

"Just like that?" challenged Emma.

"Just like that," confirmed Klein. "As brutal as that is, what you're proposing is even crueller."

"How can you say that?" she spat indignantly.

"Emma, the hard truth of the matter is that these SS men cannot be allowed to live. Not because I hate them, something I freely admit, but for sound operational reasons. What happens when we reach Eretz Yisrael? Do we hand them over to the British? Do we let them go with the chance they might make it back to Germany? The simple fact is that they've seen far too much, from far too close. That's why we didn't release them in Sète. That's why we can't set them free when we get home. Your legal charade would only provide false hope where, in reality, there is none."

"Our people have seen the same things," objected Emma. "They may not know the full secret of who you are, but your weapons and equipment are clearly not of this world. There's already a great deal of speculation about your origins. I hear it every time I'm down in the hold."

"Yes, but the point is they're our people," replied Klein. "The danger to operational security posed by gossip is something I'm prepared to tolerate among my own. Similar sufferance does not extend to the SS. Besides, I don't foresee Jewish deportees making their way back to Berlin and giving a detailed briefing to Oberkommando der Wehrmacht."

"So your decision is final?" pressed Emma.

Klein shrugged. "I don't see any alternative."

"When will this happen?"

"Now. I don't want this situation to fester, so sooner is better than later. The darkness will allow us to operate with greater discretion. Where's my uniform?"

"You're in no condition for this," Emma protested. "You're far too weak. You need to stay in bed."

Klein shook his head. "My decision, my responsibility. In the immortal words of Eddard Stark: 'The man who passes the sentence should swing the sword.'"

"Who?"

"A major character in a series of novels that will be written 65 years from now. Now ... my uniform, please."

Emma reached beneath the bunk and produced Klein's battledress. The bullet holes in his trousers' leg had been neatly darned and the bloodstains were a semi-faded black, almost imperceptible against the camouflage pattern.

Klein winced as he levered himself to his feet.

"I think I'll need a little help," he said with uncharacteristic meekness.

"Of course, mein Schatz," Emma blurted out as she rose to assist.

The unanticipated term of endearment generated a curious glance from Klein, as Emma helped maneuver his injured leg into the trousers with minimal pain. Once dressed, he limped over to his personal gear, all of which had been neatly piled in the cabin's corner. Strapping on the pistol thigh holster rig, he subjected his SigSauer P227 Tactical pistol to close examination.

Yossi Klein was a big believer in the principle of the Six P's, first coined by UK special forces founding father David Stirling. 'Proper preparation prevents piss poor performance,' he noted silently. A quick twist on the suppressor to verify it was firmly seated at the end of the barrel. Check. Retract the slide slightly to verify that a .45 ACP round was seated on the feed ramp. Check. Thumb the magazine release and extract the clip to verify a full complement of 10 bullets. Check. Reload the magazine into the pistol butt and verify two full reload clips nestled in their pouch on the thigh rig. Check.

"Emma, you should probably stay here. This won't be pleasant."

"No, Yossi. I'm also part of this enterprise. What goes for you and Edward Stark goes for me as well."

"Eddard," corrected Klein with a wry smile.

"Alright ... Eddard, then."

Klein's smile faded as a mask of grim resignation settled over his face. "Very well then, let's get to it," he said with the accompaniment of a chivalrous 'after you' bow to Emma.

Emma led the way to the bridge, where it was immediate that the run of good weather they had enjoyed had come to an inclement end.

"How long has this been going on?" asked Klein in Hebrew, as he gestured towards the rain sheeting the windows of the bridge.

"About twenty-five minutes ago," answered Farkash. "The waves have also picked up a bit, with more to come if the barometer is to be believed."

"Well, weather or no weather, the time has come to deal with the prisoners," Klein instructed. "Organise an escort detail of four men and get them up to the aft main deck. Make sure they're securely bound."

Farkash nodded sombrely and departed to carry out his orders.

Klein took off his water-resistant camouflage jacket and offered it to Emma. "You should probably wear this. It's pretty nasty out there."

"But you'll get wet," she protested.

Klein shrugged. "Perhaps the rain will wash away some of my sins."

Exiting the bridge onto the wing, they were engulfed by a driving rain that pelted their faces, propelled diagonally by a gusting wind. Ebony clouds that completely obscured the stars and moon were periodically scarred by savage streaks of lightning, ripping through the monochrome darkness.

With one hand on the ship's rails and his other arm around Emma's shoulders, Klein hobbled his way through a deluge that drenched him to the bone in the process. Emma fared somewhat better, partially protected from the elements by the oversized camo jacket that hung on her slender frame like a half-stuffed scarecrow. Their progress was aided by flashing lightning, providing episodic bouts of illumination that flickered like a dysfunctional neon light.

Arriving at their destination, Klein and Emma waited for several minutes until the hatch to the ship's superstructure opened. Soon, Farkash emerged on deck, followed by a queue of Nazi captives with their hands fettered behind their backs.

In accordance with Klein's instructions, the prisoners were arranged on their knees in a row along the deck. The hauptsturmführer glared defiantly at his captors, while the faces of his fourteen SS subordinates reflected a gamut of emotions, from shock through resignation to sheer terror. The railroad men – locomotive driver and his two firemen – were crying softly, their tears indistinguishable from the raindrops pelting their faces.

"Yossi, we can't kill the train crew," protested Emma. "They're not SS. They're not volunteers. They were simply assigned to do this job, probably without even knowing what it was. That shouldn't be a capital offence."

Klein pondered for a moment, before nodding to one of the Israeli troopers standing guard over the captives. "Yehezkel, take the three railroad men back below and secure them in the same compartment."

The trooper pulled the locomotive crewmen to their feet, gesturing with the barrel of his X95 that they should make their way to the hatch leading to the ship's interior. The railroad men stumbled off per instructions, their weeping more copious as the meaning of their eleventh-hour reprieve dawned on them.

"Will you translate for me?" Klein enquired of Emma, who nodded in sombre silence.

"Tell them that they are to be executed for crimes against the norms of civilised peoples. They have one minute to make their peace with God, or whomever else they wish."

"Als mitglieder der SS, sie sind schuldig für verbrechen gegen die normen zivilisierter völker verantwortlich," she echoed. "Die strafe für diese verbrechen ist der tod durch erschießen. Du hast eine minute zeit, um deinen frieden mit Gott zu schließen, bevor der satz vollstreckt wird."

Klein had already made the decision to shoot the men from the front. Criminals that they undeniably are, the Nazis nonetheless deserved the right to face their fate as men.

The SS officer was first. Klein limped over to stand opposite the hauptsturmführer, a true believer who shouted "Heil Hitler!" before a bullet through his forehead stilled the Nazi's voice and life.

With neither sentiment nor ceremony, Klein worked his way along the row of kneeling prisoners, dispatching each man by dispensing a single .45 ACP round to the head.

The bodies were unceremoniously cast over the side, and the rain swept the deck clean of death's detritus. Within minutes, no evidence remained of the gruesome business just transacted at that spot.

Klein dismissed Farkash and his troopers to their quarters, ordering them to remain silent on the fate of the prisoners when interacting with the Jewish civilian passengers. Exhausted and in considerable pain, he stumbled back to his own bunk, heavily reliant on Emma's support and assistance.

Ashen with fatigue, Klein didn't protest as she stripped him of his pistol rig and sopping wet uniform. Checking that his bandage was still intact, Emma bundled him into bed. She then unfurled her bedroll at the foot of the bunk and slipped within it, fully clothed to ward off the chill from the metal deck plate.

There she lay. Sleepless, heart and head locked in battle as her mind replayed the bloody episode to which she had played accomplice. It wasn't a question of naiveté. She could find no rational fault with Klein's decision. Intellectually, she understood the peril that would ensue if the German military were to gain the barest inkling about the provenance of these time-travelling Jewish warriors. Yet, despite that recognition of danger; despite everything those SS men were and everything they'd done, her moral sentiments still rebelled against the brutality of their fate.

The matter most roiling Emma's emotions at that moment was the mercuriality of her feelings for Klein. Just a single day had passed since she admitted to herself that she loved this infuriating man. Yet the tumult of the evening's events had exposed a ruthlessness of character that left her confused, unsettled and even a bit frightened. She didn't know whether to berate herself for succumbing to infatuation yesterday, or flay herself for allowing doubt to erode her romantic commitment today.

It wasn't that Emma thought him evil. Yes, Klein's callous indifference towards the SS prisoners was distressing. But, upon reflection, she had come to recognise it as the righteous contempt held by an honourable soldier toward war criminal enemies. There was some solace to be drawn from the fact that no sadism was at play. It was obvious that Klein garnered no pleasure from a task he viewed as an ugly necessity, forced upon him by impossible circumstances.

Yet, the man's capacity for remorseless violence still perturbed her. What if she was being ridiculously naïve? What if discriminate acts of brutality against evil were the only way to ensure the survival of innocents in this mad maelstrom of world war? What did she know of such matters? Who was she to judge?

Still, while reason was one thing, romantic passion was something else. As Emma lay between her blankets, the question that banished sleep from her mind was not whether she could understand this man, nor whether she loved him. It was whether she could forgive herself for doing so.

For the life of her, at that moment she couldn't say.

Sixty-five

THEN

He hadn't eaten in over 24 hours, yet the emptiness of Peter Koertig's stomach failed to alleviate the urge to dry retch. His nausea peaked in synchronicity with the pitching deck of the *Ascari*. The destroyer crested a four-five metre whitecap and slid down the far side of the wave, slamming the trough with a jarring impact that sent a sheet of foamy water over its dagger-shaped prow. A thoroughly green-in-the-gills Koertig held onto the chart table for dear life, struggling to contain the gag reflex that threatened to overwhelm him.

"Are you alright, Hauptman?" enquired Unger, as he and his Italian colleagues exchanged the smug smiles of seasoned seafarers tolerating the presence of a weak-stomached landlubber.

"Fine, sir," croaked Koertig as he gamely waved his hand. "Although I must confess that the past two days have vindicated my original decision to choose the army as my branch of service."

Buonarota translated Koertig's words into Italian, triggering a wave of guffaws from the duty complement on the destroyer's bridge, officers and ratings alike.

"Gentlemen, at the captain's behest, I'll summarise our current situation as a preface to briefing you on our next move," continued the Italian naval officer in German. "Since leaving La Spezia, we have covered eight hundred nautical miles at an average speed of 32 knots. Our course took us South of Ibiza and North up through the Balearic Sea, which is the obvious route for any ship en route from France to Gibraltar. Our superior speed meant that we were perfectly positioned to intercept a slower-travelling merchant ship moving southwards. Yet we've swept the Balearic Sea northwards to our current position just off the coast of Barcelona and found nothing."

"There's no doubt the storm has made the search considerably more difficult," observed Unger. "The seas have been heavy, and visibility has been severely limited by rain and fog. In these conditions, it's quite possible the English were able to slip past us unnoticed."

"I must regretfully agree, sir," confirmed Buonarota. "The timing of this operation is a great pity because the *Ascari* will be undergoing a refit with one of your Seektat FuMO21 radar systems in six weeks' time. As things now stand, though, we are limited to the capacity of the human eye that, in these circumstances, falls considerably short of perfection."

"I assume the captain intends to turn about and retrace our course south?" prompted Unger.

"That's correct," said Buonarota as he glanced at his watch. "The time is now 22:37 hours, 30 October. I'm sure Hauptman Koertig will be pleased to hear that our weather forecasts indicate clearing skies by 03:00 tomorrow."

"Thank God for that," muttered Koertig, triggering a grin from the Italian naval officer.

"Just before dawn tomorrow, the *Ascari* will turn about and proceed southwards at twenty-five knots. At that speed, we should be able to sweep most of the Balearic Sea during daylight hours. If your Englishmen are there, we'll find them."

Unger flashed his most diplomatic smile. "Please convey my compliments to your captain on his excellent tactical sense. His plan represents precisely the course of action I would choose, were I in command of this impressive vessel."

Buonarota blushed with pleasure, rendering a modest bow of acknowledgement. "I will convey your kind words to my captain. Now, you gentlemen are free to remain on the bridge if you wish, but I would suggest you both get a good night's rest in anticipation of seeing action tomorrow."

Both German officers heeded Buonarota's suggestion, Unger retiring to his private stateroom, and Koertig returning to the tiny cabin he shared with the *Ascari*'s gunnery officer. His compartment-mate's chainsaw-like snores did little to impede the hauptmann's solid slumber.

When Koertig awoke, he was facing the bulkhead, having been tilted to the inward edge of his bunk as the destroyer heeled around in a sharp turn. The deck plate vibrated with the throbbing urgency of an engine pushed to full throttle.

Something was clearly afoot.

Koertig clambered out of his bunk, quickly dressed and shaved in the small basin at the compartment's corner. Making his way topside, he emerged into the radiance of a cloudless morning sky. The sea was quite calm, its surface replete with myriad luminescent sparkles of sunlight reflecting off the serried wavelets. Shading his eyes from the unaccustomed brilliance, he made his way to the bridge where he joined the cluster around the chart table.

"Ah Koertig," said Unger by way of greeting. "There's news. The bastards have been very sneaky, but we're now on their trail."

"What news, sir?"

"It turns out our Englishmen aren't making for Gibraltar after all," replied Unger. "An Italian aircraft on maritime patrol from Sardinia spotted a merchant vessel sailing eastwards along the North African coast. Here," said Unger, moving his index finger to a spot on the chart marking Cap Rosa, a promontory jutting into the Mediterranean just west of the Tunisian border. "It matches the description of your commandeered ship."

"Are we certain?"

Buonarota shrugged. "Not entirely. But it's the only likely candidate we've found. No other single-stack steam freighter in the 6,000-tonne range has been sighted in the western Mediterranean. Our patrol aircraft has reported that this particular ship is flying Turkish colours. If these Englishmen are as resourceful as you report, that flag could very well be a ruse de guerre."

"Say what you will about them, their courage, resolve and imagination can't be denied," Unger confirmed.

"If not Gibraltar, then where are they going?" queried Koertig as he perused the chart. "Malta?"

Unger cast a cryptic glance towards Koertig. "Perhaps, but it's possible their final objective might be farther east."

"Whether we can intercept them before they reach Malta will come down to a balancing act between speed and fuel," said Buonarota, oblivious to the implicit messaging between the two German officers. "We've been moving at an average of thirty knots since leaving La Spezia. That has entailed a much higher level of fuel consumption than normal. If we continue at current speeds, the *Ascari* would be in position to intercept the English somewhere in the Strait of Sicily, but with very little fuel remaining. As a result, we'd be forced to break off pursuit and refuel in Trapani at the western tip of Sicily."

"Is there any opportunity for reinforcement or at-sea refuelling?" pressed Unger.

"Not likely," replied Buonarota. "As you heard from Ammiraglio Sansonetti, our primary focus is supporting our forces in Greece while preparing to counter any sortie by the Royal Navy from Egypt and Gibraltar. I seriously doubt Comando Supremo would be prepared to dispatch a fleet oiler so close to Malta, and not without a sizeable escort."

Koertig frowned. "So, in other words, we're on our own."

"Entirely," shrugged Buonarota. "As a result, the captain has decided to continue our pursuit of the English at twenty-five knots. That should be adequate to close with our quarry, while leaving adequate fuel reserves to maneuver in the event of air attack by the RAF."

"It also means we won't be able to prevent them from reaching Malta if that turns out to be their destination," said Unger.

"Kapitän, we deal with the world as it is, not as we wish it to be. The Regia Aeronautica will keep the target ship under aerial surveillance and we'll be kept informed of any changes."

"Indeed, indeed," said Unger in a conciliatory tone. "In that same spirit of cooperation, would it be possible for me to get a message off to Comando Supremo for transmission to OKW? My superiors would also appreciate an update."

"If you wish, of course," replied Buonarota. "Although, I'm sure your Wehrmacht liaison officers at the war room in Rome are already keeping Berlin fully abreast of the situation."

"I'd appreciate it nonetheless," persisted Unger.

Buonarota dragooned a nearby petty officer to serve as Unger's guide and escort. Once the senior German officer had left the bridge, he turned to address Koertig.

"Hauptman, as things now stand, we won't be within sight of the enemy until sometime tomorrow morning. I'd encourage you to spend time on deck and enjoy this fine weather. Take advantage of this opportunity to relax because, in wartime, you never know when circumstances might change."

"Thank you, sir," replied Koertig in German, maintaining his linguistic cover and politely ignoring Buonarota's between-the-lines message to stay out of everyone's way. "If you'll excuse me, I'll heed your advice and take in some sun."

The remainder of that day passed without incident, and at dusk Koertig retired to his cabin. With daybreak the following morning, he was jolted into wakefulness by a blaring claxon and pounding feet.

"Equipaggio ai posti di combattimento!" blared the loudspeaker on the wall of his compartment. "Equipaggio ai posti di combattimento!"

It took a few moments for Koertig's brain to emerge from a state of drowsy befuddlement and comprehend what he was hearing. A call to battle stations! Swinging his legs onto the deck, he scrambled to his feet, just as his Italian compartment-mate sprang from the bunk that adjoined the far wall. Both men dressed in simultaneous haste, trying to avoid the other's knees and elbows with only partial success.

By the time Koertig reached the bridge, Unger and Buonarota were standing on the wing, binoculars to their eyes as they examined a distant shape just short of the horizon.

"Guten morgen, Meine Herren," said Koertig. "Is that the English ship?"

Unger shrugged. "She's a single stacker and appears to be the correct tonnage. We can't make out the flag or lettering on her stern as yet, but my patience will endure a bit longer."

"Sir, I request permission to join any boarding party sent over to inspect the target ship," said Koertig.

The two senior officers exchanged glances, until finally Unger nodded assent.

"Very well," said Buonarota. "Note you will participate solely as an observer and will follow the orders of the boarding party commander at all times. Is that clear?"

"Capito, signore," said Koertig with a disarming simper, feigning obliviousness to Unger's glare over the younger German's unilateral decision to dispense with linguistic subterfuge.

"Così si parla Italiano?" asked a dumbfounded Buonarota.

"Così sembra," replied Koertig.

"E tue?" Buonarota enquired of Unger.

"Nein, nein," replied Unger with a shake of the head. "Deutch und Englisch nur."

Buonarota turned towards the bow, refocusing his attention and binoculars on the vessel they were pursuing. "I see a red ensign flying from her stern," he announced. "That's consistent with our aerial reconnaissance reports of a Turkish flag. Another twenty minutes should bring us close enough to identify her and fire a warning shot across her bow."

"The *Manzikert* out of Izmir," recited Unger, once the range had closed sufficiently to reveal the lettering on the freighter's stern. "Named after an

11th-century Turkish victory over the Byzantines that set the stage for the Crusades."

The *Ascari*'s forward turret barked and a large geyser erupted from the sea just off the freighter's bow. The frothy churn of the steamship's wake faded as the cargo ship slowed to a halt.

"If your impressive grasp of history is any indication, your English is likely far better than mine," said Buonarota as he proffered a simple tin megaphone to Unger. "Bitte."

The destroyer closed with the merchant vessel like a leopard chasing down a water buffalo. Within minutes, the *Ascari* hove to abreast the freighter's starboard side, the destroyer's fore and aft dual 120 mm turrets faithfully tracking the target ship.

"Merchant Vessel *Manzikert*, this is the Italian Navy warship *Ascari*, do you speak English?" yelled Unger through the bullhorn.

A man in his early 30s stood on the bridge wing of the freighter and lifted a similar megaphone to his mouth. "Yes, I speak English," came the accented reply.

"What is your port of origin, what is your cargo and where is your destination?" challenged Unger.

"We are en route from Algiers to Izmir with a cargo of wheat."

"A detachment will shortly be dispatched by motorboat to verify your bona fides," instructed Unger. "Prepare to be boarded and have your crew manifest, cargo invoice and log book ready for examination."

The man on the freighter's bridge wing acknowledged the order with a wave.

"The boarding party can now embark," reported Unger as he relinquished the megaphone to his Italian colleague.

"Tenente, si può procedure!" yelled Buonarota through the loudhailer, towards a group of a dozen sailors clustered around a 20-foot whaleboat motor launch at the destroyer's stern. He turned to address Koertig. "If you still want to join the boarding party, now's the time. As we know language isn't an impediment, please convey my compliments to Primo Tenente Rossi and let him know you'll be along as an observer."

"Yes, sir. Thank you, sir," replied Koertig, who then hastened aft. The young German officer introduced himself in fluent Italian, much to Rossi's surprise.

The dual davits holding the whaleboat were rotated over the gunwale and Rossi ordered his men aboard, assigning Koertig to a seat at the bow. With the Italian lieutenant synchronising the release of bow and aft ropes by cadence call, the sailors began to winch the boat downwards into the sea.

Sixty-six

THEN

Baruch Levinson swallowed nervously as he lay prone on the upper deck of the *Mauritz*, his back flush with the metal gunwale that hid him from the Italian destroyer's view. His unscathed emergence from the brutal firefight on the Sète docks left him with a nagging angst that he might now be a fugitive from the law of averages whose run of luck was about to expire.

But his pre-combat heebie-jeebies were suddenly interrupted by the sound of 5.56 mm rifle fire from the bridge wing above his head. The signal to act. Rising smoothly to his feet, Baruch slipped into the step-by-step series of movements he'd spent the last few minutes rehearsing in his head.

Lifting a Matador 90 mm rocket launcher atop his shoulder, he looked through the combination laser rangefinder-reflex sight that was highly accurate to a range of 400 metres. With the Italian warship lying to at less than half that distance, Levinson had no difficulty bringing his weapon to bear on the forward 120 mm gun turret that was his assigned target.

He pressed the trigger, sending a 90 mm rocket on its way, just as he heard the reports of two other Matadors being fired at the *Ascari*'s rear gun turret. All three projectiles hit their marks spot on, and the shaped penetration charges in the nose of each tandem-warhead ripped easily through the destroyer's lightly armoured turret. After one-tenth-of-a–second's delay, the primary charges detonated within those enclosed confines to devastating effect.

Ironically, it was the forward turret where the fatal blow was struck, despite receiving only a single Matador hit as opposed to the aft turret's two. Levinson's rocket exploded just as the powder hoist was in the midst of delivering propellant cases to the turret ready rack. White hot rocket fragments ripped through the thin brass cylinders, triggering a sympathetic detonation of the cordite propellant within. A fiery wave cascaded through the open turret door and down the conveyor tube to the ammunition magazine in the bowels of the ship.

The turret system was specifically designed to prevent such a catastrophic event, by means of metal doors placed at either end. When properly synchronised, the lower door would open only when the door to the turret above was sealed, thus eliminating the possibility of back flash. As it happened, a malfunctioning feed system left the lower door half open as the inferno descended.

From Levinson's vantage point, the secondary explosions ravaging the bowels of the *Ascari* were audible, but not immediately visible. While reloading his Matador, he noticed that the destroyer was in the midst of winching down a motor launch from its main deck to sea level.

A massive explosion suddenly ripped the forward turret off its mounting and an incandescent gout of orange flame shot skyward from the *Ascari's* ruptured deck. The warship immediately developed a sharp list to port, which deposited the motor launch in the water with a premature slam that sent gouts of spray through the air.

Levinson watched in sombre fascination as the launch's coxswain pulled manically at the outboard starter cord until the engine finally coughed and caught, just as the canting hull of the *Ascari* threatened to crush the cockleshell boat. Gunning the throttle to the max, the sailor steered the launch away from the mortally wounded destroyer, while his shipmates gazed open-mouthed at the death throes of their mother ship.

With one exception. A man who stood out from the blue-clad Italian navy boat crew both in the Wehrmacht feldgrau he wore and his behaviour. Rising to his feet in defiance of elementary seamanship, the German's strange behaviour didn't stop there. While his Italian boatmates were still transfixed on the demise of their home vessel, he spared not a glance at the rapidly sinking *Ascari* behind him. His attention was solely focused on the *Mauritz van Nassau*.

Leaning the Matator launcher against the gunwale, Levinson shouldered his X95 and centred its ACOG gunsight on the upright German. The man was an officer, the corded piping of his epaulette insignia clearly visible through the ACOG's 2x magnification. As was the venomous glare this out-of-place German was directing towards the bridge of the *Mauritz van Nassau*. Levinson followed the man's gaze with his own and saw that the object of wrath was Yossi Klein.

Sixty-seven

It had to be him. That same ruthless face he'd glimpsed as his Schnell Kompanie kameraden were slaughtered along the Vendôme highway. But as Peter Koertig's sense of recognition spontaneously combusted into raw red rage, his hopes of vengeance were doomed to frustration.

Even at that moment of epiphany, Koertig retained sufficient situational awareness to comprehend the forlorn truth of his tactical circumstance. From the bow of a seven-metre boat manned by a dozen Italian sailors armed with bolt-action carbines, he had no hope of surviving an armed confrontation with enemies who had just sunk a 2,500-tonne destroyer.

For all that, he didn't care. A preternatural sense of calm filled his mind as he decided that none of this mattered. Not now. Not when he was finally in a position to strike a blow, even if symbolic. If death ensued, at least it would expiate the guilt he felt for the sin of survival when his comrades had all been slaughtered.

Struggling to maintain his upright balance in the pitching launch, Koertig fumbled with the leather flap of the pistol holster attached to the belt around his waist. The Luger had only half-emerged from its nesting place when an Italian sailor, a petty officer by the look of him, snatched the handgun from Koertig's grasp and cast it over the side. Roughly pushing the German back into his seat, the Italian waved his arms towards the *Mauritz van Nassau* to signify pacific intent. The petty officer wanted to see his wife again and would shoot the crazy German himself if that's what it took to survive.

Sixty-eight

Levinson thumbed the selector switch of his X95 to the safe position and lowered the weapon. The German officer would never know how close his brush with death had been.

A horrible grinding groan of metal exceeding its tolerance prefaced the destroyer's capsizing. Sailors scrambled for their lives as the *Ascari*'s hull rolled, until its upended barnacle-encrusted keel lay exposed to the sky.

Horrified at the sight and sound of desperate men struggling amidst the choppy sea, Levinson ran to join Klein on the bridge wing. "Can we lower some of our lifeboats?"

Klein shook his head. "Not possible."

"They're Italian sailors, not SS. It's certain death by hypothermia if they remain in the water at this time of year," implored Levinson. "We can save some of them."

"No, we can't. There are eight hundred civilians on board this ship. Men, women and children. I'm not going to endanger them by giving up our lifeboats. We have lifebuoys we can throw to them. But that's all."

"Then they'll freeze to death more slowly."

"Baruch, get your head straight," barked Klein. "We're smack dab in the middle of the most destructive war in human history. Do you have some sort of crystal ball that can guarantee a smooth run over the remaining two thousand kilometres between us and home?"

Levinson shook his head.

"I've had more debates over combat ethics with Emma Cohen during the past four days than throughout the entirety of my military career. I don't need you going all Yefeh Nefesh on me as well."

"Sorry, Yossi."

Klein turned to the interior of the bridgehouse, where Farkash was posted at the ship's helm. "Get her underway."

Farkash raised his hand in acknowledgement and the deck began to vibrate as the ship's turning screws bit into the Mediterranean waters.

"May I go?" asked Levinson, as he averted his gaze from the Italian sailors they were thus consigning to death.

Klein perused his young radioman for a moment before nodding. "Go on."

Levinson made haste below deck, where he found Miriam and Emma preparing rations for the luncheon meal.

Miriam's smile at the sight of her boyfriend shifted to a frown of concern as she saw his stricken expression.

"What's wrong, Baruch?"

Levinson buried his face in her shoulder and wept.

Sixty-nine

Yossi Klein awoke some hours later with a clearer head and a rumbling stomach. Cocking open an eye, the first thing he saw was Emma dozing on the chair, head resting on her folded arms atop the chart table.

He tried to sit up, groaning as a bolt of pain coursed through his leg.

The sound was enough to rouse Emma from her nap.

"How are you feeling?"

"My leg is completely stiff," Klein groused, glancing at his wrist. "My watch is showing 21:27 hours, October 30th. Is that correct?"

She nodded. "You've been asleep for almost 12 hours."

"That explains the dilemma I'm facing right now. Putting it crudely, I have to piss but can't move."

"I'll get a pot and help you into position," rejoined a grinning Emma as she rose from her seat.

"Thanks. Afterward, I'll need a sitrep from Farkash and our navigator."

"A what?"

"Sorry. A situation report – sitrep. Army jargon."

"Captain Farkash and Mr von Stockhausen are right outside on the bridge. I'll be back momentarily."

Emma left the cabin, returning in a few moments with a metal bucket that she deposited beside the bed.

Helping Klein to a sitting position on the bunk, she waited, arms crossed, until he coughed suggestively and pointed towards the wall.

Emma twirled on her heel with a theatrical snort. "It's not as though I've never seen one before," she harrumphed.

"I'm sure," replied Klein over the tinkling sound of urine hitting the pail. "This is more a matter of my comfort zone rather than yours."

"Comfort zone? People in the 21st century have very strange expressions."

"Your era doesn't?" countered Klein, as he finished and made himself decent. "What about '23 skiddoo'. I suppose you've never heard of zoot suits?"

403

"Ach, but those are American," she scoffed with a dismissive wave. "Everyone knows the Yanks aren't really civilised."

"By the way, you can turn around now. If you could fetch my trousers, I'd appreciate it."

When she picked up his battledress pants, once again neatly folded, her facial expression changed from jocular to serious.

"Before going to bring the others, I wanted to talk about what happened with the Italians."

"Look," Klein began, his eyes rolling in exasperation, "it was a hard ..."

But Emma shut him up, mid-sentence, with a lingering kiss to the lips.

"Before you opened your mouth, I was going to say that I agree with you. You're correct that the safety of the people on this ship is paramount. You made the right decision."

With that, Emma turned and departed the cabin, leaving a thoroughly gobsmacked Klein in her wake. She reappeared several moments later, in the company of Farkash and von Stockhausen.

Klein wiped the moonstruck expression from his face, but not quickly enough to prevent the mouth of Farkash curling in a knowing smile that Klein affected not to recognise.

"Alois," said Klein in English. "Can you give me a situation report on our position and speed?"

"Certainly sir," replied the former German naval officer. "We're currently about seventy-five nautical miles south southeast of Malta, steering 91 degrees."

"Malta is a major British naval base," Klein observed. "That's good because it shields us from the Italians in Sicily, but not-so-good because we don't want to attract the attention of the RAF or Royal Navy."

"Speaking of the RAF, at around 14:00 hours we were overflown by a big flying boat with British markings," Farkash reported. "We were all wearing civvies and waved like madmen. They made two passes and flew off waggling their wings."

"How many engines?" Klein enquired.

"Four," replied Farkash.

"A Sunderland. Let's hope he fell for our false flag gambit, because the last thing we need is to tangle with the Royal Navy. What's our supply situation?"

"We'll have just enough fuel to get us home via our intended route," replied Farkash. "As for food, I'll leave that up to Ms Cohen. She's taken charge of the rationing."

"The situation is tolerable," volunteered Emma without waiting to be asked. "We're providing two meals a day to children, pregnant women and people over sixty. Everyone else gets one. There's enough to last about a week under those conditions."

"That should see us through," observed Klein. "What are the problems? Something has to be going wrong. There's no such thing as perfection in real life."

Emma shrugged. "Our primary problem is hygiene. We have a total of 861 people on board a merchant ship normally crewed by three-dozen men at most. The lavatory facilities are completely inadequate and I'm worried about the outbreak of disease."

"Any ideas?" asked Klein.

"We should have clear skies and smooth seas for the remainder of our voyage," said Farkash. "Perhaps we could rig some sort of improvised latrine on deck, so people could do their business in a bucket and then throw their waste directly over the side?"

"What about the risk of people falling overboard?" asked Emma. "These are not experienced sailors. It would be very dangerous, even in calm weather."

"Keeping a wounded man from his rest is dangerous as well," came a voice from behind them.

"Shalom, Doctor," said Klein to Yochai Lifshutz, who had materialised in the cabin doorway with a medical satchel hanging from one shoulder. "What's your view on the hygiene situation?"

"It's an issue," Lifshutz conceded. "But a manageable one that is best left to your lieutenants. Your job is to recuperate and mine is to change your dressings. So, if you could all move aside, I'd appreciate it."

Farkash and von Stockhausen left the cabin to vacate space for the medical officer who approached Klein's bunk. Lifshutz opened his satchel and produced a pair of angled bandage scissors and a sterile gauze dressing. Folding back the blanket so that Klein's wounded leg was exposed, the doctor used the scissors to remove the soiled dressing.

"Healing nicely," Lifshutz observed as he leant over to examine the angry purple entry and exit wounds on either side of Klein's thigh. "No sign of sepsis."

"Thanks to modern antibiotics," said Klein. "Just think about it, when you introduce penicillin to the medical community, you'll be a sure bet for a Nobel Prize."

"I doubt it," replied Lifshutz as he applied a fresh bandage to his commander's wound. "Alexander Fleming discovered penicillin in 1928 and Howard Florey is preparing the first clinical trials as we speak. So that particular ship has sailed, so to speak."

"Perhaps, but I'm sure there's an entire fleet of medical innovations just waiting for you to launch upon the world. There's no doubt a truly great future awaits you."

"You mean past," replied Lifshutz, reverting to bitter-toned Hebrew. "And how great will it be without Shifra and my kids?"

"Yochai, we've had this conversation already," replied Klein in the same language. "I'm happy to talk again when I'm feeling a bit stronger, but remember we all volunteered for this operation, you included."

The medical officer erupted in fury. "You think I don't know that? You think I don't regret my decision every waking moment?" He paused as his face dissolved from choler into melancholy. "It's not just that I'll never see my wife again. It's the thought that my children will now never exist. It crushes me."

Klein placed a fraternal hand on the doctor's shoulder. "I'm sorry, but think about the good we've done. Think about the lives we've saved. And in this world you're going to be an absolute star. With your base of knowledge, you'll become dean of Hebrew University Medical School at the very least. I was serious about the Nobel. The bottom line is that you'll have to beat women off with a stick. You'll have more kids. A legion of them, if you wish."

Lipshutz dried his tears and gave a non-committal shrug. "I can't think about such things right now. In any event, I apologise. It was an entirely unprofessional display."

"You're human, so don't worry about it," replied Klein. "You should go and get some rest. You look as though you could use it."

Lipshutz nodded, packed up his medical bag and left the captain's cabin without another word.

"What was all that Hebrew chatter about?" asked Emma. "It was very melodramatic."

"He had a wife and children in the old world and is having trouble reconciling to our new reality," answered Klein. "It's been festering since it became clear we wouldn't be going home."

"Small price to pay for saving millions of lives," said Emma.

"Ah, so it turns out you're a Benthamite after all!" proclaimed Klein with a 'gotcha' smile of triumph. "Here you are, engaging in precisely the same sort of utilitarian cost–benefit calculus you previously found so deplorable."

Emma pondered for a moment, then performed a bow with a stage-worthy theatrical flourish. "Mea culpa maxima. I stand condemned by my own words."

"'Hoist by your own petard', as Shakespeare put it in *Hamlet*."

"Yossi Klein, you continue to surprise me," said Emma. "Soldier, philosopher and now Shakespearean scholar. Is there anything you don't do well?"

"Math," replied Klein.

"Math?" echoed Emma.

"Mathematics. Anything more advanced than algebra has always been a struggle."

"Well that's a relief," proclaimed Emma with a disarming grin. "For a moment there, I was beginning to think you might be perfect."

"Hardly," grinned Klein. "While I'm always happy to discuss my many shortcomings and imperfections, I would very much appreciate something to eat."

"Of course. You lost a lot of blood. The doctor recommended red meat because of its high iron content and we have canned beef."

"Sounds good," answered Klein.

"Not the word I would use," she said. "But I'll be right back."

Klein drifted off to sleep, only to be awakened by the opening door that signalled Emma's return, bearing a bowl of steaming beef stew. Klein's eyes popped open and he raised himself to a seating position. "That smells delicious."

Emma sat on the chair, watching silently as Klein laid into the stew like a starving man. The bowl was soon empty and, his hunger sated, Klein glanced up at Emma with a hangdog smile

"Sorry. I was really hungry."

Emma grinned as she leaned over and gently wiped his chin with her thumb. "I'm glad you enjoyed it. But you really made a mess of yourself."

Blushing, he gently took hold of her hand. "Emma, a while ago you kissed me and called me 'schatz'. I think I understand what that means, but don't want to misread your intentions."

It was Emma's turn to blush. "Schatz means 'treasure' or 'darling'."

Klein nodded earnestly and looked squarely into Emma's sea green eyes. "Look, I've never been much of a Don Juan. I was married at age 23 and was true to my wife until ... until the end."

"We've never talked about your life before. Did you leave behind a family? Like the doctor?"

"Not exactly. The thing is, she and my daughter were killed in a traffic accident last year. Or the year before this mission, to put it in more accurate terms."

Emma's hand flew up to her mouth in shock. "Oh Yossi, that's horrible. I'm so sorry." She moved from chair to bunk and gently pulled his head to a resting place on her shoulder.

His arms encircled her waist and he nuzzled the nape of her neck. "Amazing," he whispered. "After all this, you still smell wonderful."

Klein lifted his head from Emma's shoulder and began to kiss her – slowly at first, then with a growing passion that met with full requital. They were soon engulfed by a tidal wave of desire that drowned inhibitions and washed away constraints of social convention like a sandcastle on a storm-tossed beach. Arguments over ethics and philosophy were forgotten as two wounded souls sought solace in each other's arms from a world of blood and loss and sorrow

Emma suddenly disengaged and strode to the door, locking it. She turned and unbuttoned her dress, shucking it off her shoulders to reveal a slender physique fronted by the firm upright orbs of her small perfect breasts.

"Aren't you going to let me in under the covers?" she asked, lips curved in a coy smile. "I'll get goosebumps."

Klein hastened to pull back the blanket and she slid into the bunk beside him. Emboldened by her nakedness, his hands ranged over her body with an urgency that bespoke his need. She moved to straddle him, generating a grunt of pain when her knee accidentally touched his wound.

"We have to be careful of your leg," Emma warned.

"Forget about my leg," murmured Klein, mid-kiss, while pulling her on top of him.

"You'll regret it tomorrow."

"And I'll worry about it tomorrow," he cooed as his lips caressed her beckoning nipple.

Emma gasped with pleasure as she took him within, her arms entwined around his neck as her torso settled into a primeval rhythm that dispensed frissons of equal delectation to them both.

After the fact, they would discover that their gyrations had reopened his wound, triggering a slow effusion of blood that soiled mattress and blankets alike. But Yossi Klein didn't care. Another few nights spent in a begrimed berth was an inconsequential price to pay for a glorious discovery that brought joy overflowing into a void that had plagued his spirit for so long. For the first time since his family tragedy, he truly felt content. That was all that mattered.

Seventy

"The admiral will see you now."

Colonel Ralph Neville came to his feet and straightened his uniform, which was badly creased from four days of non-stop travel. He nodded to his guide, a navy lieutenant commander whose gold and blue aiguillette signified the role of aide-de-camp to a flag rank officer.

It had been a long and onerous trip. A Boeing Clipper from Southampton to Lisbon, and then southwards along the African coast to Bathurst in the Gambia, where he transferred to a waiting de Havilland Flamingo. The next stop was Takoradi on the Gold Coast, then Kano in northern Nigeria, and on to Fort Lamy in French Equatorial Africa and El Genia in Sudan. From there he flew to Khartoum, where Neville used his ultra-priority travel warrant to divert the de Havilland direct to RAF Aboukir outside Alexandria, much to the annoyance of his Cairo-bound fellow passengers. Descending onto the tarmac, he'd been struck by the bone-chilling wind sweeping across the airfield. Never having spent much time in the Middle East, it surprised him that Egypt's Mediterranean coast was so cold in early November.

The combination of Neville's rank and travel warrant had sufficed to rate an Austin 8 Tilley plus driver for transport from Aboukir to the Ras-el-Tin Palace. Constructed by rogue Ottoman governor Muhammad Ali Pasha in the 1840s, the Ras-el-Tin was a massive complex of parkland and Italian Renaissance-style buildings that overlooked Alexandria's military harbour. It had been the obvious choice when the Royal Navy was seeking a suitable facility to house the headquarters of the Mediterranean Fleet.

The aide-de-camp conveyed Neville into a capacious office with large bay windows that afforded a panoramic view of the port area, which was packed with grey-tinted warships. A career army officer, he was no expert on ship identification – but even his unpractised eye could recognise destroyers, cruisers and battleships all moored at the quays. On the far side of the harbour, he could see submarines and the fleet's two aircraft carriers, the modern *HMS Illustrious* and the more venerable *HMS Eagle*.

Admiral Andrew Cunningham, the Mediterranean Fleet Commander, sat behind a massive oak desk perusing a sheaf of papers as Neville entered.

The bareheaded Cunningham acknowledged the army officer's salute with a lofty nod. "What can I do for you, Colonel?"

"Well, sir, may I operate on the assumption that you were notified of my impending arrival by the Admiralty?"

"Indeed," replied the admiral. "A rather opaque single paragraph informing me that a colonel from intelligence would be showing up on my doorstep, and that I should extend all possible assistance. Before we proceed any further, may I see your identification?"

"Of course, sir." Neville reached into the upper left pocket of his tunic and extracted his ID card and travel warrant.

Cunningham examined the documents carefully, before returning them to Neville with a snort of grudging acknowlegement.

"What's this about?" the admiral demanded. "I can't say I care much for your end of the business. Cloak and dagger derring-do is not at all to my taste."

"A common view, sir. I would remind you, though, that just a few months ago, we were facing the spectre of invasion and defeat. With most of its heavy weapons left in France, our army was, and still is, a hollow shell. In such circumstances, wouldn't you agree a bit of unconventional ruthlessness was the order of the day?"

"Pah," replied Cunningham with a dismissive wave of the hand. "The Home Fleet was at Scapa, just waiting to pounce. I know the Kriegsmarine. They would never risk a crossing with our main battle force still intact."

"Perhaps, sir, but you have to admit that the late and unlamented Führer's demise has greatly reduced the danger of invasion."

Cunningham fixed on Neville the same steely gaze that had reduced countless sub-lieutenants over the years to quivering terror. "Are you telling me that we had something to do with the assassination of Hitler? What about the story given out by Berlin about a rogue SS conspiracy?"

"Sorry, sir, but I'm really not authorised to elaborate," replied an unperturbed Neville. "All I can say is that our request for assistance has been afforded the highest priority by the War Cabinet and Chiefs of Staff Committee."

"Precisely what sort of assistance do you require?" asked a clearly annoyed Cunningham. "The message from London was sparse on detail."

"Well, sir, we believe there's a cargo ship making its way eastwards across the Mediterranean."

"Is this vessel linked to Hitler's killing?"

"That's something I can neither confirm nor deny, but we would greatly appreciate your assistance intercepting it."

"Where is it headed?"

"Palestine, sir ... we think."

"Interesting you should say this," said Cunningham in a pensive tone. "We've received unconfirmed reports that an Italian destroyer was sunk two days ago near Lampedusa."

"Could you show me on the map, sir?"

Cunningham rose from his desk, striding over to a large map of the Mediterranean that covered an entire office wall.

"Here," said the admiral, with a finger pointing to the small Italian island that protruded from the Mediterranean midway between Malta and the Tunisian coast. He turned to his aide-de-camp. "Simpson, wasn't there a reported sighting of a lone freighter in that general area around that same time?"

"Yes sir," replied the lieutenant commander. "An RAF Sunderland out of Malta overflew a merchant vessel on the early afternoon of October 30th. I believe the pilot reported it was Turkish-flagged and in the 6,000-tonne range."

"I can't really see how those two events could be related," mused Cunningham. "There's no way a merchant ship could sink a destroyer, not even an Italian one."

Neville pursed his lips. "Sir, with all due respect, I feel obliged to warn you that the men in question are extremely capable and exceedingly dangerous. I wouldn't necessarily rule out anything where they're concerned."

Cunningham dispatched a baleful glare in Neville's direction. "Colonel, I don't like spies, but I wouldn't presume to tell you your own business, distasteful though it may be. Please afford me the same courtesy."

"But sir ..." was all Neville could get out, before he was overridden and interrupted by Cunningham.

"Reading between the lines of what you haven't told me, these people, presumably Palestinian Jews, are supposed to have launched a raid into occupied-France, where they overcame a crack German bodyguard unit, killed Hitler and decimated the Wehrmacht high command. They then made their way through hundreds of kilometres of hostile country to the Mediterranean, where they commandeered a freighter that just happened to be available. Then they miraculously transformed an old merchant vessel into a Q-ship powerful enough to sink a modern destroyer. Colonel, do you realise how absurd this sounds? This is more of a fairy tale than a rational intelligence estimate."

"Admiral, there are other elements to this story that I'm not at liberty to disclose. In essence, your analysis is correct. Despite its implausibility, which I freely admit, we nonetheless believe it may be an accurate recounting of events. On that basis, I'm asking for the dispatch of naval assets to locate and intercept this ship."

"I'll tell you, in person, what I will shortly convey via telex to the First Sea Lord. Colonel, are you familiar with Operation Judgement?"

"No, sir."

"It's the lynchpin of a larger series of operations that will decisively shift the strategic balance in the Med. In just three days' time, most of the ships you see out there in the harbour will sortie to attack the Italian fleet at Taranto. Simultaneously, we'll be sending supply convoys to Greece and Malta. Under these circumstances, I cannot ... I will not dispatch vital naval fighting assets on a wild goose chase after some chimera dreamed up by a bunch of aspiring Mata Haris!"

Recognising defeat when it stared him in the face, Neville realised that magnanimity was his only recourse. "Of course, sir. I understand entirely and let me wish you success in this very important operation. Audentes fortuna iuvat, as Virgil so eloquently put it."

"Thank you, Colonel," replied a mollified Cunningham. "What's your next move? Back to London?"

"Oh no, sir. I'm off to Palestine."

"Is there anything I can do to facilitate your journey?" asked the admiral, relieved that this annoying spook would soon be out of his hair.

"I appreciate it, sir. My travel warrant gives me enough precedence to jump the queue if needs be, but a lift back to Aboukir would be helpful."

"Of course. But first, allow us to offer you the hospitality of the Mediterranean Fleet. Quite frankly, you look a bit worse for wear. A good bath and a freshly laundered uniform will do you a world of good. You should stay the night and be off on the morrow."

"Thank you very much, sir. That's most considerate, but I really think the sooner I get to Palestine, the better."

"Very well," said Cunningham dismissively, his mind already on other matters. "Simpson can make the necessary arrangements."

"Shouldn't be a problem, sir," Lieutenant Commander Simpson volunteered. "Now, if you'll follow me, sir, we'll organise your transport."

Neville arrived at RAF Aboukir, just as a Vickers Wellington from 70 Squadron was making final preparations for a return to its home base at Habbaniya in Iraq. The pilot congenially agreed to drop Neville at Lydda airfield outside Tel Aviv, but comfort was hard to come by in the unheated belly of an aircraft solely designed to drop high explosive on the enemy.

It wasn't so much the cold, swaddled as he was in a Sidcot flying suit and Irvin shearling jacket. Having declined the offer to displace the aircraft's navigator from his seat behind the cockpit, Neville was perched on the narrow hardwood walkway that ran the length of the Wellington's fuselage. The sharp-edged boltheads of the duralumin lattice forming the bomber's geodesic airframe were doing their best to scour grooves into his back, posterior and legs.

Yet, if any of the Wellington's crew had cause to move from one end of the aircraft to the other, they might have noticed a smile on the face of their passenger. A smile that might seem out of place given the spartan discomfort of his accommodation. The sort of smile that might grace the visage of a man about to fulfil a long-held dream.

Seventy-one

THEN

Professor Gerhard Hoffmann winced in pain as he jostled his injured arm while taking a seat on a bench in the mess. "Does anyone know why we're here?"

Levinson responded with a silent shrug, sliding a proprietary arm around Miriam's slender waist.

"We're getting close to home. Probably something to do with that," replied Weinstock in English, as he stuck his tongue out at Adele Morency. The four-year-old giggled as she nestled comfortably in the arms of a man who, just a week before, had been an utter stranger. Danielle looked on with maternal contentment at the sight of her man entertaining her daughter with silly faces.

The door opened and Hoffmann looked up to see Emma enter the mess compartment, carrying what appeared to be a rolled-up nautical chart. With her free hand, she held open the door for Klein, who hobbled unassisted to a seat at the head of the table. Klein grunted as his wounded thigh came into contact with the chair's hardwood surface. Nonetheless, he managed to greet the two-score plus people populating the mess hall with a friendly smile.

"Thank you all for coming. Professor, it's very good to see you up and about. How are you feeling?"

"Better than you, by the look of it," quipped Hoffmann.

"You sure about that?" Klein retorted. "With that bandage around your shoulder, you remind me of a trussed turkey at an American Thanksgiving."

The two friends exchanged sophomoric grins, before Klein turned his attention to the group at large.

"For Gerhard's benefit, I'll continue in English. I'll begin with a situation update. For those who've lost track, the date and time are 3 November, 18:25 hours."

Klein nodded to Emma, who spread the chart on the table. The summoned group – Gerhard, the entire Israeli contingent plus their love interests – clustered closer for a look.

"We're now steaming south about fifteen nautical miles off the coast of Lebanon," said Klein, his index finger indicating a point in the Mediterranean opposite Beirut. "In about five hours, the *Mauritz* will run itself aground on the beach at Nahariya. Passengers will then leave the ship through its two accommodation ladders and scatter to avoid arrest by British police and soldiers. Meanwhile, we disembark early in the ship's boats and sail five kilometres south to land at Shavei Tzion, the theory being that the British will be so busy rounding up eight hundred people from the freighter that we escape their notice."

"That means we're using the people from the train as decoys," protested Ohad Karmi. "Why the hell did we bother to free them? Just to let the British toss them into a detention camp on Cyprus?"

"Colonel, if I may?" interjected Hoffmann.

Klein signalled his permission with a 'go for it' wave of his hand.

Hoffmann swivelled to face Karmi directly. "It's only fair that I respond because Colonel Klein is acting on my advice. Our equipment is almost one hundred years more advanced than anything in use today. The question becomes very simple: who will be the 20th-century beneficiary of our 21st-century technology? Who gets a head-start on the science of digital electronics from access to our UAV system and radio gear? Who gets a leg-up in weapons development from exposure to our small arms?"

"And you want the 'who' to be us, not the British," volunteered Baruch Levinson.

"Precisely," Hoffmann confirmed.

"Thank you, Professor," said Klein as he turned to address the room at large. "Despite everything we've accomplished, you should have no illusions about the determination of the Arabs to oppose the creation of a Jewish state. Nothing in this regard has changed. You can be sure that there's a war coming, and I intend for the Yishuv to have every advantage when it does. That's my overriding priority."

"Even at the expense of our own people?" challenged Karmi.

"Yes, even at their expense," replied Klein. "The only consolation being that we know the British will treat those they catch in humane fashion."

"Humane fashion? That's the best you can do?" shot back Karmi in a tone that now bordered on outright insubordination.

"Ohad, if you want to accompany the civilians, I won't stop you. That goes for all of you. You've been through resistance-to-interrogation training, so I don't foresee any problems in keeping your mouth shut. But my decision stands. We act to ensure that our 21st-century gear remains in Jewish hands. Anyone who wants to remain onboard should speak now."

Klein canvassed the room, his eyes finally settling on Ohad Karmi, whose shoulders heaved in a sullen shrug.

"Alright, then. Now to a happier topic. The romantic attachments that have developed among us. For the sake of full disclosure, you should be aware that Emma and I also fall into that category."

"So, you marry Emma?" asked Miriam, her mouth curled upwards in a smile of wonderment

"That's the plan," replied Klein as he took Emma's hand in his. "If she'll have me."

Emma lifted their intertwined hands, delivering a kiss to Klein's knuckles that answered his question to the satisfaction of all present.

Miriam detached herself from Levinson and moved to embrace Emma. "We do hupa together!"

"Don't forget us," chimed Danielle as she laid a possessive hand on Weinstock's arm. "We look for a rabbi too."

"Wow, you Jewish boys work fast!" said Hoffmann, generating embarrassed smiles from Klein, Levinson and Weinstock, and sophomoric guffaws from the other Israeli troopers.

"Alright, settle down," said Klein. "The point here is that we won't be separating these couples. There's ample room in the boats, so Miriam, Danielle and little Adele and, yes, Emma, are coming with us. Emma's parents and Miriam's grandmother as well. On this point, I don't want to hear any argument."

Klein glanced at Ohad Karmi, who kept to a sullen silence.

"What about me?" enquired Hoffmann.

"You're certainly coming along," replied Klein. "We can't have the British getting their hands on the brains of the operation. Besides, who's going to explain all this science stuff to the people at the Technion and Hebrew University?"

Hoffmann smiled in relief. "Thank you."

"No thanks necessary," replied Klein. "Farkash, I want you to oversee the loading of the boats. Make sure to pack our equipment in a manner so that everything can be ditched over the side if the Brits are waiting for us on shore. Report back to me once everything's in order."

"Will do," affirmed Farkash.

"Okay, we'll convene on the main deck at 21:30. See you all then," said Klein, his mouth creasing briefly in a grimace of pain as he rose from the table. Then he hobbled through the mess compartment doorway, while the remaining meeting participants waited respectfully to follow suit.

Hoffmann remained seated, looking up as Danielle slid into the chair opposite, placing Adele on her knee.

"Bonjour," he said, his fractured French accompanied by a friendly smile.

"Guten Tag," Danielle replied with a cheeky grin of her own. "That's all the German I know," she continued in English. "I 'aven't said 'ello, so now would be a good time, I was t'inking."

"Well I have been dealing with a few distractions," said Hoffmann, his good hand gesturing towards his bandaged shoulder.

"Bien sûr ... of course," replied Danielle quickly. "I will leave you."

"No, no, not at all," he protested. "I've spent the past eight days on my back in the infirmary. It will be nice to talk to someone other than Doctor Lifshutz and the medics."

"So Azriel ... 'e tells me all this operation was ... eh ... your idea?"

Hoffmann shrugged. "Not mine alone. I had some help. The real heroes are Colonel Klein and the boys who actually put their lives on the line for this mission. I was in the rear with the gear, as the Americans say."

"But you are German, so I wonder ... why?

Gerhard sighed. "It's simple, really. The war was an absolute catastrophe for Germany. Between seven and nine million people died, and all of our major cities were destroyed by British and American bombing. The eastern part of the country was occupied by the Russians and remained a Bolshevik police state until 1989."

"Then you do this from l'égoïsme national? From patriotism?"

"No, no!" protested Hoffmann. "I'm not expressing myself clearly. "Of course, my goal was to save millions of lives that otherwise would be lost to Nazi barbarism, but I also want to save Germany's soul."

"Soul? You mean l'âme?"

"Let me explain it this way. The physical destruction caused by the war was mostly rebuilt by 1960. At least in the West ... the part not occupied by the Russians. They called this the wirtschaftswunder. The economic miracle. But material prosperity couldn't erase the sense of guilt haunting German society because of the terrible crimes committed during the Hitler-era. I, myself, am a prime example of this … phénomène, as you French would say."

"I still don' un'erstand."

"It's my family's dirty secret," he said, melancholy etched across his face. "My grandfather is a senior officer in the SS. Although, if the news out of Berlin is true, he's probably dead."

"That would make you 'appy?"

"Very. He was … is … a murderer and a thief who stole millions of dollars from his victims. I despise him."

Danielle smiled and placed her hand on his. "You are a good man. Nothing like your grandfather. Nothing like the Nazis. You save my life and the life of my daughter. I can never t'ank you enough."

Hoffmann's eyes teared up as his good hand extracted a cigarette from the packet of Galoises that lay on the table. He smiled apologetically as he pulled a lighter from the chest pocket of his battledress. "Is it alright if I smoke?"

"Of course."

Hoffmann laughed. "One of the only good things about living in the 1940s is that smoking isn't a stigma."

"Stigma?"

"Sorry … a mark of disapproval. Something considered bad."

"Ah, oui … un stigmate. Le désapprobation."

He ignited the tip of his cigarette and took a long draw, exhaling with a satisfied smile as the nicotine hit his system. "In my time, cigarettes are considered a dirty habit and a risk to public health. There are even laws that prohibit smoking in public places."

Their dialogue was interrupted by the sudden appearance of Weinstock in the compartment door.

"Excuse me, Professor," the Israeli officer said politely, "but I need Danielle's help with the packing. I want to make sure we haven't forgotten anything."

"I'm sorry, but I mus' go."

"Yes, yes," replied Hoffmann with a wave of his good arm. "Do what you have to do. I'll see you later."

Hoffmann remained seated alone at the mess table. How long, he didn't precisely know, although the seven cigarette butts neatly arrayed atop the table gave some indication of the time that had elapsed. He was brought back from reverie into situational awareness as the ship's engines fell silent and the ship palpably slowed.

Time to go.

Hoffmann made his way onto the main deck, moving to the starboard side where the motor launch and four lifeboats hung from their davits, their darkened silhouettes framed against a silvered moon.

"I'm going to need some help getting into that thing," observed Hoffmann, with a gesture towards the motor launch

"You and me both," said Klein.

The two injured men were assisted into the bow of the launch and joined by Emma and her parents, Levinson, Miriam plus grandmother, Danielle and her daughter, Adele. A quartet of Israeli troopers completed the boat's complement, with Staff Sergeant Shimshon Tzuberi positioned next to the Marston Seagull outboard engine in the stern. As a Shayetet 13 Naval Commando, Tzuberi was by far the most experienced small-boat helmsman among the Israelis. The motor launch was lowered without incident, as were the four lifeboats that arranged themselves in column formation, connected stern-to-bow by the painter ropes equipping each boat.

Tsuberi slowly opened the outboard's throttle, ensuring that the slack of the painters linking the boats behind was taken up slowly, so as to avoid them being snapped. Once the ropes were taut, he gunned the engine and the column began to pull away on a south-easterly course. The beach was visible in the distance, a strip of moonlit white that stretched between the sea's inky blackness and the duller gloom of the countryside beyond.

Seventy-two

Klein signalled the *Mauritz* with his flashlight and the sea around the ship's stern began to froth as her screws came back to life. The freighter soon disappeared into the murky darkness and the five little boats were alone, making steady progress towards a separate landfall a few kilometres to the South.

After a few minutes, the dark boxy shapes of buildings materialised from within the murk that stretched beyond the silver strip of beach.

"They'll hear us coming," yelled Emma into Klein's ear, with a nod towards the stern where the engine was belching a loud two-cycle 'putt-putt'.

That they did. The keel of the motor launch had scarcely begun to scrape along the sloping sand when a voice rang out from the darkness.

"Who are you?" came the challenge in German-accented Hebrew from an unseen sentry.

"Friends!" yelled Klein in the same language. "Ma'apilim."

"Where's your ship?"

"It should be aground on the beach at Nahariyya just about now, with a cargo of eight hundred Jews from Baden."

"Baden? Sind Sie Juden aus Deutschland?"

"Over to you," said Klein to Emma with a big grin on his face.

"Ja!" she yelled to the unseen questioner. "Mein Name ist Emma Cohen und ich bin von Heidelberg."

A lanky man with glasses and curly dark hair materialised from the darkness with a welcoming smile and Lee–Enfield rifle slung over his shoulder. He and Emma began to chatter away in German until Klein interjected in Hebrew.

"Sorry to interrupt, but it's important that I speak to the moshav secretary. It's an issue of vital security importance."

The lanky sentry nodded and departed to summon the Shavei Tzion's leadership team.

"You knew this was a German community," said Emma with a tint of reproach.

"I knew it was founded by Yekkes," replied Klein. "I thought it would be a nice surprise."

She answered with a playful punch to his shoulder.

Some minutes later, the sentry returned, accompanied by two men and a woman looking bleary-eyed after having been roused from their beds.

"Who's in charge here?" asked the woman, whose German-accented Hebrew exuded an unequivocal aura of authority.

"That would be me. My name is Yossi Klein."

"Well, Mister Klein, my name is Gisella Rosenblum and I am the Secretary of this Moshav. Perhaps we can start with you telling me how you happened to wash up on our beach?"

"Could we speak privately?" Klein requested.

With a nod, Rosenblum led the way to the nearby moshav secretariat building.

Once inside her office, Rosenblum got straight to the point. "Nu?" she asked, using the classic one-word Yiddish interrogatory expression.

"I am the commander of a special Haganah unit that has returned from a highly classified operation in Europe. The details of our primary mission are off limits, but I will tell you that we encountered a trainload of German Jews being deported by the SS. We liberated the train and brought these people home with us. As we speak, a freighter carrying those eight hundred Jews is running itself aground two kilometres north of here at Nahariya."

On hearing this news, Rosenblum's gruff, no-nonsense demeanour slipped and she broke into a friendly smile. "Is this connected to recent events in France?"

Klein simply shook his head. "Sorry, but I can't discuss our mission."

"I think I understand," grinned Rosenblum. "So how can we help?"

"We are carrying top-secret military technology that will be vital to the defence of the Yishuv," explained Klein. "It is imperative that we hide this material from the British until our scientists can analyse it properly. I presume you have a 'slik?'" – the Hebrew slang term for a secret weapons cache.

Rosenblum nodded.

"We'll store our material there. Then I'll be needing a meeting with Ben Gurion."

"Ben Gurion?" she said, with a wide-eyed look of surprise. "You don't ask for much, do you?"

"It's of the utmost importance," replied Klein with deadpan seriousness.

Rosenblum shrugged. "Such a meeting will take time to arrange. Until then, we'll have to take care of your group. How many are you?"

"Forty, including two wounded," Klein replied.

"You mean three wounded," Rosenblum dryly observed. "Unless that limp of yours is the result of an old sporting injury?"

"Don't worry about me, I've had top-quality medical treatment."

"It's my job to worry," said Rosenblum. "Our nurse can have a look at all the injured, you included. We also have to think about keeping the lot of you away from the British. Their police and the army are nothing if not methodical. They may spend the next few days rounding up the people who landed at Nahariya, but then they'll broaden the net. Sooner or later, they'll show up here to conduct a search, and by the time that happens you and your people need to be gone."

"What's the plan?"

"We'll farm you out to some of the other settlements in the area. Shavei Tzion has only two hundred residents and we won't be able to hide forty people when His Majesty's finest come calling."

"Hanita, then?" Klein suggested.

Rosenblum shook her head. "Too isolated. I was thinking Kfar Masarik and Ein Hamfratz. They have bigger populations and are close to Haifa. In the meantime, I'll send your request for a meeting with the Old Man through the system. I'm sure Dori and the Haganah command will be eager to talk with you as well."

"I appreciate your help."

"It's the least we can do. Welcome home."

423

Seventy-three

Neville squinted in discomfort as the blindfold was finally removed from his head. He had no idea of his location, the sightless drive having fully achieved its disorienting purpose. As his eyes adjusted to the bright white light cast by the neon lamp from above, he observed his surroundings – a non-descript room in what he presumed would be a non-descript building in a non-descript location.

Far more intriguing was the lithe man in his early 30s sitting across the table. He radiated an aura of soldierly competence and, clearly, was someone to be reckoned with.

"Colonel Ralph Neville of British Military Intelligence," the man announced, "it's come to our attention that you've been asking questions, so we've decided to accommodate your curiosity. To a point."

"By 'we' you mean the Haganah underground militia?"

The Israeli man nodded. "I apologise for the blindfold, but our relations with the local British authorities are a bit tense at present. I'm sure you'll understand our need to take precautions. Now that you're here, can I get you anything?"

"A cup of tea wouldn't go amiss," croaked Neville through a dry throat.

"Of, course," the man said, with a nod to someone standing behind. "You may call me Yossi and I'm here to answer your questions. Or not, as I see fit. Fire away."

"I'm sorry, I didn't catch your last name?"

"That's correct," replied Klein. "You didn't."

Neville smiled in amused respect. "Very well, straight to the business at hand. As you know, the story put about publicly by Berlin is that their Führer was assassinated by rogue elements of the SS. Of course, this narrative serves the interests of the Wehrmacht High Command by providing a perfect rationale for a purge against the army's only real competitor for power. Some of our sources, however, inform us that the German military secretly believes the attack against Hitler's special train was conducted by Palestinian Jews. To put it simply, I'm here to ascertain the truth of that hypothesis."

"Why would this be of such interest to you? The deed is done and the facts are what the facts are. Unless you're conducting due diligence for an award of the Victoria Cross to those involved in that enterprise?"

Neville couldn't help but laugh. He was beginning to like this Yossi fellow. "That would be a matter for his Majesty – but nonetheless, we'd like to know."

"No doubt," replied Klein. "For the sake of argument only, let's delve into your hypothetical for a moment. Say we were involved. Would such an action on our part bring about a change in British government policy towards Palestine? After all, the United Kingdom has benefitted tremendously from Hitler's death. At the very least, you're no longer facing the threat of imminent invasion. In return, hypothetically speaking, would London be prepared to rescind that obscene White Paper on Jewish immigration brought into force last year?"

Neville shrugged, his good humour replaced by flush-faced embarrassment. "You know full well that such policy decisions are the sole preserve of Cabinet."

"Indeed they are," replied Klein. "In view of that fact, let me give you a message for transmission to the powers-that-be in London. The strategic logic underpinning their White Paper is facile and wrongheaded. The Grand Mufti of Jerusalem has been in league with Berlin for years, and the current Prime Minister of Iraq is an unrepentant Nazi sympathiser. Pro-German sentiment is rampant within the Egyptian officer corps and, in that regard, you might want to keep a close eye on a young lieutenant named Anwar Sadat. The bottom line is that the Arab elites are fascist in sympathy, and nothing Britain can do will change that ugly reality. In the end, all you've done is spurn your natural Jewish allies in order to plight your troth with a bunch of Arab autocrats who despise you and side with your enemies. Earlier this year, Mr Churchill described appeasers as those who feed the crocodile in the hopes of being eaten last. You'd think he'd know better."

The end of Klein's oration was met by stunned silence on the part of his British interlocutor. Put simply, the power of the Jewish case, and the eloquence with which it was expressed, left Ralph Neville speechless.

A few awkward moments ensued until Klein spoke again, this time in a much more conciliatory tone.

"I apologise for speaking so harshly. Particularly in view of the fact that I'm reliably informed you're sympathetic to our cause."

"I'm sorry, but I don't follow."

"We've looked into your background, Colonel. We know you come from a family of Plymouth Brethren whose members follow the teachings of John Nelson Darby."

"Ah," said Neville, his head canting forward in a nod of understanding. "That's why you let me hang around at loose ends in Jerusalem for ten days until agreeing to schedule this meeting."

Klein smiled enigmatically. "As a veteran intelligence officer, you know that these things take time. Now, back to the faith of your fathers. Darby's Christian theology advocated for the return of the Jews to their ancestral home in the Land of Israel. Do you subscribe to that belief, Colonel?"

"I am a serving officer in the British Army. With that caveat, I'm prepared to say that what the Zionist movement has managed to achieve over the space of a few short decades is quite remarkable. You've taken a decrepit corner of the Ottoman Empire that was left moribund by centuries of neglect and transformed it into a vibrant society. Your land reclamation projects are world-class and the revivification of the Hebrew language is historically unprecedented."

Klein smiled. "Elizier Ben Yehuda was an amazing man."

Neville nodded. "Ah, yes, the linguist. Well, I can muddle through the Hebrew Bible with the aid of a dictionary, but your rapid-fire delivery of Mr Ben Yehuda's vernacular leaves me utterly confused."

Klein laughed. "It's different, yet very much the same. For example, do you know how to say you like something in modern Hebrew?"

Neville shook his head.

"You say "zeh motzai chen beh aynai" ... it finds favour in my eyes."

"'And Noah found favour in the eyes of the Lord', intoned Neville. "Genesis 6."

Klein's lips pursed in a smile of approval. "You're quite a scholar. I'm impressed."

"Just a humble student. In answer to your previous question, yes, I personally believe the Land of Israel was promised to the Jewish People. I think everything Zionism has accomplished stands as a testament to that divine commitment. By the way, this is all entirely off the record."

"While I find your point of view refreshing, Colonel, it appears to be very much a minority perspective. Most of your countrymen seem to share the sympathies of Thomas Edward Lawrence in favour of 'our cousins', as we colloquially refer to the Arabs."

"There's no denying Lawrence was academically brilliant. He graduated with a First from Oxford. But intellect and wisdom are two separate things, the title of his book notwithstanding. His brilliance did not prevent him from succumbing to foolish notions of Orientalist romanticism. He failed to recognise that the Arabs are a retrograde tribal culture that has never recovered from the Mongol invasions of the 13th century. He should have cast his lot with the Jews."

"Like Orde Wingate?" asked Klein.

"Precisely like Wingate, who was three years ahead of me at Charterhouse."

"Also a Plymouth Brother."

"Correct. In fact, our families are well-acquainted," said Neville, as an epiphanic look spread across his face. "Where is Orde these days? I assume your knowledge of his whereabouts is more up-to-date than mine."

Klein grinned. "He's currently in Abyssinia, as a matter of fact. Which made the task of contacting him relatively easy. In the neighbourhood, in a manner of speaking. You know, we have a special name for Wingate."

"A special name?"

"Yes. We call him 'the friend' on account of the aid he provided to the Jewish community during the Arab rebellion a few years ago."

"Can I assume that Orde gave testament to my bona fides?" asked Neville.

"Indeed he did. Which is why I'd like to offer you our hospitality during your visit."

"Hospitality?"

"Yes. I assumed you'd like to visit the major Christian holy places. I took the liberty of laying on a guided tour with one of our leading authorities in biblical history from the Hebrew University."

"That's very generous of you, but I must be getting back to London."

"Colonel, the war effort will surely survive without you for a few days. I think we can be reasonably sure that the Germans won't be crossing the Channel now that we're midway through November. Professor Casuto has organised visits to the Church of the Nativity in Jerusalem and Holy Sepulchre in Bethlehem. Then up north to the Sea of Galilee."

"Very tempting, but I must still regretfully decline," replied Neville as he rose to his feet, hand extended. "I must say that making your acquaintance has been both enlightening and enjoyable."

The grimace of pain that flashed across Klein's face as he stood to reciprocate the courtesy did not escape Neville's notice.

"I'm sorry to see you've been injured. May I be so bold as to enquire how it happened?"

"Stubbed my toe against the bed," replied Klein with a flippant stare.

Neville's mouth creased in an urbane smile. "Then I hope the bed isn't too much worse for the wear. In any event, perhaps we might be able to meet again one day in less adversarial circumstances."

"Once we gain our independence."

"Time will tell," replied Neville diplomatically.

"Oh, you should consider it a certainty," replied Klein with just a touch of defiance before his tone softened. "I do have one more question. What will be done with the refugees you picked up around Nahariya? The ones who came off the ship?"

"Ah," replied Neville. "Why do you ask?"

Klein shrugged. "Simple curiosity. It was in the headlines."

"Of course. Well, if my recommendation carries any weight, they'll be released and counted against the Jewish immigration quota for next year. After all, I can't imagine they'd be sent back to Germany."

"One would hope not. In any event, we owe you a debt of gratitude for that recommendation. I hope I'll be able to repay the favour one day. Consider it a standing invitation."

"I will. Thank you."

There being nothing left to say, Neville turned and, with a gesture, invited his escort to reaffix the blindfold. Within the hour, he was deposited three blocks from his lodgings in Jerusalem – the King David Hotel that doubled as British military headquarters. He bypassed the cipher-room, deciding that the inferences and extrapolations that would mark the core of his report were best delivered in person. To that end, he commenced travel arrangements for his return to London. With any luck, he would be back at Whitehall by the middle of next week.

Seventy-four

Only a slight limp remained in evidence as Klein made his way up the front steps of Haifa City Hall, an imposing sandstone edifice in the Hadar HaCarmel section of the city. From the information desk in the central atrium, he was ushered to a nearby waiting room, where Gerhard Hoffmann greeted him with a thousand-watt smile.

"How's the arm, Professor?" Klein enquired as he slid into the bench alongside the German physicist.

"Better by the day, thanks," replied Hoffmann. "I see your leg is on the mend."

"Not quite ready to run a marathon, but last week I gave up the crutches."

"Glad to hear. I also wanted to thank you for inviting me along today. This is a tremendous opportunity to meet a man I've long admired."

"Hell," rejoined Klein with a self-deprecating grin, "I'm a mathematical moron. You had to come in case the discussion delves into scientific matters."

"Speaking of things scientific, you're aware I've been talking to some of the senior staff at the Technion?"

"I hope you haven't mentioned ... the unmentionable," murmured Klein, as he glanced around in search of potential eavesdroppers.

"No, no," protested Hoffmann. "I've stayed on script. They're fascinated by our radios, so I've focused the conversation on digital electronics. These are very intelligent people, though, and broader questions have been asked."

"Left unanswered, I hope."

Hoffmann nodded. "Absolutely. My discussions have led to another unexpected development. It seems I've been deemed worthy of a position at the Technion's Faculty of Physics. They're calling it a senior research fellowship, which apparently is something created specifically for my benefit. They also promise that, when my Hebrew is up to standard, I'll be able to teach as well."

"I'm pleased, but not surprised," said Klein. "I imagine they decided to move quickly, just in case the Hebrew University tried to poach you. There's quite a rivalry between …"

The sound of a door handle being turned caused Klein to fall silent as an obvious bodyguard entered the waiting room. "He will see you now."

Klein and Hoffmann were conducted down the hall to an office that was marked, not by ostentation, but by a spartan lack thereof. Rising from behind a desk was a short, portly man of late-middle-age who was immediately recognisable by his trademark balding pate, flanked by two unruly shocks of white hair.

"Welcome gentlemen," said David Ben Gurion in Russian-accented English. "Please be seated. Mr Hoffmann, I've heard very good things about you from our people at the Technion."

"Thank you, sir," Hoffmann responded in a tone of awed reverence.

"Yet I'm told you also present something of a conundrum," Ben Gurion continued. "You offer a wealth of advanced scientific knowledge while refusing to divulge anything about where and how such expertise was acquired."

"Because I've sworn him to silence," Klein interjected.

"Have you indeed?" mused Ben Gurion as he scoped the Israeli special forces officer up and down. "You're quite the enigma in your own right, Mr Klein. A speaker of perfect idiomatic Hebrew with a Sabra's accent, yet no-one in the Yishuv has ever heard of you. You bring us weapons and equipment that feature technology far beyond the imagination of our most gifted scientists. The people you liberated from that train absolutely idolise you as some latter-day Joshua, smiting the Amorites hip and thigh. The Haganah high command has also been extremely impressed by your military expertise. So much so, that you were permitted to represent us at the meeting with that Englishman who was making a nuisance of himself with speculative questions."

"As a matter of fact, that particular initiative came from me," Klein replied, "my argument being that I'm uniquely qualified to deduce what the British know, as opposed to what they only suspect. I was a bit surprised when Shaltiel agreed."

"The decision was mine," said Ben Gurion. "Made in the hope that we might learn a bit more about you as a result. We had very little interest in this particular Englishman and your cooperation with us has been

430

described as selective at best. Your men have been equally disobliging when it comes to disclosing information."

"As I told Shaltiel and the others, we are operating under strict 'need to know' protocols that restrict what can be said and to whom," declared a deadpan Klein. "Those are our orders."

"Am I included among those select few who need to know?"

"Yours is the only name on the list, until you authorise otherwise," Klein disclosed in a sober voice.

"Very well then. I believe the relevant expression in English is 'coming clean'. So, Mister Yosef Klein, now is the time to come clean about who you really are."

"Yes sir," replied Klein with a glance at the hovering bodyguard, "but my report contains extremely sensitive information that would best be discussed in confidence."

Ben Gurion responded with a decisive shake of the head. "Yakoutiel has full access to everything that comes across my desk. You said I could authorise otherwise, so I'm authorising otherwise. He's in the loop."

Klein nodded and reached to open his satchel, causing Yakoutiel to go for what looked like an M1911 .45 calibre pistol in a shoulder rig. Ben Gurion motioned for his bodyguard to stand down and the security man resumed his ever-watchful pose.

Klein produced a package encased in a protective layering that immediately attracted Ben Gurion's interest.

"This is called bubble wrap," explained Klein as he extracted a flat rectangular object from the wrapping, popping one of the inflated cells between his fingers before proffering the plastic sheeting to Ben Gurion. "A very effective packaging device. Patent it and the Yishuv will make billions."

Ben Gurion accepted the wrap and smiled as he popped one of the cells.

"Many people find popping bubble wrap to be therapeutic," explained Klein as he pushed a button on the side of the flat rectangle. The logo of a white apple with a bite missing materialised on a dark gray screen.

"This is called an iPad and, in a few moments, you'll understand more."

The Apple logo was soon replaced by a series of rectangular shapes atop a light blue background. Ben Gurion watched with obvious fascination as Klein's fingers deftly manipulated this strange device until a photograph materialised, showing a business-suited man seated behind a desk with a Zionist flag hanging in the background.

Klein looked up from the device. "Are you ready?"

Ben Gurion nodded, placing the now-decimated bubble wrap to one side.

Klein pushed another button and the still image came to life in the form of a film clip.

"Shalom Mr Ben Gurion," announced the man on the screen in fluent Hebrew. "This might seem difficult to believe, but my name is Yair Etzioni, and I am Prime Minister of Israel. The man you are now meeting is an emissary from my time to yours who was tasked with a mission to prevent the greatest cataclysm in our long history from descending upon the Jewish People. His name is Yossi Klein and he is a Lieutenant Colonel in the Israel Defense Force. The fact you are watching this video, which is our word for film, is an indication that the operation commanded by Lieutenant Colonel Klein was a success and that Adolf Hitler is dead.

"Your scientists will no doubt be thrilled by the opportunity to examine this iPad, as it is called, as well as other pieces of 21st-century technology Colonel Klein has been able to deliver. However, he is also the source of something even more valuable, and that's 'foreknowledge'. I'm pleased to report that my Israel is an economically thriving, culturally vibrant democracy. Hence, you have much cause for pride in your achievements. While things are good, we now have a unique opportunity to make them even better. To that end, you now have at your disposal one of the sharpest minds in our military. We will miss him, but our loss is your gain. Which, in the end, will make it our gain as well. You would be well advised to see Yossi Klein as a most precious national resource. I will now bid you goodbye and leave you in Colonel Klein's capable hands. Good luck."

The screen of the iPad faded into darkness as Ben Gurion sat quietly for a few moments, hand on chin. "Quite a story," mused Israel's founding father.

"From your perspective, I imagine so," replied Klein. "At first, I found the idea of time travel hard to believe. I can assure you that all this is one hundred per cent true. Technical questions should be directed to Doctor Hoffmann, as it was his discovery that made this possible."

"Everything you've shown me leaves no room for doubt, which brings me to my next question. Doctor, would it be possible to recreate your time travel device for our use?"

"Why is that the first thing everyone asks?" exclaimed Hoffmann with ill-concealed exasperation. Then he stopped, baring his teeth in a grimace of embarrassment. "I apologise, sir."

Ben Gurion responded with a hand gesture that was part 'don't worry about it' and part 'go on'.

"The simple answer is no," explained Hoffmann. "The scientific equipment you have is not nearly powerful enough."

"Not even this iPad thing of yours?" questioned Ben Gurion. "It's an amazing device."

Klein and Hoffmann exchanged amused smiles. "Sir, the machine we used to calculate the necessary data is several million times more powerful than the iPad. It took up most of an entire room."

"A pity," mused Ben Gurion, "but no matter. We operate in the realm of the real rather than the ideal. Mr Hoffmann, have our Technion people spoken to you about a position in their physics department?"

"Yes sir," replied Hoffmann, "the offer was extended yesterday. It's a great honour that, needless to say, I have already accepted."

"Excellent. We'll be expecting great things from you. Now, would you mind if Mr Klein and I switch to Hebrew? It's more out of convenience than anything else. I'm afraid my English isn't that good."

"Your English is excellent, Mr Ben Gurion," replied Hoffmann with a smile. "Rest assured I take no offence. In fact, perhaps it's best that I should get back to the Technion. I'm eager to have a look at my new lab."

"Yakoutiel will arrange transport," Ben Gurion replied, nodding to his bodyguard.

As Hoffmann rose from his seat, Klein stood up and enveloped the German in a bear hug.

"Thank you for everything, Gerhard," said Klein, using the physicist's given name for the very first time. "Emma asked me to tell you don't be stranger. You're always welcome in our home and we'll have you over for Shabbat dinner soon."

"Th ... thank you," stuttered Hoffmann, his voice breaking and eyes filling with tears. The display of fraternal affection lasted for several moments before the physicist recovered his composure. With a dignified nod to Ben Gurion, he followed Yakoutiel out of the room.

"Amazing man," said Klein.

"Indeed," observed Ben Gurion, "and not even one of us."

"Part of what makes him so remarkable."

"True enough," agreed Ben Gurion. "Tell me, Mr Klein, while we're on the subject of Doctor Hoffmann, was he married? Did he leave anyone behind?"

Klein shrugged. "You know, the topic never came up, and I never asked. We only ever talked business. Why?"

"It's just that I know someone who might suit him quite well."

Klein's face cracked into wide grin. "Are you telling me the leader of the Yishuv and future prime minister of Israel is going to spend time arranging a shidduch for Gerhard Hoffmann?"

"Let's not get ahead of ourselves, but even a future prime minister should be entitled to a hobby, don't you think?" rejoined Ben Gurion with a twinkle in his eye. "In the meantime, you and I have other matters to discuss. The Haganah high command is planning to create an elite unit that will be tasked with raiding operations in the enemy's rear areas. Am I correct in understanding that you have considerable experience in such matters?"

"I did most of my military service in special forces. Like all Israelis, I'm quite familiar with the Palmach, which in my history was established mid-next year. In May 1941, as I recall."

"How would you feel about becoming the Palmach's first commander? You'll be able to shape its organisation as you see fit and select the personnel you deem appropriate. You'll have a free hand in all but one respect."

"That would be?"

"You will not go into the field. You're much too valuable an asset for that sort of risk."

"To be effective, a commander has to pull his men forward by personal example," protested Klein.

"Then you'll leave the pulling to your lieutenants. This is non-negotiable and I think your Emma – who I am eager to meet, by the way, will thank me."

"No doubt she will," Klein conceded. "What about Yitzhak Sadeh? In my world, he was the one who oversaw the creation of the Palmach."

"It's not as though we're suffering from an undersupply of serious challenges. We'll find something important for him to do. Now, enough business talk for one day. I want to hear all about your operation in France."

"It's a story that's neither short, nor simple," warned Klein. "I was hoping to get back home for dinner."

"Did you tell your Emma that you might have to stay overnight in Haifa?" Klein nodded in the affirmative.

"Then you can indulge an old man's wish for one evening. Dinner and a spare bed are on me."

"You're only 55," Klein pointed out didactically.

"And what are you, a lawyer all of a sudden?" rejoined Ben Gurion. "I want to hear all the details, particularly how you sent that bastard Hitler, yimach shmo, to hell."

"Fine," sighed Klein, and settling back in his chair, he began to recount what, with the exception of a select few, would always be the greatest story never told.

Epilogue

Emma's index finger tapped idly on the stem of the fountain pen as she perused the sheaf of papers on the desk. Not for her, one of those Tapuach Model 1001 personal computers that had generated so many billions for the Israeli economy since their introduction three years earlier. She was old school, favouring handwritten annotations in red ink on pages typed with her 1954 Olympia manual typewriter that included additional keys for the ä, ü and ö of the Germanic alphabet.

Emma was in the midst of inscribing a scarlet-hued comment in the margin of page 17 when a bellowed "breakfast!" echoed through the house from the ground floor. Concentration broken, she capped the fountain pen, laying it aside with a sigh. She glanced up from the desk, her gaze skipping over the familiar testaments of merit that adorned the white plaster walls of the study where she worked. Academic diplomas from Heidelberg and Cambridge universities, a licence of legal practice from the Israel Bar Association, and a certificate of membership in the Institute de Droit International, to mention just a few. A brass-framed group photograph perched at the corner of the desk showed two boys and two girls aged from six to sixteen, smiling against the backdrop of the Western Wall in Jerusalem's Old City.

Emma made her way down the stairs, turning towards the wafting aroma of breakfast. Entering the kitchen, she observed the back of a man who was busy applying a garnish of chives and parsley to a pair of omelettes just transferred from frying pan to plates.

"Sorry, beautiful," he said, still facing the kitchen counter, "but I wanted to make sure you got yours while it's still hot. Coffee's incoming."

The man who turned away from the stove, a plate in each hand, was easily recognisable. The broad shoulders and athletic physique had changed little. But the blue eyes gazing out above Yossi Klein's smile were now filtered through a pair of bifocal glasses and the hair across his pate was streaked with grey.

Setting the plates of omelette and salad on the kitchen table, Yossi began to fiddle with the Bezzera expresso machine that stood beside the sink. It was the only extravagance on display in the home's otherwise mundane décor. Quality cappuccino was more necessity than luxury in the Klein household.

"What's new in the world?" Emma enquired. "I haven't seen this morning's paper."

"I'm not surprised," her husband replied above the steamy hiss of the Bezzera's milk frothing wand. "You've been holed up in the study since ... when?"

"The conference is next week. I got up at five to work on my speech."

"Well, the domestic news is mostly focused on the prospect of Ben Gurion's impending retirement. Both *Ha'aretz* and *Ma'ariv* are predicting a resignation announcement within the next few weeks."

Emma nodded thoughtfully. "You're still close to him after all these years. Why don't you just call and ask?"

Klein shook his head. "That would be presumptuous."

"Even for you?"

"Especially for me, now that I'm no longer working in government. Now I'm just another businessman trying to earn a living in the private sector."

She laughed. "Yeah, just another businessman who happens to be CEO of the company that holds global patents for the silicon microchip. Speaking of global issues, what's happening internationally?"

"The pundits are saying that Joseph Kennedy's re-election prospects are looking good. Conventional wisdom holds that Henry Cabot Lodge will win the Republican nomination, but won't stand a chance in November."

"Let's go with Joe," intoned Emma, the sarcasm in her elocution unmistakable.

"It's catchy, you have to admit, and the Kennedys do have a certain panache."

"Panache isn't the word I'd apply to the President's younger brothers. The poor-little-rich-boy antics of John, Robert and Teddy keep generating the wrong types of headlines."

"Aside from gossip page fodder, what's your problem?"

Emma shrugged. "A second Kennedy administration means four more years of inaction on the League."

Klein sighed. "Emma, we've had this conversation before. I told you what an absolute disaster global government was in that other place."

"Just because your version failed the first time doesn't mean it won't be a success the second."

"The third time, ontologically speaking," noted Klein in a tone of mock didacticism, "when the League of Nations is included in your calculus."

Emma's brow arched theatrically. "Ontologically, eh? A very big word for the likes of you."

Klein grinned, sweeping Emma into a lascivious embrace. "That's the sort of thing that happens when simpletons like me start spending time with egghead intellectuals like you."

The long kiss that followed was interrupted by the entrance of their youngest child into the kitchen.

"Ughhh!" muttered 14-year-old Noam, his groan accompanied by an eye roll tailor-made to convey a full quota of teenage melodrama. "Can't you guys get a room?"

"We have several," replied Klein, his eyes still locked on Emma, "including the one where you sleep every night."

Noam responded to his father's retort with an even more ostentatious eye roll as he pulled a box of cornflakes from the pantry shelf.

"Would you like an omelette, Liebchen?" asked Emma. "I'm sure your father would be happy to make you one."

"A Klein special just the way you like it, complete with mushrooms and labneh on the side," added Yossi.

"No time," mumbled Noam through a mouthful of cereal scarfed directly from the box. "Don't want to be late for school."

"Have some juice, at least," urged Emma as she filled a glass.

"Okay, okay," capitulated Noam, taking the glass and guzzling its contents over the space of two seconds. "Gotta run or I'll miss my bus."

"Kiss your mother goodbye," instructed Klein.

Noam dutifully pecked Emma's cheek, leaving orange juice residue in his wake. "See you later," the boy called over his shoulder as he departed.

Emma cast an affectionate glance after her son, before turning to address the still-steaming omelette in front of her. She was midway through her second bite when the rotary telephone on the wall began to trill.

"Eat your breakfast," said Klein. "I'll get it."

Emma watched as her husband lifted the receiver from its cradle, straightening the twisted spiral cord with a shake of his hand. "Klein here." He listened intently for some twenty seconds before concluding the conversation with a hasty, "We'll be here."

"Nu?" enquired Emma.

"The Mushkin wants to speak with us. He'll be here in half an hour."

"Us? As in you and me? What does the Head of Mossad want with me?"

Klein shrugged. "Don't know, but they were specific that you're to be part of the discussion."

It was just over thirty minutes later that a knock sounded from the front door. Klein disappeared into the foyer, returning moments later in the company of three men – two twentysomething athletic types with telltale bulges showing through their jackets, and one in his fifties who was clearly in charge.

"Hello Mrs Klein," said the older man with his hand extended. "My name is Nahum Mushkin. I feel as though you and I are already acquainted because Yossi has sung your praises so often. And, of course, your eminence as a professor of law is well known."

"Call me Emma," she replied, her mouth creasing in a perfunctory smile. "May I enquire what this is all about?"

"You and Avi can wait outside," said Mushkin to the closest of his bodyguards. "I'll be fine here."

The senior security officer acknowledged the command with a silent nod and led his colleague out of the kitchen.

The coast now clear, the Mossad chief lifted the briefcase he was carrying onto the table. Then he clicked it open and extracted a folded document that he pushed across the table top towards the couple.

Klein unfolded what turned out to be an architectural schematic diagram adorned with a logo in the upper left corner: EUROPÄISCHES ZENTRUM FÜR LUFT- UND RAUMFAHRT/CENTRE EUROPÉEAN D'AÉROSPA-TIALES.

Yossi and Emma studied the diagram for a few moments before looking up in unison at Mushkin.

"European Center for Aerospace," Emma recited. "So?"

"Those are the plans for a new satellite relay centre that will be built outside Montoir-sur-le-Loir," answered Mushkin. "Ground-breaking is scheduled for next March at a site within the Prunay Forest," explained the Mossad chief.

Emma watched with concern as her husband's face blanched in shock. "What does this mean, Yossi? Why are you so upset?"

"The Forêt de Prunay was our transition point," explained Yossi in a quiet, sombre tone. "It's where we travelled through time." He turned to address the Mossad chief. "How big will this facility be?"

"Massive. Twenty-eight buildings spread over an 85-hectare campus. If our calculations are correct, the main control centre will be sited at La Hubardière. This three-storey brick building right here." The Head of Mossad pointed to a large L-shaped structure drawn in the diagram's centre right.

Yossi sat in pensive silence as Emma reached over and clasped his hand supportively. After several moments of silence, he glanced up at Mushkin, his mouth set in a frown of grim finality. "So now we know."

"Yes," the Israeli spymaster confirmed with a nod, "now we know. Or, at least, we're reasonably certain we do."

Klein shrugged. "I'm no physicist, but isn't this the only logical explanation?"

Mushkin nodded. "That's what the experts tell us."

"Time out," interjected Emma. "If I understand correctly, you're saying this control centre will be constructed next year at the precise location where Yossi and his men travelled to 1940. That means the first group of Yossi's soldiers will collide with that building upon their return? Presumably, its brick construction will cause the disintegration of the vehicle?"

"There's some debate among the scientists on that last point," noted Mushkin. "Because time travel occurs at a molecular level, some of our physicists believe that any obstacle, even a flimsy canvas tent, would be enough to generate a process of atomic fusion. Theory aside, there's absolute consensus that a solid brick structure like the control centre would trigger a massive explosion that would level the entire facility and then some."

Klein's mouth quivered. "Gerhard would have been the best person to consult on this."

Attuned to her husband's distress, Emma administered another gentle squeeze to his hand.

"Just one more reason to mourn the passing of Professor Hoffmann," said Mushkin. "While I admired his devotion to Israel, I'd be lying if I didn't admit my frustration over his stubborn refusal to divulge the technical secrets of time travel. Although, he was certainly a man of great principle."

"And a dear friend," said Emma, in a quiet tone of sombre reflection.

"I need to ask something else," interjected Klein. "Does the Mossad have a rabbi?"

"I beg your pardon?"

"Someone with clearance to give a Halachic psika about this."

"I don't follow," replied Mushkin, his shaking head in perplexity. "Why would you need a rabbinic ruling on a point of Jewish law? You're not Shabbat-observant, unless you've had some sort of mid-life epiphany?"

The Chief of Mossad cast a questioning glance at Emma, who answered with a negative shake of her head.

"It's quite simple," explained Klein. "We're in 1964, and I'm 57 years old. That means there's no way I'll be around when this catastrophe occurs. Hence, I need to know whether it's permissible to say prayers of bereavement prospectively. Some of the boys were religious, while others were non-observant – but they were all Jews. Every one of them deserves to have the Mourners Kaddish and El Malehi Rahamim recited in their honour."

Mushkin pondered silently for several seconds. "There is someone. A former fighter pilot who found religion and is now lead rabbi at one of the big yeshivot in Jerusalem. I'll couch the question in opaque terms and let you know what he says."

So it came to pass, four months later, that Emma and Yossi walked, hand in hand, through the gates of the national cemetery on Mt Herzl in Jerusalem. The couple passed in silence through the ordered rows of military headstones towards an obelisk of white Jerusalem stone.

A crowd of roughly three dozen was already assembled, some of them chatting quietly while others gazed silently upon the 53 sets of initials carved into the flanks of the monument.

Emma exchanged hugs with the matronly Miriam and Danielle, while Yossi worked his way through a cluster of former comrades, whose balding pates and generous waistlines attested to the passage of years. Azriel Weinstock, Baruch Levinson and Doctor Yochai Lifshutz were there, as were the other members of the Agag force who were hale enough to attend. The only down-timers present were the Chief of Mossad and the three wives who had married into the time travel secret.

"Let's begin," announced Yossi in a voice loud enough to cut through the buzz of conversation. Emma interlocked arms with her female compatriots as silence settled over the assembly.

"We all know why we're here," Yossi continued, "so there's no cause for me to blather on. After almost 25 years, we've finally learned what happened to our missing brothers – and what happened to us, as a consequence. It's been a hard path to tread and I know you all miss your families from that other place. I also hope you've built fulfilling lives in this one. Something I've been able to do with the help of my Emma."

Yossi paused to exchange a loving smile with his wife.

"Now we have an opportunity to honour those among us who didn't make it through. I've asked Azriel to lead us because he's a rabbi's son and, as I recall, his voice isn't too bad."

A brief smattering of laughter swept through the group as Yossi beckoned his former team commander forward. As Azriel Weinstock began to intone the El Malei Rahamim, the soulful beauty of its melody and lyrics cast an aura of melancholy on those assembled.

At first, Emma was able to hold it together, but then came the names – that segment of the El Malei where the list of dead was declaimed in memoriam. There were just so many. So many names representing so many lives.

It was midway through this catalogue of lamentation that Emma felt herself slipping over the edge of self-control. She lost it. She wasn't alone. Through her own veil of tears, she saw glistening tracks of liquid sorrow coursing down the creased and weathered faces of those around her.

It mattered not that Emma Klein né Cohen never met the men for whom she mourned. She wept. Tears of grief over what was sacrificed, tears of gratitude over what was accomplished. Tears of hope that, somehow, those who remained might reap a measure of solace so richly earned and deserved.

Author's note

GENESIS

The genesis of this novel can be traced to the summer of my 14th year, when I purchased Sir Steven Runciman's three-volume *History of the Crusades*. In those pages, I read how Crusader armies massacred Jewish community after Jewish community while advancing up the Rhine during the summer of 1096. In response, my adolescent imagination propelled me back to that time and place armed with an AK47 and a copious supply of ammunition. The Al Pacino remake of *Scarface* had yet to be filmed, but the scenario I envisaged always climaxed with a 'say hello to my lil' friend' moment on the ramparts of medieval Mainz.

My publisher, Humfrey Hunter, describes this book as *Back to the Future* meets *Zero Dark Thirty* meets *Inglorious Basterds*. A more accurate allegorical description of the teenage daydream that started all this would be: Jewish Tony Montana meets the Golem of Prague meets Detective Yonatan McClane. Yippee-kai-yay, yah mamzerim!

VERISIMILITUDE

Beyond its sci-fi/time travel component, I wanted *Righteous Kill* to be historically accurate and militarily plausible. To that end I spent many hours scouring topographical maps, 1940s-era aerial photographs, unit orders of battle and technical weapons specifications. I also relied heavily on the amazing suite of resources provided by Geoportail, the French government cartographic website. When I put boots on the ground at those locations where key chapters of the book take place, I was gratified to find that the storyline fitted perfectly with the actual lay of the land. Merci au gouvernement Français.

While fictionalised for the sake of this novel, the account of the Wagner-Bürkel Aktion that appears in *Righteous Kill* provides a faithful depiction of this event as it unfolded. On the morning of 22 October 1940, Gestapo officers and Ordnungspolizei appeared at the front doors of every Jewish home in Baden and the Saar-Palatinate. More than 6,500 men, women and children were taken at gunpoint to their local railroad station. There they were crammed into nine passenger trains that set out on a two-day journey to the Vichy detention camp at Gurs in the foothills of the Pyrenees.

This route took these deportees into France and southwards along the Saône River where, in the pages of *Righteous Kill*, the leading train has a rendezvous with our time travelling detachment of Israeli special forces troopers. In order for this plotline to compute, I was obliged to adjust the date of Wagner-Bürkel by four days, from 22 to 26 October. In my view, this is a modest calibration that falls well within the bounds of creative licence.

We learn from Shoah history that the Jews detained at Gurs were deported to Auschwitz in August 1942. I far prefer the *Righteous Kill* version.

Acknowledgements

First and foremost, I acknowledge and thank my beloved wife Sharon, without whose faith, love and support this book would never have been written. Her keen editorial expertise was also essential in burnishing my prose to a more incandescent lustre. To the kids, thank you for brightening my life.

Gratitude as well to Humfrey Hunter of Silvertail Books, who was quick recognise the potential of this book. It's a rare privilege to work with such a kindred spirit on artistic and other matters. Appreciation is also due to Robert Dinsdale for his initial edit and words of praise for *Righteous Kill*. I must also acknowledge how Ollie Ray's brilliant cover design hits the elusive sweet spot by managing to be both eye-catching and nuanced at the same time.

Fraternal fondness and gratitude to Stephen Elder and Brian Lovison, my partner in digital Machiavellianism. A special thanks to Andrew Hastie MP and Senator Kimberly Kitching who agreed to launch *Righteous Kill* in Melbourne, even though the public event was derailed by the force majeure of COVID-19.

Merçi aussi à André Michel de la mairie de Montoire-sur-Le Loir pour sa généreuse assistance en fournissant des témoignages contemporains de la conférence au sommet d'Hitler-Pétain.

Ted Lapkin
Melbourne, Australia
April, 2020

Glossary

Adjudant	French Gendarmerie Nationale rank of equivalent to warrant officer (E-8)
Ahalan	Arabic word for 'hi' that is often used in informal Hebrew conversation
Aliya	Immigration to Israel, literally translated as 'ascent'
Aliya Bet	Underground program in operation during the 1940s by the Yishuv that smuggled Jews into mandatory Palestine in defiance of British immigration restrictions
Aman	Hebrew portmanteau of 'Agaf Modi'in' – Intelligence Branch, the IDF department that oversees intelligence collection and analysis at the strategic level, commanded by a major general
Am Yisrael	The 'People of Israel
Anabasis	Classical Greek for 'The Ascent' and the title of Xenophon's account of the epic march by the Ten Thousand
Arschloch	German for 'asshole'
Amerika	Code name for Führersonderzug (Führer Special Train)
Bacha	Hebrew portmanteau of 'B'sis Heyl Avir' – Air Force Base
Bahad	Hebrew portmanteau of 'B'sis Hadracha' – Training Base
Bahad Echad	Training Base No. One – IDF Officer Training School located outside Mitzpeh Ramon in the Negev Desert
Bahad Sheva	Training Base No. Seven – IDF School of Telecommunications and Computers
Bahad Eser	Training Base No. Ten – IDF School of Military Medicine
BMNT (Begin Morning Nautical Twilight)	Dawn hour when the centre of the sun is geometrically 12 degrees below the horizon when objects become visible to the naked eye
Crye Six12	Semiautomatic 12-gauge shotgun with six round magazine that is mounted on an X95 assault rifle
Dan .338	Bolt-action sniper rifle manufactured by Israel Weapons Industries chambered for the .338 Lapua cartridge with 3/8 MOA standard of accuracy
Depth Command	IDF equivalent of Special Operations Command
Dicke, der	German for 'the fat one', a derisive nickname for the obese Hermann Göring

446

Dvekut Bah-Misimah (Mission Tenacity)	IDF combat doctrine that preaches the pre-eminent virtue of perseverance in pursuit of operational objectives despite obstacles, casualties or enemy opposition.
Egoz	Battalion-sized tier-two special forces unit specializing in counter-guerrilla warfare
El Malei Rahamim	Hebrew for 'G-d full of mercy,' the prayer of mourning recited at Jewish funeral and memorial services
Escadron	'Squadron' – company-sized unit of the Gendarmerie Nationale Française's Gendarmerie Mobile, numbering 108 gendarmes at full strength
Enemy – Eyeball/ Non-Eyeball	IDF combat doctrine divides enemy forces into two categories: 'eyeball enemy' who are in the immediate vicinity of the target area and will almost certainly be encountered by friendly forces; and more distant 'non-eyeball enemy' (such as reinforcements or a reaction force) who may or may not be encountered
Eretz Yisrael	Land of Israel
Fallshirmjäger	German paratroopers
Fieseler Storch	Luftwaffe light reconnaissance and liaison aircraft capable of short-take-off and rough field landings, similar in size and function to the USAAF Piper Cub or the Westland Lysander
Feldgendarmerie	'Field-gendarmes' – Wehrmacht uniformed military police distinguishable by the large metallic gorget on a chain worn around the neck
Feldgrau	'Field-gray' – the standard colour of Wehrmacht uniforms and equipment
Feldkommandatur	Administrative unit of the Wehrmacht occupation regime in France equivalent to a regimental command; the Orleans Feldkommandatur's zone of responsibility was divided into three battalion-sized 'kreiskommandaturen' based in Vendôme, Orléans and Romorantin
Führer-Begleit-Bataillon	Führer Escort Battalion (FBB), the Wehrmacht unit tasked with providing outer-perimeter security for Hitler's headquarters
Führerbegleitkommando	Hitler's close bodyguard unit that in October 1940 was composed of sixteen SS officers under the command of Bruno Gesche
Führersonderzug	Führer Special Train (code-named 'Amerika')
Generalleutnant	Wehrmacht (Heer/Luftwaffe) commissioned officer rank equivalent to US Major General (O-8)
Generalmajor	Wehrmacht (Heer/Luftwaffe) commissioned officer rank equivalent to US Brigadier General (O-7)

Ger Toshav	Talmudic term for a righteous non-Jew
Gill	IDF nomenclature for medium-range variant of the Spike 4th generation fire-and-forget anti-tank missile with a range of 2,500 metres
GL 40	40 mm single shot grenade launcher mounted on an X95 assault rifle
Gomed	IDF nomenclature for longer-range variant of the Spike 4th generation fire-and-forget anti-tank missile with a range of 4,000 metres
Green	IDF slang reference to the ground forces as opposed to the 'blue' air force or navy. The IDF equivalent of British 'brown jobs' slang term for the army
Harduf (pl Hardufim)	'Oleander' – IDF radio voice procedure code for a dead soldier
Hatirah Le Magah (Striving for Contact)	IDF combat doctrine that preaches the categorical imperative of seizing the initiative in battle by aggressively assaulting or counterattacking the enemy
Heer	German army
Hormah	Hebrew for 'devoted to destruction' derived from the name of the Israelite city built in present-day southern Israel on the ruins of the sacked Canaanite city of Tzfat
Hysteria Margin	IDF slang for principle of ensuring sufficient redundancy in scheduling and/or allocation of forces in an operational plan to ensure victory in the event of unforeseen problems or setbacks
Judenfrei	'Jew-free,' the Nazi term employed to describe a region ethnically cleansed of its Jewish population
Ju-88	Junkers 88, a versatile two-engine aircraft used by the Luftwaffe as a bomber, heavy dive bomber and night-fighter
Khmelnytsky	Seventeenth century Cossack leader who led a rebellion against Ukraine's Polish rulers that included the mass slaughter of 20,000 Jews
Kinneret	Hebrew for Sea of Galilee
Kirya	Tel Aviv neighbourhood where IDF headquarters is located
Kodkod	IDF radio voice procedure call sign of a unit commander who 'owns' that particular network
Kreiskommandatur	Administrative unit of the Wehrmacht occupation regime in France equivalent to a battalion command
Kriegsmarine	German Navy
Kriminalrat	Gestapo rank roughly equivalent to captain (O-3)
Kristallnacht	'Night of Broken Glass', an orchestrated Nazi pogrom against German Jews that took place in November 1938
Kübelwagen	German light utility vehicle roughly equivalent to the US jeep, although lacking 4-wheel-drive

Kus Emak	Extremely vulgar Arabic curse that has made its way into Hebrew slang usage, referring to the genitalia of the cursee's mother
Lamed Hey	Hebrew gematria for the number thirty-five refers to a platoon of thirty-five Palmach fighters who were discovered and massacred by local Arabs as they made their way with relief supplies to the besieged Etzion Block in January 1948
Lamed Vavnik	Hassidic belief that at any one time there are 36 righteous individuals alive on earth; derived from Hebrew gematria in which the letters 'lamed' and 'vav' equal the number 36
Landgerichte	Mid-level regional German court empowered to try serious criminal cases and serve as appellate court of first instance
Lotar	Hebrew portmanteau of 'Lohama BahTerror' – Counter Terrorism, the informal designation of Unit 707, IDF Counter Terrorism School at Mitkan Adam base near moshav Beit Nehemia
Luftwaffe	German air force
Ma'apil (pl Ma'apilim)	Hebrew for an illegal immigrant/s smuggled into Mandatory Palestine in violation of British policy; pre-Israeli version of Oleh
Maschinenpistole	Wehrmacht slang term for the MP38 submachine gun known amongst the allies as the 'Schmeisser'
Maglan	IDF special operations unit specializing in deep penetration missions behind enemy lines to designate strategic and tactical targets for air and missile strike
MK47	Automatic grenade launcher that fires 40 mm explosive shells like a large calibre machinegun
Maslul	Hebrew for 'route' or 'trajectory'; in IDF terms the training course that qualifies Israeli combat soldiers as full-fledged combatants. The length of the maslul varies from 7-8 months for conventional infantry brigades to 24 months for tier-one special operations units.
Matkal	Hebrew portmanteau of 'Mateh K'lali – General Staff, the IDF high command and is also slang term of reference for Sayeret Matkal
Mavo	Hebrew for 'entrance', or 'opening', or 'introduction'
Meshuga (pl Meshuga'im)	Hebrew for insane person/s
Me-110	Messerschmitt 110 two-engine aircraft used as a fighter-bomber and night fighter by the Luftwaffe, one of the fastest piston engine aircraft in the German inventory
Miluim	IDF reserve duty
Mishneh Kodkod	IDF radio voice procedure call sign of a unit Second-in-Command (2iC)

Mitkan Adam	IDF special forces training centre located near moshav Beit Nehemia in central Israel; home to 'Lotar' Unit 707 Counter Terrorism School
Mission Tenacity (Dvekut Bah-Misimah)	IDF combat doctrine that preaches the pre-eminent virtue of perseverance in pursuit of operational objectives despite obstacles, casualties or enemy opposition.
Moshavnick	Resident of Israeli Moshav collective farming community
Mossad	Hebrew short-name for 'Mossad leModi'in uleh Tafikidim Mehuhadim' – Institute for Intelligence and Special Operations, Israeli's foreign intelligence agency
MP	Abbreviation of 'maschinenpistole '– Wehrmacht slang reference to the MP38 submachine gun known amongst the allies as the 'Schmeisser'
Nahal Zavitan	Zavitan Stream that flows from the Golan Heights into the Sea of Galilee
Negev 7	7.62 mm NATO version of the Negev light machinegun
Neuordnung Europas	'New European Order, the Nazi vision of a racially purified Europe
Nu	'So' – Yiddish colloquial expression often used in the interrogative at the beginning of a conversation, e.g. "Nu? What have you been up to lately?"
Obergefrieter	Wehrmacht (Heer) enlisted rank equivalent to Corporal (E-4)
Oberleutnant	Wehrmacht (Heer/Luftwaffe) commissioned officer rank equivalent to 1st Lieutenant (O-2)
Obersturmbannführer	SS commissioned officer equivalent to US Lieutenant Colonel (O-5)
Oleh (pl Olim)	Hebrew for 'one who ascends', the term for a Jewish immigrant making Aliya to Israel
OODA Loop	'Observe, Orient, Decide, Act' (OODA) Loop is a theory that describes the human decision-making cycle; by getting inside the enemy's OODA Loop one gains tactical advantage by reacting more quickly and effectively to unfolding events
Opel 'Blitz'	Wehrmacht utility truck
Paintmunitions	Non-lethal training system that allows realistic live-fire force-on-force exercises by means of marking rounds fired from real weapons equipped with conversion kids (think paintball on steroids)
Pakal	Hebrew portmanteau of 'Pkudot Keva laKrav' – Standing Battle Order, an IDF term that can refer to a wide variety of matters ranging from standard doctrinal issues to the table of organization & equipment (TO&E) that details the manpower, weapons and equipment complement of a given unit

Palsar (pl Palsarim)	Hebrew portmanteau of 'Plugat Siyur'– Reconnaissance Company; each IDF infantry brigade has an elite reconnaissance company tasked with long-range reconnaissance, raids and direct-action missions; infantry brigade palsarim are classified as tier-two special forces units
Papiersoldat	'Paper soldier' – Wehrmacht slang for a rear-echelon clerk
Pazatzta	Hebrew portmanteau composed of the verbs 'poll, z'chal, tzpeh, tavayach, esh' – 'fall, crawl, observe, range and fire', the standard operating procedure for Israeli infantry coming under enemy fire
Perach (pl Prachim)	"Flower' – IDF radio voice procedure code for a wounded soldier
Prinz-Albrecht-Straße	Colloquial name for SS headquarters derived from its address at No 8 Prinz-Albrecht-Straße, Berlin
Putain	French derogatory word whose literal translation means prostitute, but can also be employed as a general term of abuse in present participle form, as in "fix the fucking (putain) tire"
Ramatkal	Hebrew portmanteau of 'Rosh Mateh HaKlali' – Chief of the General Staff; Lieutenant General who is the highest-ranking uniformed officer in – and the commander of – the IDF
Rassenschander	'Race-defiler', a Nazi term derived from the Nuremberg laws passed in 1935 outlawing sexual relations between Jews and Aryans
Reichsspritzenmeister	'Injection Master of the Reich' – derogatory nickname for Dr Theodore Morell, Hitler's personal physician who was widely regarded as a drug-administering quack
Reentrant	Terrain feature formed by low ground found that runs perpendicular to the main ridgeline of the higher ground in which is it located; in US parlance often called a draw
Rittmeister	Wehrmacht commissioned officer rank (cavalry) equivalent to captain (O–3)
Rosh Aman	Hebrew for 'Head of Aman' – Major General who commands the Intelligence Directorate (Aman) of the IDF
Rosh Mossad	Hebrew for 'Head of Mossad'
Rosh Yeshiva	Hebrew for "Head of Yeshiva," the senior rabbi who presides over a yeshiva seminary
SA	'Sturmabteilung' paramilitary wing of the Nazi Party whose members were identifiable by their tan uniforms and colloquially known as 'brownshirts' or stormtroopers

Sayeret Matkal	Israel's preeminent tier-one special operations unit modelled on the British SAS tasked with deep penetration intelligence gathering and direct-action missions
Schwärme	Luftwaffe day fighter tactical formation of four aircraft copied by the RAF and USAAF under the name 'finger-four'
Shabak	Hebrew portmanteau of 'Shirut Bitachon Klali' – General Security Service, the branch of the Israeli intelligence community tasked with domestic intelligence and counter-terrorism and VIP personal security
Shaldag	Formally designated as Unit 5101, Shaldag is the Israeli Air Force tier-one special operations unit that is tasked with deep penetration raids against strategic enemy installations and bomb damage assessment. Named after the Kingfisher bird of prey
Shayetet 13	'Flotilla 13', Israeli Navy tier-one special operations unit, specializing in maritime direct action, amphibious reconnaissance and underwater demolitions
Shidduch	Hebrew/Yiddish term for matchmaking
Sicherheitsdienst des Reichsführers-SS	SS intelligence service
Sicherheitspolizei	SS security police
Sirkin	Home base of Sayeret Matkal located at a disused former RAF airfield at Kfar Sirkin near Petach Tikva
Sous-Lieutenant	French Gendarmerie Nationale commissioned officer rank equivalent to Sub-Lieutenant (O-1)
Striving for Contact (Hatirah leMaga)	IDF combat doctrine that preaches the categorical imperative of seizing the initiative in battle by aggressively assaulting or counterattacking the enemy
Sykes-Picot	Secret agreement drafted in 1916 by Sir Mark Sykes and François George-Picot that divided the post-Ottoman Middle East into British and French spheres of influence, laying the foundations for the post-WWI creation of Iraq, Syria, Lebanon and the British Mandate in Palestine
Technion	Scientific and engineering university located in Haifa – in essence Israel's MIT or Caltech equivalent
Tier-One/Two	Three tier-one IDF special forces units (Matkal, Shaldag and Shayetet 13) have the most selective recruiting/training regimes and are under the operational control of the 'Depth Command' Israel's Special Operations Command; by contrast, tier-two units are subordinate to lower level formations, e.g. the palsarim that belong to each infantry brigade.

Tzahal	Hebrew portmanteau of 'Tzva Haganah Le'Yisrael' – Israel Defense Force
Unit (the)	Colloquial reference to Sayeret Matkal
Unit 669	Israeli Air Force special forces combat pararescue unit tasked with search and extraction of downed aircrew in enemy territory and evacuation of wounded troops under fire
Unit 707	Official designation of IDF Counter Terrorism School at Mitkan Adam outside moshav Beit Nehemia
Unit 8200	IDF signals intelligence unit (pronounced 'eight, two hundred)
VLUP	Vehicle Laying Up Position – a camouflaged position in close proximity to friendly troops in contact where patrol vehicles are concealed for rapid exfiltration
Wachtmeister	Ordnungspolizei NCO rank equivalent to corporal (E-4)
Yamam	Hebrew portmanteaus of 'Yehida Merkazit Meyuhedet' – Special Central Unit, the elite Israeli Border Police counter-terrorism unit
Yekke Potz	Mildly derogatory term used by native-born Israelis in reference to German Jews that refers to their stereotypical pedantic tendencies as sticklers for protocol and formality
Yimach Shmo	Ancient Hebrew curse 'may his name be obliterated'
Yishuv	Informal term for the Jewish community in British mandatory Palestine prior to the establishment of the Israeli state
X95	5.56 mm NATO calibre bullpup rifle developed by Israel Weapons Industry to replace the M-4 carbine as the IDF's standard service weapon

Made in the USA
Monee, IL
20 July 2020